THE SINGLE MOM DIARIES:

First comes baby,
then comes happily-ever-after.

The Darling sisters, both single moms, have always
supported each other through the ups and downs of life
and love. But they'll need each other's advice more than
ever when the possibility of true love comes knocking!

Playboy Connor McNair thinks life behind a picket
fence isn't his speed—until Jill Darling, the girl he
secretly loves, traps him with kisses and Bundt cake.
How can he turn away from the woman he's always
wanted and her twin baby boys?

Don't miss:
A DADDY FOR HER SONS

Sara Darling's joy at adopting her deceased half-
sister's baby turns into a bad dream when she realises
that the rough, handsome man she's just met has
come to claim that same child. Could a marriage
of convenience with Sara be exactly the medicine
the tortured Jake Martin needs?

Find out in
MARRIAGE FOR HER BABY

Dear Reader,

This story is about a woman who bakes such lovely Bundt cakes she's hoping to build a business on it. What a fun way to make a living! Personally, I'm pretty much a disaster in the baking department, but I do have one favorite Bundt cake that makes friends *ooh* and *aah*. Hope it works for you!

Measurements are according to US custom. I grew up with Dutch cookbooks, but converting recipes to metrics is just too risky for me. Sorry!

Chocolate Overload Bundt Cake

1 package chocolate cake mix
1 small package instant chocolate pudding
4 eggs
1 cup sour cream
¼ cup cold coffee
¼ cup water
12 ounces fine-quality semi-sweet chocolate chips

Heat oven to 350 degrees F.

Beat eggs until well mixed, add sour cream, then water and coffee, and mix thoroughly. Add cake mix, beating in slowly, then the pudding. Mix the same way. When smooth, fold in chocolate chips and pour it all into a prepared Bundt pan.

Bake for about one hour. Test with pick and take out when pick comes clean. Cool, but glaze while still somewhat warm.

Rum Glaze (a chocolate or coffee glaze will do as well)

Mix together in a saucepan:

½ cup butter
1 cup white sugar
¼ cup white rum
¼ cup water

Bring to boil and simmer for 2 minutes, then pour over warm cake that has been poked all over with a toothpick.

You don't want to think about the calories, carbs and fat per slice. If you let that bother you, you wouldn't bake this in the first place!

Eating Bundt cake goes perfectly with reading romances! Enjoy!

Raye Morgan

A DADDY
FOR HER SONS

BY
RAYE MORGAN

MILLS & BOON

Raye Morgan has been a nursery school teacher, a travel agent, a clerk and a business editor, but her best job ever has been writing romances—and fostering romance in her own family at the same time. Current score: two boys married, two more to go. Raye has published more than seventy romance novels, and claims to have many more waiting in the wings. She lives in Southern California, with her husband and whichever son happens to be staying at home at the moment.

This is dedicated to Lauri, for everything wonderful
that comes out of her oven!

CHAPTER ONE

A NIGHTMARE. That was what this had to be. She must be dreaming. But what had she expected from a blind date?

Jill Darling was no shy innocent, but her face was blazing. She could feel it. The man was trying to… Ugh, it was just too creepy to even try to name what he was doing. She couldn't really be sure unless she took a look under the table. And that would cause a scene. She couldn't do that. She knew people in this restaurant.

But…was that really his foot sliding up and down her leg?

He was leaning close, talking on and on, his breath hot on her neck. Okay, maybe that was all in the game. But what the heck was that foot doing?

She tried to move away, but she was trapped, huddled right up against the edge of the planter that sat right beside their table, tickling her nose with its palm fronds. They were eating in the restaurant of the nicest hotel in this part of town. It had Irish linen tablecloths, real sterling silverware and a small combo playing for dancers on a tiny dance floor to the side.

She took a long drink from her water glass, then

looked over at him. She tried to smile, but she knew it was wobbly and pretty darn unconvincing if he should happen to actually notice it.

Karl Attkins was his name. Her friend's brother. He was good looking enough, but somehow cold, as though she could have been anyone with an "available female" label stamped on her forehead. Should she ask him about the foot? And maybe warn him not to lose sight of his shoe. It wouldn't be easy to replace that here in this crowded restaurant.

Oh, Lord, he was using his toes now. She was going to have to say something. If she didn't, her nice steak dinner just might come back up. And all that wine she drank, trying to keep busy. This just wasn't cool. She took a deep breath and tried to think of a way to say it without being insulting.

But then he gave her the out she needed.

"Would you like to dance?" he asked, cocking an eyebrow as though he knew she must consider him quite debonair.

Dance. No, not at all. But she steeled herself to the effort. Dancing ought to give him a reason to put his shoe back on, and if so, it would all be worth it.

"Sure," she said breathlessly. "Why not?"

Well, the fact that they were playing a tango at that very moment might have been a reason to sit this one out. But it hardly mattered. At least the man was shod once more. She tried to keep the electric smile painted on her face as he led her to the proper position. And then she glanced at her watch and wondered how much longer she was going to have to endure this torture. She had to put in a good chunk of time or the friends who'd got her into this wouldn't believe she'd really tried.

Oh, Mary Ellen, she groaned silently as Karl pushed her to and fro dramatically across the dancing floor, leaving her to lunge about like a puppet with its strings cut. *I love you dearly, but this is just too high a price to pay for your friendship.*

"But, Jill," all her friends had counseled solemnly, "you've got to do it. You've got to get back into the swim of things. It's been over a year since Brad…well, since you've been alone." The timing had helped make her receptive. Changes were making her feel vulnerable. Her sister was probably moving away, and her younger half-sister had recently died. Loneliness was looming large in her life. "Time is streaking by," another friend lectured. "Don't let it leave you behind. Don't be a coward. Get out there and fight!"

Fight? For what?

"A man, of course," said Mary Ellen. "Once you hit your age, they don't come a dime a dozen any more. You've got competition."

"But, what if I…?"

"No! You can't give up!" her friend Crystal had chimed in. "Your kids need a father figure in the home."

Mary Ellen had fixed her with a steely stare. "And you want to show old Brad, don't you?"

Show old Brad. The need to do just that surged in her. Of course she wanted to show old Brad. Sure. She would date. If he could do it, so could she. Stand back. She was ready for the challenge.

But where would she find someone to date? Mary Ellen knew just the man for her.

"My brother Karl is a real player," she said airily. "He'll get you back into the swing of things in no time. He has so many friends. You'll be dating like crazy before you know it."

Dating. She remembered dating. The way your heart raced as you waited for him to come to the door, the shy pauses, the way your eyes met his and then looked quickly away. Would he kiss you on the doorstep? Were you really going to let him?

Fun!

But that was then. This was a completely different thing, seemingly from a galaxy far, far away. She was older now. She'd been married and she had two kids. She knew how things worked. She could handle it. Or so she thought.

No. This was a nightmare.

At least her dress was pretty, and she didn't get many chances to wear something like this anymore. A sleek shift dress in teal-blue, it was covered with sequins and glistened as she walked, making her feel sexy and pretty and nice. Too bad she was wasting that on a man who spent more time looking at himself in the mirror than she did.

The tango was over. She turned back toward the table in relief, but Karl grabbed her free hand and twirled her around to face him. The band was playing a cha cha. He grinned. "Hey mambo!" he cried out and began to sway. He seemed to consider himself quite the ballroom dancer, even if he couldn't tell one Latin dance from another.

Jill had a decision to make. Would she rather dance, or go back to playing footsie? She wasn't sure she knew how to cha cha. But she knew she didn't want to feel that foot on her leg again.

What the hell.

"Everybody loves to cha-cha-cha," she murmured as she let him twirl her again.

And then she looked up and saw Connor McNair staring at her in horror.

Her blood ran cold. She was still moving, but no one could accuse her of dancing at this point. The music didn't mean a thing.

Connor. Oh, no.

First, it appalled her to think that anyone she knew might see her here like this. But close on that thought came the shock question—was Brad with him?

No. She glanced around quickly and didn't see any sign of her ex-husband at all. Thank heaven for small blessings. Connor must have come to town and was staying here at the hotel—alone. But still, it was Connor, Brad's best friend, the one person most likely to report to him. She could hardly stand it.

He was mouthing something to her. She squinted, trying to make it out. What was he trying to say?

She couldn't tell, but he was coming out onto the dance floor. Why? She looked around, feeling wild, wanting to run. What was he going to do?

"May I cut in?" he asked Karl.

He was polite, but unsmiling, and Karl didn't seem to be in a friendly mood.

"What? No. Go get your own girl," Karl told him, frowning fiercely. And just to prove his point, he grabbed Jill and pulled her close.

She looked over his shoulder at Connor. He offered a safe harbor of sorts, but there was danger there, too. She didn't want to talk to Connor. She didn't want to have anyone close to Brad anywhere near. The pain of Brad's desertion still ached inside her like an open wound and she didn't want anyone from his side of the rift to see her like this—much less talk to her.

So she glared at Connor. Let him know she didn't need him or his rescue. She was doing fine. She was here enjoying herself. Sort of.

She got back to dancing, swaying her hips, making her sequins sparkle, and trying hard to smile at Karl. Let Connor see that she was having the time of her life. Let him take that bit of news back to Brad, if that was what he was after.

"Mambo!" she cried out, echoing Karl. Why the heck not?

Connor gave her a look of disbelief as he stepped back to the sidelines, but he didn't leave. The next dance was a simple two-step, but that meant Karl's arms around her again, and she couldn't disguise the shudder that gave her.

And there was Connor, taking in every nuance. She glowered at him. He was very handsome in his crisp white shirt with the dark slacks that looked tailor-made. But that was beside the point. Didn't he have a table to go to? What gave him the right to stand there and watch her? Biting her lip, she tried to keep him out of her line of vision and blot him out of her head.

But then he was back, right at Karl's elbow again, stopping them in their tracks.

"Excuse me," he said, looking very serious. "Listen, do you have a silver BMW in the parking lot?"

Karl blinked. His eyes narrowed suspiciously, but he couldn't resist the question. "Why, yes I do. What about it?"

Connor's brows came together in a look of sorrow. "I'm afraid your car's on fire."

Karl dropped Jill like a hot potato and whirled to face Connor. "What?" he cried, anguish contorting his face.

Connor was all sympathy. "I think they've called the fire department, but you might want to get out there and…"

No more words were necessary. He was already gone.

Connor took Jill by the arm, looking annoyed when she balked and tried to pull away.

"Come on," he said impatiently. "I know a back way out."

Jill shook her head, not sure what he thought he was doing here. "But…I can't just leave."

Connor looked down at her and suddenly grinned, startling her. She'd forgotten how endearing he could be and she stared up at him. It was like finding a beloved forgotten toy in the attic. Affection for him trembled on the edge of her mood, but she batted it back.

"Why not?" he said. "Do you want to spend the next two hours with the guy?"

She tried to appear stern. She wanted to deny what he was implying. How could she go? What would she say to her friends? What would she tell Mary Ellen?

But in the end, his familiar grin did her in. "I'd rather eat dirt," she admitted, crumbling before him.

"There you go." He led her gently across the dance floor, only hesitating while she scooped up her sparkly little purse. They headed for the exit and he winked at a waiter who was holding the door for them, obviously primed to help with the escape. He paused only long enough to hand the man some folded money and then they were out the door.

"But what about his car?" Jill asked, worrying a bit. She knew the sense of guilt would linger long after the evening was gone. "He loves that car."

"Don't give it a second thought," he advised, steering her toward his own souped-up, twenty-year-old Camaro, a car she remembered from the past, and pulling open the passenger door.

"His car isn't really on fire, is it?" she asked as she plunked down into the leather seat.

"No." He sank into the driver's seat and grinned at her again. "Look, I'll do a lot for an old friend, but setting a guy's car on fire...no, that's a step too far."

She watched him start the engine and turn toward the back exit.

"But you will lie to him about it," she noted.

"Oh, yeah."

She sighed and settled back into the seat. All in all,

at least she didn't have a naked foot exploring her leg at the moment. That alone was worth its weight in gold.

"Rickey's on the Bay?" he asked in the shorthand they both remembered from earlier years.

"Of course," she responded without thinking. That was where everyone always went when the night was still young enough to make the last ferry to the island. She turned and looked at the lights of Seattle in the distance. If only you could go back in time as easily as you could go back to the places where you hung out in your youth.

"I can't believe I'm letting you do this," she said with a sigh.

"I can't believe you needed me to do it."

She laughed. "Touché," she muttered. So much for the great date that was supposed to bring her out of her shell and into the social whirl.

She pulled her cell phone out of her purse and checked it.

"What are you doing?" Connor asked with just a hint of suspicion in his tone.

She glanced up at him and smiled impishly. "Waiting for Karl to call. I've got to explain this to him somehow."

He shuddered. "Is Karl the mambo king?" he asked.

She gave him a baleful look.

"Don't worry. I gave the waiter a little money to tell old Karl what the score was."

She raised an eyebrow. "And just what is the score, pray tell?"

He hesitated, then shrugged. "I told him to tell Karl I

was a made guy from the mob and we didn't take kindly to outsiders poaching on our women."

"What?"

He looked a little embarrassed. "Yeah, I know. Definitely corny. But it was the best I could think of on the spur of the moment."

She had to hold back her laughter. He didn't deserve it.

"I didn't even know you were Italian."

"There are a lot of things you don't know about me." He gave her a mocking wink. "A lot of things you don't want to know."

"Obviously."

She frowned, thinking the situation over. "So now you've single-handedly destroyed my chances of dating anyone ever again in this town. Thanks a lot."

"I'm just looking out for you, sweetheart."

She rolled her eyes, but she was biting back a grin.

Rickey's was as flamboyant as a fifties retro diner should be, with bright turquoise upholstery and jukeboxes at every table. They walked in as though they ought to see a lot of old friends there, but no one looked the least bit familiar.

"We're old," he whispered in her ear as he led her to a booth along the side with windows on the marina. "Everyone we used to hang out with is gone."

"So why are we still here?" she asked, a bit grumpy about it. This was where so much of her life had played out in the old days. And now, the waitresses didn't know her and the faces all looked unfamiliar.

"Lost souls, searching for the meaning of life," he said, smiling at her across the linoleum-covered table. His smile looked wistful this time, unlike the cheerful grin from before.

"The meaning of life is clear enough," she protested. After all, hadn't everyone been lecturing her on it for months? "Get on with things. Make the world a better place. Face reality and deal with it. Or something along those lines."

He shrugged. "Sounds nice, until you start analyzing definitions. What exactly does 'better' mean? Better for whom? How do you get the whole world involved, anyway?"

She made a face at him. "You always were the great contrarian," she said accusingly. "And now I've let you kidnap me. Someone should call the police."

The waitress, a pretty young girl in a poodle skirt who'd just arrived at their table blanched and took a step backward.

"No, no," Jill told her quickly. "I'm only joking. Please don't take me seriously. Ever."

The waitress blinked rapidly, but risked a step closer in to take their order. She didn't hang around to chat, however.

"You scared her," Connor suggested as she hurried away.

"I scare everyone lately," Jill admitted. "What do you think? Am I too intense? Are my eyes a little wild?"

He looked at her uncertainly, not sure if the truth would be accepted in the spirit he would mean it. His gaze skimmed over her pretty face. She had new lines between the brows, a new hint of worry in her eyes. Her hands were clenched around her water glass, as though she were holding on to a life preserver. Tense was hardly a strong enough word. His heart broke just a little bit. What had happened to his carefree girl?

But that was just it. She wasn't "his," never had been.

He knew she'd been through a lot since Brad had left her. She had a right to a few ragged edges. But when you came right down to it, she was as beautiful as she'd ever been. Her golden hair sprang into curls in an untamed mass all around her head. Her dark eyes were still warm, her lips were still full and sexy. Still gorgeous after all these years.

And looking at her still sent him over the moon. It happened every time. She was like a substance he had to be careful he didn't mess with, knowing it would be too dangerous to overdose.

But he could see a difference in her and silently he swore at himself. Why had he stayed away so long? She probably could have used a friend. She'd lost her young girl sparkle and he regretted it. He loved that sparkle.

But now he frowned, studying her face as though he was worried about what he found there. "How are you doing, Jill?" he asked her quietly. "I mean really. How've you been?"

She sat back and really looked at him for the first time, a quiver of fear in her heart. This was what she really wanted to avoid. Silly banter was so much safer than going for truth.

She studied his handsome face, his crystal-blue eyes sparking diamond-like radiant light from between those inky black eyelashes that seemed too impossibly long. It had been over a year since she'd seen him last and he didn't seem quite so much like a kid living in a frat house anymore.

He'd always been such a contrast to Brad, like a younger brother who didn't want to grow up. Brad was the serious one, the ambitious one, the idea man who had the drive to follow through. Connor was more likely to be trying to make a flight to catch a party in Malibu or volunteering to crew on a sailing trip to Tahiti. Brad was a man you could count on. Connor—not so much.

Only that had turned out to be a lie, hadn't it? It was hard to trust anything much anymore once the man you'd considered your rock had melted away and wasn't there for you anymore.

She closed her eyes for a moment, then gave him a dazzling smile. "I've been great," she said breezily. "Life is good. The twins are healthy and my business is actually starting to make a profit, so we're good."

He didn't believe her. He'd known her too long to accept the changed woman she'd become. She'd always been careful—the responsible sort—but she'd also had a sense of fun, of carefree abandon. Instead, her eyes, her tone, her nervous movements, all displayed a wary tension, as though she was always looking over her shoulder to see what disaster might be gaining on her now.

"So good that you felt it was time to venture out into the dating world again, huh?" he noted, being careful to smile as he said it.

"Why not? I need to move on. I need to…to…" She couldn't remember exactly what the argument was, though she'd heard it enough from her friends lately. Something about broadening her horizons. Something about reigniting her womanly instincts. She looked at Connor as though she might read the words in his eyes, but they just weren't there.

"So who talked you into that fiasco tonight?" he asked her.

She frowned at him. "It was a blind date."

"No kidding. Even *you* wouldn't be nutty enough to go out with that guy voluntarily."

"Even me?" His words stung. What did he think of her, anyway? Her eyes flashed. "Just how nutty am I, Connor?"

He reached out and grabbed her hand, gazing at her earnestly. "Will you stop? Please?"

She glanced back, her bottom lip trembling. Deep breaths. That was what she needed. And no matter what, she wasn't going to cry.

"So where have you been all this time?" she asked, wishing it didn't sound quite so petulant.

"All what time?" he said evasively.

"The year and a half since I last saw you."

Her gaze met his and skittered away again. She knew he was thinking about exactly what she was thinking about—that last time had been the day Brad left her. Neither one of them wanted to remember that day, much less talk about it. She grimaced and played with her spoon. The waitress brought their order so it was a moment or two before they spoke again.

"So you said your business is doing okay?" he noted as he spread his napkin on his lap.

"Yes." She stared down at the small dish of ice cream she'd ordered and realized she wasn't going to be able to eat any of it. Her throat felt raw and tight. Too bad. It looked creamy and delicious.

He nodded, reaching for a fork. It was pretty clear he wasn't going to have any problem at all. "What business?"

She blinked at him. "Didn't you know? Didn't Brad tell you?"

He shook his head and avoided saying anything about Brad.

She waited a moment, then sighed. "Okay. When Brad left, he took the electronics business we had developed together. And told me I might as well go out and get a job once the babies were born."

He cringed. That was enough to set your teeth on edge, no matter who you were.

She met his gaze with a touch of defiance in her own. "But I gave birth to two little boys and looked at them and knew there was no way I was handing them over to someone else to raise for me. So I racked my brain, trying to find something I could do at home and still take care of them."

He nodded. That seemed the resourceful thing to do. Good for her. "So what did you decide on?"

She shrugged. "The only thing I was ever really good at. I started a Bundt Cake Bakery."

He nodded, waiting. There had to be more. Who could make a living baking Bundt cakes? "And?"

"And that's what I'm doing."

"Oh." He frowned, puzzled. "Great."

"It *is* great," she said defensively. She could hear the skepticism in his voice. "It was touch and go for a long time, but now I think I'm finally hitting my stride."

He nodded again, wishing he could rustle up some enthusiasm, but failing on all fronts. "Okay."

The product Jill and Brad had developed together had been a bit different from baked goods and he was having a hard time understanding the connection. Jill had done the bookkeeping and the marketing for the business. Brad had been the electronic genius. And Connor had done some work with them, too. They'd been successful from the first.

With that kind of background, he couldn't imagine how the profits from cakes could compare to what they'd made on the GPS device for hikers to be used as a map App. It had been new and fresh and sold very well. He wasn't sure what he could say.

He looked up across the restaurant, caught sight of someone coming in the door and he sighed. "You know how legend has it that everyone stops in at Rickey's on a Saturday night?"

Her eyes widened warily. "Sure."

"I guess it's true." He made a gesture with his head. "Look who just walked in. Mr. Mambo himself."

She gasped and whirled in her seat. Sure enough, there was Karl starting in their direction. He was coming through the restaurant as though he thought he owned the place, giving all the girls the eye. He caught sight of her and his eyes lit up.

Her heart fell. "Oh, no!"

CHAPTER TWO

AND THEN, KARL'S jaunty gaze fell on Connor and he stopped dead, visibly paling. Shaking his head, he raised his hands and he seemed to be muttering, "no, no," over and over again, as though to tell Connor he really didn't mean it. Turning on his heel, he left so quickly, Jill could almost believe she'd been imagining things.

"Wow." She turned back slowly and looked at Connor accusingly. "I guess he believed your cockeyed story." She put a hand to her forehead as though tragedy had struck. "Once he spreads the word, my dating days are done."

"Good," Connor said, beginning to attack his huge piece of cherry pie à la mode. "No point wasting your time on losers like that."

She made a face and leaned toward him sadly. "Are they all like that? Is it really hopeless?"

"Yes." He smiled at her. "Erase all thoughts of other men. I'm here. You don't need anybody else."

"Right." She rolled her eyes, knowing he was teasing. "You'd think I would have learned my lesson with Brad, wouldn't you?"

There was a catch in her voice as she said it. He looked up quickly and she knew he was afraid she might cry. But she didn't cry about that anymore. She was all cried out long ago on that subject.

Did he remember what a fool she'd been? How even with all the evidence piling up in her daily life, she'd never seen it coming. At the time she was almost eight months pregnant with the twins and having a hard time even walking, much less with thinking straight. And Connor had come to tell her that Brad was leaving her.

Brad had sent him, of course. The jerk couldn't even manage to face her and tell her himself.

That made her think twice. Here was Connor, back again. What was Brad afraid to tell her now?

She watched him, frowning, studying his blue eyes. Did she really want to know? All those months, all the heartbreak. Still, if it was something she needed to deal with, better get it over with. She took a deep breath and tried to sound strong and cool.

"So what does he want this time?"

Connor's head jerked back as though what she was asking was out of line. He waved his fork at her. "Do you think we could first go through some of the niceties our society has set up for situations like this?" he asked her.

She searched his face to see if he was mocking her, but he really wasn't. He was just uncomfortable.

"How about, 'How have you been?' or 'What have you been up to lately?' Why not give me some of the details of your life these days. Do we have to jump right into contentious things so quickly?"

So it wasn't good. She should have known. "You're the messenger, not me."

His handsome face winced. It almost seemed as though this pained him more than it was going to pain her. Fat chance.

"We're friends, aren't we?" he asked her.

Were they? She used to think so. "Sure. We always have been."

"So…"

He looked relieved, as though that made it all okay. But it wasn't okay. Whatever it was, it was going to hurt. She knew that instinctively. She leaned forward and glared at him.

"But you're on his side. Don't deny it."

He shook his head, denying it anyway. "What makes you say that?"

She shrugged. "That day, the one that ended life as I knew it, you came over to deliver the fatal blow. You set me straight as to how things really were." Her voice hardened. "You were the one who explained Brad to me at the time. You broke my heart and then you left me lying there in the dirt and you never came back."

"You were not lying in the dirt." He seemed outraged at the concept.

She closed her eyes and then opened them again. "It's a metaphor, silly."

"I don't care what it is. I did not leave you lying in the dirt or even in the sand, or on the couch, or anything. You were standing straight and tall and making jokes, just like always."

Taking a deep breath, he forced himself to relax a bit. "You seemed calm and collected and fine with it. Like you'd known it was coming. Like you were prepared. Sad, but okay." He shook his head, willing her to believe what he was saying. "Or else I never would have left you alone."

She shrugged carelessly. How could he have gotten it all so wrong? "And you think you know me."

He pushed away the pie, searching her eyes, looking truly distressed. "Sara was with you. Your sister. I thought…"

He looked away, frowning fiercely. He remembered what he'd thought. He'd seen the pain in her face and it had taken everything in him not to reach out and gather her in his arms and kiss her until she realized…until she knew… No, he'd had to get out of there before he did something stupid. And that was why he left her. He had his own private hell to tend to.

"You thought I was okay? Wow." She struck a pose and put on an accent. "The corpse was bleeding profusely, but I assumed it would stop on its own. She seemed to be coping quite well with her murder."

He grimaced, shaking his head.

"I hated you for a while," she admitted. "It was easier than hating Brad. What Brad had done to me was just too confusing. What you did was common, everyday cowardice."

He stared at her, aghast. "Oh, thanks."

"And to make it worse, you never did come back. Did you?"

He shook his head as though he really couldn't understand why she was angry. He hadn't done anything to make her that way. He'd just lived his life like he always did, following the latest impulse that moved him. Didn't she know that?

"I was gone. I left the country. I…I had a friend starting up a business in Singapore, so I went to help him out."

She looked skeptical and deep, deep down, she looked hurt. "All this time?"

"Yeah." He nodded, feeling a bit defensive. "I've been out of the country all this time."

Funny, but that made her feel a lot better. At least he hadn't been coming up here to Seattle and never contacting her.

"So you haven't been to see Brad?"

He hesitated. He couldn't lie to her. "I stopped in to see Brad in Portland last week," he admitted.

She threw up her hands. "See? You're on his side."

He wanted to growl at her. "I'm not on anybody's side. I've been friends with both of you since that first week of college, when we all three camped out in Brad's car together."

The corners of Jill's mouth quirked into a reluctant smile as she remembered. "What a night that was," she said lightly. "They'd lost my housing forms and you hadn't been admitted yet. We had no place to sleep."

"So Brad offered his car."

"And stayed out with us."

"We talked and laughed the whole night."

She nodded, remembering. "And that cemented it. We were best buds from that night on."

Connor smiled, but looked away. He remembered meeting Jill in the administration office while they both tried to fight the bureaucracy. He'd thought she was the cutest coed on campus, right from the start. And then Brad showed up and swept her off her feet.

"We fought the law and the law won," he noted cynically.

"Right." She laughed softly, still remembering. "You with that crazy book of rules you were always studying on how to make professors fall in love with you so they'd give you good grades."

He sighed. "That never worked. And it should have, darn it all."

Her eyes narrowed as she looked back into the past a little deeper. "And all those insane jobs you took, trying to pay off your fees. I never understood when you had time to study."

"I slept with a tape recorder going," he said with a casual shrug. "Subliminal learning. Without it, I would have flunked out early on."

She stared at him, willing him to smile and admit he'd made that up, but he stuck to his guns.

"No, really. I learned French that way."

She gave him an incredulous look. *"Parlez-vous francais?"*

"Uh…whatever." He looked uncomfortable. "I didn't say I retained any of it beyond test day."

"Right." She laughed at him and he grinned back.

But she knew they were ignoring the elephant in the room. Brad. Brad who had been with them both all through college. Brad who had decided she was his from the start. And what Brad wanted, Brad usually got. She'd been flattered by his attention, then thrilled with it. And soon, she'd fallen hard. She was so in love with him, she knew he was her destiny. She let him take over her life. She didn't realize he would toss it aside when he got tired of it.

"So what are you doing here?" she asked again. "Surely you didn't come to see me."

"Jill, I always want to see you."

"No kidding. That's why you've been gone for a year and a half. You've never even met the twins."

He looked at her with a half smile. Funny. She'd been pregnant the last time he'd seen her, but that wasn't the way he'd thought of her all these months. And to tell the truth, Brad had never mentioned those babies. "That's right. I forgot. You've got a couple of cookie crunchers now, don't you?"

"I do. The little lights of my life, so to speak."

"Boys."

"Boys." She nodded.

He wanted to ask how they got along with Brad, but he wasn't brave enough to do it. Besides, it was getting late. She had a pair of baby boys at home. She looked at her watch, then looked at him.

"I've got to get home. If you can just drop me at the dock, the last ferry goes at midnight and…"

He waved away her suggestion. "You will not walk home from the ferry landing. It's too late and too far."

She made a face. "I'll be fine. I've done it a thousand times."

"I'll drive you."

She gave him a mock glare. "Well, then we'd better get going or you won't make the last ferry back."

"You let me worry about that."

Let him worry—let him manage—leave it to him. Something inside her yearned to be able to do that. It had been so long since she'd had anyone else to rely on. But life had taught her a hard lesson. If you relied on others, they could really hurt you. Best to rely on nobody but yourself.

The ferry ride across the bay to the island was always fun. He pulled the car into the proper space on the ferry and they both got out to enjoy the trip. Standing side by side as the ferry started off, they watched the inky-black water part to let them through.

Jill pulled her arms in close, fending off the ocean coolness, and he reached out and put an arm around her, keeping her warm. She rested her head on his shoulder. He had to resist the urge to draw her closer.

"Hey, I'm looking forward to meeting those two little boys of yours," he said.

"Hopefully you won't meet them tonight," she said, laughing. "I've got a nice older lady looking after them. They should be sound asleep right now."

"It's amazing to think of you with children," he said.

She nodded. "I know. You're not the only one stunned by the transformation." She smiled, thinking of how they really had changed her life. If only Brad…

No, she wasn't going to start going back over those old saws again. That way lay madness.

"It's also amazing to think of how long we've known each other," she added brightly instead.

"We all three got close in our freshman year," he agreed, "and that lasted all through college."

She nodded. "It seemed, those first couple of years, we did everything together."

"I remember it well." He sighed and glanced down at her. All he could see was that mop of crazy, curly blond hair. It always made him smile. "You were sighing over Brad," he added to the memory trail. "And I was wishing you would look my way instead."

She looked up and made a face at him. "Be serious. You had no time for stodgy, conventional girls like I was. You were always after the high flyers."

He stared at her, offended despite the fact that there was some truth in what she said. "I was not," he protested anyway.

"Sure you were." She was teasing him now. "You liked bad girls. Edgy girls. The ones who ran off with the band."

His faint smile admitted the truth. "Only when I was in the band."

"And that was most of the time." She pulled back and looked at him. "Did you ever actually get a degree?"

"Of course I got a degree."

She giggled. "In what? Multicultural dating?"

He bit back the sharp retort that surfaced in his throat. She really didn't know. But why should she?

He had to admit he'd spent years working hard at seeming to be a slacker.

"Something like that," he muttered, thinking with a touch of annoyance about his engineering degree with a magna cum laude attached. No one had been closer friends to him than Brad and Jill. And they didn't even realize he was smarter than he seemed.

It was his own fault of course. He'd worked on that easygoing image. Still, it stung a bit.

And it made him do a bit of "what if?" thinking. What if he'd been more aggressive making his own case? What if he'd challenged Brad's place in Jill's heart at the time? What if he'd competed instead of accepting their romance as an established fact? Would things have been different?

The spray from the water splashed across his face, jerking him awake from his dream. Turning toward the island, he could see her house up the drive a block from the landing. He'd been there a hundred times before, but not for quite a while. Not since the twins were born and Brad decided he wasn't fatherhood material. Connor had listened to what Brad had to say and it had caused a major conflict for him. He thought Brad's reasons were hateful and he deplored them, but at the same time, he'd seen them together for too long to have any illusions. They didn't belong together. Getting a divorce was probably the best thing Brad could do for Jill. So he'd gone with his message, he'd done his part and hated it and then he'd headed for Singapore.

He turned to look at her, to watch the way the wind blew her hair over her eyes, and that old familiar pull began somewhere in the middle of his chest. It started slow and then began to build, as though it was slowly finding its way through his bloodstream. He wanted her, wanted to hold her and kiss her and tell her…. He gritted his teeth and turned away. He had to fight that feeling. Funny. He never got it with any other girl. It only happened with her. Damn.

A flash of panic shivered through him. What the hell was he doing here, anyway? He'd thought he was prepared for this. Hardened. Toughened and ready to avoid the tender trap that was always Jill. But his defenses were fading fast. He had to get out of here.

He needed a plan. Obviously playing this by ear wasn't going to work. The first thing he had to do was to get her home, safe and sound. That should be easy. Then he had to avoid getting out of the car. Under no circumstances should he go into the house, especially not to take a peek at the babies. That would tie him up in a web of sentiment and leave him raw and vulnerable to his feelings. He couldn't afford to do that. At all costs, he had to stay strong and leave right away.

He could come back and talk to her in the morning. If he hung around, disaster was inevitable. He couldn't let that happen.

"You know what?" he said, trying to sound light and casual. "I think you really had the right idea about this. I need to get back to the hotel. I think I'll take the ferry right on back and let you walk up the hill on your own. It's super safe here, isn't it? I mean…"

He felt bad about it, but it had to be done. He couldn't

go home with her. Wouldn't be prudent, as someone once had famously said.

But he realized she wasn't listening to him. She was staring, mouth open, over his shoulder at the island they were fast approaching.

"What in the world is going on? My house is lit up like a Christmas tree."

He turned. She was right. Every window was ablaze with light. It was almost midnight. Somehow, this didn't seem right.

And then a strange thing happened. As they watched, something came flying out of the upstairs window, sailed through the air and landed on the roof next door.

Jill gasped, rigid with shock. "Was that the cat?" she cried. "Oh, my God!"

She tried to pull away from him as though she was about to jump into the water and swim for shore, but he yanked her back. "Come on," he said urgently, pulling her toward the Camaro. "We'll get there faster in the car."

CHAPTER THREE

JILL'S HEART WAS racing. She couldn't think. She could hardly breathe. Adrenaline surged and she almost blacked out with it.

"Oh, please," she muttered over and over as they raced toward the house. "Oh, please, oh, please!"

He swung the car into the driveway and she jumped out before he even came to a stop, running for the door.

"Timmy?" she called out. "Tanner?"

Connor was right behind her as she threw open the front door and raced inside.

"Mrs. Mulberry?" she called out as she ran. "Mrs. Mulberry!"

A slight, gray-haired woman appeared on the stairway from the second floor with a look close to terror on her face. "Oh, thank God you're finally here! I tried to call you but my hands were shaking so hard, I couldn't use the cell phone."

"What is it?" Jill grabbed her by the shoulders, staring down into her face. "What's happened? Where are the boys?"

"I tried, I really tried, but...but..."

"Mrs. Mulberry! What?"

Her face crumpled and she wailed, "They locked me out. I couldn't get to them. I didn't know what to do…."

"What do you mean they've locked you out? Where? When?"

"They got out of their cribs and locked the door. I couldn't…"

Jill started up the stairs, but Connor took them two at a time and beat her to the landing and then the door. He yanked at the handle but it didn't budge.

"Timmy? Tanner? Are you okay?" Jill's voice quavered as she pressed her ear to the door. There was no response.

"There's a key," she said, turning wildly, trying to remember where she'd put it. "I know there's a key."

Connor pushed her aside. "No time," he said, giving the door a wicked kick right next to where the lever sat. There was a crunch of wood breaking and the door flew open.

A scene of chaos and destruction was revealed. A lamp was upside down on the floor, along with pillows and books and a tumbled table and chair set. Toys were everywhere, most of them covered with baby powder that someone had been squirting out of the container. And on the other side of the room were two little blond boys, crowding into a window they could barely reach. They saw the adults coming for them, looked at each other and shrieked—and then they very quickly shoved one fat fluffy pillow and then one large plastic game of Hungry Hungry Hippos over the sill. The hippos could be heard hitting the bricks of the patio below.

"What are you doing?" Jill cried, dashing in as one child reached for a small music toy. She grabbed him, swung him up in her arms and held him close.

"You are such a bad boy!" she said, but she was laughing with relief at the same time. They seemed to be okay. No broken bones. No blood. No dead cat.

Connor pulled up the other boy with one arm while he slammed the window shut with the other. He looked at Jill and shook his head. "Wow," was all he could say. Then he thought of something else. "Oh. Sorry about the door. I thought…"

"You thought right," she said, flashing him a look of pure relief and happiness. Her babies were safe and right now that was all that mattered to her. "I would have had a heart attack if I'd had to wait any longer."

Mrs. Mulberry was blubbering behind them and they both turned, each carrying a child, to stare at her.

"I'm so sorry," she was saying tearfully. "But when they locked me out…"

"Okay, start at the beginning," Jill told her, trying to keep her temper in check and hush her baby, who was saying, "Mamamama" over and over in her ear. "What exactly happened?"

The older woman sniffled and put a handkerchief to her nose. "I…I don't really know. It all began so well. They were perfect angels."

She smiled at them tearfully and they grinned back at her. Jill shook her head. It was as though they knew exactly what they'd done and were ready to do it again if they got the chance.

"They were so good," Mrs. Mulberry was saying,

"I'm afraid I let them stay up longer than I should have. Finally I put them to bed and went downstairs." She shook her head as though she still couldn't believe what happened next. "I was reading a magazine on the couch when something just went plummeting by the bay window. I thought it was my imagination at first. Then something else went shooting past and I got up and went outside to look at what was going on. And there were toys and bits of bedding just lying there in the grass. I looked up but I couldn't see anything. It was very eerie. Almost scary. I couldn't figure out what on earth was happening."

"Oh, sweetie boys," Jill muttered, holding one closely to her. "You must be good for the babysitter. Remember?"

"When I started to go back in the house," the older lady went on, "one of these very same adorable children was at the front door. As I started to come closer, he grinned at me and he…" She had to stop to take a shaky breath. "He just smiled. I realized what might happen and I called out. I said, 'No! Wait!' But just as I reached the door, he slammed it shut. It was locked. He locked me out of the house!"

Jill was frowning. "What are you talking about? Who locked you out of the house?"

She pointed at Timmy who was cuddled close in Jill's arms. "He did."

Jill shook her head as though to clear it. He's only eighteen months old. "That's impossible. He doesn't know how to lock doors."

Mrs. Mulberry drew herself up. "Oh, yes he does," she insisted.

Jill looked into Timmy's innocent face. Could her baby have done that? He smiled and said, "Mama-mama." No way.

"I couldn't get in," Mrs Mulberry went on. "I was panicking. I didn't know what I was going to do." Tears filled her eyes again.

Jill stared at her in disbelief and Connor stepped forward, putting a comforting hand on her shoulder. "We believe you, Mrs. Mulberry," he said calmly. "Just finish your story. We want to know it all."

She tried to give him a grateful smile and went on. "I was racing around, trying all the doors, getting more and more insane with fear. Finally I got the idea to look for a key. I must have turned over twenty flower pots before I found it. Once I got back into the house, I realized they were up here in the bedroom, but when I called to them, they locked the bedroom door."

She sighed heavily, her head falling forward on her chest. "I thought I would go out of my mind. I tried to call you but I couldn't do it. I thought I ought to call the police, but I was shaking so badly..." She shuddered, remembering. "And then you finally came home."

Jill met Connor's gaze and bit her lip, turning to lay Timmy down in his crib. He was giving her a warning glance, as if to say, "No major damage here. Give her a break."

For some reason, instead of letting it annoy her, she felt a surge of relief. Yes, give her a break. Dear soul, she didn't mean any harm, and since nothing had really happened, there was no reason to make things worse. In fact, both boys were already drifting off to sleep. And why not? They'd had a busy night so far.

Turning, she smiled at the older woman. "Thank goodness I got back when I did," she said as lightly as she could manage. "Well, everything's alright now. If you'll wait downstairs, I'll just put these two down and…"

Connor gave her a grin and a wink and put down the already sleeping Tanner into his crib as though he knew what he was doing, which surprised her. But her mind was on her babies, and she looked down lovingly at them as they slept. For just a moment, she'd been so scared….

What would she do if anything happened to either one of them? She couldn't let herself think about that. That was a place she didn't want to go.

Connor watched her. He was pretty sure he knew what she was thinking about. Anything happening to her kids would just about destroy her. He'd seen her face when she first realized she was losing Brad. He remembered that pain almost as if it had been his own. And losing these little ones would be ten times worse.

He drove Mrs. Mulberry home and when he got back, all was quiet. The lights that had blazed out across the landscape were doused and a more muted atmosphere prevailed. The house seemed to be at peace.

Except for one thing—the sound of sniffles coming from the kitchen where Jill was sitting at the table with her hands wrapped around a cup of coffee.

"Hey," he said, sliding in beside her on the bench seat. "You okay?"

She turned her huge, dark, tragic eyes toward him.

"I leave the house for just a few hours—leave the boys for more than ten minutes—the first time in a year. And chaos takes over." She searched his gaze for answers. "Is that really not allowed? Am I chained to this place, this life, forever? Do I not dare leave…ever?"

He stared down at her. He wanted to make a joke, make her smile, get her out of this mood, but he saw real desperation in her eyes and he couldn't make light of that.

"Hey." He brushed her cheek with the backs of his fingers. "It's not forever. Things change quickly for kids. Don't let it get you down. In a month, it will be different."

She stared up at him. How could he possibly know that? And yet, somehow, she saw the wisdom in what he'd said. She shook her head and smiled. "Connor, why didn't you come back sooner? I love your smile."

He gave her another one, but deep down, he groaned. This was exactly why he had to get out of here as soon as he could. He slumped down lower in the seat and tried to think of something else reassuring to say, but his mind wouldn't let go of what she'd just said to him.

I love your smile.

Pretty pathetic to grasp at such a slender reed, but that was just about all he had, wasn't it?

Jill was back on the subject at hand, thinking about the babysitter. "Here I hired her because I thought an older woman would be calmer with a steadier hand."

She rolled her eyes. "A teenage girl would have been better."

"Come on, that's not really fair. She got a lot thrown at her at once and she wasn't prepared for it. It could have happened to anyone."

She shook her head as though she just couldn't accept that. "I'm lucky I've got my sister close by for emergencies. But she's getting more and more caught up in her career, and it's a pretty demanding one. I really can't count on her for too much longer." She sighed. "She had to be at a business dinner in Seattle tonight, or she would have been here to take care of the boys."

"Family can be convenient." He frowned. "Don't you have a younger sister? I thought I met her once."

Instead of answering, she moaned softly and closed her eyes. "Kelly. Yes. She was our half sister." She looked at him, new tragedy clouding her gaze. "Funny you should remember her tonight. She was killed in a car crash last week."

"Oh, my God. Oh, Jill, I'm so sorry."

She nodded. "It's sad and tragic and brings on a lot of guilty feelings for Sara and me."

He shook his head, not understanding. "What did you have to do with it?"

"The accident? Oh, nothing. It happened in Virginia where I guess she was living lately. The guilt comes from not even knowing exactly where she was and frankly, not thinking about her much. We should have paid more attention and worked a little harder on being real sisters to her."

There was more. He could tell. But he waited, letting her take her time to unravel the story.

"She was a lot younger, of course. Our mother died when we were pretty young, and our father remarried soon after. Too soon for us, of course. After losing our mother, we couldn't bear to share our beloved father with anyone. We resented the new woman, and when she had a baby, we pretty much resented her, too." She shook her head. "It was so unfair. Poor little girl."

"Didn't you get closer as she got older?"

"Not really. You see, the marriage was a disaster from the start and it ended by the time Kelly was about five years old. We only saw her occasionally after that, for a few hours at a time. And then our father died by the time she was fifteen and we didn't see either one of them much at all after that."

"That's too bad."

She nodded. "Yes. I'm really sorry about it now." She sighed. "She was something of a wild child, at least according to my father's tales of woe. Getting into trouble even in high school. The sort of girl who wants to test the boundaries and explore the edge."

"I know your father died a few years ago. What about your stepmother?"

"She died when I was about twenty-three. She had cancer."

"Poor lady."

"Yes. Just tragic, isn't it? Lives snuffed out so casually." She shook her head. "I just feel so bad about Kelly. It's so sad that we never got to know her better."

"Just goes to show. Carpe diem. Seize the day. Don't let your opportunities slip by."

"Yes." She gave him a look. "When did you become such a philosopher?"

"I've always been considered wise among my peers," he told her in a snooty voice that made her laugh.

A foghorn sounded its mournful call and she looked up at a clock. "And now here you are, stuck. The last ferry's gone. You're going to have to stay here."

He smiled at her. "Unless I hijack a boat."

"You can sleep on the couch." She shrugged. "Or sleep in the master bedroom if you want. Nobody else does."

The bitter tone was loud and clear, and it surprised him.

"Where do you sleep?" he asked her.

"In the guest room." Her smile was bittersweet. "That's why you can't use it."

He remembered glancing in at the master bedroom when he was upstairs. It looked like it had always looked. She and Brad had shared that bed. He looked back at her and didn't say a word.

She didn't offer an explanation, but he knew what it was. She couldn't sleep in that bed now that Brad had abandoned it.

He nodded. "I'll take the couch."

She hesitated. "The only problem with that is, I'll be getting up about four in the morning. I'll probably wake you."

"Four in the morning? Planning a rendezvous with the milkman?"

"No, silly. I've got to start warming the ovens and mixing my batter." She yawned, reminding him of a sleepy kitten. "I've got a day full of large orders to fill tomorrow. One of my busiest days ever." She smiled again. "And hopefully, a sign of success. I sure need it."

"Great."

"Wait here a second. I think I've got something you can use."

She left the room and was back in moments, carrying a set of dark blue men's pajamas.

He recoiled at the sight. "Brad's?" he said.

"Not really." She threw them down in his lap. "I bought them for Brad but he never even saw them. That was just days before he sent you to tell me we were through."

"Oh." That was okay, then. He looked at them, setting aside the top and reserving the pants for when he was ready for bed. Meanwhile, she was rummaging through a linen closet and bringing out a sheet and a light blanket. That made her look domestic in ways he hadn't remembered. He thought about how she'd looked with Timmy in her arms.

"Hey," he said gently. "That's a pair of great little boys you've got there."

She melted immediately. "Aren't they adorable? But so bad!"

"I'll bet they keep you busy every hour of the day."

She nodded. "It's not easy running a business from home when I've got those two getting more and more mischievous." She sighed and sat back down. "Can you believe they were locking doors? I had no idea they knew what a lock was."

"Time to dismantle some and add extra keys for others," he suggested.

"Yes. And keep my eyes on them every minute."

"Can't you hire a daytime babysitter?"

"Yeah, hiring a babysitter really works out well, doesn't it?" She shook her head. "Actually Trini, my bakery assistant, helps a lot. She doubles as a babysitter when I need her to, and does everything else the rest of the time. And then, Sara comes by and helps when she has a free moment or two." She gave him a tremulous smile. "We manage."

He resisted the impulse to reach out and brush back the lock of hair that was bouncing over her eyebrow. The gesture seemed a little too intimate as they sat here, alone in the dim light so late at night.

But Jill didn't seem to have the same reservations he harbored. She reached out and took his hand in hers, startling him. Then she gazed deep into his eyes for a moment before she spoke. His pulse began to quicken. He wasn't sure what she wanted from him, but he knew he couldn't deny her much.

"Well?" she said softly.

He could barely breathe. His fingers curled around hers and he looked at her full, soft lips, her warm mouth, and he wanted to kiss her so badly his whole body ached with it. The longing for her seared his soul. What would she do if he just…?

"Well?" she said again. "Out with it."

"What?" His brain was fuzzy. He couldn't connect what she was saying to what he was feeling.

"Come on. Say it."

He shook his head. What was she talking about? Her brows drew together and her gaze was more penetrating.

"My dear Connor," she said, pulling at his hand as though to make him say what she wanted to hear. "It is time for you to come clean."

"Come clean?"

He swallowed hard. Did she know? Could she read the desire in his eyes? Did she see how he felt about her in his face? Hear it in his voice? Had he really let his guard down too far?

"On what?" he added, his voice gruff with suppressed emotion.

"On why you're here." She was looking so intense. "On why Brad sent you." She searched his eyes again. "Come on, Connor. What exactly does he want this time?"

Brad. His heart sank, and then he had to laugh at himself. Of course that was what she was thinking about. And why not? What right did he have to want anything different? What he wanted didn't mean a thing. This was all about Jill—and Brad. As usual. He took a deep breath and shook his head.

"What makes you think Brad sent me?" he said, his voice coming out a bit harsher than he'd meant it to.

"You're his best friend." She frowned and looked pensive. "You were my best friend once, too."

There you go. Too many best friends. He was always the odd man out. That was exactly why he'd opted for

Singapore when he had the chance. And maybe why he would go back again.

He raised her hand and brought it to his lips, touching her gently with a kiss, then setting her aside and drawing away.

"Jill, you've had enough excitement for tonight. Let's talk in the morning."

"No, tell me. What does Brad want me to do?"

It was the question in her eyes that scared him— the hint of hope. She didn't really think that there was a chance that Brad might want her back….did she? It wasn't going to happen. He'd seen it with his own eyes.

Brad was a selfish bastard. It had taken him years to accept that. Maybe Jill didn't realize it yet. Brad was a great guy to hang out with. Playing poker with him was fun. Going waterskiing. Box seats at a Mariners game. But as far as planning your life with him, he wouldn't recommend it.

"Jill, I didn't come for Brad. I came to see you because I wanted to come."

Okay, so that was partly a lie. But he had to say it. He couldn't stand to see the glimmer of hope in her eyes, knowing it would only bring her more heartbreak. He had a message from Brad all right. But right now, he wasn't sure if he would ever tell her what it was. She thought he was on Brad's side, but she was wrong. If it came to a showdown, he was here for her—all the way.

He just wasn't sure how much she cared, one way or the other. She still wanted Brad. He could see it in her face, hear it in her voice. He shouldn't even be here.

No worries. He would leave first thing in the morn-

ing. He couldn't leave before six when the ferry started
to run, but he would slip out while she was busy. No
goodbyes. Just leave. Get it over with and out of the
way and move on. That was the plan. He only had to
follow it.

The couch was comfortable enough but he could
only sleep in short snatches. When he did doze off, he
had dreams that left him wandering through crowds of
Latin American dancers in huge headdresses, all swaying wildly to exotic music and shouting "Mambo!" in
his face.

He was looking for something he couldn't find. People kept getting in his way, trying to get him to dance
with them. And then one headdress changed into a huge
white parrot before his eyes, the most elegant bird he'd
ever seen. He had to catch that parrot. Suddenly it was
an obvious case of life or death and his heart was beating hard with the effort as he chased it through the
crowd. He had to catch it!

He reached out, leaped high and touched the tips of
the white feathers of its wings. His heart soared. He had
it! But then the feathers slipped through his fingers and
the bird was swooping away from him. He was left with
nothing. A feeling of cold, dark devastation filled his
heart. He began to walk away.

But the parrot was back, trailing those long white
fathers across his face—only it wasn't white feathers.
It was the sleeve of a lacy white nightgown and it was
Jill leaning over him, trying to reach something from
the bookcase behind the couch.

"Oh, sorry. I didn't want to wake you up," she whispered as though he might go back to sleep if she was quiet about it. "It's not time to get up. I just needed this manual. I'm starting to heat the ovens up."

He nodded and pretended to close his eyes, but he left slits so he could watch her make her way across the room, her lacy white gown cascading around her gorgeous ankles. The glow from the kitchen provided a backlight that showed off her curves to perfection, making his body tighten in a massive way he didn't expect.

And then he fell into the first real deep and dreamless sleep of the night. It must have lasted at least two hours. When he opened his eyes, he found himself staring into the bright blue gaze of one of the twins. He didn't know which one. He couldn't tell them apart yet.

He closed his eyes again, hoping the little visitor would be gone when he opened them. No such luck. Now there were two of them, both dressed in pajamas, both cute as could be.

"Hi," he said. "How are you doing?"

They didn't say a word. They just stared harder. But maybe they didn't do much talking at this age. They were fairly young.

Still, this soundless staring was beginning to get on his nerves.

"Boo," he said.

They both blinked but held their ground.

"So it's going to take more than a simple 'boo,' is it?" he asked.

They stared.

"Okay." He gathered his forces and sprang up, waving the covers like a huge cloak around him. "BOO!" he yelled, eyes wide.

They reacted nicely. They both ran screaming from the room, tumbling over each other in their hurry, and Connor smiled with satisfaction.

It only took seconds for Jill to arrive around the corner.

"What are you doing to my babies?" she cried.

"Nothing," he said, trying to look innocent. He wrapped the covers around himself and smiled. "Just getting to know them. Establishing pecking order. Stuff like that."

She frowned at him suspiciously. To his disappointment, she didn't have the lacy white thing on anymore. She'd changed into a crisp uniform with a large apron and wore a net over her mass of curly hair.

He gestured in her direction. "Regulation uniform, huh?"

She nodded. "I'm a Bundt cake professional, you know," she reminded him, doing a pose.

Then she smiled, looking him over. "You look cute when you're sleepy," she told him, reaching out to ruffle his badly mussed hair. "Why don't you go take a shower? I put fresh towels in the downstairs bathroom. I'll give you some breakfast before you leave."

Leave? Leave? Oh, yeah. He was going to leave as fast as he could. That was the plan.

He let the sheet drop, forgetting that his torso was completely naked, but the look on her face reminded him quickly. "Oh, sorry," he said, pulling the sheet back. And then he felt like a fool.

He glanced at her. A beautiful shade of crimson was flooding her face. That told him something he hadn't figured out before. But knowing she responded to him like that didn't help matters. In fact, it only made things worse. He swore softly to himself.

"You want me gone as soon as possible, don't you?" He shouldn't have said it that way, but the words were already out of his mouth.

She looked a little startled, but she nodded. "Actually you are sort of in the way," she noted a bit breathlessly. "I...I've got a ton of work to do today and I don't really have time to be much of a hostess."

He nodded. "Don't worry. I'm on my way."

He thought about getting into his car and driving off and he wondered why he wasn't really looking forward to it. He had to go. He knew it. She knew it. It had to be done. They needed to stay away from each other if they didn't want to start something they might not be able to stop. Just the thought made his pulse beat a ragged rhythm.

She met his gaze and looked almost sorry for a moment, then took a deep breath, shook her head and glanced at her watch.

"So far, so good. I'm pretty much on schedule," she said. "It can get wild around here. My assistant, Trini, should show up about seven. Then things will slowly get under control."

Despite her involuntary reaction to seeing him without a shirt—a reaction that sent a surge through his bloodstream every time he thought of it—there was still plenty of tension in her voice. Best to be gone before he really felt like a burden. He shook his head as he went off to take a shower.

It can get wild around here, she'd said. So it seemed. It couldn't get much wilder than it had the night before.

That reminded him of what those boys were capable of, and once he'd finished his shower, he took a large plastic bag and went outside to collect all the items the boys had thrown down from the bedroom. Then he brought the plastic bag into the house and set it down in the entryway.

"Oh, good," Jill said when she saw what he'd done. She looked relieved that he'd changed back into the shirt and slacks he'd been wearing the night before. "I forgot. I really did want all the stuff brought in before the neighbors saw it."

"This is quite a haul," he told her with a crooked smile. "Are you sure your guys aren't in training to be second-story men?"

"Very funny," she said, shaking her head at him, then smiling back. "There are actually times when I wonder how I'm going to do it on my own. Raise them right, I mean." She turned large, sad eyes his way. "It's not getting any easier."

It broke his heart to see her like this. If only there was something he could do to help her. But that was impossible, considering the situation. If it weren't for Brad… But that was just wishful thinking.

"You're going to manage it," he reassured her. "You've got what it takes. You'll do it just like your parents managed to raise you. It comes with the territory."

She was frowning at him. "But it doesn't always

work out. Your parents, for instance. Didn't you used to say…?"

He tried to remember what he'd ever told her about his childhood. He couldn't have said much. He never did. Unless he'd had too much to drink one night and opened up to her. But he didn't remember anything like that. Where had she come up with the fact that his parents had been worthless? It was the truth, but he usually didn't advertise it.

"Yeah, you're right," he said slowly. "My parents were pretty much AWOL. But you know what? Kids usually grow up okay anyway." He spread his arms out and smiled at her. "Look at me."

"Just about perfect," she teased. "Who could ask for anything more?"

"My point exactly," he said.

She turned away. She knew he was trying to give her encouragement, but what he was saying was just so much empty talk. It wouldn't get her far.

"Come on," she said. "I've got coffee, and as long as you want cake for breakfast, you can eat."

The cake was slices from rejects—Dutch Apple Crust, Lemon Delight and Double Devil's Food—but they were great and she knew it. She watched with satisfaction as he ate four slices in a row, making happy noises all the while.

The boys were playing in the next room. They were making plenty of noise but none of it sounded dangerous so far. Her batters were mixed. Her first cakes were baking. She still had to prepare some glazes. But all in all, things were moving along briskly and she was feeling more confident.

A moment of peace. She slipped into a chair and smiled across the table at him.

"You look like a woman expecting a busy day," he noted, smiling back at her and noticing how the morning light set off the faint sprinkling of freckles that still decorated her pretty face.

She nodded. "It's my biggest day ever. I've got to get cakes to the charity auction at the Lodge, I've got cakes due for six parties, I've got a huge order, an engagement party at the country club today at three. They want 125 mini Bundt cakes. I was planning to get started on them last night, but after the baby riot, I just didn't have the energy." She shook her head. "As soon as Trini gets here, we'll push the 'on' switch and we won't turn it off until we're done."

He grinned at her. "You look like you relish the whole thing. Or am I reading you wrong?"

"You've got it right." She gave him a warm look. "I really appreciate you being here to help me last night," she said, shaking her head as she remembered the madness. "That was so crazy."

"Yeah," he agreed, polishing off the last piece of Lemon Delight. "But nobody got hurt. It all turned out all right."

She nodded, looking at him, at his dark, curly hair, at his calm, honest face. She felt a surge of affection for him, and that made her frown. They'd been such good friends at one point, but she hardly knew anything about what he'd been doing lately. He'd walked out of her life at the same time Brad had. Both her best friends had deserted her in one way or another.

What doesn't kill you makes you stronger. Yeah, right.

"So the way I understand it," she said, leaning forward, "you've been in Singapore for the last year or so."

"That's right."

"Are you back for good?"

"Uh…" He grimaced. "Hard to say. I've got some options. Haven't decided what I want to do."

She thought about that for a moment. Did Connor ever have a solid plan? Or was it just that he kept his feelings close to the vest? She couldn't tell at this point. She resented the way he'd walked off over a year ago, but that didn't mean she didn't still love him to death.

Best friends. Right?

She narrowed her eyes, then asked brightly, "How about getting married?"

He looked at her as though she'd suddenly gone insane. "What? Married? Who to?"

She laughed. She could read his mind. He thought she was trying out a brand-new idea and he was ready to panic. "Not to me, silly. To someone you love. Someone who will enhance your life."

"Oh." He still looked uncomfortable.

"I'm serious. You should get married. You could use some stability in your life. A sense of purpose." She shrugged, feeling silly.

Who was she to give this sort of advice? Not only was she a failure at marriage, but she'd turned out to be a pretty lousy judge of character, too. "Someone to love," she added lamely.

His blue eyes were hooded as he gazed at her. "How do you know I don't have all those things right now?"

She studied his handsome face and shook her head. "I don't see it. To me, you look like the same old Connor, always chasing the next good time. Show me how I'm wrong."

She knew she was getting a little personal, but she was feeling a little confused about him right now. What was he doing here? Why was he sticking around?

In the bright light of day she thought she could see things more clearly, and that fresh sight told her he'd come with a goal in mind. If he'd just wanted to see her, make a visit, he'd have called ahead. No, Brad had sent him. Coming face-to-face in the hotel dining room had been a fluke. But what did Brad have in mind? Why didn't Connor just deliver the message and go?

She was beginning to feel annoyed with him. Actually she was becoming annoyed with everything. Something was off-kilter and her day was beginning to stretch out ominously before her.

"Okay, let's stop avoiding the real issue here." She stared at him coolly. "No more denials. What does Brad really want?"

CHAPTER FOUR

"Brad?"

Jill saw the shift in Connor's eyes. He didn't want to talk about this right now. He was perfectly ready to avoid the issue again. Well, too bad. She didn't have all the time in the world. It was now or never.

"Yes, Brad. You remember him. My ex-husband. The father of my children. The man who was once my entire life."

"Oh, yeah. That guy."

She frowned. He was still being evasive. She locked her fingers together and pulled.

"So, what does he want?" she insisted.

Connor looked at her and began to smile. "What do you think Brad wants? He always wants more than his share. And he usually gets it."

She shook her head, surprised, then laughed softly. "You do know him well, don't you?"

Connor's smile faded. He glanced around the kitchen, looking uncomfortable. "Does he have visitation rights to the boys? Does he come up here to see them or does he…?"

"No," she said quickly. "He's never seen them."

For once, she'd shocked him. His face showed it clearly. "Never seen his own kids? Why? Do you have a court injunction or...?"

The pain of it all would bring her down if she let it. She couldn't do that. She held her head high and met his gaze directly.

"He doesn't want to see them. Don't you know that? Didn't he ever tell you why he wanted the divorce?"

Connor shook his head slowly. "Tell me," he said softly.

She took a deep breath. "When Brad asked me to marry him, he told me he wanted a partner. He was going to start his own business and he wanted someone as committed to it as he was, someone who would stand by him and help him succeed. I entered into that project joyfully."

Connor nodded. He remembered that as well. He'd been there. He'd worked right along with them. They'd spent hours together brainstorming ideas, trying out options, failing and trying again. They'd camped out in sleeping bags when they first opened their office. They'd been so young and so naive. They thought they could change the world—or at least their little corner of it. They'd invented new ways of doing things and found a way to make it pay. It had been a lot of hard work, but they'd had a lot of fun along the way. That time seemed a million miles away now.

"I knew Brad didn't want children, but I brushed that aside. I was so sure he would change his mind as time went by. We worked very, very hard and we did really well together. The business was a huge success. Then I got pregnant."

She saw the question in his eyes and she shook her head. "No, it was purely and simply an accident."

She bit her lip and looked toward the window for a moment, steadying her voice.

"But I never dreamed Brad would reject it so totally. He just wouldn't accept it." She looked back into his eyes, searching for understanding. "I thought we could work things out. After all, we loved each other. These things happen in life. You deal with them. You make adjustments. You move on."

"Not Brad," he guessed.

"No. Not Brad." She shrugged. "He said, get rid of them."

He drew in a sharp breath. It was almost a gasp. She could hear it in the silence of the kitchen, and she winced.

"And you said?"

She shrugged again. "I'd rather die."

Connor nodded. He knew her well enough to know that was the truth. What the hell was Brad thinking?

"Suddenly he was like a stranger to me. He just shut the door. He went down to Portland to open up a branch office for our business. I thought he would think it over and come back and…" She gave him a significant look. "But he never came back. He began to make the branch office his headquarters. Then you showed up and told me he wanted a divorce."

Connor nodded. His voice was low and gruff as he asked her, "Do you want him back?"

She had to think about that one. If she was honest, she would have to admit there was a part of her—a part she wasn't very proud of—that would do almost anything to get him back. Anything but the one thing he asked for.

She stared at him and wondered how much she should tell him. He was obviously surprised to know about how little Brad cared about his sons. A normal man would care. So Brad had turned out to be not very normal. That was her mistake. She should have realized that and never married him in the first place.

She also had to live with the fact that he was getting worse and worse about paying child support. There were so many promises—and then so many excuses. What there wasn't a lot of was money..

The business was floundering, he said. He was trying as hard as he could, but the profits weren't rolling in like they used to in the old days—when she was doing half the work. Of course, he didn't mention that. He didn't want her anywhere near the business anymore.

She knew he resented having to give her anything. After all, he'd given her the house—not that it was paid off. Still, it had been what she wanted, what she felt she had to have to keep a stable environment for the boys.

But now she was having a hard time making the mortgage payments. She had to make a go of her cake business, or else she would have to go back to work and leave the boys with a babysitter. She was running out of time.

Time to build her business up to where it could pay for itself. Time to stabilize the mortgage situation before the bank came down on her. Time to get the boys old enough so that when she did have to go for a real, paying job, it wouldn't break her heart to leave them with strangers.

So, yes. What Brad wanted now mattered. Had he gone through a transformation? Had he come up with second thoughts and decided to become a friend to the family? Or was it all more excuses about what he couldn't do instead of what he could? Women with husbands in a stable situation didn't realize how lucky they were.

Funny. Sometimes it almost seemed as though Brad had screwed up her marriage and now he wanted to screw up her single life as well.

She shook her head slowly. "I want my life back," she admitted. "I want the life I had when I had a loving husband. I want my babies to have their father. But I don't see how that can ever happen."

Her eyes stung and she blinked quickly to make sure no tears dared show up.

"Unless…" She looked up into Connor's eyes. "Unless you have a message from Brad that he wants it to happen, too."

Whistling in the wind. She knew how useless that was. She gave Connor a shaky smile, basically absolving him of all guilt in the matter. She saw the look in his eyes. He felt sorry for her. She cringed inside. She didn't want pity.

"Don't worry. I don't expect that. But I do want to know what he sent you for."

Connor shook his head. Obviously he had nothing

to give her. So Brad must have sent him on a scouting expedition, right? To see if she was surviving. To see if she was ready to hoist the white flag and admit he was right and she was wrong. She couldn't make it on her own after all. She should have listened to him. And now, she should knuckle under and take his advice and give it all up.

She bit her lip. She wasn't disappointed, exactly. She knew the score. But she was bummed out and it didn't help her outlook on the day.

A timer went off and she hopped up to check on her cakes. This was where she belonged, this was where she knew what she was doing. The realm of human emotions was too treacherous. She would take her chances with the baked goods.

Connor watched her getting busy again and he wished he could find some way to help her deal with the truth— that Brad didn't want her. He couldn't say it might never happen. Brad could change his mind. But right now, he didn't want Jill at all. What he wanted was to be totally free of her. At least, that was how he'd presented things a few days ago when they'd talked.

Brad wanted that, and he wanted her to give up her remaining interest in the company. That was the message he was supposed to make her listen to. That was the message he just couldn't bring himself to tell her. Maybe later.

He took his cup to the sink, rinsed it out and headed back into the living room. He was folding up the covers he'd used when the front door opened and a young woman hurried in.

Connor looked up and started to smile. It was Sara Darling, Jill's sister, and she stopped dead when she saw who had been sleeping on her sister's couch.

"You!" she said accusingly, and he found himself backing up, just from the fire in her eyes.

He knew that Sara and Jill were very close, but he also knew they tended to see things very differently. Both were beautiful. Where Jill had a head full of crazy curls that made you want to kiss her a lot, Sara wore her blond hair slicked back and sleek, making her look efficient and professional. Today she wore a slim tan linen suit with a pale peach blouse and nude heels and she looked as though she was about to gavel an important business meeting to order.

"What are you doing here?" she demanded of him. "Oh, brother. I should have known you'd show up. Let a woman be vulnerable and alone and it's like sharks smelling blood in the water."

"Hey," he protested, surprised. He'd always been friendly with this woman in the past. "That's a bit harsh."

"Harsh? You want to see harsh?"

He blanched. "Not really."

Okay, so Sara was being extra protective of her sister. He got it. But she'd never looked on him as a bad guy before. Why now? He tried a tentative smile.

"Hey, Sara. Nice to see you."

She was still frowning fiercely. "You have no right to complicate Jill's life."

He frowned, too, but in a more puzzled way. That was actually not what he wanted to do, either. But it seemed he was right. Sara was circling the wagons around her sister. How to convince her she didn't need to do that with him?

"Listen, staying for the night wasn't how I planned this."

"I'll bet." She had her arms crossed and looked very intimidating. "Just what *did* you have in mind, Casanova?"

What? Did she really think he was hovering around in order to catch Jill in an emotional state? If only! He wanted to laugh at her but he knew that would only infuriate her further.

"Listen, I saved your sister from a blind date gone horribly wrong. Seriously. Do you know the guy she went out with?"

Sara shook her head, looking doubtful.

"I think his name was Karl."

She shook her head again.

"Well, if you knew him, you'd see why Jill needed rescuing. He was flamboyantly wrong for her."

"Okay." Sara looked a little less intimidating. "Good. I'm glad you were there to help her out."

He breathed a sigh of relief. She was approachable after all.

"So I brought her back here, planning to drop her off and come back to see her in the morning, but there was a riot going on in the house. The twins had taken the babysitter hostage. I had to stay and help Jill regain the high ground. There was no choice."

It was as though she hadn't heard a word he'd said. She paced slowly back and forth in front of him, glaring like a tiger. It was evident she thought he was exaggerating and she'd already gone back to the root of the problem.

"So...what's the deal?" she said, challenging him with her look. "Brad sent you, didn't he?"

Uh-oh. He didn't want to go there if he could help it. He gave her a fed-up look. "Why does everyone assume I can't make a move on my own?"

She glared all the harder. "If he's trying to get her to come back to him, you can tell him..."

He held up a hand to stop her. It was time to nip this supposition in the bud. "Sara, no. Brad is not trying to get her back."

"Oh." Her look was pure sarcasm. "So the new honey is still hanging around?"

He ran his fingers through his thick, curly hair and grimaced. "Actually I think that was two or three honeys ago," he muttered, mostly to himself. "But take my word for it, Brad isn't looking for forgiveness. Not yet, anyway."

Her dark eyes flared with outrage, but she kept her anger at a slow simmer. "That's our Brad. Trust him to make life and everything in it all about him and no one else."

He nodded. That was one point they could agree on. "Brad does like to have things go his way."

Sara's gaze had fallen on the plastic bag of items picked up in the yard. She scowled, touching it with the toe of her shoe.

"What's all this?"

"Oh. Uh. I left it there. I'll get it…."

She looked up in horror. "What are you doing, moving in?"

Now he couldn't help it. He had to laugh. "Sara, you don't need to hate me. I'm not the enemy."

"Really? What are you, then?"

"A friend." He tried to look earnest. He'd always thought Sara liked him well enough. He certainly hadn't expected to be attacked with guns blazing this way. "I'm Jill's friend. And I really want what's best for her."

"Sorry, Connor. You can't be a true friend to Jill while you're still any sort of friend to Brad. It won't work."

His head went back and he winced. "That's a little rigid, don't you think?"

She moved closer, glancing toward the kitchen to make sure they weren't being overheard. "If you'd seen what she's gone through over this last year or so, you might change your tune."

"What?" He caught her by the upper arm. "What happened?"

She shook her head, looking away.

"Has Brad been here to see her?"

She looked up at him. "Not that I know of. But he manages to make life miserable for her by long distance."

He frowned, wishing she would be more specific.

She looked at him, shook her head and her shoulders drooped. All her animosity had drained away and tears rimmed her eyes. "Oh, Connor, she deserves so much better. If you could see how hard she works… And every time she turns around, there's some new obstacle thrown in her path. I just can't stand it anymore. It's not fair."

She pulled away and he let her go. And now he was the one whose emotions were roiling. Damn Brad, anyway. Why couldn't he just leave her alone?

He ran his hand through his hair again, tempted to rip chunks of it out in frustration. He had to get out of here. If he wasn't careful, he would get caught up in the need to protect Jill. From what? He wasn't even sure. Life, probably. Just life. As Sara had said, it wasn't fair. But it also wasn't his fight. No, he had to go.

He would drive back to his hotel, check out and head for Portland. He would tell Brad he couldn't help him and advise him to leave Jill alone. Maybe he would even tell his old friend what he really thought of him. It was way past time to do that.

Jill was in a hurry and things weren't working out. She had Tanner dressed in his little play suit, but she couldn't catch Timmy, and now he was streaking around the room, just out of her reach, laughing uproariously.

"Timmy!" she ordered. "You stop right there."

Fat chance of that. He rolled under the bed and giggled as she reached under, trying to grab him.

"You come out of there, you rascal."

She made a lucky grab and caught his foot and pulled him out, disarming grin and all. "Oh, you little munchkin," she cried, but she pulled him into her arms and held him tightly. Her boys were so precious to her. She'd given up a lot to make sure she would have them. Tears stung her eyelids and she fought them back. She couldn't let herself cry. Not now. She had a day to get through.

She had a huge, wonderful day full of work ahead. A day like this could turn things around, if it started a trend. She heard Sara's voice downstairs and she smiled. What a relief. Good. Sara was here. She would be able to help with the children.

She so appreciated Sara giving her some time like this. She knew she was applying for a promotion. She'd been a contributing editor to the design section of *Winter Bay Magazine* for almost two years and she'd done some fabulous work. If she got the new job, she would be working more hours during the week and wouldn't be able to help out as much. Still, she hoped she got it. She certainly deserved the recognition.

She was thankful for small blessings. Right now, if she had Sara here to help with the twins, and then Trini coming in a half hour to help with the baking and delivery, she would be okay. She would just barely be able to fulfill all the commitments she'd made for the day.

It was a challenge, but she could do it. In fact, she had to do it.

Sara appeared at the doorway just as she finished dressing her boys and sent them into the playroom.

"Hey there," she said, ready to greet her sister with a smile until she saw the look on her face. "What's the matter? What's wrong?"

Sara sighed and shook her head.

"Did you see Connor?" Jill asked brightly. "He looks

so much the same, you'd never know he'd been gone for a year and a half, would you?"

Sara gave her a look. "Jill, we've got to talk."

Jill groaned and grabbed her sister's hand. "Not now, sweetie. Not today. I've got so much I've got to get to and…"

Sara was shaking her head. "You've got to get rid of him, Jill."

She frowned. "Who?"

Sara pointed back down the stairs as though he were following her. "Connor. You've got to make him go right away."

Dropping her hand, Jill turned away, feeling rebellious. She'd been thinking the same thing but she didn't want to hear it from anyone else. Connor was hers. She resented anyone else—even her beloved sister—critiquing their relationship. She would make him go when she was good and ready to make him go.

Sara grabbed her by the shoulders. "You know he's just here spying for Brad," she said in a low, urgent voice. "You don't want that, do you?"

Sara had never warmed to Jill's ex-husband, even during the good times. And once he'd gone off and left her high and dry, she'd developed what could only be described as a dogged contempt for the man.

Jill took a deep breath and decided to ignore everything she'd said. Life would be simpler that way.

"What are you doing here so early?" she asked instead, trying to sound bright and cheery. "I appreciate it, but…"

"Oh." Sara's demeanor changed in an instant and she

dropped her hold on her sister's shoulders. "Oh, Jill, I came early to tell you…I'm so sorry, but I won't be able to help you today. They want me to fly down to L.A. There's just no way I can get out of it. I'll be meeting with the editorial staff from Chicago and…"

"Today?" Jill couldn't stop the anguish from bursting out as she realized what this meant.

Sara looked stricken. "It's a really bad day, right?"

"Well, I told you I've got a huge stack of orders and…" Jill stopped herself, set her shoulders and got hold of her fears. "No, no." She shook her head. "No, Sara. It's much more important for you to go do this, I'm sure."

Sara grabbed her hand again. "Oh, honey, I'm so sorry, but I really can't turn them down. They want to see how I handle myself with the visiting members." She bit her lip and looked as though she was about to cry. A range of conflicting emotions flashed through her wide dark eyes and then she shook her head decisively. "Oh, forget it. I'll tell them something has come up and I just can't do it. Don't worry. They'll understand. I think."

Jill dismissed all that out of hand. "Don't be ridiculous. Of course you have to go. This is your career. This is something you've worked so hard for."

"But I can't leave you if you really need me."

"But I don't." Jill dug deep and managed a bright smile. "Not really. Trini will be here soon and we'll be able to handle it."

Sara looked worried. "Are you sure?"

"Positive." She smiled again.

"Because I can stay if you really need me. I can tell them…"

"No." She hugged her sister. "You go. You have to go. I will lose all respect for you if you let silly sentiment keep you from achieving your highest goals. Say no more about it. You're gone. It's decided."

"But…"

"Come on. Do it for me. Do it for all of us. Make us proud."

Her smile was almost painful by now, but doggone it—she wasn't going to stop. Sara had to go. No two ways about it. And she would just have to cope on her own. Thank God for Trini.

"So she's really going?" Connor had watched Sara rushing off and then turned to see Jill come down from upstairs with a tense look on her face.

"Yes. Yes, she is."

He noted that her hands were gripped together as though she could hardly stand it. He frowned.

"Do you think you can do it without her?"

She took a deep breath. "It won't be easy. But once Trini gets here, we'll put our noses to the grindstone and work our little tushes off for the next twelve hours. Then you'll see."

He was bemused by her intensity. "What will I see?"

She looked up at him wide-eyed. "That this is serious. Not just a hobby job. It's real."

He frowned. He wanted to tell her that he respected her immensely and that he was impressed with what she was attempting to do here, but before he could get a word out, she went on, pacing tensely as she talked.

"You know, I thought I had everything pretty much under control. My life was running on an even keel. I was beginning to feel as though I might make it after all." She stopped and looked at him with a sense of foreboding wonder. "And then you hit town. And everything went to hell."

She was trying to make it sound like a joke, but there was too much stress in her voice to carry it off. He winced.

"So you blame me now?"

"Why not? There's nobody else within shouting distance. You're going to have to take the fall." She tried to smile but her mouth was wobbly.

He looked at her, saw the anxious look in her eyes and he melted beyond control. "Jill…" He took her hands in his and drew her closer. "Listen, why don't I stay? I could help you with the boys. I could run errands, answer phones."

She was shaking her head but he didn't wait to hear her thoughts.

He pulled her hands up against his chest. "I want to help you. Really. I know you've had a lot of setbacks lately and I want to help smooth over some rough spots if I can. Come on, Jill. Let me stay."

Her lower lip was trembling as she looked into his eyes. He groaned and pulled her into his arms, holding her tightly against his body. She felt like heaven and he wanted the moment to go on forever, but she didn't let it happen. She was already pulling out of his embrace, and he could have kicked himself for doing it.

Too blatant, Connor old chap, he told himself ruefully. *You really tipped your hand there, didn't you?*

"No, Connor," she said as she pushed him away.

She looked at him, shaken. She'd wanted to melt into his arms. She still felt the temptation so strongly, she had to steel herself against it. She knew it had to be mostly because she was so afraid, so nervous about her ability to meet her challenges. If she let him hold her, she could pretend to forget all that.

And then there was the fact that it had been so long since a man—a real man, a man that she liked—had held her. Karl didn't count. And she hungered for that sort of connection.

But not with Connor. Not with Brad's best friend.

"No. It's sweet of you to offer, but I really can't let you stay. We are going to need to focus like laser beams on this task and having you here won't help." She smiled at him with affection to take the bite out of her words.

He stepped farther from her and avoided her eyes. The sting of her rejection was like a knife to his heart. "Okay then. I guess I'd better get going."

"Yes. I'm sorry."

He started to turn away, then remembered. "Hey, I didn't fix the door I kicked in last night."

She shook her head. "Don't worry. I've already called a handy man I use."

"Oh." He hesitated, but there didn't seem to be much to say. He was superfluous, obviously. Just in the way. Might as well get the hell out.

"Okay. It was good to see you again, Jill."

She smiled at him. "Yes. Come back soon. But next time, don't stop off to see Brad first."

He nodded. "You've got my word on that one," he said. He shoved his hands down into the back pockets of his jeans and looked at her, hard.

"What?" she asked, half laughing.

"I just want to get a good picture of you to hold me over," he told her. "Until next time."

The look in her eyes softened and she stepped forward and kissed his cheek. "Goodbye," she whispered.

He wanted to kiss her mouth so badly, he had to clench his teeth together to stop himself from doing it.

"Goodbye," he said softly, then he turned and left the house.

Outside, he felt like hell. He'd had hangovers that hadn't felt this bad. Everything in him wanted to stay and he couldn't do it. He looked down at the ferry dock. There was a ferry there now, loading up. He'd catch it and then it would be all over. How long before he saw her again? Who knew. He would probably go back to Singapore. At least he knew where he stood there.

Swearing softly with a string of obscenities that he rarely used, he slid into the driver's seat and felt for the keys.

"Goodbye to all that," he muttered, then turned on the engine. About to back out, he turned to glance over his shoulder—just in time to see a small economy car come sailing in behind him, jerk to a stop, and block him in.

"Hey," he said.

But the young woman who'd driven up didn't hear him and didn't notice that his engine was running. She flew out of the car and went racing up the walk, flinging herself through the doorway.

Okay. This had to be the famous Trini he'd heard so much about. She'd trapped him in his parking space and he wasn't going to make the ferry. Now what?

CHAPTER FIVE

JILL HADN'T RECOVERED from Connor leaving when Trini came bursting in. The boys ran to her joyfully and she knelt down and collected them into her arms, then looked up. Jill knew immediately that something was wrong.

"Trini, what is it?" she cried.

Trini was young and pretty with a long, swinging ponytail and a wide-eyed expression of constant amazement, as though life had just really surprised her once again. And in this case, it seemed to be true.

"You'll never guess!" she cried, and then she burst into tears. "Oh, Jill," she wailed, "this is so good and so bad at the same time."

"What is it, sweetheart?" Jill asked, pulling her up and searching her face. But she thought she knew. And she dreaded what she was about to hear.

"Oh, Jill, I just got the call and…" She sobbed for a moment, then tried again. "I got in. I was on the wait list and they just called. I got accepted into the program at Chanoise Culinary Institute in New York."

"But…hasn't the quarter already started?"

"Yes, but they had two people drop out already. So they called and said if I could get there by tomorrow, I'm in."

"Trini! That's wonderful! You deserve a space in the class. I always knew that."

But did it have to be today? She couldn't help but wish the timing had been different. Still, this was wonderful for Trini.

"What can I do to help you?"

Trini shook her head. "You've already done enough. You wrote the recommendation that got me in." She sighed happily, and then she frowned with worry. "The only bad part is I have to leave right away. My flight leaves at noon. The Jamison engagement party..."

"Don't you think twice, Trini. You just get out of here and go pack and prepare for the best experience of your life. Okay?"

Trini threw her arms around Jill's neck and Jill hugged her tightly. "I'm so excited," Trini cried. "Oh, Jill, I'll keep you posted on everything we do. And when I come back..."

"You'll teach me a thing or two, I'm sure." She smiled at her assistant, forcing back any hint of the panic she was feeling. "Now off with you. You need to get ready for the rest of your life."

"I will. Wish me luck!"

"I'll definitely wish you luck. You just supply the hard work!"

Trini laughed and dashed out the door. Jill reached out to put her hand on the back of a chair to keep herself from collapsing. She could hardly breathe. She saw

Connor standing in the entryway. She didn't know why he'd come back and right now, she couldn't really think about it or talk to him. She was in full-scale devastation meltdown mode.

What was she going to do? What on earth was she going to do? She couldn't think a coherent thought. Her mind was a jumble. She knew she was standing on the edge of the cliff and if she lost her balance, she was going over. She couldn't let that happen. She had to get herself together.

But what was the use? She'd fought back so often. So much kept going wrong and she kept trying to fix things. They just wouldn't stay fixed. She was so tired. Today, right now, she wanted to quit. There had to be a way to give up, to surrender to reality. She just couldn't do this anymore.

Looking at her reflection in the hall mirror, she muttered sadly, "Okay. I get it. I'm not meant to do this. I should quit banging my head against the wall. I should quit, period. Isn't that what a sane, rational person would do?"

She stared at herself, feeling cold and hollow. She knew Connor was still watching her, that he'd heard what she said, but she hardly cared. She was in such deep trouble, what did it matter if he saw her anguish? But a part of her was grateful for his presence—and that he was keeping back, not trying to comfort her right now. She didn't need that since there was no comfort, was no real hope.

She stared at herself for a long moment, teetering between the devil and the deep blue sea. That was how it felt. No matter what she did, disaster seemed inevitable.

Then, gradually, from somewhere deep inside, she began to put her strength back together and pull her nerve back into place. She took a giant breath and slowly let it out. She wouldn't surrender. She would go down fighting, no matter what it cost her. Let them try to stop her! She had glaze to prepare. She had cakes to bake. She would try her best to get this done and on time. She could only do what she could do—but she would do the best she could.

She looked at herself in the mirror again and gave herself a small, encouraging smile. She needed a joke right now, something to help her put things into perspective. She was a baking woman—hear her roar! They would have to pry her baking mitts off her cold, dead hands.

Revived and reinvigorated, she turned to face Connor. "There," she said. "I'm better now."

He still appeared a bit worried, but he'd watched her mini-breakdown and the instant rebuild in awe.

"Wow," he said. "Jill, you are something else."

She sighed. "You weren't supposed to see that."

"I'm glad I did. I've got more faith in you than ever."

She laughed. "I've got to get back to work." She frowned. "Why are you still here?"

"Because I'm not going to go while you still need me."

"What makes you think I need you?" Turning, she headed into the kitchen.

"So," he said tentatively, following her. "Now your

number one assistant has bailed on you. And your sister has bailed on you." He shrugged. "Who you gonna call? You need someone else. Who can come to your rescue?"

She met his gaze. "There's nobody. Really. I've tried to find backup before. There's really nobody. This island is too small. There aren't enough people to draw on."

He nodded. "That's what I thought." He picked up an apron someone had thrown on the chair and began to tie it on himself. "Okay. Tell me what to do."

Her eyes widened. "What are you talking about?"

His face was so earnest, she felt her breath catch in her throat. He really meant it.

"How can I help you, Jill? What can I do?"

This was so sweet of him, but it couldn't work. He didn't have the skills, the background. And anyway, he wasn't here for her. He was here for Brad. There was no denying it.

"Just stay out of the way." She shrugged helplessly. He shouldn't be here at all. Why was he? "Go back to your hotel. You don't belong here."

He shook his head. "No."

"Connor!"

He shook his head again. "You're like a fish flopping around on the pier, gasping for breath. You need help, lady. And I'm going to give it to you."

She shook her own head in disbelief. "You can't cook."

"The hell I can't."

Her gaze narrowed. "I don't believe it."

He stepped closer, towering over her and staring down with cool deliberation. "There are a whole lot of things about me you just don't have a clue about, Miss Know-it-all."

She shook her head, still wary. "Look, just because you can fry up a mean omelet after midnight for your Saturday night date doesn't mean you can cook. And it certainly doesn't mean you can bake."

"I'm not proposing to be your baker. You've got that slot nailed. I'm signing on as an assistant. I'm ready to assist you in any way I can."

He meant it. She could see the resolve in his eyes. But how could he possibly be a help rather than a hindrance? There was no way he could get up to speed in time. Still, she was in an awful bind here.

"So you can cook?" she asked him skeptically.

"Yes."

"There's a difference between cooking and baking."

"I know that." He shook his head impatiently. "Jill, you're the baker. But you need a support staff and I'm going to be it."

"But…what are you planning to do?"

"Prep pans, wash pans, drizzle on glaze, pack product for delivery, deliver product, go for supplies, answer the phones…"

She was beginning to smile. Maybe she was being foolish, but she didn't have much choice, did she? "And the most important thing?" she coached.

He thought for a moment, then realized what she was talking about.

"Keep an eye on the boys," he said and was rewarded with a quick smile. "You got it. In fact, I'll do anything and everything in order to leave you room to practice your creative artistry."

"My what?" She laughed and gave him a push. "Oh, Connor, you smooth talker you."

"That's what it is." He took her by the shoulders and held her as though she was very, very special. "I've eaten some of your cake wizardry, lady. *Magnifique!*"

The word hung in the air. She gazed up at him, suddenly filled with a wave of affection. Had she ever noticed before how his eyes crinkled in the corners? And how long his beautiful dark lashes were? Reaching out, she pressed her palm to his cheek for just a moment, then drew it back and turned away so that he wouldn't see the tears beginning to well in her eyes.

"Okay," she said a little gruffly. "We'll give it a try. As long as you turn out to be worth more than the trouble you cause." But she glanced back with a smile, showing him that she was only teasing.

"I won't get in your way, I swear. You just wait and see. We'll work together like a well-oiled machine."

She blinked back the tears and smiled at him. "You promise?"

"Cross my heart and hope to die."

"Ooh, don't say that. Bad vibes." She shook her head. "Okay then. Here's the game plan. I'm going to go back over all my recipes and check to make sure I've got the right supplies before I start mixing new batters. You go and see what the boys are up to. Then you come back and help me."

He saluted her like a soldier. *"Mais oui, mon chef."*

"Wow. Those sleepy-time French lessons really did do some good. And here I was a non-believer."

He looked a bit nonplussed himself. "Every now and then a few French words just seem to burst out of me, so yeah, I guess so."

He turned his attention to the twins not a moment too soon. There was a ruckus going on in the next room. The boys were crying. Someone had pushed someone down and grabbed away his toy. The other one was fighting to get it back. Happened all the time. They needed supervision.

But there was really no time today to deal with it properly. He went back to discuss the situation with Jill.

"If you can think of any strenuous activities, something that might make them take their naps a bit earlier…" she mused, checking the supply of flavorings and crossing them off a list, then handing the list to him to start working on an inventory of the flour she had in storage.

"Say no more," He gave her a wise look. "I've got a trick or two up my sleeve. As soon as I finish counting up the canisters, I'll deal with those little rascals."

Time was racing by. Her convection oven could accommodate four cakes at a time, but they had to be carefully watched.

"We've got to get these done by noon," she told him. "I can't start the mini Bundts any later than that. We've got to get the minis done by three, glazed and packed by four-thirty, and off for delivery by five."

He nodded. He knew she wasn't completely resigned

to him being there with her. This was her biggest day and her eyes betrayed how worried she was. Her shoulders looked tight. She wasn't confident that they could do it, even working hard together.

He only hoped he could—what? Help her? That went without saying. Protect her? Sure. That was his main goal. Always had been. If only he'd realized earlier that his vague distrust of Brad was based on more than jealousy. It seemed to be real in ways that were only now becoming more and more clear to him. It was a good thing she'd reconciled herself to accepting his help, because he knew he couldn't go. He couldn't leave her on her own. He had to be here for her.

Meanwhile, he had to find a way to wear out the boys. He tried to recall his own childhood, but eighteen months old was a little too far back to remember much. Still, he had a few ideas.

He took the boys out into the backyard. There was a big sloping hill covered with grass. Improvising, he set up a racetrack with different stations where the boys had to perform simple modified gymnastic elements in order to move on to the next station.

They loved it. They each had a natural competitive spirit that came out in spades as they began to understand the goals involved. Each wanted to win with a naive gusto that made him laugh out loud. They were a great pair of twins.

They were so into it. Running up the hill took a lot of their time. Shrieking with excitement was a factor. And Connor found he was having as much fun as they were.

At one point, he had them racing uphill, each pulling a red wagon filled with rocks to see who could get to the top first. He'd brought along lots of prizes, including pieces of hard candy that they loved. He knew they were sure to rot teeth, but he would only use them today and never again. Or not often, anyway. He also made sure to keep the winnings pretty equal between the two of them, so that each could shine in turn.

But, as he told Jill a bit later, the one drawback was— no matter how tired he made them, he was even more so. He was pitifully out of shape.

But it was fun. That was the surprising part. The boys were a couple of great kids, both so eager, so smart. He wondered what Brad would think if he could see them. How could he possibly resist these two?

He brought them back in and settled them down to watch an educational DVD while he went down to the kitchen to see what he could do to help Jill. She had recently pulled four cakes out of the oven and she was ready to put on a glaze.

"Show me how," he told her. "You're going to need help when you glaze all those small cakes for the engagement party, aren't you?"

She looked at him with some hesitation, and he saw it right away. Reaching out, he took her hands in his.

"Jill, I'm not here to take over," he said. "I don't expect to start making decisions or judging you. I'm here to do anything you tell me to do. You talk. I'll listen."

She nodded, feeling a little chagrined. She knew he meant well. He was just here to help her. Why couldn't she calm her fears and let him do just that?

As she glanced up, her gaze met his and she had an

impulse that horrified her. She wanted to throw herself into his arms, close her eyes and hold on tightly.

The same thing she'd felt before when he'd held her came back in a wave and she felt dizzy with it. She wanted his warmth and his comfort, wanted it with a fierce craving that ached inside her. She couldn't give in to that feeling. Turning away quickly, she hoped he couldn't see it in her eyes.

She was just feeling weak and scared. That was what it had to be. She couldn't let herself fall into that trap.

"Okay. I'm going to teach you everything I know about putting on a glaze," she said resolutely. "And believe me, it's simple. We'll start with a basic sugar glaze. You'll pick it up in no time at all."

He learned fast and she went ahead and taught him how to make a caramel glaze as well, including tricks on how not to let the sugar burn and how to roast the chopped pecans before you added them to make them crisper and more flavorful. She then showed him how to center the cakes on the lacy doilies she used in the fancy boxes she packed the cakes in before transporting them.

"Each cake should look like it's a work of art on its own," she told him. "Never ever let a cake look like you just shoved it into a box to get it where it needs to go. They should look like they're being carried in a golden coach, on their way to the ball."

He grinned. "Cinderella cakes?"

"Exactly. They have to look special. Otherwise, why not pick up a cake at the grocery store?"

That was when his phone rang. It made him jerk. He

knew before he even looked at the screen who it was. Brad. Brad wondering how things were going. Brad, wondering if he'd talked her into committing to his plan. Brad, trying to control everything, just like always.

He put the phone on vibrate and shoved it into his pocket.

Once they'd finished the glazing, he went back to babysitting, making peanut butter and jelly sandwiches for the boys. They looked so good, he made one for himself. Then he raided the refrigerator and made a cool, crisp salad for Jill.

"Lunchtime," he told her, once he'd set the boys down to eat at their little table in their playroom.

She gave one last look at her boxed creations, snuck a peek at the new cakes in the oven and turned to him with a smile.

"So far, so good," she said as she sat down across from him at the kitchen table. "Though one disaster can throw the whole schedule off."

"Relax," he said. "No disaster would dare ruin this day for you."

"Knock on wood," she said, doing just that. She took a bite of salad and made a noise of pleasure. "Ah! This is so refreshing." She cocked her head to the side. "The boys are being awfully good."

He nodded. "So it seems. I gave them their sandwiches."

She frowned. "You left them alone with food?"

"They seemed to be doing great when I looked in on them." He glanced toward the doorway. "Though they sure seem quiet."

Jill's eyes widened. "Too quiet," she cried, vaulting out of her chair and racing for the playroom. Visions of peanut butter masterpieces smeared on walls and teddy bears covered in sticky jam shot through her head.

Connor came right behind her. He didn't have as much experience with what might go wrong, but he could imagine a few things himself.

They skidded around the corner and into the room, only to find a scene of idyllic contentment. The peanut butter sandwiches were half eaten and lay on the table. The boys were completely out, both lying in haphazard fashion wherever they were when sleep snuck up on them. Jill turned and grinned at him.

"You did wear them out. Wow."

They lifted them carefully and put them down in the travel cribs that sat waiting against the far wall. Jill pulled light covers over each of them and they tiptoed out of the room and back to the kitchen.

"They look like they'll sleep for hours," she said hopefully.

"Maybe days," he added to the optimism, but she laughed.

"Doubtful. Besides, we'll miss them if they stay away that long."

"Will we?" he questioned, but he was smiling. He believed her.

She glanced at her watch. "We've got time for a nice long lunch," she said. "Maybe fifteen whole minutes. Those cakes have to be delivered by noon, but the church hall where they're going is only two blocks away. So let's sit down and enjoy a break."

She watched as he settled in across from her and began to eat his sandwich. She was so glad he'd talked her into letting him stay to help. Without him, she would surely be chasing her children up and down the stairs by now, with cakes burning in the background. She raised her glass of iced tea at him.

"To Connor McNair, life saver," she said. "Hip, hip, hooray."

He laughed. "Your Bundt cakes aren't all out of the fire yet," he told her with a crooked grin. "Don't count your chickens too soon."

"Of course not. I just wanted to acknowledge true friendship when it raises its furry head."

He shook his head and had to admit it was almost as covered with curls as hers. "Anytime," he told her, then tried to warble it as a tune. "Anytime you need me, I'll be there."

Her gaze caught his and she smiled and whispered, "Don't get cocky, kid."

His gaze deepened. "Why not?" he whispered back. "What's the fun of life if you don't take chances?"

She held her breath. For just a few seconds, something electric seemed to spark between them. And then it was gone, but she was breathing quickly.

"Chances. Is that what you call it?" she said, blinking a bit.

He nodded. "Chances between friends. That's all."

She frowned at him. "Some friend. Where were you to stop me from marrying Brad?"

The look in his face almost scared her. She'd meant it in a lighthearted way, but being casual about a subject that cut so deep into her soul didn't really work. Emotions were triggered. Her joke had fallen flat.

"I tried," he said gruffly, a storm brewing in his blue eyes.

He was kidding—wasn't he?

"What do you mean?" she asked, trying to ignore the trembling she heard in her own voice.

He leaned back in his chair but his gaze never left hers. "Remember? The night before your wedding."

She thought back. "Yes. Wait. You didn't even go to the bachelor party."

He snorted. "I went. Hell, I was hosting it." He seemed uncomfortable. "But I couldn't stay. I couldn't take all the celebration."

"Oh."

"So I went off and left all those happy guys to their revelry. I got a bottle of Scotch and took it to a sandy beach I knew of."

She nodded slowly, thinking back. "As I remember it, you were pretty tanked when you showed up at my apartment."

He took a deep breath and let it out. "Yes. Yes, I was. I was a tortured soul."

"Really? What were you so upset about that night?"

He stared at her. Couldn't she guess? Was she really so blind? He'd been out of his head with agony that night. He knew what a wonderful girl Jill was, knew it and loved her for it. And he knew Brad wasn't going to make her happy. But how could he tell her that? How could he betray a friend?

The problem was, he had to betray one of them. They

were both his best friends and he couldn't stand to see them getting married. And at the same time, he didn't think he should interfere. It was their decision. Their misfortune. Their crazy insane absolutely senseless leap into the brave unknown.

But he knew a thing or two, didn't he? He knew some things he was pretty sure she didn't know. But how could he hurt her with them? How could he explain to her about all the times Brad had cheated on her in the years they'd all been friends?

She would chalk it up to pure jealousy, and in a way, she would have been right. He was jealous. He wanted her. He knew Brad didn't value her enough. He knew Brad didn't deserve her. But how could he tell her that? How could he tell her the truth without ending up with her despising him more than she now did Brad? If she really did.

Besides, what could he offer her in place of her romance with Brad? He wasn't even sure he would ever be ready for any sort of full-time, long-term relationship. Every now and then he thought he'd conquered his background and the wariness he felt. But then he would see examples among his friends that just brought it back again. Could you trust another human in the long run? Was it worth the effort, just to be betrayed in the end?

And so—the Scotch. The alcohol was supposed to give him the courage to do what had to be done. But it didn't work that way. It made him sick instead, and he babbled incoherently once he had Jill's attention. She never understood what he was trying to say.

He couldn't even tell her now. She'd asked him a direct question. What was he so upset about that night? And still, he couldn't tell her the truth.

Because I knew you were marrying the wrong man. You should have been marrying me.

Reaching out, he caught her hand and looked deep into her eyes.

"Jill, tell me what you want. What you need in your life to be happy."

She stared back at him, and he waited, heart beating a fast tattoo on his soul.

"Connor," she began, "I... I don't know how to explain it exactly, but I..."

But then she shook her head and the timer went off and they both rose to check the cakes. Whatever she'd been about to say was lost in a cloud of the aroma of delicious confections.

The last full-size cakes came out and were set to cool and they began to fill the large mini Bundt cake pans. Twelve little cakes per pan. And each had to be filled to exactly the same level.

"They'll take about fifteen to twenty minutes," she told him nervously. "Then the ovens have to be back up to temperature before we put the next batch in. If we time it right, we might just make it. But it's going to be close."

One hundred and ten little cakes, she thought with a tiny surge of hysteria. Oh, my!

Connor left to deliver some of the full-size cakes. Jill checked on the babies. They were still sleeping in their travel cribs. She was thankful for that. Back to the kitchen, she began to prepare the rectangular boxes with the small dividers she was going to put the mini cakes in once they were ready to go. Then Connor was back and they pulled a batch out.

"These are perfect," she said with a sigh of relief. "You get the next batch ready. I'll make the Limoncello glaze."

They both had their eyes on the clock. Time seemed to go so quickly. Minutes seemed to evaporate into thin air. Jill was moving as fast as she could.

And then the phone started ringing. People who hadn't had their deliveries yet were wondering why.

"We're working as fast as we can," she told them. "Please, every minute I spend on the phone means your cake will get there that much later."

It was starting to feel hopeless. A batch overflowed its pan and they had to pull it out, clean up the mess and start again. She mixed up three batches of glaze and accidentally knocked them over onto the floor. That had to be done again.

And the clock was ticking.

She felt as though the beating of her heart was a clock, racing her, mocking her, letting her know she wasn't going to make it. Biting her lip, she forced back that feeling and dug in even harder.

"Last batch going in," Connor called.

She hurried over to see if it was okay. It was fine. Connor was turning out to be a godsend.

It was almost time. The phone rang. It was the Garden Club wondering where their cake was.

"Their party isn't until seven tonight," she said in full annoyance mode. "Can't they wait?"

"I'll run it over," Connor offered.

"You will not," she told him. "The engagement party is next. We have to deliver to them by five or we will have failed."

The twins woke up and were cranky. Connor tried to entertain them but there was very little hope. They wanted their mother.

Jill had to leave Connor alone with the cakes while she cuddled her boys and coaxed them into a better mood. She knew they needed her and she loved them to pieces, but all the while she felt time passing, ticking, making her crazy. She had to get back to the cakes.

Connor had his own problems. His phone was vibrating every fifteen minutes. Every call was from Brad. He knew that without even checking. He had no intention of answering the phone, but every time it began to move, he had that sinking feeling again.

Brad. Why couldn't he just disappear?

Instead he was texting. Connor didn't read the texts. There was no point to it. He knew what they said.

Brad wanted answers. He wanted to know what was going on. He wanted to get the latest scoop on Jill. All things Connor had no intention of giving him. But knowing Brad, that wasn't going to satisfy him. He was going to intrude, one way or another. And he wouldn't wait long to make his influence felt. Connor looked at his phone. If only there was some way to cut the link to Brad and his expectations.

CHAPTER SIX

IT WAS TIME. They had to move. But the twins wouldn't stop clinging to Jill.

Connor had an idea. He brought in a huge plastic tub he found in the garage, placing it in an empty corner of the kitchen, far from the oven and the electric appliances. Using a large pitcher, he put a few inches of barely warm water in the bottom.

"Hey kids," he called to them. "Want to go swimming?"

He didn't have to offer twice. They were excited, getting into their swimsuits and finding swim toys. Jill could get back to packing up her cakes and Connor could supervise the play area while he worked on glazing at the same time.

The long, rectangular boxes were filled with cakes for the Jamison engagement party. It was time to go. Connor packed them into Jill's van and took off. Jill sat down beside the tub of water to watch her boys pretend to swim and she felt tears well up in her eyes. They had made it. Now—as long as they didn't poison everyone at the engagement party, things would calm down. There were still a few cakes to deliver, but nothing was the hectic job the engagement party had been. She'd come through. And she couldn't have done it without Connor.

She wrapped her arms around her knees and hugged tightly. "Thank you, Connor," she whispered to the kitchen air. "You saved my life. I think I love you."

And she did. Didn't she? She always had. Not the way she loved Brad. But Brad was always such a problem and Connor never was.

She remembered when Brad had been the coolest guy around. The guy everyone looked up to, the hunk every girl wanted to be with. He drove the coolest convertible, had the best parties, knew all the right people. At least, that was the way it seemed back then. And he had chosen her. It was amazing how much you could grow up in just a few years and learn to see beyond the facade.

"Cool" didn't mean much when you had babies to feed in the middle of the night. And it only got in the way when it was time to separate your real friends from the posers. Back then, she'd been a pretty rotten judge of character. She'd improved. She had a better idea of what real worth was.

A half hour later, Connor was back. She rose to meet him, ready to ask him how it went, but he didn't give her time to do that. Instead he came right for her, picked her up and swung her around in a small celebratory dance.

"You did it," he said, smiling down into her face. "The cakes are delivered and the customer is in awe. You met the challenge. Congrats."

"We did it, you mean," she said, laughing as he

swung her around again. "Without you, all would be lost right now."

He put her down and shrugged. "What do we still have to get delivered?" he asked. "I want to get this job over with so we can relax." He looked down at the boys, still splashing about in the water. "Hey, guys. How are you doing?"

Timmy laughed and yelled something incomprehensible, and Tanner blew bubbles his way.

"Great," Connor said back, then looked at Jill. "Your orders, *mon chef?*" he asked.

"We do have two deliveries left," she said. "The last cakes are baking right now. We should be ready to call it a day in about an hour. Can you make it until then?"

"Only if I get a fair reward," he said, raising an eyebrow. "What are you offering?"

"I've got nothing," she said, making a face. "Unless you'll take kisses."

She was teasing, just having fun, but it hit him like a blow to the heart. "Kisses are my favorite," he told her gruffly, his eyes darkening.

She saw that, but it didn't stop her. Reaching up, she planted a kiss on his mouth, then drew back and laughed at him.

He laughed back, but his pulse was racing. "Hey, I'll work for those wages any day," he told her, and then he had to turn away. There was a longing welling up in him. He'd felt it before and he knew what it was.

He'd been yearning for Jill since the day he met her. His own background and emotional hiccups had worked against him letting her know over that first year, and by the time he actually knew what he wanted, Brad had taken over, and it was too late.

"What kind of glaze are we putting on these last cakes?" he asked her.

Jill didn't answer right away. She'd seen the look that had come over his face, noticed his reaction to her friendly kiss. For some reason, her heart was beating in a crazy way she wasn't used to.

"Those get a rum caramel with roasted chopped pecans sprinkled on top," she said at last.

They worked on it together, but there was a new feeling between them, a sort of sense of connection, that hadn't been there before. And she had to admit, she rather liked it.

He took out the last deliveries and stopped to pick up a pizza on his way home. She had the boys dried and put into their pajamas by then. They got their own special meals and then were put into the playroom to play quietly and get ready for bed. Jill set out the pizza on the kitchen table and she and Connor ate ravenously.

"Wow," he said with a groan. "What a day. I've worked in a lot of places, but I've never been put through the wringer like I was today."

"You did great," she responded. "I couldn't have met the deadlines without you."

He sighed. "What's the outlook for tomorrow?"

Tomorrow? She hadn't allowed herself to think that far ahead. Was he going to leave tonight? She didn't think so. He didn't seem to be making any of the pertinent preparations. And if he stayed tonight, what about tomorrow? Would he stay then, too? Should she let him?

"Just a couple of orders," she said. "And then, for the rest of the week, not a thing."

"Oh." He looked at her with a guilty grimace. "Uh, maybe you'd better take a look at some of the orders I took over the phone today. I wrote them down somewhere."

That started a mad scramble to locate the paper he'd written them down on.

"I have to set up a system," she muttered once they'd found it. "What if you'd gone and never told me about these?"

Gone? Where was he going?

Their gazes met and the question was there and neither of them wanted to answer it.

She looked at him, at his handsome face, his strong shoulders, and she felt a wave of affection. There was no one else she would have rather spent this day with. It had to be him.

She stopped in front of him and smiled, putting a hand flat on his chest. "Thank you," she said solemnly. "I can never stop thanking you enough. You really did make the difference today."

He didn't smile, but there was a dark, cloudy look in his eyes and he put his own hand over hers. "I wish I could do more," he said, and she could have sworn his voice cracked a little.

She shook her head, wishing she had the right to kiss him the way you would a lover. "You saved me from the nightmares," she murmured.

He frowned. "What nightmares."

She shrugged, wishing she hadn't brought it up.

"Sometimes I have this dream where I'm all alone on an island that's being attacked by huge black birds. They look sort of like vultures. They peck away at me. I run and run and they swoop down. Every time I turn to fight one off, others attack from behind me." She shuddered.

His hand tightened over hers. "Bummer."

She tried to smile but her lips were trembling. "No kidding."

"Hey." He leaned forward and dropped a soft kiss on her mouth. "I had a dream about birds last night, too. Only my dream was about a beautiful huge white bird with lacy wings. I was desperately trying to catch her. And you know what? That bird was you."

She smiled, enchanted, and he kissed her again. "Connor," she whispered warningly, trying to draw back, and a shout from one of the boys gave her statement emphasis. He straightened and watched as she left him.

They both went up to put the boys to bed.

"They're just going to climb out of these cribs again," Connor whispered to her.

"Shh. Don't remind them of the possibilities."

They covered the boys and turned out the lights and left, hoping for the best.

"How about a glass of wine?" he asked her.

She hesitated, knowing it would put her right to sleep. "I'd better not," she said. "But you go ahead."

The phone rang. She sighed. She was completely exhausted and ready to go to bed early and try to recoup. Hopefully this wasn't one of her friends asking about the date last night. She'd already ignored a couple of those calls on her cell. And if it was an order for a cake, she only hoped she would be able to get the facts straight.

"Hello?" she said, stifling a yawn. "Jill's Cakes."

"Oh, thank goodness," said the lady on the other end of the line. "You're there. Now please, please don't tell me you're closed for the night."

Jill frowned. What the heck did that mean? Was it someone at the engagement party who thought some of their order was missing? Or something different? "Well, uh, we're here and cleaning up but our workday is pretty much over. Was there something you needed?"

"Oh, Jill, this is Madeline Green," she responded in a voice that could summon cows. "You know me from the church choir."

"Of course." She pulled the phone a bit away from her ear and glanced up at Connor who had come close and was listening. She gave him a shrug. "Nice to hear from you, Madeline."

"Honey, listen. I'm here at the Elks lodge. We've had a disaster. Our caterer has failed us. We have one hundred and two people here for dinner and we have no dessert."

"Oh." No. Her brain was saying, *"No!"* Her body was saying, *"No!"* "I see. Uh….maybe you should go out and buy some ice cream."

"Impossible. We have to have a special dessert. It's traditional. People expect it. This is Old Timers' Night. Some only come to this annual award dinner because of the fancy desserts we usually serve. It's everyone's favorite part."

"But you had some ordered?"

"Oh, yes. They never showed up. The caterer disavows all knowledge of what the pastry chef was up to. He washes his hands of it entirely."

"I see." Her brain was still shrieking, "No!"

"Have you tried the Swedish bakery?"

"They're closed. In fact, everyone is closed. You're our only hope."

Jill blinked. "So you called everyone else first?"

"Well…"

"Never mind." She made a face, but the lady couldn't see it. She took a deep breath. "Madeline, I'm afraid we just can't…"

Suddenly she was aware that Connor had grabbed her upper arm and was shaking her gently.

"Say 'yes,'" he hissed at her intensely.

"What?" she mouthed back, covering the receiver with her hand. "Why?"

"Say 'yes.' Never ever say 'no.'"

He meant it. She groaned.

"You're trying to build up a reputation," he whispered close to her ear. "You need to be the go-to person, the one they can always depend on. If you want to build your business up, you have to go the extra mile."

He was right. She knew he was right. But she was so tired. She really didn't want to do this.

"Say 'yes'," he insisted.

She was too limp to fight it. Uncovering the mouthpiece, she sighed and handed the phone to him. "You do it," she said.

She turned around and looked at the mess they would have to wade through to get this done. Everything in her rebelled.

"You realize how many they need, don't you?" she asked when Connor hung up.

"Yes. We can do it."

"Can we? What makes you think you can say that?"

"I've seen you work. And I'm here to help you."

She winced. "How long do we have?"

"One hour."

Her mouth dropped open but no sound came out.

"Okay," Connor said quickly, hoping to forestall any forecasts of doom. "Think fast. What do you make that cooks in less than an hour?"

She shrugged. She felt like a wrung-out rag. "Cookies."

"Then we make cookies."

She frowned. "But that's not special."

"It is the way we make them." He looked at her expectantly. "What'll we do?"

She looked at him and she had to smile, shaking her head. She knew he was as beat as she was, but the call for desserts seemed to have given him new life. "You're the one who made the promises. You tell me."

"Come on. What's your signature cookie?"

She closed her eyes. "I'm too tired to think."

"Me, too," he agreed stoutly. "So we'll go on instinct instead of brainpower."

She began to laugh. This was all so ridiculous.

They'd just produced more baked product than she'd ever done before in one day, and now they were going to do more? Impossible.

"Cookies?" he coaxed.

"I guess."

They made cookies. Pecan lace cookies with a touch of cardamom, pressed together like sandwiches with mocha butter cream filling between them. Chocolate ganache on the base. A touch of white butter cream around the edges, like a lacy frill.

Connor used the mixer while Jill prepped the pans and got the chocolate ready to melt. Just as the first pan went into the oven, they heard the sound of giggling from the next room.

Jill looked at Connor. "Oh, no."

He nodded. "They climbed out again. We should have known they would." He looked at her. There was no time to spare and she was the chef. "I'll take care of them," he told her. "You just keep baking."

It took a couple of minutes to catch the boys and carry them back up, and all the while, he was racking his brain to think of some way to keep them in their beds. There was only one idea that just might work, but he knew instinctively that Jill wasn't going to like it. They didn't have much choice. He was going to have to do it and deal with the consequences later.

CHAPTER SEVEN

BY THE TIME Connor got back to the kitchen, Jill had at least sixty cookies cooling and was beginning assembly of the desserts.

"I don't hear the boys," she said. "What did you do?"

"Don't worry. I took care of it."

She stopped and looked at him through narrowed eyes. "You didn't tie them up or anything like that, did you?"

"No, nothing like that. I'd show you, but right now, we've got to hurry with this stuff."

She gave him a penetrating glance, but she was in the middle of the drizzle across the top of each confection and her attention got diverted.

"What do you think?" she asked him.

Connor looked the sample over with a critical eye.

"I don't know. It still needs something. Something to make it look special."

They both stared for a long sixty seconds.

"I know," he said. "We've got plenty of buttercream left. Get your decorating thingamajig."

"Why?"

"I've seen the flowers you can make with butter cream frosting. You're going to make one hundred and two rose buds."

"Oh." She looked at the clock. "Do you really think we can get them out in time?"

"I know we can." He grinned at her, then swooped in and kissed her hard on her pretty mouth. "We can do anything. We already have."

He took her breath away, but she stayed calm. At least outwardly. She stared at him for a few seconds, still feeling that kiss. Why was he doing things guaranteed to send her into a tailspin if she didn't hold herself together?

But she went back to work and she kept control and the job got finished. And at the end, they stared at each other.

"We did it."

"We did, didn't we?"

"But the delivery…"

"Quick. We're five minutes late."

He piled the desserts in boxes and headed for the door. Just before he disappeared, he called back, "Better check on the twins."

She was already on her way. There wasn't a sound as she climbed the stairs. When she opened the door, nothing moved. But somehow everything looked a little wrong. In the dark, she couldn't quite figure out what it was and she hated to turn on the light, but she had to. And what she saw left her speechless.

"What?"

One crib stood empty. The other had been turned

upside down. The mattress was on the ground, but the rest of the crib was above it like a cage. And on the mattress, her two little boys were sound asleep.

Her first impulse was to wake them up and rescue them, but then she realized they were probably better off where they were. After all, how was she going to get them to stay in their cribs without the bars?

She went back down, not sure what to do. She started cleaning up the kitchen, but then she heard Connor driving up and she went to meet him at the door.

He came in smiling. "They loved it," he announced. "People were asking for our card and I was handing them out like crazy."

She put her head to the side and raised her eyebrows as she listened to him. *"Our"* card? When had that happened? But she could deal with that later. Right now she had something else on her mind.

"Now do you want to explain what happened to the crib?"

"Oh." His face changed and suddenly he looked like a boy with a frog in his pocket. "Sure. I, uh, I had to turn it upside down."

"So I see."

He gave her a guilty smile. "Are they okay?"

She nodded. "Sound asleep."

"Good." He looked relieved. "That was the goal."

"But Connor…"

"They wouldn't stay in the cribs," he told her earnestly. "They kept climbing out. And that was just so dangerous. This was the only thing I could think of on the fly. And luckily, they loved it when I put them into their own special cage. I told them to be monkeys and they played happily until they went to sleep. Didn't they?"

"I guess so, but…"

"If I hadn't done it, they would still be climbing out and running for the hills. And we wouldn't have finished in time."

"Okay." She held up a hand and her gaze was steely. "Enough. I understand your logic. What I don't understand is how you could do such a crazy thing without consulting me first."

That stopped him in his tracks. He watched her and realized she was right. He thought he was doing what was best for her, but without her consent, it was really just what was best for him. He had no right to decide for her. They were her kids.

He'd goofed again and it pained him. Why was he always putting his foot in it where she was concerned? He had to apologize. He swallowed hard. That wasn't an easy thing to do. Taking a deep breath, he forced himself to do what had to be done.

"Jill, you're absolutely right," he said sincerely. "And I'm really sorry. I was wrong to take your agreement for granted. I won't do that again."

Now she had a lump in her throat. Few had ever said that sort of thing to her before, especially not a man. Could she even imagine Brad saying such a thing? Hardly. She felt a small sense of triumph in her chest. She'd asked for an apology and she got one. Wow.

"I guess the first order of business is to figure out

how to make a crib they can't climb out of," she noted, looking at him expectantly.

He feigned astonishment. "Who? Me? You want me to build a crib they can't climb out of?"

"Either that, or come up with a plan," she said, teasing him flirtatiously. "Aren't you here to help?"

His grin was endearingly crooked and he pulled her to him, looking down like a man who was about to kiss a very hot woman. She looked up at him, breath quickening, and she realized she really wanted that kiss. But a look of regret and warning flashed in his eyes. He quickly released her and turned away.

"You ready for that glass of wine now?" he asked, walking toward the wet bar at the end of the room.

She took a deep breath and closed her eyes before she answered. "Sure," she said. "Why not?"

He poured out two crystal glasses of pinot noir and they sat in the living room on a small couch. There was a gentle rain falling and they could see it through the huge glass windows that covered one side of the room.

"What a day," he said, gazing at her as he leaned back in his corner of the couch. The dim light left the wine in their glasses looking like liquid rubies. "It feels like it must have lasted at least a day and a half."

"Or maybe three and a half," she agreed. "And a few shocks to the system." She sighed. "But you came through like a trooper. I couldn't have done it without you."

"I'm glad I was here to help."

She met his gaze and then looked away too quickly. She felt her cheeks reddening and groaned inside. There was nothing to be embarrassed about. Why had she avoided his eyes like that? She coughed to cover up her feelings.

"So tell me the story of this cooking talent you seem to have discovered in the mysterious East," she said quickly.

He grinned. "So you can see the evidence of my expertise in my work even here," he said grandly.

The corners of her mouth quirked. "No, but you told me you were good, so I believe it."

"Ah." He nodded. "Well, it's all the fault of a young chef named Sharon Wong. We dated each other for most of the last year in Singapore. She taught me everything I know." He made a comical face. "Of course, that was only a small fraction of what *she* knows, but it was a start."

A woman was behind it all. She should have known. But it gave her a jolt. Connor had never seemed to have a special woman in his life. Lots of women, but no one special. Had that changed?

"A chef. Great. I'm partial to chefs. What kind of cuisine?"

"She specializes in Mandarin Chinese but she mostly taught me French basics. She claims every chef needs French cooking as a standard, a baseline to launch from. Sort of like learning Calculus for science classes."

She nodded. "That's why it's so important for Trini to go to the school she just left to attend. She'll get a great grounding in the basics."

He watched her for a moment, then asked, "Why didn't you ever go there?"

She shrugged and stretched back against the pillows, beginning to feel her body relax at last. "I took classes locally, but nothing on that level." Her smile was wistful. "Funny. I applied a few years ago. I got accepted on my first try. A scholarship and everything. But I didn't get to go."

"Why not?"

She gave him a bemused smile. "I married Brad instead."

"Wow, that was a bad decision." He looked pained at the thought. "You gave up going to the school of your dreams to marry Brad?"

"Yes." She threw him a reproving look. He was getting a little adamant about her life choices. "And I do regret it. So that's why I won't let her give it up for anything. She's got to go. She'll learn so much."

He was quiet and she wondered what he was thinking about. Something in the look on his face told her it still bothered him to think of her giving up her dream that way and she wasn't sure why he cared.

Everybody had to make choices. Everybody had to give something up now and then. It was part of life.

"I was just thinking about that time we went to San Francisco," she said a few minutes later. "Remember?"

He looked up and his smile completely changed his face. "Sure I remember. You had set up a weekend to celebrate Brad's birthday with a surprise trip to San Francisco and then you ended up taking me instead."

She nodded, still captivated by that smile.

"It was senior year, wasn't it?" he went on. "You got

a hotel just off Union Square and tickets to the ballet—or so you said."

She nodded again. "That was my big mistake. Once I told Brad that, he suddenly had somewhere else he had to be that weekend."

She could hardly believe it. What a fool she'd been in those days. "I was so mad, I told him I was going to take you instead. And he said, sure, go ahead."

Connor smiled, recalling that sunny day. He thought he'd died and gone to heaven. He was walking on air when she asked him to go with her.

A whole weekend with Jill and no Brad. He hadn't even cared if it was the ballet. But the beauty of it was, she was just setting up a surprise, because the tickets that she had were for the Giants in Candlestick Park. The ballet thing was just a ruse to tease Brad and the baseball game was supposed to be his big surprise. Instead it was Connor's.

She gazed at him speculatively. "Sometimes when I look back I wonder why I didn't notice."

His heart gave a lurch. What was she reading into his responses? "Notice what?"

She shrugged. "How little Brad actually cared for me."

Oh, that. It had always been obvious to most of those around her. Brad wanted her when he wanted her, but he didn't confine his activities too close to home. Still, looking at her now, he couldn't stand the haunted expression in her eyes. The last thing in the world she should do was beat herself up over the past.

"He cared plenty," he said gruffly. "He wanted you for himself right from the first. Don't you remember?"

She shook her head and gave him a sad smile. "I think you know what I mean. Anyway, we had a great time in San Francisco, didn't we?"

"Yes, we did." He let his head fall back as he thought of it. That trip had planted dreams in his head. You could say he might have been better off without them, but he didn't think so. His feelings for Jill were a part of that time, even if she never knew it.

"Remember that night? We talked until almost dawn, and then we slept until noon."

"Yeah." They had two rooms, but he never went to his own. There were two beds in hers, one for each of them, and he just stayed with her. He never touched her, but he sure wanted to.

And best of all, it was on that night that he knew he was ready to try to have a real relationship. He'd spent the first few years in college wary of making any sort of commitment to any girl. His background had argued strenuously against it.

But Jill was different. He made up his mind that night that he was going to tell her how he felt about her once they got back to the university. And he was resolved— he was going to take her away from Brad. Somehow, someway, he would do it. He spent hours going over what he wanted to say, how he wanted to make her understand his feelings.

And then they got back to school, and there was Brad on crutches. He'd gone waterskiing and broken his leg. Suddenly he needed Jill. Connor felt himself fading into the background, like some sort of invisible man, and wondering why his timing was always so bad.

It was shortly afterward that he signed up to go to Europe for a semester. When he got back, he learned that Jill and Brad had broken up just after he left. From what he could see, Brad was busy dating every pretty girl on campus while Jill was busy trying to pretend she didn't care.

He took her to his favorite little Italian restaurant and they ate pasta and talked for hours. He ended up with his arm around her while she cried on his shoulder about how awful Brad was being to her. He restrained himself. He was going to do it right. He was going to take it one step at a time.

But once again, the timing wasn't in his favor. By the next afternoon, Brad was back in her life and all was forgiven.

That was when he'd hardened his heart. It had happened to him one too many times. He wasn't going to let it happen again—ever. Even today he was wary. What seemed like the opportunity to strike so often ended up as the chance to fall on his face instead. It wasn't worth it.

"I think of that trip to San Francisco as an island of happiness in an ocean of stress," she said softly. She looked at him with gentle speculation and a touch of pure affection. "Everything is always so easy with you. And it was always so hard with Brad."

Really? Really?

He stared at her, wondering how she could say such a thing. If that was so, why had she married the hard guy? He was tempted to come right out and ask her that question. That just might clarify a lot of things between them. But before he could think of a way to put it, she spoke again.

"So, was it serious?" she asked him.

He was startled. "Was what serious?"

"You and Sharon Wong?"

"Oh." He laughed, then considered for a moment. "Who knows? It might get to be. If I go back to Singapore."

She turned away. Why did she have such a sick feeling in the pit of her stomach? Was she jealous? Ridiculous. He deserved to fall in love. He deserved some happiness. Hadn't she just been counseling him to find someone to marry? And now she was going to go all green-eyed over a woman he obviously had some affection for? What a fool she was acting.

Connor was probably the best man she knew. He'd always been there for her—except when he took off for places like Singapore. Still, he'd always been a playboy in so many ways. She couldn't imagine him in love.

"I never knew any of your girlfriends in college," she noted. "Why was that? You never showed up with a girl on your arm. I knew they existed, because I heard about them. How come you never brought them around?"

He gazed at her and didn't know what to say. He'd dated plenty of girls in college. But why would he take any of them to meet the one girl he cared about above all others? They would have seen through his casual act in no time.

Funny that she never did.

He stared at her for a long, pulsing moment. "You could have had me anytime you wanted me," he said in a low, rough voice.

There. He'd said it. Finally a little hunk of truth thrown out into this sea of making everyone feel good about themselves. What was she going to do about it?

"Connor!"

She didn't seem to want to take it as truth. More like teasing. Did she really think he was making a joke?

"Be serious," she said, waving that away. "You know that's not true. You didn't want anyone to be your steady girl. You wanted fun and excitement and games and flirting. You didn't want a real relationship. You admitted it at the time." She made a face at him. "You have to realize that back then, what you wanted didn't seem to have anything to do with what I wanted."

He shook his head sadly. "I don't know how you could have read me so wrong."

"I didn't." She made a face at him. "You just don't remember things the way they really were. I was looking for the tie that binds, just like a lot of women at that age. It's a natural instinct. Nesting. I felt a deep need for a strong male, someone to build the foundation of a family with."

He almost rolled his eyes at her. Was she really so self-delusional? "So you chose a guy who didn't want kids."

Her shoulders sagged. He got her on that one. What had she been thinking? He was right. She'd known from the first that he didn't want children. Somehow she had buried that fact under everything, pretending to herself that it didn't matter. Maybe she wouldn't want children, either. Or, more likely, he would change his mind. After all, once it was a clear possibility, surely he would think twice and begin to waver. After all, he loved her. Didn't he?

"I didn't say I chose wisely." She hated to face it, but he had hit the nail on the head. Her mistakes had been easy to avoid, if she'd only been paying more attention. Sighing, she rose. "I want to check on the kids. And I think I'll change out of this uniform. Will you still be up or should I not come back and let you get some sleep?"

He looked at her and realized he wanted her back above all else. He wanted her in his bed, in his arms, in his life. But for now he would have to do with the minimum.

"Sure, come on back," he said, holding up his wine-glass. "I've still got a long way to go."

She was glad he'd said that. As she stopped in to look at her sleeping children, she sighed. The upturned crib was not a long-term solution. Something would have to give. She only hoped it wasn't her peace of mind.

She stopped by the guest room where she slept and changed into something more comfortable, then hurried back down, wondering if he would be asleep before she got back. But he was still staring at the light through his wine and he smiled to welcome her as she entered the room.

She flopped down on the little couch, sitting much closer this time. She was drawn to his warmth, drawn to his masculinity. Might as well face it. She loved looking at him, loved the thought of touching him. Would he kiss her good-night? That would be worth a little loss of sleep.

"Connor, how come I don't really know anything about your childhood? How come you never talk about it?"

He took a long sip of wine and looked at her through narrowed eyes. Then he put on his Sam Spade tough-guy voice. "It's not a pretty story, sweetheart. Full of ugliness and despair. You don't want to worry your pretty little head over it."

"Be serious for a moment," she asked. "Really. I want to know you better."

"Why? What more can there be? We've known each other for more than ten years and suddenly you don't know me?"

"Exactly. You've used our friendship as cover all this time. And now I want to know the truth. What were your parents really like? Not the cartoon version you dredge up for jokes. The real people."

He appeared uncomfortable for a moment, then thought for a second or two, and began.

"Let's just put it this way. As they say in the head-shrinking crowd, I've had lifelong relationship com-mitment problems, which can probably be traced back to my childhood environment."

"And that means?"

He stared at her. Did she really want him to go there? Okay.

"I learned early and firsthand just what kind of power women have," he said softly. "I watched my mother purposefully drive my father crazy. Payback, I think, for never making as much money as she felt she needed."

"Ouch." She frowned.

"Yes." He glanced at his ruby-red wine and thought back. "My father was a sweet guy in many ways. He tried hard to please her. But he just didn't have what it took to bring in a high salary, and she rubbed his nose in it every day."

"Oh, Connor," she said softly.

"I watched him go through all sorts of contortions to find some little way to bring a smile to her face, but that was virtually impossible. She nitpicked everything. Nothing was ever good enough for her." He threw her a lopsided grin. "Especially me."

"So she nitpicked you, too?"

"Oh, yeah. I think finding something to make me stammer out 'gee, I'm sorry, Mom,' was what made her day for her." He looked at her. "So I avoided going home. I hung around school in the afternoon, joined every sports team, every debating society, every club that would give me a place to hang out." His gaze darkened. "Meanwhile my father drank himself to death."

"Oh, Connor. I'm so sorry."

He nodded. "It was a waste, really. He was a smart guy. He should have had a better life."

"Yes."

He gazed at her levelly, wondering if he really wanted to get into the next level of this discussion. Did he want to cut a vein and just let it bleed all over the night? Not really. But he might as well explain a little more about why he'd been the way he was when they were younger.

"You know, for years I really was leery of having a relationship with a woman that lasted more than twenty minutes. It just didn't seem worth the risk from what I'd seen."

She wrinkled her nose at him, as if she thought he was being silly. Still, he plowed on.

"But I have a new perspective on it now. I spent the last eighteen months or so in Singapore working with a great guy name George who is married to a wonderful woman named Peggy. I lived in their house and saw their entire interaction, and it helped me understand that decent, loving relationships are possible. I had to look harder at myself and wonder if I had what it takes to have that. I mean, it may be possible, but is it possible for me?"

Jill stared at him. She'd had no idea he had such deep misgivings about lifetime relationships. It made her want to reach out to him, to hold his hand and reassure him. There were plenty of women in the world who didn't treat men the way his mother had. Didn't he know that?

"And what did you decide?" she asked tentatively.

He flashed her a quick grin. "The verdict isn't in yet."

She started to argue about that, but she stopped herself. How could she wrestle him out of opinions that had developed from real life experiences? She didn't have as many bad ones as he did. Maybe it got harder as they piled up.

"Where's your mother now?" she asked.

He shrugged. "I'm not sure. I think she moved to Florida to live with her sister, but we don't keep in touch."

She thought that was a mistake, but she held her tongue. Maybe later she would try to talk to him about how much could be lost when you lost your parents. Instead of going into it directly, she decided to tell him about her background.

"Here's what happened to me," she said. "And Sara. When my mother was alive, we were a happy family. At least, that's the way I remember it. But my father's second marriage was a horror show right from the beginning. That's why Sara and I never warmed to our stepmother, Lorraine." She shook her head.

"She was such a terrible choice for him. And it probably didn't help the marriage that we couldn't like her. He was a good guy, gentle, warm. And she was a shrew."

"Wow," he said, somewhat taken aback. He wasn't used to such strong disapproval from Jill. "That's a pretty negative judgment on the woman."

She shrugged. "Of course, I saw the whole thing through the perspective of a child who had lost her mother and found her father bringing home a new, updated version that didn't please her at all. We were very resentful and probably didn't give her much of a chance, especially after she had a baby. Little Kelly was cute, but it didn't make up for Lorraine. And she didn't like us any better than we liked her and she made it pretty obvious."

"Little Kelly is the one who died last week in a car crash?"

She nodded. "The one I wish we'd been kinder to." She shrugged, but her eyes were sad and haunted. "Too late now." She looked at him again. "And that's what I want you to think about. Don't wait until it's too late to contact your mother again."

He gave her a quizzical look. "Okay. Point taken."

She nodded, then yawned. He smiled.

"You look like a sleepy princess."

She'd traded in her uniform for a short fuzzy robe over the long lacy white nightgown and she looked adorable to him.

"What?" she said, laughing.

"In that gown thing. Even with the little robe over it. You look like you should be in a castle."

She was blushing. Connor had a way of letting her know how pretty he thought she was and she was so hungry for that, it almost brought tears to her eyes.

She smiled back. "I guess we'd better go to bed."

"You're right. We need sleep. I'm only glad we survived the day."

He rose and turned to pull her up beside him and he didn't let go of her hands once they were standing face-to-face, looking at each other.

"I'm glad you came back," she told him, her breath catching in her throat as her pulse began to race. Was he going to kiss her? Or was she going to have to do it herself?

"Me, too." His eyes went so dark, they could have been black instead of blue. He leaned closer, pulling her body up hard against his. "Jill..." he began, and at the same moment, the cell phone in his pocket began to vibrate.

She felt it right away. Sharply drawing in her breath, she stepped back and looked at him. He pulled the phone out, looking for a place to set it down. She reached out and took it from him. Flipping it up, she glanced at the screen and handed it back to him.

"Message for you," she said, and her voice showed no emotion. "How interesting. It's Brad." Her face didn't reveal a thing, but her eyes were strangely hooded as she turned away and started for the stairs. "Good night," she said over her shoulder.

He cringed, though he wouldn't show it. He stuck the phone back in his pocket and didn't answer it. He hadn't been answering Brad's calls all day. Why should he start now?

But he wished she hadn't seen that.

CHAPTER EIGHT

SLEEPING ON THE couch was getting old fast. Connor stretched and hit the armrest before he had his legs out straight.

"Ouch," he muttered grumpily, wondering why he was awake so early when he was still so tired. Then he noticed the problem. The twins were running around the furniture and yelling at the top of their lungs. He groaned. He really preferred a normal alarm clock.

He opened his eyes just enough to see them. They were pretty cute. But loud. He was going to have to give up any chance for more sleep. He stretched again.

"Great game, kids," he told them groggily, swinging his legs over the side of the couch and sitting up with a yawn.

The boys stopped and stared at him. He stared back. Tanner pretended to bark like a puppy. Timmy made a sound like a growling monster. He shook his head. They wanted him to respond. He could tell. And he couldn't resist.

Just like the day before, he burst up off the couch,

waving the covers to make himself look huge, and gave them a monster growl they wouldn't soon forget.

They screamed with scared happiness and charged out of the room, pushing and shoving to both fit through the door at once.

Jill came in and glared at him. "They won't be able to eat their breakfast if you rile them up too much," she warned.

He waved his sheet-covered arms at her and growled. She shook her head and rolled her eyes.

"How come you're not scared?" he complained.

"Because you look so ridiculous," she told him. She laughed softly, letting her gaze slide over his beautiful body. What on earth did he do in Singapore that kept him so fit? His muscles were hard and rounded and tan and a lot of that was on display. His chest was all male and his pajama bottoms hung low on his hips. He took her breath away.

"But you do look cute as a scary monster," she allowed, trying to avoid an overdose of his sexiness by looking away. "We might be able to use your skills at Halloween."

"Hey, no fair," he said as he looked her over sleepily. "You already changed out of your princess dress."

"I'm going incognito for the day," she told him. "They don't let princesses bake Bundt cakes."

"They should."

"I know." She smiled at him then asked with false cheerfulness, "What did Brad want last night?"

He shrugged. "I didn't answer it."

She stared at him for a moment, then looked away.

"I just checked my email. There are already two more orders from people who had cake last night. That makes four who want their cakes today, and two more for the weekend."

"I said you had star power. Didn't I?"

She reached out to take the sheet from him and he leaned forward and dropped a quick kiss on her mouth before she could draw back. She looked up into his eyes and the room began to swim around her.

"They should let princesses do whatever they want," he said softly, and then he reached out and pulled her closer and she slipped her arms around his neck and his mouth found hers.

Finally!

She'd been waiting for this kiss forever—or anyway, it seemed that way. She melted in his arms, taking in his taste and letting her body feel every hard part of him it could manage. His rounded muscles turned her on and his warm, musky smell sent her senses reeling.

And then the doorbell rang.

She collapsed against him, laughing and shaking her head. "Why does fate hate me?" she protested.

He held her close and buried his face in her hair, then let her go.

A timer went off.

"Oh, no, I've got to check that," she said.

"I'll go to the door," he offered.

"Really?" She looked at him skeptically, wondering who was going to get a stunning view of that magnificent chest and hoping it wasn't the church people. Then she rushed on into the kitchen to check her cake.

It definitely needed to come out. She set it on the cooling rack and looked around at the mess that still existed from yesterday. She usually made it a practice never to go to bed with a dirty pan left in the sink, but she'd broken that rule last night. Now she had a couple of counters full of pans that needed washing. She was working on that when Connor came into the kitchen.

"Who's at the door?" she asked distractedly.

Connor made a face. "The Health Department Inspector."

She turned to stare at him. "What? He just came last week."

He shrugged. "I guess he's back."

And so he was, coming into the kitchen and looking around with massive disapproval all over his face. Tall and thin, he wore glasses and had a large, fluffy mustache, along with a pinched look, that made him look like a bureaucratic force to be reckoned with.

Connor made a face at her and left to put on some clothes. The inspector sniffed at him as he left, then looked back at the kitchen.

"What the hell is going on here?" he demanded, looking at the pot and pan strewn counters.

Jill had a smart-alecky answer right on the tip of her tongue, but she held it back. This was the health inspector. He could ruin her if he wanted to. Shut her down. She had to be nice to him, much as it stuck in her craw.

"Look, this is such a bad time for you to show up. Unannounced, I might add. Aren't you supposed to make appointments?"

He glared at her. "Aren't you supposed to be ready at all times for inspection?"

She gave him a fake smile. "Sorry about the mess. I'm in the middle of cleaning it up. We had a huge, huge day yesterday. Things will be back in order in no time."

"That would be wise," he said. "I wouldn't want to have to write you up for kitchen contamination."

She gaped at him in outrage. "There's clutter, there's mess, but there's no contamination. Please!"

He shrugged, then turned as Connor reappeared, dressed in the same shirt and slacks he'd been wearing for three days now.

"What are you doing here?" he asked.

"Moral support," Connor responded simply. "I'm just a friend. I'm helping."

His eyes narrowed. "Helping how?"

Connor shrugged, instinctively knowing this might be a time to be careful and wary. "Odd jobs. Deliveries."

"Ah." He appeared skeptical. "Let's hope you aren't doing any of the baking. Because if you are, you're going to need to be screened for medical conditions. You'll need a blood test. And more. We don't want you touching the food if you're not healthy. Your papers must be in order."

Connor frowned at the man. "What papers?"

"The ones you need to qualify to do any cooking whatsoever."

Connor sighed and looked away. "Ah, those papers."

"Yes. Records of shots and tests, etc. Medical problems in the last ten years. You understand."

Connor made a face, but he said as pleasantly as possible, "Of course."

The man glared at him. "So? Where are your papers?"

"Really?" Connor said, beginning to get belligerent. "Hey, Mr. Health Inspector, let's see *your* papers."

The man produced a badge and a license and Connor stared at them, realizing he had no idea if they were authentic or not. But he was beginning to have his doubts about this guy.

Jill winced. Connor looked about ready to do something that would jeopardize her business and she had to stop him. Standing behind the inspector, she shook her head and put her finger to her lips, then jerked her thumb toward the other room. Connor hesitated, then followed her out into the hallway, leaving the inspector to poke around at will.

"Connor, don't antagonize him, for heaven's sake," she whispered. "He'll probably write me up for some little thing and then he'll have to come back to check if I've fixed it. But at least he'll go. So leave him alone."

Connor was frowning. "How often does this guy show up here?" he asked her.

"Too much if you ask me. I almost feel like it's harassment at this point. And the funny thing is, every time he comes, something seems to go wrong. I don't know if it's just that I get nervous and then I don't keep focused on what I'm doing or what."

Connor's gaze narrowed. "What sort of things go wrong?"

"Oh...one time the oven wouldn't work anymore and

I had to get a repairman out. Another time somehow the refrigerator got unplugged and it was hours before we knew it. A lot of supplies spoiled and I had to throw them out."

"No kidding." He frowned. "Is he the same official who comes every time?"

"No. But he does come the most. And he says the goofiest things. In fact, I called the health department to complain about him a few weeks ago. They claimed they hadn't sent anyone."

Connor's face was hard as stone. "That doesn't seem right."

"I know. But what can I do? I don't dare confront him. What if he pulls my license?"

Connor shook his head. "Jill, I don't buy it for a minute."

She stared at him. "What do you mean?"

"I think he's a phony. He's got to go."

"What?" She grabbed at his arm to stop him, but he pulled away and marched back into the kitchen, catching the stranger with a tiny camera in his hand.

"Get the hell out of here," he told the inspector in a low, furious voice.

"Connor!" Jill cried, coming in behind him. "You can't talk that way to the inspector!"

But the man seemed to take Connor quite seriously. He raised his hands as though to show he didn't mean any harm and said, "Okay, okay. Take it easy. I'm going."

And he turned around and left as quickly as he could.

Jill stared after him, then looked at Connor. "What the heck?" she cried.

He turned and gave her a look. "Jill, that man's not a real health inspector. Can't you see that?"

"No." She blinked in bewilderment. "What is he then?"

"A private investigator pretending to be a health inspector."

"But why would…?" Her face cleared. "Brad!"

Connor nodded. "That's my guess."

She sank into a chair. "Oh, my gosh. I can't believe that. Brad sent him to spy on me."

"And to sabotage your business, I would guess."

She closed her eyes and took a deep breath. "Why didn't I think of that? I knew there was something fishy about the way he kept showing up." She looked up at Connor. "I should have known."

But Connor was still thinking things over. "Okay, I'm ready to believe that was Brad at work. So the question is, what else has he been meddling in?"

She thought for a moment, then put a hand over her mouth. "Oh, my gosh." She grabbed his hand and held it tightly. "Connor, I don't know this for sure, but I was told that Brad tried to get them to disallow my license. Right at the beginning."

He lowered himself into the chair beside her, still holding her hand. "Why would he do that?"

"Well, he never wanted me to keep this house. He thought I ought to move to the mainland and get an apartment, put the kids in day care and get a regular job. He sort of acted like he thought I was trying to extort money from him by doing anything else."

His face was cold as granite. "Tell me more."

"It took a while to get started. At first, I didn't have any of the right equipment. I used every penny I got from Brad to help pay for the commercial oven, but I still needed to buy a three-unit sink and the special refrigeration I needed. When he found out what I was doing, he was furious."

"And stopped giving you money," he guessed.

She nodded. "Pretty much. Which only made it more important that I find a way to grow my business." She laced her fingers with his.

"You know, you hit a place where you can either move forward, or settle for something less, and get stuck in that great big nowhere land." She sighed. "In order to get to where I might make some actual profit, I had to take the chance. I needed funding. So…"

She met his gaze and looked guilty. "So, yes, I took out a loan so that I could finish buying the supplies I needed."

"What did you use to get a loan? The house?"

She nodded. "That's why it's so scary that this house is still underwater and they won't give me a mortgage modification."

"You've tried?"

"Countless times."

"You're in a tight spot."

She nodded. "I'm standing at the edge of the cliff, you mean. And the ground is starting to crumble under my feet."

His free hand took her chin and lifted her face toward his, then he leaned in and kissed her softly. "I'll catch you," he said, his voice husky. "I'm here, Jill. I won't let you hit the rocks."

She smiled, loving his generous spirit, but not really believing his words. How could he stop the chain of events that seemed to be overwhelming her? It wasn't likely. They'd had a good day yesterday and he'd made that possible. But goodwill—and cake sales—could only go so far. Every step forward seemed to bring on two steps back. She was beginning to lose hope.

He hesitated, then shook his head and drew back from her. "Okay, here's what I don't understand. This just really gets to me. Why do you let Brad still be such a huge part of your life?"

"I...I don't."

"Yes, you do. You're divorced. He's not even giving you the money you should be getting for the kids. He doesn't want anything to do with the children." He frowned, searching her eyes. "Why let him affect you in any way? Why maintain any ties at all?"

She blinked. It was hard to put this in words. How to explain how alone she felt in the world? In some ways, Brad was still her only lifeline. It was too scary to cut that off.

"The only real, legal ties we still have is the business," she said instead of trying to explain her emotional connection to her past. "I still own fifteen percent of it."

He nodded. He knew that. "Do you have a voting position on the board?"

She shrugged. "I'm not really sure if I do or not. I

think I'm supposed to but I've never tried to use it. I suppose I should ask a lawyer."

"At the very least."

"The only reason I keep it, to tell you the truth, is that emotionally, I just can't give up on it yet. It's still a part of my life, a part of my past, all those years we spent building it into the enterprise it is today."

He nodded. Did that answer the question? Her ties to Brad were still too strong. But were they that way from fear…or love? Hard to pull those two apart for analysis. And the answer to that meant everything.

Connor was so angry inside, both at Brad and at himself, he couldn't stay near her for now. Instead he went out and walked down to the ferry and then around the quaint little village and back again. He finally had something he wanted to say to Brad, but when he tried calling him, he found his old pal had turned the tables, and now he wasn't taking calls from Connor.

Voice mail was his only recourse. He waited for the beep.

"Hey, Brad. I just wanted to let you know that I know the health inspector is a phony. He's someone who works for you. If he comes here again, I'll have him arrested for impersonating a government employee.

"About those shares. If you really want them so badly, why don't you come and ask her for them like a man? Why don't you face her? And why don't you offer her something real? You never know what might happen.

"In the meantime, other than that, leave Jill alone. Go live your own life and forget about hers."

He clicked off and tried to tame the rage that roiled in him. Jill didn't deserve any of this. He only hoped she would let him stay here to help her get out from under all this. He knew she couldn't get Brad out of her system, but there wasn't much he could do about that. He didn't care about his own emotional involvement anymore. So, he was probably going to get his heart broken. So what? His love for Jill was too strong to try to deny any longer. And all he wanted was what was good for her. He had to stay.

When he walked into the house, he heard Jill singing in the kitchen. He had to stop for a moment and listen, marveling at her. What was she, some kind of angel? Whatever—she was everything he knew he wanted. And would probably never have.

"Hey," he told her as he came up behind her, putting his arms around her. She leaned back into him and smiled. "I'm getting pretty funky in these clothes," he said. "I think I'll run into town and get some fresh things from the hotel room. Can I bring anything back for you?"

She turned in his embrace and kissed him. "Just bring yourself back. That's all I need," she said.

He kissed her again and the kiss deepened. The way he felt about her grew every time he touched her. Right now, it seemed like fireworks going off in his chest. This was the way he wished it could always be.

Jill stood at the sliding glass door looking out at the grassy hill that was her backyard. Connor was outside playing with the twins, chasing them up and down the hill, laughing, picking up one and then the other to whirl about and land gently again. Her heart was full of bittersweet joy. Tears trembled in her eyes.

If only Brad could be this way. If he really met the boys, if he tried to get to know them, wouldn't he realize how wonderful they were? Wouldn't he have to love them? Wouldn't that make everything better?

As she watched, Connor fell, iron-cross style, into a huge bed of leaves, and the boys raced each other to jump on top of him. She could hear the laughter from where she was behind glass and it answered her own questions.

No. Brad would never love the boys, because he didn't want to. He wouldn't let himself. It was time she faced facts.

She heard the front door open and she turned that way.

"Jill!"

"In here, Sara." She frowned. Her sister's voice sounded high and strained. What had happened now?

Sara appeared, looking a little wild. "Did you get the letter?"

"What letter?"

"From Social Services." She waved an official-looking envelope. "Did you get one, too?"

"I don't know. Connor brought in the mail. I think he left it on the entryway table. Let me get it."

She stepped into the foyer and found the envelope Sara was talking about. Connor and the boys were coming back into the family room as she returned to it. The boys were jumping around him like puppies.

"I promised them ice cream," he said after nodding at Sara. "I'm hoping you actually have some."

"Don't worry." Jill put the envelope down and went into the kitchen. They all followed her and she pulled two Popsicles out of the freezer for them. "They'll accept this as a substitute," she said. "Now go on out and play in the sunroom. I don't care if you drip all over that floor."

They did as they were told, dancing happily on their toes. Connor laughed as he watched them go, then looked at Jill. They shared a secret smile.

Sara groaned. "Come on. Open the mail. You won't believe this."

"What does it say?"

"You need to read it for yourself. Go ahead. Read it. I'll wait."

Connor looked at Sara and said, "Hey, you look really upset."

Her eyes flashed his way. "Did Jill tell you about our stepsister? She died in a car accident last week."

"Yes, she did tell me. I'm sorry."

Sara nodded, then looked at Jill, waiting.

Moments later, Jill handed the letter to Connor and he noticed right away that her fingers were trembling. She turned and looked at her sister, wide-eyed. "I don't believe it."

Sara nodded, looking flushed. "Told you."

Connor glanced at the letter. It seemed to be about someone named Kelly Darling. Then he connected the name. It was the stepsister who had died the week before. Kelly Darling. It seemed that Kelly had a baby. A three-month-old baby. Jill and Sara were her only living relatives that could be found. Would either of them care to claim the child?

"A baby," he said. "And you didn't know?"

"No." Jill shook her head. "I guess she wasn't married. We hadn't heard from her for so long."

Sara nodded mournfully. "And now, a baby."

Jill felt tears threatening again. "Poor little thing."

Sara flashed her a look. "Kelly's baby." She shook her head. "I don't think we've seen Kelly more than three times in the last fifteen years."

"And that's our fault," Jill said mournfully. "We should have made more of an effort."

Sara shrugged. "Why? She never liked us. The last time I saw her, she was furious with me."

Jill looked surprised. "What happened?"

"She wanted to borrow five thousand dollars to help pay for a certification class she wanted to take."

"Some kind of computer class?"

"No. It was to qualify as a professional dog trainer. When I pointed out that I didn't see how she was going to be able to pay me back on the salaries beginning dog trainers make, she told me I was ruining her life and she never wanted to see me again."

Jill sighed. "Well, she was an awfully cute little baby."

Sara looked at Jill and bit her lip. "I'm sure they'll find some relative we don't even know about to take the child."

Jill frowned. "Maybe. But…"

"Jill!" Sara cried. "Don't you dare! There is no way you can take on another baby."

Jill looked pained. "What about you?" she asked.

"Me?" Sara's face registered shock. It was obvious that option hadn't even entered her mind. "Me?" She shook her head strenuously. "I don't do babies. I can barely manage to watch your little angels for more than an hour without going mad."

"Sara, she's our flesh and blood. She's our responsibility."

"How do you figure that? I don't see it. She was Kelly's responsibility, and now they'll find someone to adopt her. Tons of people want babies that age."

Jill was shaking her head. "I don't know...."

Sara groaned and looked tortured. Stepping closer, she took her sister's hands in her own. "Jill, I haven't come right out and told you this. I've tried to hint it, just to prepare you, but... I'm going to be moving down to Los Angeles. And my job is going to include almost constant travel, especially to New York. There's no room for a baby in that scenario." She had tears sliding down her cheeks. "And that also means I won't be here to help you. You can't even begin to think of taking this baby."

Jill looked at her and didn't say a thing.

Connor watched her. She was going to take the baby. He could tell. He tried to understand the dynamics here. This was another blow to Jill, another obstacle in her struggle to survive. And yet, that wasn't the way she was taking it. She didn't look at it as the end of her hopes and dreams, a financial and emotional disaster.

She was seeing it as another burdensome responsibility, but one that she would accept. He'd known her for years but he'd never realized how deep her strength went. Where had that come from? Where had she found the capacity to take on everyone else's problems? Was being the oldest sister the key? Or was it just the way her soul was put together?

"They'll find a good home for the baby somewhere, I'm sure," Sara was insisting. "Don't they have agencies to do things like that?"

Jill frowned. That just wasn't right and she knew it. "Sara…"

Sara closed her eyes and turned away.

"I've got to go. I'm expecting half a dozen calls and I've got to prepare myself." She looked back and hesitated, then said with fierce intensity, "Jill, you can't be considering taking that baby. I won't let you."

Jill winced. She knew what was going to happen. It was inevitable. She couldn't expect Sara to understand. Babies…life…family—that was what she'd been put on earth to deal with. So Brad hadn't worked out. Too bad. So her cake business was trembling on the brink and might just crumble. Okay. But turn down taking care of a baby? Her father's grandchild? Her own niece? No. Impossible. If Sara couldn't face it, that baby had only one chance.

She followed Sara to the door and touched her arm before she could escape. "Sara, I'm going to call them. I want that baby here with us."

A look of abject terror flared in her sister's eyes. Slowly, she shook her head, her lower lip trembling.

"You're crazy," she whispered. "Jill, I beg you. Don't do it." And then she turned on her heel and hurried to her car.

Jill came back into the house and went straight to Connor as though drawn by a magnet.

"Are you sure?" he asked her.

"About the baby?" She smiled. "Yes. There is no way I could let Kelly's baby go to strangers. I'm going to get in touch with these people right away. The sooner we get her here the better."

"Jill, your heart is definitely in the right place. But can you do it? You're already overextended. You're on the ragged edge with these two little boys. Can you take on another child like this?"

"I have no choice. I couldn't live with myself if I didn't do it."

His heart was overflowing with love for her, and he knew what she was doing courted disaster. His brain told him Sara was right, but his heart—it was all for Jill. "Come here. I have to hold you. You are so special…"

"Oh, Connor." She started to cry and he held her while she sobbed in his embrace. "It's scary, but it's wonderful, too. It's the right thing to do."

"I just hope it won't be too much for you," he said, kissing her tears away.

She kissed him back. "Sometimes I feel like I'm at my breaking point, but something always comes through to save the day. And right now, it's your arms around me. Connor, I'm so glad you're here."

And she started to sob again. He held her close, enjoying the feel of her and the sweet, fruity scent from her hair. He loved her and he would be there for her as long as she let him stay. But deep inside, he knew a time would come when she would want him to leave. He was prepared for that. He only hoped it didn't come for a long, long time.

CHAPTER NINE

AN HOUR LATER, Jill invited Connor to help her take the boys to the park to play on the swings and in the sandbox. They took little shovels and pails and made the trek on foot, through the residential streets and over the low-lying berm that marked the edge of the park area. The boys ran ahead, then came back for protection when dogs barked or a car came on the end of the street. Then they reached the park and the twins were in heaven.

When they tired of the swings, they got to work with the shovels, tossing sand and shrieking with happiness. After making a vain attempt to keep order, Jill and Connor sat back and let them play the way that seemed to come naturally to them. There weren't many other children around, so they gave them their freedom.

"I heard from Trini this morning," she told him. "I got an email. She's behind in a few classes, but she thinks she can catch up. She's thrilled to be there." She smiled happily. "She's going to keep me apprised with daily bulletins. That'll be great. It's just like vicariously going myself."

"I wish you could go yourself. We ought to be able to figure out a way…."

"We"? She looked at him sideways. But that seemed like a silly thing to have an argument about, so she moved on.

"So tell me more about what you were doing in Singapore all this time," she said, looking at the way his unruly hair flew around his head, much the way hers did, though his was dark as coal and hers was bright as sunshine. "You told me about the nice couple you lived with and worked for, and you told me about the chef you fell in love with—"

"Whoa! Hold on. I never told you that."

"Really?" Her eyes twinkled with mischief. "Gee, I don't know where I picked that up. I must have misheard it."

He knocked against her with his shoulder. "Come on, Jill. You know you're the only woman I've ever loved."

"Wow." She pressed closer to him. "It would be nice to think that was true."

He turned his head and said, close to her ear, "Count on it."

There was something in the way he said it that made her look up into his eyes. They were just kidding each other, weren't they?

"So tell me," she said after they sat down at the edge of the play area. She was sifting sand through her fingers. "Are you really going back or not?"

"That depends."

"On what?"

On whether I can make you fall in love with me. On

*whether you can wipe Brad out of your calculations for
your future. On whether you can believe in me.*

But he sighed and actually said, "The company got
bought out by a huge corporation. George made a fine
haul on it. And under our contract, he gave me a nice
chunk of change, too. So if I went back, it would be to
link up with old George again and work on the next
big idea."

She smiled with happy memories. "Just like the three
of us did when we started MayDay."

"Exactly."

"Only Brad hasn't been bought out by anyone."

"No. Not yet."

She frowned, thinking that over. "And what are you
going to do with your profits?"

He shrugged. "I don't know. Right now I'm pretty
much looking around for a company to invest in. Some
nice, clean little start-up. Preferably in the food business."

She looked at him suspiciously. "Are you teasing
me?"

"Teasing you?" He looked shocked at the concept.
"Why would I tease you?"

"Because you love to knock me off balance," she said
with mock outrage. "You always have."

He leaned back against the rock behind him and
laughed at her. She began to poke him in the ribs.

"You love it. Admit it. You love to have a good gig-
gle over my naïveté. Fess up!"

He laughed harder and she began to tickle him. He
grabbed her and pulled her down beside him and kissed

her nose, making her laugh, too. And then he kissed her
for real and she kissed him back and the warmth spread
quickly between them.

"You're like a drug," he whispered, dropping kisses
on her face. "I don't dare take too much of you."

"Good thing, too," she whispered back. "Because I
only have that little tiny bit to give."

"Liar," he teased, kissing her mouth again.

She sighed, holding back the sizzle that threatened
to spill out and make this inappropriately exciting. That
would have to wait. But she had no doubt they would
be able to explore it a bit more later.

"Hey," she said, pulling back up. "We're supposed
to be watching the boys."

Luckily the two toddlers were still enchanted with
the pails and shovels. Connor and Jill sat up and shook
off the sand and grinned at each other.

"Okay," she said. "Now tell me what you're really
going to do with the money."

"Just what I said. I've got my eye on a nice little
Bundt cake bakery."

She didn't laugh this time. "No, Connor. I will not
take charity from you."

He'd known she would react that way but it didn't
hurt to start setting the background and give her a
chance to think about it. "I'm talking about investing.
I wouldn't put my money anywhere that I didn't expect
to make a profit on it."

She was shaking her head adamantly. "I don't have
shares to sell. That just won't work and you know it."

No, he didn't know it, but he had known she would be

a hard sell on the idea. Hopefully he would have more time to see what he could develop to do for her. "Jill…"

"Connor, I'm still bound to Brad by his company. I refuse to play that game again."

Ouch. That could make all the difference. He nodded slowly, frowning. "Jill, when you say you're still bound to Brad, what do you mean?" He looked her full in the face, searching her eyes for hints of the truth. "Do you still want him back?"

She thought for a moment, then looked at him, clear-eyed. "Connor, for a long time, I wanted Brad back. But not for me. I wanted him back for his children. What will it be like for them to go through life wondering why their father didn't want them? It breaks my heart." Her voice caught and she paused. "For so long, I was so sure, once he saw them, once he held them in his arms…"

He couldn't stand to see her still hoping. He wanted to smash something. Carefully he tried to tell her.

"He's just not made that way, Jill. Brad doesn't want to love a child. He doesn't want to complicate his life like that. He doesn't even want a wife at this point. He thinks he needs to keep the way clear so that he can think big thoughts and make cool-headed decisions. Human relationships only mess things up as far as he's concerned." He shrugged, grimacing. "I don't know why we didn't see that more clearly from the beginning."

"Maybe we did and we just didn't want to believe it."

She closed her eyes. She still had her dreams. She sometimes thought that maybe, if he saw her again, if they did come face-to-face, he would see what he'd once loved in her and realize what he'd lost—and want it back.

No. It wasn't going to happen. She'd given up on that fantasy a long time ago. So why did she still cling to the shards of that relationship?

"When did you start to figure out the truth about Brad?" Connor asked her softly.

Her smile was mirthless. "When I realized he was cheating on me."

He drew his breath in sharply. "You knew?"

She looked at him. "Connor, I'm not stupid. Gullible, maybe. Too weak to stand up for myself when I should, sometimes. But not dumb."

They were silent for a long moment, then Connor asked, "What do you think Brad will say about you taking on another baby?"

She laughed. "Luckily it doesn't matter what he says. Does it?"

The boys were tussling. One was hitting the other with a plastic pail and both were starting to cry. The inevitable end to a lovely time being had by all. Jill and Connor rose from their sitting place and started across the sand to mediate the battle, but on the way, they held hands.

Jill baked two more cakes once they got home and Connor put the boys down for their naps. They both fell asleep as soon as their heads hit their mattresses. He watched them for a while, amazed at how much he cared for them already. Then he went down to help Jill with the bakery business.

"So what's next?" he asked, sitting at the kitchen table and eating a nice large slice of Strawberry Treat. "What's the plan?"

She glanced back at him as she mixed up a fresh glaze. "Stay out of the way of the inspectors. Obey all regulations scrupulously. Grow my business. Hire some employees and get my own shop." She threw him a smile. "In other words, succeed."

He took another bite and nearly swooned with the deliciousness of it all. "You're the best Bundt cake baker on the island. Probably the best in all of Seattle. But all of Seattle isn't going to come here for their cakes. Your customers are basically the people on this island. Are there enough of them to let you be successful?"

She came to the table and dropped down into a seat across from him. "This is exactly my nightmare question. How can I get a large customer base?"

"And what's your answer?"

She shook her head. "I haven't really dealt with it because I'm scared of what it will take."

"And what is that?"

She frowned. "I have to branch out. I know it. I have to develop a full-blown bakery out of this. I have to make cookies and pies and éclairs and bear-claws and dinner rolls. I have to learn to do everything. It's my only hope."

"And your competition?"

She nodded. "There are two bakeries here, both run by older bakers who are about at the end of their bakery careers, I would think. So there should be room for me." She made a face. "If I can come up to the challenge."

He was impressed that she'd thought this out so fully. It gave him the reassurance that she really meant to make a go of it. Because she was going to have to work very hard to last.

"You've really developed a good business brain, haven't you?"

"I developed it right next to you. Remember when we used to brainstorm together during the early days at MayDay?"

"I do." He smiled at her. "But how are you going to do all this without someone here to help you? I can't even understand how you've done this much so far."

"It isn't easy."

He thought about that for a moment, then turned back and said, "You're going to have to have some help. Face it."

She nodded. "I know. I'm thinking of giving Mrs. Mulberry another chance."

"Great. I think she deserves it."

"She means well and she wants to do it. So there you go."

He nodded. "If you're with her most of the time, you can train her. And she'll begin to understand what the twins need. I'm sure it will go well."

She grinned at him. "I never realized what an optimist you are. Just a regular what-me-worry-kid."

"Sure. I learned long ago that being happy is better than being angry all the time."

He watched her work, nursing a cup of coffee and enjoying the smells of a working bakery. It all seemed too quiet and idyllic. Until you remembered that Brad was probably on his way. Most likely he would drive up from Portland. And then he would come here. Connor wanted to be here when he arrived. There was no way he was going to let Jill face him alone.

Jill was chatting about something or other. He wasn't paying much attention. He was too busy enjoying her, smiling at the flour on her face, watching the way her body moved, the way her breasts were swelling just inside the opening of her shirt, those long, silky legs. She'd always been his main crush, but now she was becoming something more. He wanted her and his body was letting him know the need was getting stronger.

From the beginning, it had seemed she was strangely dominated, almost mesmerized, by Brad. She'd been Brad's and he'd been crazy jealous, but he'd never thought he would have a chance with her. Now, he did. It all depended on how strong that bond between them still was.

He had his own bond with her—didn't he? Even if she didn't feel it, he did. She walked out toward where he was sitting at the table, talking about something he wasn't really listening to and stopping near him. Reaching out, he caught her wrist and tugged her closer. She looked down at him, saw the darkness in his eyes, and her own eyes widened, and then her mouth softened and she sank down beside him.

She hadn't hesitated. She'd come to him as soon as she saw he wanted her to. That filled him with a bright new sense of wonder. He wanted to hold her forever, make a declaration, make love to her and make her his own.

He wrapped her in his arms and she sighed as he

began to drop small, impatient kisses along the line of her neck. She turned, giving him more access to her body in a way he hadn't expected.

His heart was pounding now, filling him with a sort of excitement he hadn't felt for a long, long time. She was warm and soft and rounded in the best places for it. He kissed just under her ear and suddenly she was turning in his arms, moaning, searching for his mouth with hers, and then that was all there was.

The kiss. It took his breath away at the same time it put his brain into orbit. He couldn't think. He could only feel. And taste. And ache for her.

Jill felt his release, his acceptance of the desire swelling between them, and she was tempted to give way to it as well. She knew this had to stop but for the moment, she couldn't find the strength to make it happen. She hungered for his heat, longed for his touch, moved beneath his hands as though she couldn't get enough of him.

There was no way to stop this feeling. Was it love? Was it loneliness that needed healing? Or was it a basic womanly demand that smoldered deep inside all the time, hidden by the events of the day, and only revealed when the right man touched her?

That was it. She'd known passion before, but this was different. She not only wanted his body, but she also needed his heart and soul, and for once, she thought she just might have a chance to get that.

She was drowning in his kiss. His mouth tasted better than anything she'd ever known. She writhed with it, moaned and made tiny cries as though she could capture the heat and keep it forever in her body. And then reality began to swim back into focus and she tried to pull away.

It wasn't easy. His kisses were so delicious and his hands felt so good. But it had to be done. There were cakes in the oven. There were children waking up from their naps.

Reality. Darn it all.

"Jill," he murmured, his face buried in her curly hair, "we're going to have to find a way to do something about this."

"Are we?" But she smiled. Her body was still resonating with the trembling need for him, and she totally agreed. Somehow, they had to do something about it—soon.

The shadows were longer. Afternoon was flowing into evening. The boys were stirring and Connor went up to supervise their waking. He got them changed and brought them down to play in the playroom, listening as they called back and forth with what seemed like their own special language.

The doorbell rang and he stiffened. He didn't think Brad could have gotten here this fast unless he flew. But it was a possibility.

He went out into the entryway. It wasn't Brad. Jill was talking to the mailman and signing for a certified letter. She closed the door and ripped the letter open.

"What in the world is this going to be?" she muttered, her mind on her cakes. Then she looked at the letter. Frowning, she looked at it again.

"What does this mean?" she asked Connor.

He glanced over her shoulder and frowned. "It looks like the bank is calling your loan."

She gasped. "Are they allowed to do that?"

"Let me see the letter." He read it over more carefully. "Okay, it says here that their investigation has revealed that you have insufficient security and they don't trust your collateral." He looked at her. "You used this house, didn't you?"

She nodded, her eyes wide with alarm.

He went back to the letter. "They also claim that, if you study your contract, you will find it has a 'Due for Any Reason Clause' which allows them to call the loan without having to justify it." He stared at her in distaste. "Just because they want to." His face darkened as he thought that through. "Or because someone bribes them to do it," he suggested.

She stared at him and then she whispered, "Brad?"

He shrugged. "You probably won't ever be able to prove it."

She took the letter and read it again. That was what it said. Her loan was being called. There was no doubt in her mind that Brad had something to do with this.

She was shaking. Everything she tried to do seemed to fail. She wasn't getting anywhere. It was so hard—it was like running in quicksand. In her worst nightmares, she'd never thought of this. How could he do this to her?

"He won't ever cut me free, will he?" She raised her tragic gaze to Connor's blue one. "He doesn't want me, but he still wants to manipulate me. He still wants to control my life." Her voice got higher. "Am I doomed

to be tied to this man forever? That's like being married without any of the perks. I just have to obey, forget
the love and all that other stuff."

Connor took her shoulders and held her firmly.

"Jill, calm down. I know it's frustrating, but maybe
if you find out exactly what he thinks he wants."

"Like what? For me to get rid of the boys?" She knew
she looked wild. And why not? She felt wild. "You
actually think I would consider something like that?"

"No, of course not." He hesitated. "But I don't think
that's what he's after right now."

"Really? And why do you know so much about what
he's after? Did he tell you?" Her face changed as she
realized what she'd said. "That's it, isn't it?" She stared
at him. "You know what he wants. You just haven't
told me yet."

He had a bad feeling about where this train of thought
was leading. He took a deep breath. "Jill…"

She backed away from him. "Okay, Connor," she
said coldly, her face furious. "Are you finally ready to
tell me what Brad wants from me? What he sent you
to tell me?"

He tried to touch her but she pulled away.

"Tell me," she demanded.

He shook his head, knowing she was in no mood
to hear this and think logically. But he didn't have any
choice. He had to tell her. He should have done it sooner.
But still he hesitated, not sure how to approach it.

"Brad asked me to talk to you," he admitted. "But
I never told him I would. And once I saw you again,
I knew I would never do his dirty work for him. If he

wanted to ask you something he had to come and do it himself."

"I see," she said cynically. At this point, she was ready to believe the worst of anyone and everyone. "So you decided for some reason, I wasn't ready. I wasn't softened up enough. You decided to go slow. You needed to sweeten me up, flatter me a little, get me ready for the slaughter."

"Jill..." He shook his head, appalled that she would think that.

She drew in a trembling breath. "I can't believe you would gang up on me with Brad this way."

That was like a knife through his heart. "I'm not."

She wasn't listening. "So how about it, Connor? Am I ready now? Are you going to stop lying and tell me the truth?"

He shook his head. He might as well get this over with. "Okay, Jill. What Brad wants is those company shares he gave you when you divorced. He thinks he needs them back."

She looked surprised. "Why?"

He shrugged. "I think he's having a fight with some of the other shareholders. He wants to stop a power play by some who are getting together to outvote him on some company policies."

She pressed her lips together and thought about that for a moment. Then she glared at him again.

"Is that all? Really? Then why didn't you tell me the truth from the beginning?"

He turned away, grimacing. Then he turned back. "I asked you before, Jill, and I'm going to ask you again.

You've hinted now and then that you would take Brad back if you could. Do you still feel that way?"

She thought for a moment, pacing from him to the glass door and back again. "What I really want is to have my life back. Do you understand that? I chose Brad to be at my side forever and I gave birth to two angels, two gifts for him." She stared at him with haunted eyes. "So why did he reject them? Why did he reject me and the life we'd both created together? I want that life."

He winced. That wasn't really what he'd wanted to hear.

"I want things to be like they used to be. I want my life back."

"So you still want Brad back."

She didn't answer that.

Who was he to tell her it couldn't happen? Stranger things had.

"Nothing has changed?" he asked her, incredulous.

She shook her head. "Of course. Everything has changed." Anger flashed through her eyes like flames from a fire. "And now you've proven you stand with Brad."

He grimaced. He couldn't let her think he wasn't behind her one hundred percent. "Jill, listen to me. Seeing you again, I realized how much I care for you. How much I missed you and all you've always meant to me. I want you for myself. I don't want Brad to have anything to do with...with our relationship."

She stared at him as though she hadn't heard a word he'd said. "But you've kept in constant contact with him, haven't you? Isn't he always calling on your phone?"

"Yes, but…"

"Connor, you lied to me!"

"No, I didn't. That's ridiculous."

"Yes, you did. You led me to believe Brad didn't really want anything. And now I come to find out, he wanted it all."

Tears filled her eyes and she turned away, walking back into the kitchen. That was her default position. The kitchen was the center of her world. She went to the counter and turned to face him, hugging her arms in around herself.

"Jill," he said as he caught up with her. "I know this looks bad to you, but I didn't lie. When you asked, I just didn't answer."

"That's the same as a lie." She shook her head. "I can't trust you."

"Okay, Jill. I understand that you're really angry, and I'm sorry. But…"

She narrowed her eyes and hardened her heart. "I think it's time for you to leave, Connor. Way past time."

He shook his head. Pain filled him, pain and regret. "Don't do this, Jill. Wait until you've calmed down. Think it over. I…I don't want to leave you here on your own."

"You have to. I can't trust you. I want you to go."

His eyes were tortured but she didn't relent. She had to have some time and space to think, to go over all that had happened in the last few days and decide if she could ever, ever talk to him again.

He winced. "You know that at some time soon, Brad will be coming, don't you?"

She blinked at him. "Why?"

"Because he wants those shares. He's not going to rest until he gets them. If he has to come here to do that, he will."

She was seething. "If you knew that, why didn't you tell me before? Why didn't you warn me?"

He had no answer for that.

"Go," she said. "You've helped me with some things, but you've undermined me at the same time. I need you to go."

He started to say something, but she pointed toward the door. Shaking his head, he turned away. Then he looked back and said over his shoulder, "Call me if you need me," and he left.

She watched him walk away until tears flooded her eyes and she couldn't see anything anymore.

"Connor, Connor, how could you betray me like this?" she murmured.

The one person she thought she had in her corner, that she could count on when things got rough, the only one that she could really trust in this world besides Sara had turned out to be lying to her. And now it turned out all she had left was Sara.

She sank to the floor of the kitchen and hung her head and cried.

Connor was headed back to the mainland, but before he went, he had one last thing he had to do. He knew Sara lived only about a mile away, but her bungalow was right on the beach. Turning down the narrow road, he found her house easily. He'd been there before.

Walking up to the front door, he saw Sara in the side yard, trimming roses. He approached carefully but she still jumped when she saw him.

"Hey, Sara," he said. "We need to talk."

She backed away looking wary. "Connor, I don't want to talk to you. I already know how I feel about everything and I don't need you messing with my mind."

"Sara, come on. You know we both love Jill. Right?"

Sara made a face, but she nodded reluctantly.

"And you know that she's not going to let that baby go anywhere else, don't you? Not if she can help it."

Sara looked away.

"If you won't take her, your sister will. There's just no two ways about it."

Sara turned and looked at him pleadingly. "Can't you talk her out of it?"

"You know the answer to that. Nobody can talk her out of it." He looked down and kicked the dirt. "And we both know that taking on another baby is going to be hard. She doesn't need to have something that hard. She's already got far too much on her plate, far too much that she has to handle alone." He looked up at her. "So there's only one thing left to do. And you know what it is."

She shook her head with a jerky motion. Her face was a study in tragedy. "No," she said. "I can't."

He was quiet for a minute and she snipped off a few more dead blossoms. He listened to the water lapping against the shore not too far from where they stood. Seagulls called and a flock of low-flying pelicans swooped by.

Her hair was still slicked back into a bun at the back of her head. She'd changed into slacks and a fuzzy pullover, but she managed to look like a fully functioning professional anyway. There was something about her that spoke of competence and dignity. But when he looked at her face, all he saw was fear and sadness.

Finally he spoke to her quietly.

"Sara, come sit down with me."

She edged closer, but she still acted as though she was afraid he might have something catching.

"Come on." He sat down on a wicker chair and nodded toward the little wicker couch. She walked over slowly and sat down, but she wouldn't look at him.

"Thanks, Sara. I want to tell you about someone I got to know well in Singapore. Her name is Sharon Wong. She's a very fine chef. A few years ago, her neighbor died, leaving behind a three-year-old girl. Sharon had gotten to know them both during the neighbor's illness. She took her broths and things and watched the child for her at times.

"When the woman died, Social Services came to take away the child, and Sharon realized what a nightmare that baby faced. Who knew who would end up caring for her? Maybe someone good. Maybe not. Maybe she would be in an institution for the rest of her childhood. She watched how the Social Services people treated that little girl and she made up her mind that she couldn't let this happen.

"So she stepped in and took the baby herself. When I met her, the girl was six years old, bright as a penny and sweet as candy. A delight. And Sharon told me that this little girl had enriched her life like nothing she'd ever dreamed might happen to her."

"And then she told me about a saying she'd heard lately. No one on their deathbed ever says they should have spent more time at the office. When you get down to what really counts, it's family."

Sara turned tragic eyes his way. "But I don't really have that kind of family," she said softly.

"Not now. But that doesn't mean you won't."

She stared at him, shaking her head. "Connor, if I had a choice right now between having a terrific career, or meeting a terrific guy, I'd take the career. I've had enough disappointment with terrific guys."

He shrugged as he rose to leave. "Guys are one thing. Babies are another." Reaching over, he kissed her cheek. She didn't turn away. She caught his hand and held it for a moment, looking deep into his eyes.

"See you later, Sara. Do the right thing, okay?"

And he walked away.

Jill was wandering through her house like a ghost. It was after dark and she hadn't put on any of the downstairs lights yet. The boys were in bed and sound asleep. She was alone.

Her mind was a jumble of thoughts, none of them very coherent. She was so angry with Connor, and at the same time, she was so hurt that he would still be on Brad's side after all he'd seen her go through. Why had he come all the way back just to prove to her that she really wanted him—only to say, "Sorry, I'm with

Brad. He's such an old friend." That thought made her furious all over again.

She heard the front door opening and she stopped in her tracks, heart beating wildly. Who was this going to be?

"Anybody home?"

She let her held breath out in a whoosh. It was Sara.

Seconds later, Sara came into the family room where Jill was standing.

"What's going on? How come no lights?"

She wasn't going to tell her it was to hide her swollen eyes and tear-stained face. She would see that for herself soon enough.

Sara went ahead and turned on the overhead without asking permission. It must have seemed a natural thing to do.

"Hey, Jill. I've got to talk to you." Compared to the last time Jill had seen her, she seemed to be brimming with energy.

Slowly Jill shook her head, staying to the shadows as much as she could. "Sara, sweetie, not now."

She thought Sara would notice from her voice that this was not a good time, but no. Sara charged ahead as though she hadn't said a thing.

"Wait. I'm sure you're busy, but this will just take a minute and it may help take a load off your mind."

Jill threw up her hands in surrender. "Anything that will do that," she muttered and tried to smile. "What is it?"

Sara came and stood before her, looking as earnest as Jill had ever seen her look.

"I've thought about this long and hard. I've looked at all the angles. And I've decided. I want to take Kelly's baby."

That was a jolt from the blue. "What are you saying? You can't possibly do that and take the job in L.A. Can you?"

"No." She shook her head. "I'm turning the job down."

"What? Oh, Sara, no!"

"Yes. A job is just a job. A baby is a human being. And this human being is even a part of our family, whether we like it or not." She smiled. "And I've decided to like it."

It was true that she looked much better, much healthier, than she had earlier that day when she had been so frightened of the entire concept. That was good. If it was really going to last.

She took her sister's hands in hers. "But, Sara, why?"

"It's a funny thing. I wanted a traditional life so badly. I planned my wedding from the time I was five years old. You know that. But every romance I tried to have ended badly. I just couldn't seem to find a man who fit me. I finally got hurt one too many times and I gave up all that. It's just too painful. No more romance. No more man who was wrong for me."

Jill nodded. She'd been there and watched it all. "I know all this. But what does it have to do with taking the baby?"

"I decided maybe I was going at it from the wrong side. Maybe if I find a baby who fits me, I'll have my family without having to find a man first."

Oh, no. Sara had lost her mind.

"Sara, babies don't provide miracles. Please don't go into this thinking it's going to be a piece of cake. Don't depend on a baby to make you happy, to solve all your problems."

She waved that away. "Oh, please, Jill. Give me some credit. I know that. I've been with you enough with the twins to know that raising a child is no picnic."

"You got that right."

"But anyway, you're the one who always picks up the slack for everyone else. You do your big sister routine and go all noble on me, and I let you, because then I get out of doing things I don't want to do."

"Oh, Sara, please. We're not kids anymore."

"No, but we're still sisters." She gave Jill a hug. "So I decided. It's time I took my turn. I want Kelly's baby."

Jill took a deep breath and realized, suddenly what a weight she'd been carrying. "Oh, Sara, I hope you know what you're doing."

"I do."

She hugged her again and held her close, then leaned back and looked at her. "What changed your mind? What made you see it that way?"

"Connor."

"Connor?" She was thunderstruck.

She heaved a heavy sigh. "Yes, it was Connor. He gave me a good talking-to and then told me about a friend of his. Some woman in Singapore…"

"Sharon Wong?"

"That's the one. Do you know her?"

"No."

"Well, he sat me down and made me take a more realistic look at life."

"He did?" Jill felt dizzy.

"Yeah. Where is he?"

"He's a…"

"You know, that is one great guy. You'd better not let him slip away. He's a treasure." She looked around the room and toward the back porch. "So where is he, anyway?"

"I, uh, he left."

Her head swung around. "Left? Where did he go? What happened?"

"I told him to leave."

"Oh, Jill… You didn't!"

"I did. I told him to go. I was so angry."

"Why?"

She took a deep breath and tried to remember it all, including the incredible pain she'd felt. Quickly she explained to Sara about the loan being called, and how Connor thought Brad was behind it. Then she went on to fill in her problems with Connor.

"He didn't tell me the truth about what Brad wanted and when I found out that he wanted me to sell him the shares I swore I would never give up, I just…I felt like he was manipulating me. Like I couldn't trust him. Like he was on Brad's side again. Why didn't he prepare me to know what Brad was up to?"

"You think he's on Brad's side?"

Jill nodded.

Sara stared at her. "What are you, nuts? You do realize he's crazy in love with you, don't you?"

She shook her head. "Sara, I don't think—"

"You can see it in the way he looks at you."

She hesitated. "Do you really think so?"

"Come on, he's always had a crush on you. And now I think it's developed into full-blown mad love. He's insanely in love with you."

Jill was feeling dizzy again. "We've always been friends."

"No. It's more than that." Sara threw up her hands. "He wants you, babe. Don't let that one get away."

"I just got so frustrated. And…and so jealous."

"Jealous?"

She nodded. "I mean—is he my friend or Brad's? It makes a difference."

Sara nodded wisely. "I told him that the first day he was here. I told him if he was going to be your friend, he had to get rid of Brad. And you know what? He was ready to do it."

Jill wasn't so sure. Sara could go off like a runaway train at times. But she listened to her sister and they talked about how she was going to manage to take care of a baby, and after she left, she went back over what she'd said about Connor and she felt more confused than ever.

There was no doubt about it, she wanted Connor back. For the past couple of days, he'd been her shelter against the storm. Why on earth was she making him go?

But maybe it was for the best. After all, she didn't want him to be here if he was Brad's friend more than he was hers. What was the truth? She was overwhelmed by the emotions churning inside her.

But she knew one thing: it was time to face facts. She loved Connor. She'd probably loved him for years and hadn't been able to admit it to herself. But she could re-member countless times that she'd been frustrated with Brad and wished he could be more like Connor. She'd known forever that Connor fit her better than Brad did. They looked at life through much the same lens. They liked the same things, laughed at the same jokes. Brad always seemed restless and disapproving. Why had she put up with it for so long?

And Connor was so darn sexy. She'd always felt a certain buzz around him. Brad was more demanding, more dominant. Connor was more easygoing. More her type. What a fool she'd been all these years.

She loved Connor. Wow.

Except for one little tiny problem. No matter what Sara said, she was pretty sure he didn't love her. He liked her fine, he always had. But he liked a lot of girls. And when push came to shove, he was better friends with Brad than he was with her. And that hurt.

In fact, it cut deep. Brad had been so awful to her. It had taken time, but she'd finally come to a place where she could look into the past and face the truth. She'd been blinded by a lot of things when she'd thought she loved Brad. A lot of those things were not too flatter-ing to her. She'd been a fool. Now she could look Brad squarely in the eye and say, "Brad, you're a real jerk." At least, she thought she could.

She had to get that out of her system because, like it

or not, Brad was her boys' father. There was no hiding from that. Even Brad couldn't pretend it didn't matter. They would always be tied to him in ways he couldn't control.

So Connor had tried to help her in his way, and now she'd kicked him out. Maybe that wasn't the wisest thing to do, but she couldn't pretend with Connor. She was in love with him. What if he knew that? What if he saw it in her face, in her reactions? Would he use it against her? She didn't know, because she really couldn't trust him.

Why hadn't he told her the truth right from the beginning so that she could get prepared for any sort of attack from Brad? Now she was going to have to deal with Brad on her own.

That was going to be hard to do. Brad had a domineering way about him and she'd been trained over the years to yield to him. It almost came naturally to her. She was going to have to fight against that impulse. She couldn't let him walk all over her. And once he realized she wasn't going to obey him, what next? He would find some way to make her pay. Brad was capable of doing almost anything.

Life was becoming impossible. What was she going to do? She was probably going to lose her house and lose her business. She couldn't meet the loan call. She was going to go under like a small boat in heavy swells.

The only way out she could see was to sell her shares to Brad. She didn't want to do it. She especially hated to do anything that might make him happy. But she wasn't going to have any choice. Her options had just become even more limited.

Well, she might end up that way, but she intended to put up a fight as long as she could. She would see how well she could stand up to Brad when she really tried. Live and learn.

In the meantime, all she could do was sit here and wait for Brad to show up.

CHAPTER TEN

CONNOR CHECKED BACK into his hotel. As he started for the elevators, he heard "Mambo!" coming from the dining room dance floor and he couldn't resist looking in to see if Karl was back. Sure enough, and dancing with a bewildered looking redhead. Connor ducked back out quickly. He didn't want to scare Karl off.

He ordered something from room service and watched the news and then he turned off the TV and went out and walked the Seattle streets for a couple of hours. This was a city he knew well. He'd grown up not far away in a small town, and then gone to the University. The years after college had been spent right here. It was home in a sense. He could live here. He didn't need anything else.

Except Jill. He needed Jill more than he needed air to breathe.

His cell received a text and he flipped it out to see who it was. Brad had finally answered him.

"You're right," he said. "I need to come and get what I need myself. I'll be there in the morning."

So Brad was coming to work his magic on Jill. What

did he think—that he could walk in and hypnotize her into doing things his way? Or was he ready to give her what she'd always wanted—marriage and a promise to try to be a father to his kids?

That night he couldn't sleep. He spent the time staring at the ceiling and going over what had happened over the last few days. He knew he was following a familiar pattern. He'd begun to let his feelings for Jill come out and actually show themselves, but once Jill backed away, so did he. He'd walked off and left the field to Brad so many times, it seemed the natural thing to do.

But it wasn't. It was time he made up his mind, declared himself, and claimed Jill for himself. This was probably his last chance to do it. What the hell was he waiting for?

Damn it, she needed him. He was the only one who loved her the way she needed to be loved. He was the only one ready to protect her and make her happy, the only one who was ready to help her raise her kids. The only other person he needed to convince was Jill herself. And that was the only part he still a little shaky on.

He was a realist and he knew there was a chance that Brad would offer to take Jill back, and he knew there was a chance she would take him up on it. She yearned to have the boys' father back fulfilling his role, giving them what they needed. Whether she yearned for the man himself in the same way, he wasn't sure. But he wasn't going to let things take their natural course and see what happened. No. Not this time. He was going to fight for the woman he loved.

He ate an early breakfast in the coffee shop and then he headed for the ferry landing. He got out of the car during the crossing and looked up at the house Jill and Brad had bought together when their marriage was young and the company was all they cared about. How quickly things could change.

He was pretty sure Brad would show up sometime today. And how Jill reacted to that would tell the tale. He meant to play a part, regardless. And if he had to tell a few home truths to his old friend, he was ready to do it. He drew in a lungful of sea air and began to prepare for what he was going to do.

Jill had the children up and dressed and ready to go first thing in the morning. She'd hardly slept at all but she had done a lot of thinking. She was definitely staring at a fork in her life's road. Would she bow to Brad, or would she fight for Connor? Could she find a way to make Connor want her more than he wanted to be friends with Brad? If she couldn't do that, it was all over. But if she didn't even try, how would she ever know?

She planned to leave the twins with Sara and then she was heading to the mainland. She was going to go and find Connor and tell him she loved him. Her blood pounded in her ears. She was so scared. But she had to take the chance. Like Sara said, she couldn't let him slip away.

She'd let the boys out to play in the backyard while she got things ready and she was just about to get them and put them into the car when she heard the front door close. She stopped, listening.

"Sara?" she called at last. "Is that you?"

There was no answer. She swallowed hard, glancing toward the side door and thinking of making a run for it, one child under each arm. But before she could try that out, Brad appeared in the doorway to the kitchen.

"No," he said, watching her coolly. "It's me."

It was still early and once Connor got across the channel, he decided to take a run around the island before he went up to the house. The trip was as pretty as it had ever been, with trees and a lush growth of flowers that was almost tropical in its glory. What a wonderful place to choose to raise a family.

As he came back around, he stopped at a light and looked down at the ferry landing. The next one had arrived, and the first car coming off was a silver Porsche. He knew right away that had to be Brad.

Staying where he was, he watched as the car climbed the hill and turned into Jill's driveway, then parked in front of the entryway. Brad got out and headed for the front door, and Connor gritted his teeth and counted to ten. He had to force back the rage that threatened to overwhelm him. If he came face-to-face with Brad right now, he would surely end up bloodying the man's nose. He had to give it a minute.

Once he was calmer, he turned his car up toward the house, parking on the street. He got out just as he saw Brad disappearing inside.

Striding quickly up the hill, he went around back,

quietly opening the door to the screened-in porch, which opened onto the kitchen. Ten to one she would be there. He stopped and listened.

Jill was shaking. She only hoped Brad couldn't tell. How many times had she imagined this scene? Here he was, in the flesh.

This was the first time he'd been back to their house since the divorce. The first time she'd seen him in over a year. She shoved her unruly hair back behind her ears and tried to smile.

"It's good to see you, Brad," she said breathlessly.

His eyes had been cold as steel when he'd first come in, but as she watched, they began to warm. "Jill," he said, and held out his hands to her.

She hesitated for a few seconds, but she took them. They were warm. He was so cool and confident. And here she was, rattled and skittish as a baby bird.

"I've missed you," he said.

She blinked at him. Why did his lies always sound so sincere?

"Where's Connor?" he asked.

"Oh, he…he left. Last night."

"Ah," he said, and she could tell he thought Connor had left because he was coming. "Probably a good thing," he said almost to himself. "Did he ever give you my message?" he asked.

She took a deep breath. "Why don't you just tell me what that message is?"

"I don't want to rush things. How about a cup of coffee while we talk over old times?"

He was so cool, so ready to treat her like dirt and pretend she deserved it. She dug deep inside. She couldn't let him maneuver her. This was her home and he was the invader.

"I...I don't have any coffee ready," she told him. "Why don't you just get on with it? I'd like to know where we stand."

He didn't like that. She could see the annoyance flash in his eyes. "Okay," he said shortly. "Here's the deal. I need those shares, Jill. You have fifteen percent of my company. I'm going to have to ask for them back."

"Really? And what if I want to keep them?"

He looked as though he could hardly believe she was being so obstinate. "No, don't you understand? I need them. I'm fighting off a mini rebellion and I need them to regain the advantage." He frowned. He could see she wasn't bending for him the way he thought she should. "Listen, I'll make it worth your while. I'm prepared to pay you quite handsomely for them."

He named a figure that didn't sound all that handsome to her. If he could pay that for shares, why couldn't he pay child support? But she knew the answer to that. Because he didn't want to.

"I'm being attacked by some of the other shareholders who are conspiring against me. I need those shares to defend myself. And of course, if you ever hope to get any more money out of me, you'd better help."

She found herself staring at him. The fear had melted away. He was just a big jerk. There was no reason to let him intimidate her.

"Brad, I'm not interested in selling. I feel that those

shares are a legacy of sorts for the boys. I want them to be there for them when they grow up, both as an investment and for traditional reasons."

His jaw tightened. "All right, I'll double the offer."

She shook her head. "But that's not the point. I want the boys to have something from their father. I'm just sorry you don't feel the same way."

"Are you crazy? What do those brats have to do with my company?"

She glared at him. Didn't he have any human feelings at all? "We built that company together, you, me and Connor. It was a work of joy and friendship between us all at the time."

"That's a crock. I had the idea, I worked out the plans, I did the development. You two were filler. The company is mine. You had very little to do with it." He grunted. "And those kids didn't have anything to do with it."

Her fingers were trembling but she was holding firm. "Whether or not you want to acknowledge them, those kids are yours. They have your DNA. They wouldn't exist without you. Though you may never be a real father to them, this will give them something to know about you, to feel they've been given a gift from you."

"That's ridiculous. It's sentimental garbage." He shook his head as though he just couldn't understand her attitude. "Jill, what's happened to you? You were once my biggest supporter. You would have done anything to help me. And now…"

For just a moment she remembered him as he used to be, so young and handsome, with the moonlight in his eyes and a kiss on his mind. She thought of how it was when they were first married and he had let her know how much he wanted her, every minute of the day. She'd thought it would always be like that. She'd been wrong.

But thinking about what used to be had the effect of cooling her anger. They did have a past. She couldn't ignore that. She took a deep breath and made her voice softer, kinder, more understanding.

"Brad, I did support you for so many years. But what you've done has undermined that. Lately you have done nothing but stand in my way. And you expect me to bend over backward for you?"

He controlled his own anger and tried to smile. "You know what, you're right. And that wasn't really fair of me." He tried to look sincere. "But everything I do is for the good of the company. You know that."

She shrugged. That wasn't good enough to justify what he'd done.

He stared at her for a long moment, then nodded and adjusted his stance. He was good at sizing up the other side and finding a way to adapt to new facts.

"Okay, Jill. I understand. You need something more." He nodded, thinking for a moment. "Here's the deal. I want full ownership of the company. I need it. I'm willing to take you back to get it."

She almost fell over at his words. "You'll take me back?"

"Yes, I will."

Unbelievable. "And the boys?"

He turned and looked at the twins playing on the hill behind the house. "Is that them?"

She nodded.

"Sure, why not?" He turned back, his eyes hard and cold as steel. "Have we got a deal?"

She stared at him. What could she say? Did she have a right to hand away her children's connection with their father? But what was that connection worth? Why hadn't she ever seen the depths of his vile selfishness before? His soul was corrupt.

"Brad, you've really surprised me with this. I never thought you would make such an offer."

"So what do you say?"

"She says 'no.'" Suddenly Connor was in the room with them.

"Hello, Brad," he said, his tone hard and icy. "She says 'no deal.' Sorry."

She looked from Brad to Connor and back again, confused. Where had he come from? She wasn't sure, but suddenly he was there and suddenly Brad didn't look so smooth and sure of himself.

"Connor," Brad said, looking annoyed. "I thought you were gone."

"I was. But I'm back."

Brad looked unsure. "This is just a matter between me and Jill."

"No, it's not. I'm afraid there's been a change." Connor stood balanced, his stance wide, like a fighter. In every way, he was exuding a toughness she didn't think she'd ever seen in him before. "I'm involved now."

Brad looked bewildered. "What the hell are you talking about?"

"You're not married to Jill anymore. In fact, since

you won't acknowledge your own children, and from what I understand, you hardly ever give them any money, the only real substantial tie they have with you is those shares."

He turned and looked at Jill. "Here's my advice. Give him the shares. Let him buy them from you. Once they're gone, and you and I are married, he won't have any reason left to contact you in any way or have any part in your life. You'll be free of him." He reached out and touched her shoulder. "But of course, it's up to you. What do you say?"

Jill stared at Connor. She heard his words but she was having some trouble understanding them. Did he mean…? Wait, what did he say about marrying her? A bubble began to rise in her chest—a bubble of happiness. She wanted to dance and laugh and sing, all at once.

"Connor?" she said, smiling at him in wonder. "Are you feeling okay?"

He gave her a half smile back. "I'm feeling fine. How about you?"

"I think I'm going to faint." She reached out and he caught hold, steadying her against him. She put an arm around his waist and pulled even closer, looking up at him with laughter bubbling out all over.

He gazed down at her and grinned. He had a good feeling about how this was turning out. There was only one last test. Was she ready to cut all ties to Brad? "What do you think about selling back the shares?" he asked her.

She nodded happily. Suddenly she knew that she just

didn't care about the shares. All her excuses had been hogwash meant to give her an excuse to not do what Brad wanted. But she didn't care about that anymore. She didn't have to care about Brad. She was going to care about her family, and he wasn't in it. He'd given up that chance long ago.

"I think you're right," she said. "I liked that second offer."

Brad looked uncertain.

Connor shrugged at him. "There you go. Hand over the money, Brad. Let's see the glint of your gold."

"Hey, she just said…"

"I don't care what you heard. She'll take the second offer. Or would you rather have her contact the people in the company who are fighting you and see how much they'll offer?"

Brad frowned at him, shooting daggers of hate, but he pulled out his checkbook. He wrote out a check and handed it to Jill. She looked at it, held it up to the light, then nodded and put it down, leaving the room to get her documentation. In a moment she was back.

"Here are the shares," she said. "There you go. It's all you now, Brad. You don't need me for anything anymore. Right?"

Brad didn't say a word.

"Let's make a pact," Jill said. "Let's not see each other ever again. Okay?"

He seemed completely bewildered. "Jill. Don't you remember what we once had together?"

She snorted. "Don't you remember what you did to me eighteen months ago?"

One last disgruntled look and Brad headed for the door. Connor pulled Jill into his arms and smiled down at her.

"I hope you don't feel like I coerced you into that."

"Not at all. I think it was the perfect solution. If he'd come and asked me in a humble, friendly way, I would have handed them back to him at any time. It was just when he acted like such a jerk, I couldn't stand the thought of giving in to him."

"At least you made him pay for them."

She shook her head and laughed. "It is so worth it to get him out of my life."

He searched her dark eyes. "You're sure there's nothing left? You don't love him?"

"How can you even ask that?" She touched his face with her fingertips. "I love you," she said, her voice breaking on the word. "It's taken a while to get that through my skull, but it's true."

He shook his head, laughing softly. "That's quite a relief. I wasn't sure."

She smiled and snuggled into his arms. "I'm not even going to ask if you still consider Brad your best friend. Actions speak louder than words. You showed me."

"You're my best friend," he told her lovingly.

She pursed her lips, looking up at him with her brows drawn together. "And the new baby?" she asked, just testing reality. "Are you really willing to take that one on with me?"

"Of course. It's going to be crazy around here with all these kids, but I think I can handle it." He went to the sliding glass door and called the boys and they came running.

"Well," Jill said, "the truth is, Kelly's baby is going to be living with Sara."

He turned and looked at her. "Ah. She came around, did she?"

"Thanks to you."

He shook his head. "She was going to get there eventually. It just took some time for the shock to wear off."

Jill looked at him with stars in her eyes. He was so good and so ready to be a part of this family and commit to them all, even to her sister. And the new baby. She hardly knew how to contain her happiness.

The twins roared in and headed for the sunroom and she went back into Connor's arms. This was where she really belonged. This is where she was going to stay. Forever was a long, long time, but she was ready to promise it.

"I love you," she whispered to him.

"I've always loved you," he told her, his gaze dark with adoration and longing. "So I win."

"Oh, no, my handsome husband-to-be. If anyone is a winner here, it's me." And she kissed him hard, just to make sure he knew it.

* * * * *

"Allie, I care," he said, and it was as if someone else was talking.

"How can you care?"

He had no answer. He only knew that he did.

He only knew that it felt as if a part of him was being wrenched out of place. He was a banker, for heaven's sake. He shouldn't feel a client's pain.

But this was Allie's pain. Allie—a woman he'd known for less than a day. A woman he was holding with comfort, and something more. He looked down at her, and she looked straight back up at him, and he knew that now, for this moment, he wasn't her banker.

In a fraction of a moment things had changed, and he knew what he had to do. He knew for now, for this moment in time, what was inevitable—and she did, too.

He cupped her face in his hand, he tilted her chin— and he stooped to kiss her.

Dear Reader,

I was raised in a farming community, so neighbours' visits and Christmas were almost the extent of family excitement. Once a year, however, the circus came to town.

I thought it was the most exotic, amazing event in the world. They had camels and trapeze artists and clowns and popcorn and hot dogs... I remember watching with my heart in my mouth, sure that the lady in the pink sparkles would come crashing down. My dad must have worried as much as I did, for most years we repeated the five-mile drive into town, to see the performance all over again.

So I guess it's no wonder I've finally written a circus book, complete with heroine landed with a run down circus and a billionaire hero who has to step in to save not only the lady in sparkles but her assortment of circus animals and her extended circus family.

To research this book, of course I had to go to the circus. My husband complained all the way—'*Why are we going to the circus without the kids?*' But who needs kids? We sat up the back and ate popcorn, we watched the lady in pink sparkles and I fell in love all over again. Sometimes I love being a romance writer.

Enjoy,

Marion

SPARKS FLY WITH THE BILLIONAIRE

BY
MARION LENNOX

MILLS & BOON

First published in Great Britain 2013
by Mills & Boon, an imprint of Harlequin (UK) Limited,
Eton House, 18-24 Paradise Road, Richmond, Surrey TW9 1SR

© Marion Lennox 2013

ISBN: 978 0 263 90108 5
ebook ISBN: 978 1 472 00478 9

23-0513

Printed and bound in Spain
by Blackprint CPI, Barcelona

Marion Lennox is a country girl, born on an Australian dairy farm. She moved on—mostly because the cows just weren't interested in her stories! Married to a "very special doctor", Marion writes for Mills & Boon® Medical Romance™ and Mills & Boon® Cherish™. (She used a different name for each category for a while—readers looking for her past romance titles should search for author Trisha David as well). She's now had more than seventy-five romance novels accepted for publication.

In her non-writing life Marion cares for kids, cats, dogs, chooks and goldfish. She travels, she fights her rampant garden (she's losing) and her house dust (she's lost). Having spun in circles for the first part of her life, she's now stepped back from her "other" career, which was teaching statistics at her local university. Finally she's reprioritised her life, figured what's important and discovered the joys of deep baths, romance and chocolate. Preferably all at the same time!

For Dad,
who took me to the circus.
With thanks to Trish, who sent me back.

CHAPTER ONE

HE WAS HOPING for a manager, someone who knew figures and could discuss bad news in a businesslike environment.

What he found was a woman in pink sequins and tiger stripes, talking to a camel.

'I'm looking for Henry Miski,' he called, stepping gingerly across puddles as the girl put down a battered feed bucket and turned her attention from camel to him. A couple of small terriers by her side nosed forward to greet him.

Mathew Bond rarely worked away from the sterile offices of corporate high-flyers. His company financed some of the biggest infrastructure projects in Australia. Venturing into the grounds of Sparkles Circus was an aberration.

Meeting this woman was an aberration.

She was wearing a fairy-floss pink, clinging body-suit—really clinging—with irregular sparkling stripes twining round her body. Her chestnut hair was coiled into a complicated knot. Her dark, kohled eyes were framed by lashes almost two inches long, and her make-up looked a work of art all by itself.

Marring the over-the-top fantasy, however, was the ancient army coat draped over her sparkles, feet encased in heavy, mud-caked boots and a couple of sniffy dogs. Regardless, she was smiling politely, as any corporate director might greet an unexpected visitor. Comfortable in her own position. Polite but wary.

Not expecting to be declared bankrupt?

'Hold on while I feed Pharaoh,' she told him. 'He's had a cough and can't work today, but unless he thinks he's getting special treatment he'll bray for the entire performance. No one will hear a thing for him.' She emptied the bucket into the camel's feed bin and scratched the great beast's ears. Finally satisfied that Pharaoh was happy, she turned her attention to him.

'Sorry about that, but the last thing I want is a camel with his nose out of joint. What can I do for you?'

'I'm here to see Henry Miski,' he repeated.

'Grandpa's not feeling well,' she told him. 'Gran wants him to stay in the van until show time. I'm his granddaughter—Alice, or The Amazing Mischka, but my friends call me Allie.' She took his hand and shook it with a shake that would have done a man proud. 'Is it important?'

'I'm Mathew Bond,' he said and handed over his card. 'From Bond's Bank.'

'Any relation to James?' She peeped a smile, checking him out from the top down. It was an all-encompassing scrutiny, taking in his height, his bespoke tailored suit, his cashmere overcoat and his classy, if mud-spattered, brogues. 'Or is the resemblance just coincidental? That coat is to die for.'

To say he was taken aback would be an understatement. Matt was six feet two, long, lean and dark, as his father and grandfather had been before him, but his looks were immaterial. Bond's Bank was a big enough mover and shaker to have people recognise him for who he was. No one commented on his appearance—and he had no need to claim relationship to a fictional spy.

Allie was still watching him, assessing him, and he was starting to feel disconcerted. Others should be doing this, he thought, not for the first time. He should have sent the usual repossession team.

But he was doing this as a favour for his Aunt Margot. This whole arrangement had been a favour and it was time it stopped. Bankers didn't throw good money after bad.

'Your grandfather's expecting me,' he told her, trying to be businesslike again. 'I have an appointment at two.'

'But two's show time.' She tugged a gold watch on a chain out from a *very* attractive cleavage and consulted. 'That's in ten minutes. Grandpa would never have made an appointment at show time. And on Sunday?'

'No. Henry said it was the only time he was available. I told you, I'm from the bank.'

'Sorry, so you did.' Her cute pencilled brows furrowed while she watched him. 'Bond's Bank. The bank Grandpa pays the mortgage into? He must be just about up to the final payment. Is that why you're here?'

Mortgage? There was no mortgage. Not as far as he knew. Just a pack of geriatric animals, eating their heads off.

But he wasn't about to discuss a client's business with an outsider. 'This is between me and your grandfather,' he told her.

'Yes, but he's not well,' she said, as if she was explaining something he really should have got the first time round. 'He needs all his energy for the show.' She glanced at her watch again, then wheeled towards a bunch of caravans and headed off with a speed he struggled to keep up with. He was avoiding puddles and she wasn't. She was simply sloshing through, with her dogs prancing in front.

'Isn't this weather ghastly?' she said over her shoulder. 'We had major problems trying to get the big top up last night. Luckily the forecast is great for the next two weeks, and we have most of the crowd in and seated now. Full house. Look, you can have a quick word but if it's more than a word it'll have to wait till later. Here's Grandpa's caravan.' She raised her voice. 'Grandpa?'

She paused and thumped on the screen door of a large and battered van, emblazoned with the Sparkles Circus emblem on the side. Matt could see armchairs through the screen, a television glowing faintly on the far bench—and mounds of sparkles. Cloth and sequins lay everywhere.

'Gran's overhauling our look for next season,' she told him, seeing where he was looking. 'She does colour themes. Next season it's purple.'

'But pink this year?'

'You guessed it,' she said, and hauled her overcoat wide, exposing pink and silver in all its glory. 'I kinda like pink. What do you think?'

'I… It's very nice.'

'There's a compliment to turn a girl's head.' She chuckled and banged some more. 'Grandpa, come on out. It's almost show time and Mathew Bond is here from the bank. If you guys want to talk, you need to schedule another time.'

Silence.

'Grandpa?' Allie pulled the screen wide, starting to look worried—and then she paused.

Henry was coming.

Henry Miski was a big man. Looking closely, Matt could see the telltale signs of age, but they were cleverly disguised.

This was Henry Miski, ringmaster, tall and dignified to suit. He was wearing jet-black trousers with a slash of gold down each side, and a suit coat—tails—in black and gold brocade, so richly embroidered that Mathew could only blink. His silver hair was so thick it seemed almost a mane. His outfit was topped with a black top hat rimmed with gold, and he carried an elegant black and gold cane.

He stepped down from the caravan with a dignity that made Matt automatically step aside. The old man was stiffly upright, a proud monarch of a man. All this Matt saw at first glance. It was only at second glance that he saw fear.

'I don't have time to speak to you now,' Henry told Matt with ponderous dignity. 'Allie, why are you still wearing those disgusting boots? You should be ready. The dogs have got mud on their paws.'

'We have two minutes, Grandpa,' she said, 'and the dogs only need a wipe. You want us to give Mathew a good seat so he can watch the show? You can have your talk afterwards.'

'We'll need to reschedule in a few days' time,' Henry snapped.

But the time for delay was past, Matt decided grimly. A dozen letters from the bank had gone unanswered. Registered letters had been sent so Mathew knew they'd been received. Bond's didn't make loans to businesses this small. It had been an aberration on his grandfather's part, but the loan was growing bigger by the minute. There'd been no payments now for six months.

In normal circumstances the receivers would be doing this—hard men arriving to take possession of what now belonged to the bank. It was only because of Margot that he'd come himself.

'Henry, we need to talk,' he said, gently but firmly. 'You made this appointment time. We've sent registered letters confirming, so this can't be a surprise. I'm here as representative of the bank to tell you officially that we're foreclosing. We have no choice, and neither do you. As of today, this circus is in receivership. You're out of business, Henry, and you need to accept it.'

There was a moment's silence. Deathly silence. Henry stared at him as if he was something he didn't recognise. He heard a gasp from the girl beside him—something that might be a sob of fright—but his eyes were all on the old man. Henry's face was bleaching as he watched.

The ringmaster opened his mouth to speak—and failed.

He put his hand to his chest and he crumpled where he stood.

To Allie's overwhelming relief, her grandpa didn't lose consciousness. Paramedics arrived reassuringly fast, and decided it seemed little more than momentary faintness. But faintness plus a slight fever plus a history of angina were enough to have them decreeing Henry needed hospital. Yes, his pulse had stabilised, but there had been heart pain and he was seventy-six and he needed to go.

Allie's grandmother, Bella, summoned urgently from the ticket booth, was in total agreement.

'You're going, Henry.'

But Henry's distress was obvious. 'The circus…' he stammered. 'The tent's full. All those kids…I'm not letting them down.'

'You're not letting them down.' Allie was badly shaken. Henry and Bella had cared for Allie since her mother left when she was two. She loved them with all her heart, and she wasn't risking Henry's health for anything. 'We'll cope without you,' she told him. 'You always said the circus isn't one single person. It's all of us. Fluffy and Fizz are keeping the audience happy. You go and we'll start properly.'

'You can't have a circus without a ringmaster,' Henry groaned.

He was right. She was struggling to think of a plan, but the truth was she didn't have one.

They could lose an individual act without it being a disaster. Given notice, one of the clowns could step into Henry's shoes, but they were down to two today because Sam had flown up to Queensland to visit his new granddaughter and Fluffy and Fizz were already costumed, prancing in the ring, warming up the crowd.

'We'll manage,' she said but her head was whirling. Without a ringmaster…

'Without a circus master the circus is nothing,' Henry moaned. 'Get me off this thing and give me back my hat.'

'No.'

'Allie…'

'No,' Allie said more forcibly. 'We'll manage. Maybe I can do the announcing myself.'

But she couldn't. She knew she couldn't. Apart from the fact that a girl in pink sparkles didn't have the same gravitas as her grandfather, she could hardly announce her own acts.

What they needed was a guy. A guy in a suit.

Or… Or… She was clutching at straws here, but a guy in a cashmere coat?

The banker had picked up Henry's hat from the mud. He was standing on the sidelines looking almost as shocked as she was.

He had presence, she thought. He was tall, dark and forceful, he had a lovely deep voice and, in his way, he was almost as imposing as her grandfather. Maybe even more so.

She looked at the hat in his hands—and then she looked fully at him. Not seeing a banker, but…something else. 'You're Grandpa's size,' she whispered.

'What?'

'With his jacket and hat…you're perfect.' This was a lifeline—a slim one, admittedly, but she was clutching it hard. Maybe they could run the circus without a ringmaster but it'd be a sad imitation of what it should be—and Henry would know it and worry all the way to hospital and beyond.

'He can do it.' She turned back to Henry, stooping over the stretcher, taking his hands. 'Of course he can. I'll write out the introductions as we go. The thing's a piece of cake.'

'The banker?' Henry whispered.

'He's already in a suit. All he needs is the trimmings. He's Mathew Bond, a close relative of James, who does so much scary stuff that ringmaster pales in comparison. He made you collapse two minutes before show time and he's happy to make amends. Aren't you, Mathew? Have you ever seen a circus?'

'What on earth are you talking about?'

'Have you seen a circus?'

'Yes, but…'

'Then you know the drill. Dramatics R Us. *Ladies and Gentlemen, announcing the arrival all the way from deepest, darkest, Venezuela, the Amazing Mischka…*' Can you do that? Of course you can. Grandpa's coat, hat and cane…a spot of make-up to stop you disappearing under the lights… Surely that's not so scary for a Bond.' She smiled but her insides were jelly. He had to agree. 'Mr Bond, we have a tent full of excited kids. Even a banker wouldn't want them to be turfed out without a show.'

'I'm no circus master,' he snapped.

'You hurt my grandfather,' she snapped back. 'You owe us.'

'I'm sorry, but I owe you nothing and this is none of my business.'

'It is. You said you're foreclosing on the circus.' She was forcing her shocked mind to think this through. 'I have no idea of the rights and wrongs of it, but if you are then it's your circus. Your circus, Mr Bond, with an audience waiting and no ringmaster.'

'I don't get involved with operational affairs.'

'You just did,' she snapped. 'The minute you scared Grandpa. Are you going to do this or am I going to march into the big top right now and announce Bond's Bank have foreclosed and the head of Bond's Bank is kicking everyone out right now?'

'Don't be ridiculous.'

'I'm not being ridiculous,' she said, standing right in front of him and glaring with every ounce of glare she could muster. 'I'm telling you exactly what I'm going to do if you don't help. You caused this; you fix it.'

'I have no idea...'

'You don't have to have an idea,' she said. She'd heard the hesitation in his voice and she knew she had him. No bank would want the sort of publicity she'd just threatened. 'You wear Grandpa's hat and jacket and say what I tell you to say and there's no skill involved at all.'

'Hey,' Henry said weakly from his stretcher and Allie caught herself and conceded a smile. To her grandpa, not to the banker.

'Okay, of course there's skill in being a ringmaster,' she admitted. 'This guy won't be a patch on you, Grandpa, but he's all we have. We'll feed him his lines and keep the circus running. We'll do it, I promise. Off you go to hospital,' she said and she bent and kissed him. 'Mathew Bond and I are off to run the circus.'

'If you agree to my requirements,' Mathew said in a goaded voice. 'We're foreclosing; you'll accede quietly without a fuss.'

'Fine,' Allie said, just as goaded. 'Anything you like, as long as this afternoon's show goes on.'

How had that happened?

He couldn't think of any circumstances—*any circumstances*—that'd turn him into a ringmaster.

He was about to be a ringmaster.

But in truth the sight of the old man crumpling onto the dirt had shocked him to the core. For a couple of appalling moments he'd thought he was dead.

He shouldn't be here. Calling in debts at such a ground roots level wasn't something he'd done in the past and he wasn't likely to do again.

What had his grandfather been thinking to lend money to these people? Bond's Bank was an illustrious private bank, arranging finance for huge corporations here and abroad. If things got messy, yes, Matt stepped in, but he was accustomed to dealing with corporate high-flyers. Almost always the financial mess had been caused by administrative mismanagement. Occasionally fraud took a hand, but the men and women he dealt with almost always had their private assets protected.

He was therefore not accustomed to old men collapsing into the mud as their world shattered.

Nevertheless, his news had definitely caused the old man to collapse. He watched the ambulance depart with a still protesting Henry and his white-faced wife, and he turned to find he was facing a ball of pink and silver fury.

Seemingly Allie's shock was coalescing into anger.

'He'll be okay,' Allie said through gritted teeth, and he thought her words were as much to reassure herself as they were to reassure him. 'He's had angina before, but he's had a rotten cold and it'll be the two combined. But you…I don't care what bank you come from or what the rights and wrongs are of this absurd story you're telling me, but you tell him two minutes before a performance that you're about to foreclose? Of all the stupid, cruel timing… This has to be a farce. I know Grandpa's finances inside out. We're fine. But meanwhile I have two hundred kids and mums and dads sitting in the big top. I'd like to kick you, but instead I need to get you into costume. Let's go.'

'This is indeed a farce.'

'One you're involved in up to your neck,' she snapped. 'Grandpa's obsessive about his role—he's written it all down ever since he introduced the camels instead of the ponies last year. You'll have a script and gold-embossed clipboard. We have two minutes to get you dressed and made up and into the ring. We have two hundred kids and parents waiting. Let's get them satisfied and I'll do my kicking later.'

'It'll be me who does the kicking,' he said grimly. 'I'm not used to being pushed around, especially by those who owe my bank money.'

'Fine,' she snapped. 'All out war. But war starts after the show. For now we have a circus to run.'

Which explained why, five minutes later, Mathew Bond, corporate banker, was standing in the middle of the big tent of Sparkles Circus, wearing tails, top hat and gold brocade waistcoat, and intoning in his best—worst?—ringmaster voice…

'Ladies and gentlemen, welcome to the one, the only, the stupendous, marvellous, exciting, magical once-in-a-lifetime experience that is Sparkles Circus. One hundred and forty years of history, ladies and gentlemen, unfolding before your very eyes. Sit back, but don't relax for a moment. Prepare to be mesmerised.'

To his astonishment, once he got over shock and anger, he even found he was enjoying himself.

He did have some grounding. After his parents' death, Matt had spent every summer holiday in Fort Neptune with his beloved Great-Aunt Margot. Margot was the great-aunt of every child's dreams. Her sweetheart had died in the war and she'd refused to think of replacing him, but it didn't stop her enjoying life. She owned a cute cottage on the waterfront and a tiny dinghy she kept moored in the harbour, and she always had a dog at her heels. She'd been a schoolteacher, but in summer school had been out for both of them. Child and great-aunt and dog had fished, explored the bay, swum and soaked up the beach.

He'd loved it. In this tiny seaside town where no one knew him, he was free of the high standards expected of the heir to the Bond Banking dynasty. He could be a kid—and at the end of every summer holiday Margot had taken him to Sparkles Circus as a goodbye treat.

Margot always managed to get front row seats. He remembered eating popcorn and hot dogs, getting his clothes messy and no one cared, watching in awe as spangly ladies flew overhead, as men ate fire, as tightrope walkers performed the impossible, as clowns tumbled and as elephants made their stately way around the ring.

There were no elephants now—or lions or any other wild animals, for that matter. That was at the heart of the circus's problems, he thought—but now wasn't the time to think about finance.

Now was the time to concentrate on the clipboard Allie had handed him.

'Here it is, word for word, and if you could ham it up for us, we'd be grateful.'

The look she'd cast him was anything but grateful, but two hundred mums and dads and kids were looking at him as if he *was* the ringmaster—and a man had to do what a man had to do.

He was standing to the side of the ring now, still on show as the ringmaster was expected to be, as he watched Bernardo the Breathtaking walk on stilts along a rather high tightrope.

It had seemed higher when he was a kid, he thought, and there hadn't been a safety net underneath—or maybe there had, he just hadn't noticed.

Bernardo was good. Very good. He was juggling as he was balancing. Once he faltered and dropped one of his juggling sticks. A ringmaster would fetch it, Matt thought, so he strode out and retrieved it, then stood underneath Bernardo, waited for his imperceptible nod, then tossed it up to him. When Bernardo caught it and went on seamlessly juggling he felt inordinately pleased with himself.

He glanced into the wings and saw a lady in pink sequins relax imperceptibly. She gave him a faint smile and a thumbs-up, but he could tell the smile was forced.

She was doing what was needed to get through this show,

he thought, but that faint smile signalled more confrontation to come.

Did she really not know her grandparents' financial position? Was she living in a dream world?

Bernardo the Breathtaking was finished, tossing his juggling sticks down to one of the clowns who Matt realised were the fill-in acts, the links between one act and another. Fluffy and Fizz. They were good, he thought, but not great. A bit long in the tooth? They fell and tumbled and did mock acrobatics, but at a guess they were in their sixties or even older and it showed.

Even Bernardo the Breathtaking was looking a little bit faded.

But then…

'Ladies and gentlemen…' He couldn't believe he was doing this, intoning the words with all the theatrical flourish the child Mathew had obviously noted and memorised. 'Here she is, all the way from deepest, darkest Venezuela, the woman who now will amaze us with her uncanny, incredible, awesome…' how many adjectives did this script run to? '…the one, the only, the fabulous Miss Mischka Veronuschka…'

And she was in the ring. Allie.

Her act included three ponies, two camels and two dogs. The animals were putty in her hands. The dogs were identical Jack Russell terriers, nondescript, ordinary, but with tricks that turned them into the extraordinary. She flitted among her animals—her pets, he thought, for there was no hint of coercion here. She was a pink and gold butterfly, whispering into ears, touching noses, smiling and praising, and, he thought, they'd do anything for her.

He understood why. The audience was mesmerised, and so was he.

She had the camels lying down, the ponies jumping over the camels, the dogs jumping over the ponies, and then the dogs were riding the ponies as the ponies jumped the camels. The dogs' tails were wagging like rotor blades and their excitement was infectious.

Allie rode one of the camels while the ponies weaved in and out of the camels' legs, and the little dogs weaved through and through the ponies' legs. The dogs practically beamed as they followed her every whispered command.

Matt thought of stories of old, of animal cruelty in circuses, and he looked at these bouncing dogs, the camels benignly following instructions as if they were doing Allie a personal favour, at the ponies prancing around the dogs—and he looked at the girl who knew them from the inside out and he thought...he thought...

He thought suddenly that he'd better think nothing.

This was a lady in pink spangles. She was the granddaughter of a client. Where were his thoughts taking him? Wherever, they'd better get back where they belonged right now.

He didn't get involved. Not personally. The appalling sudden deaths of his parents and his sister had smashed something inside him so deep, so huge, that he'd spent the rest of his life forming armour against ever feeling that sort of hurt again.

He'd looked at Allie's face as she'd seen her grandfather collapse and he'd seen a glimpse of that hurt. It should be reinforcing that armour, yet here he was, looking at a girl in pink spangles...

And then, thankfully, she was gone. The clowns swooped in again, making a game of the pan and shovel they needed—the camels were clearly not house trained—and the show was ready to move on.

He needed to focus on his next introduction.

'Ladies and Gentlemen...' he said, and the circus proceeded.

Interval.

Since when did standing in a circus ring make you sweat?

He felt wiped. He headed out through the pink and gold curtains—and was struck by the sheer incongruity of the difference between front and behind the curtains.

The ring was all gold and glitter—a fantasy. Back here was industry. Men and women were half in and out of costumes, hauling steel rods and ropes and shackles, lining up equipment so it could be carried out neatly as needed.

Allie was back in her boots again, heaving like the best of the men. She had a denim jacket over her sequins.

'Time for you to change, Allie, love,' a very large lady yelled. 'Fizz's selling popcorn instead of Bella. We're cool. Allie, dressing room, now.'

'Someone give Mathew the words for the next half,' Allie yelled and shoved the last iron bar into place and disappeared.

He watched her go and he felt the slight change in atmosphere among the women and men behind the scenes.

She was the boss, he thought.

Henry was the boss.

Henry was seventy-six years old.

Matt had thought he was coming to deal with an elderly ringmaster, to tell him it was time to close down. It seemed, however, that now he'd be dealing with Allie, and something told him dealing with Allie would be a very different proposition altogether.

He pretty much had things down pat by the second half.

He introduced acts. He was also there as general pick-up guy—and also…set-up guy for the clowns?

'The gag's on page three of the cheat sheet,' Fizz had growled at him at half-time. 'Henry sets it up for us so you'll need to do it. It'll be weird you reading it but it's the best we can do.'

Right now the Exotic Yan Yan—Jenny Higgs, wife of Bernardo, or Bernie Higgs, according to the staff sheet he'd read '…*fresh from the wilds of the remotest parts of Tukanizstan*'—

was there such a place?—was doing impossible things with her body. She was bending over backwards—like really backwards. Her head was touching her heels! Matt was appalled and fascinated—and for some weird reason he was thinking he was glad it wasn't Allie doing the contorting.

He glanced ahead at the feed lines for the gag and thought...he could do this better if he stopped looking at the Exotic Yan Yan.

And he could do this better if he stopped thinking about Allie?

Do it. He read it twice, three times and he had it.

Yan Yan unknotted and disappeared to thunderous applause. Out came the clowns. It was time to take centre stage himself.

Deep breath. Remember the first line.

'Fluffy, I have a present for you,' he called in a *Here Kitty, nice Kitty* voice, and set the clipboard down, preparing—against all odds—to play the ham. 'It's your birthday, Fluffy, and I've bought you a lovely big cannon.'

'A cannon?' Fluffy squeaked, somersaulting with astonishment.

The clowns responded with practised gusto and foolishness as the great fake cannon was wheeled in. The joke went seamlessly, water went everywhere and the audience roared their appreciation.

Exit stage left, two dripping clowns with cannon.

Matt headed back to the sidelines for his clipboard as the ropes and pulleys and shackles were heading out at a run.

Allie, dressed now in brilliant hot pink, with her trademark tiger stripes making her look spectacular, was in the wings and she was staring at him with incredulity.

'You memorised it?'

'I had time.'

'You had two minutes.'

'Plenty of time,' he said and felt a little smug. Banker

Makes Good. He motioned to the bars, ropes, pulleys and shackles, set up in well drilled order. 'Let's get this show moving.' He picked up his clipboard and strode out again.

And then Allie was flying in from the outer, twisting and clinging to a rope that looked like the sort of rope you'd hang over a river. She swung to the middle, seized another rope, changed direction—and swung herself up to a bar far up in the high reaches of the big top.

There was a guy up there waiting, steadying her.

It was his turn again.

'Ladies and gentlemen, hold onto your hats. From the wilds of outer Mongolia, from the great, wild warrior hunting grounds of the Eastern nations, ladies and gentlemen, the great Valentino, to be catcher for our very own Mischka. Watch with bated breath while Mischka places life and limb in his hands and see if he lets her down.'

He didn't let her down.

Mathew had watched this act when he was six years old and he'd been convinced the spangly lady would fall at any moment. In fact he'd remembered hiding under his seat, peeping through his hands, afraid to come out until the gorgeous creature flying through the air was safely on the ground.

He didn't watch with quite the same sense of dread now. For a start, he'd seen how big, quiet and competent 'Valentino'—alias Greg—was. He was six feet eight at least, and pure muscle. He hung upside down and swung back and forth, steady and unfaltering, as Allie somersaulted and dived.

Terrifying or not, it was an awesome act.

And Allie…Mischka…was stunning. *She was gorgeous.*

He wasn't the only one who thought so. Matt had fallen in love with the circus when he was six years old. Now he was watching other children, other six-year-olds, falling in love in exactly the same way.

He was foreclosing. He was declaring these people bank-

rupt. He was putting Mischka out of a job and he was making this circus disappear.

It's business, he told himself harshly. What has to be done, has to be done.

Right after the show.

Now.

For the circus was over. Clowns, acrobats, all the circus crew, were tumbling out to form a circle in the ring, holding hands, bowing.

Allie took his hand and dragged him into line with the rest of them. She was bowing and forcing him to do the same. She was smiling and smiling as the kids went wild and Mathew smiled with her—and for a weird, complex moment he felt as if he'd run away with the circus and he was part of it.

Part of them.

But then the performers backed out of the ring with practised ease. The curtain fell into place and Allie turned to face him, and all the pretence of the circus was stripped away. She looked raw, frightened—and very, very angry.

The other performers were clapping him on the back, saying 'Well done', grinning at him as if he was a lifesaver.

He wasn't.

The team dispersed and he was left with Allie.

'I suppose I should say thank you,' she said in a tone that said thank you was the furthest thing from her mind.

'You don't need to.'

'I don't, do I?' She was no longer Mischka. She'd reverted to someone else entirely. Even the brilliant make-up couldn't stop her looking frightened. 'But how can I? The rest of the team think Grandpa's sick and you stepped in to save us. They're grateful. Grateful! Ha. To threaten him with bankruptcy…. Of all the stupid… If Grandpa dies…'

She stopped on an angry sob.

'The paramedics said it was only a faint.'

'So they did,' she managed. 'So why should I worry? But

I'm worrying, Mr Bond, and not just about Grandpa's heart. How dare you threaten our circus? Give me one good reason.'

There was no easy way to do this. By rights, this was between Bond's Bank and Henry, but Henry was in hospital and this girl had proved conclusively that she was fundamental to the running of Sparkles Circus. More, she was Henry's granddaughter.

She had a right to know.

He had the file in his car, but he hadn't brought it in with him. He'd thought he'd come quietly and put the facts to Henry, facts Henry must already know. But he had a summary.

He reached into his back pocket and tugged out a neatly folded slip of paper, unfolded it and handed it over.

'This is your grandfather's financial position with Bond's Bank,' he told her. 'The balances for the last ten years are on the right. We've been as patient as we can, but no capital's been paid off for three years, and six months ago even the interest payments stopped. The circus's major creditor is winding up his business and is calling in what he's owed. We can't and won't lend any more, and I'm sorry but the bank has no choice but to foreclose.'

She read it.

It made not one whit of sense.

She'd done financial training. One thing Henry and Bella had insisted on was that she get herself professional qualifications, so that she had a fallback position. *'In case you ever want to leave the circus. In case you want to stay in one place and settle.'*

They'd said it almost as a joke, as if staying in the same place was something bred out of the Miski family generations ago, but they'd still insisted, so in the quiet times of the circus, during the winter lay-off and the nights where there weren't performances, she'd studied accountancy online.

It'll be useful, she'd told herself, and already she thought it was. Henry left most of the bookkeeping to her. She therefore knew the circus's financial position from the inside out. She didn't need this piece of paper.

And it didn't correlate.

She stared at the figures and they jumbled before her. The bottom line. The great bold bottom line that had her thinking she might just join Henry in his ambulance.

It didn't help that Mathew was watching her, impassive, a banker, a judge and jury all in one, and maybe he'd already decided on the verdict.

Enough.

'Look, I need to contact the hospital,' she told him, thrusting the sheet back at him, then hauling the tie from her hair to let loose a mass of chestnut curls around her shoulders. She had a stabbing pain behind her eyes. The shock of seeing Grandpa collapse was still before her. These figures... She couldn't focus on these figures that made no sense at all.

'Of course,' Mathew said quietly. 'Would you like me to come back tomorrow?'

'No.' She stared blindly ahead. 'No, I need to sort this. It's stupid. Go back to Grandpa's van. It's not locked. I'll ring the hospital, then come and find you—as long as everything's okay.'

Mathew dealt with corporate high-flyers and usually they came to him. His office was the biggest in the Bond Bank tower. It had a view of the Sydney Opera House, of the Sydney Harbour Bridge, of the whole of Sydney Harbour.

Allie was expecting him to sit in a shabby caravan among mounds of sequins and calmly wait?

But Allie's face was bleached under her make-up. With her hair let down, she suddenly seemed even less under control. The pink and silver sparkle, the kohl, the crazy lashes seemed nothing but a façade, no disguise for a very frightened woman.

Her grandpa was ill. Her world was about to come crashing down—as his had crashed all those years ago?

Not as bad, he thought, but still bad.

So…the least he could do was take off this crazy outer jacket, fetch the file from the car, turn back into a banker but give her time to do what she must.

'Take as long as you need,' he said. 'I'll wait.'

'Thank you very much,' she said bitterly. 'I don't think.'

'The doctor says he's sure he'll be okay.'

Allie's grandmother, Bella, sounded tremulous on the other end of the phone, but she didn't sound terrified, and Allie let out breath she didn't know she'd been holding. 'Did the circus go on?' Bella asked.

'Yes.'

'Without Henry?'

'We used the banker.'

There was a moment's silence and then, astoundingly, a chuckle. 'Oh, Allie, you could talk anyone round your little finger. See if you can talk him into lending us more money, will you, love?'

Allie was silent at that. She thought of the figures. She thought…what? Why did they need to borrow?

'Gran…'

'I have to go, dear,' Bella said hurriedly. 'The nurse is bringing us both a cup of tea. The doctor says your grandpa should stay here for a few days, though. He says he's run down. He hasn't been eating. I wonder if that's because he knew the banker was coming?'

'Gran…'

'I gotta go, love. Just get an extension to the loan. It can't be too hard. Banks have trillions. They can't begrudge us a few thousand or so, surely. Bat your eyelids, Allie love, and twist him into helping us.'

And she was gone—and Allie was left staring at her phone thinking...thinking...

Mathew Bond was waiting for her in Grandpa's caravan.

Twist him how?

Twist him why?

CHAPTER TWO

SHE CHANGED BEFORE she went to meet him. For some reason it seemed important to get rid of the spangles and lashes and make-up. She thought for a weird moment of putting on the neat grey suit she kept for solemn occasions, but in fact there'd only ever been one 'solemn' occasion. When Valentino's mother died, Valentino—or Greg—had asked them all to come to the funeral in 'nice, sober colours' as a mark of respect.

Allie looked at the suit now. She lifted it from her tiny wardrobe—but then she put it back.

She could never compete with that cashmere coat. If she couldn't meet him on his terms, she'd meet him on her own.

She tugged on old jeans and an oversized water proof jacket, scrubbed her face clean, tied her hair back with a scrap of red sparkle—okay, she could never completely escape sparkle, and nor would she want to—and headed off to face him.

He was sitting at her grandparents' table. He'd made two mugs of tea.

He looked…incongruous. At home. Gorgeous?

He'd taken off his ringmaster coat but he hadn't put his own coat back on. Her grandparents' van was always overheated and he'd worked hard for the last three hours. He had the top couple of buttons of his shirt undone and his sleeves rolled up. He looked dark and smooth and…breathtaking?

A girl could almost be excused for turning tail and running, she thought. This guy was threatening her livelihood. Dangerous didn't begin to describe the warning signs flashing in her head right now.

But she couldn't turn and run.

Pull up those big girl panties and forget about breathtaking, she told herself firmly, and she swung open the screen door with a bang, as if she meant business.

'Milk?' he said, as if she was an expected guest. 'Sugar?'

She glared at him and swiped the milk and poured her own. She took a bit longer than she needed, putting the milk back in the fridge while she got her face in order.

She *would* be businesslike.

She slid onto the seat opposite him, pushed away a pile of purple sequins, cradled her tea—how did he guess how much she needed it?—and finally she faced him.

'Show me the figures,' she said, and he pushed the file across the table to her, then went back to drinking tea. He was watching the guys packing up through the screen doors. The camels—Caesar and Cleopatra—were being led back to the camel enclosure. He appeared to find them fascinating.

Like the figures. Fascinating didn't begin to describe them.

He had them all in the file he'd handed her. Profit and loss for the last ten years, expenses, tax statements—this was a summary of the financial position of the entire circus.

She recognised every set of figures except one.

'These payments are mortgage payments,' she said at last. 'They're paying off Gran and Grandpa's retirement house. There's no way the loan's that big.'

'I don't know anything about a house,' he said. 'But the loan is that big.'

'That's monstrous.'

'Which is why we're foreclosing.'

'You can just…I don't know…' She pushed a wisp of hair from her eyes. 'Repossess the house? But there must be some mistake.'

'Where's the house?'

She stared across the table in astonishment. 'What are you talking about?'

'The house you're talking of,' he said gently. 'The house that matches this mortgage you seem to think exists. Is it in Fort Neptune?'

'Yes,' she said blankly. 'It's a street back from the harbour. It's small but it's perfect.'

'Have you ever been inside?'

'It's rented. Gran and Grandpa bought it ten years ago. It's for when they need to leave the circus.'

'Have you ever seen the deeds?'

'I… No.'

'So all you've seen is the outside?'

She felt…winded. 'I…yes,' she managed. 'They bought it while I was away and it's been rented out since.' She was thinking furiously. She would have been, what, seventeen or eighteen when they'd bought it? It was just after that awful fuss about the elephants…

The elephants…Maisie and Minnie. Two lumbering, gentle Asian elephants she'd known and loved from the moment she could first remember.

Elephants.

House.

'They sold the elephants,' she whispered, but already she was seeing the chasm where a house should be but maybe elephants were instead.

'There's not a big market for second hand circus elephants,' Mathew said, still gently, but his words were calmly sure. 'Or lions. Or monkeys, for that matter.'

'Grandpa said he sold them to an open-range zoo.'

'Maybe your grandpa wanted to keep you happy.'

She stared at him—and then she snatched up the paper and stared at it as if it was an unexploded bomb, while Mathew Bond's words washed around her.

'Bond's Bank—meaning my grandfather—was approached ten years ago,' he told her as she kept staring. 'We were asked to set up a loan to provide for the care of two elephants, three lions and five monkeys. A wildlife refuge west of Sydney provides such care, but, as you can imagine, it's not cheap. Elephants live up to seventy years. Lions twenty. Monkeys up to forty. You've lost one lion, Zelda, last year, and two of the monkeys have died. The rest of the tribe are in rude health and eating their heads off. The loan was worked out based on costs for ten years but those costs have escalated. You've now reached the stage where the interest due is almost as much as the loan itself. Henry's way overdue in payments and the refuge is calling in its overdue bills. They're winding down. Your grandfather's seventy-six, Allie. There's no way he can repay this loan. It's time to fold the tent and give it away.'

Silence.

She was staring blindly at Mathew now, but she wasn't seeing him. Instead she was seeing elephants. She'd watched them perform as a child, she'd learned to work with them and she'd loved them. Then, as a teenager she'd started seeing the bigger picture. She'd started seeing the conditions they lived in for what they were, and she'd railed against them.

She remembered the fights.

'Grandpa, I know we've always had wild animals. You've lived with them since you were a kid, too, but it's not right. Even though we do the best we can for them, they shouldn't live like this. They need to be somewhere they can roam. Grandpa, please...'

As she'd got older, full of adolescent certainty, she'd laid down her ultimatum.

'I can't live with you if we keep dragging them from place to place. The camels and dogs and ponies are fine—they've

*been domestic for generations and we can give them decent
exercise and care. But not the others. Grandpa, you have to
do something.'*

'The circus will lose money...' That was her grandfather,
fighting a losing battle.

'Isn't it better to lose money than to be cruel?'

She remembered the fights, the tantrums, the sulky si-
lences—and then she'd come home from one of her brief
visits to her mother and they'd gone.

'We've sent them to a zoo in Western Australia,' Gran had
told her, and shown her pictures of a gorgeous open range zoo.

Then, later—how much later?—they'd shown her pictures
of a house. Her mind was racing. That was right about the
time she was starting to study bookkeeping. Right about the
time Henry was starting to let her keep the books.

'The house...' she whispered but she was already accepting the house was a lie.

'If they've been showing you the books, maybe the house
is a smokescreen. I'm sorry, Allie, but there is no house.'

Her world was shifting. There was nothing to hold on to.

Mathew's voice was implacable. This was a banker, here
on business. She stared again at that bottom line. He was calling in a loan she had no hope of paying.

No house.

The ramifications were appalling.

She wanted this man to go away. She wanted to retreat
to her caravan and hug her dogs. She wanted to pour herself
something stronger than tea and think.

Think the unthinkable?

Panic was crowding in from all sides. Outside, the circus
crew was packing up for the night—men and women who
depended on this circus for a livelihood. Most of them had
done so all their lives.

'What...what security did he use for the loan?' she whispered.

'The circus itself,' Mathew told her.

'We're not worth...'

'You are worth quite a bit. You've been running the same schedule for over a hundred years. You have council land booked annually in the best places at the best times. Another circus will pay for those slots.'

'You mean Carvers,' she said incredulously. 'Ron Carver has been trying to get his hands on our sites for years. You want us to give them to him?'

'I don't see you have a choice.'

'But it doesn't make sense. Why?' she demanded, trying desperately to shove her distress to the background. 'Why did Bond's ever agree to such a crazy loan? If this is true... You must have known we'd never have the collateral to pay this back?'

'My Great-Aunt Margot,' he said, and he paused, as if he didn't quite know where to go with this.

'Margot?'

'Margot Bond,' he said. 'Do you know her?'

She did. Everyone knew Margot. She'd had a front row seat for years, always present on the first and last night the circus was in Fort Neptune. She arrived immaculately dressed, older but seemingly more dignified with every year, and every year her grandparents greeted her with delight.

She hadn't been here this year, and Allie had missed her.

'My grandfather and Margot were brought to Sparkles as children,' Mathew told her. 'Later, Margot brought my father, and then me in my turn. When your grandfather couldn't find anyone to fund the loan, in desperation he asked Margot. He knew she was connected to Bond's. When Margot asked my grandfather—her brother—he couldn't say no. Very few people can say no to Margot.'

He hesitated then, as if he didn't want to go on, and the words he finally came out with sounded forced. 'Margot's dying,' he said bleakly. 'That's why I'm in Fort Neptune. We could have foreclosed from a distance but, seeing I'm here, I decided to do it in person.'

'Because now she's dying you don't need to make her happy any more?'

Her tea slopped as she said it, and she gasped. She stood up and stepped away from the table, staring at the spilled tea. 'Sorry. That…that was dreadful of me—and unfair. I'm very sorry Margot's dying, and of course it's your money and you have every right to call it in. But…right now?'

'You've been sent notices for months, Allie. Contrary to what you think, this is not a surprise. Henry knows it. This is the end. I have authority to take control.'

She nodded, choked on a sob, swiped away a tear—*she would not cry*—and managed to gain composure. Of a sort. 'Right,' she managed. 'But there's nothing you can do to-night. Not now.'

'I can…'

'You can't,' she snapped. 'You can do nothing. Otherwise I'll go straight to the local paper and tomorrow's headlines will be Bond's Bank foreclosing on ancient circus while its almost-as-ancient ringmaster fights for his life in the local hospital.'

'That's not fair.'

'Fair,' she said savagely. 'You don't know what fair looks like. I haven't even started. Now, I'm going to the hospital to see how Grandpa really is. Meanwhile, you need to get off circus land.'

'Are you threatening me?'

'Yes,' she said, and suddenly the emotion, the anger, the distress built up and she could no longer contain it. 'Now. If I so much as see you skulking…'

'I do not skulk…'

'Or any of your heavies…'

'I don't have heavies.'

'I'll call the police.'

'I have the right…'

'You have no rights at all,' she yelled, and she'd really lost it but right now she didn't care. 'The moral high ground is mine and I'm taking it. Get off circus land, Mathew Bond. I'll sort this mess, somehow, some way, but meanwhile I have my grandfather in hospital, I have a circus to tend and you have no place here.'

She grabbed his half-full mug and her spilled one and she thumped them both into the sink so hard one broke.

She stared at the shattered remains and her face crumpled.

'Well, that's one thing you won't be able to repossess,' she said at last, drearily, temper fading, knowing she was facing inevitable defeat.

Enough. She stalked out of the caravan and thumped the door closed behind her.

Business shouldn't be personal, Matt thought bleakly. He didn't do personal, and he didn't cope with emotion. It had been a huge mistake to come here himself. He should have sent his trained, impersonal staff who'd do what had to be done and get out of here.

That was what he had to do now, he told himself. Do what had to be done and get out of here.

So he did.

He filed his papers together, making sure every page was in order and the file was complete. He rolled down his sleeves, he buttoned his shirt and he put back on his grey silk tie.

He put on his cashmere coat and walked out of the caravan, out of the circus, out of personal and back to the controlled world of Mathew Bond, banker.

Henry was lying in his hospital bed, and he looked old and white and defeated. Bella just looked sick.

The doctor she'd met on the way in had given her good news. 'There doesn't seem to be any damage to his heart.

We're fairly sure it was simply a bad attack of angina, but your grandmother says he's losing weight. He's running a slight fever and we need to get his angina under control, so we'd like to keep him in for a few days, run a few tests, see if we can get him looking a bit stronger before we send him back to the wilds of circus living.'

He won't be going back to the wilds of circus living, Allie thought drearily, but she pushed the ward door open with her smile pinned in place and spent the first few minutes telling her grandparents of the unlikely success of their banker as a ringmaster.

It made them smile—but the big issue couldn't be avoided.

She didn't have to bring it up. Mathew was right. Both Henry and Bella had a clear idea of what was happening, and why.

'Why didn't you tell me?' she whispered, holding her grandpa's hand, and he snorted.

'Telling you wouldn't have made a difference. We figured we'd keep the circus cheerful and functioning right up till the moment they pulled the rug.'

Great, Allie thought bleakly. They had two weeks of advance bookings. Almost every show for the time they were in Fort Neptune was sold out. She couldn't conceive of folding the big top tomorrow and leaving a gap in the heart of the town at the height of summer.

She couldn't bear thinking today had been their last day.

And wages? To go back to the crew now and say it's over, no more pay as of now…

Was there any money to pay wages already owed? She should have asked. She should have demanded to see what powers Mathew had.

Her head was spinning, and Bella put her wrinkled hand on hers so there were three hands combined, Henry's, Bella's and Allie's. 'It's okay, dear,' she said. 'Something will come up.'

'Something already has come up,' she muttered. 'Mathew Bond.'

'But he has to be a nice young man. He's the great-nephew of Margot and Margot's lovely. Why don't you talk to her?'

'Mathew says she's dying.'

There was a pause at that. A really long pause.

Then…

'Just because you're dying, it doesn't mean you're dead,' Bella said at last, with a lot more asperity than usual. 'Your grandpa and I are almost eighty and if people treat us like we're on our last legs we might as well be. Don't you think Margot would want to know how appallingly her nephew is acting?'

'He has the right…'

'The moral right?' Bella said. 'Maybe he has and maybe he hasn't. We've given his aunt a lot of pleasure over the years. At least he can let us have our last two weeks here without refunding tickets. Bond's is huge. Our loan must be a drop in the ocean. Go and see Margot, love. Talk to her.'

'But she's dying,' Allie repeated, horrified.

'Yes, but she's not dead,' Bella repeated impatiently. 'Just like our circus isn't dead until we take down the big top. And just like your grandpa isn't dead yet. He'll be fine, Allie, love, as long as he has hope.'

'That's blackmail. You want me to front a dying Margot and her cashmere-coated nephew so Grandpa will get better?'

'That's the one,' Bella said and beamed.

'You're such a good girl,' Henry said and gave a wee feeble cough and sank further back into his pillows.

Allie glared. 'You're a fraud. Grandpa, was that collapse real this afternoon?'

'Of course it was,' Henry said, affronted, possibly with stronger affront than the wee feeble cough signified should be possible.

'Go and see Margot, Allie,' Bella urged. 'It's the least you can do.'

'I...'

'At least talk again to the nephew.'

She did have to do that. There were so many complications.

'Do you know where Margot lives?' Henry asked. 'The second house from the point along the esplanade. It's a little blue fisherman's cottage.'

'You've been there before—asking for money?'

'I had to keep the animals safe,' Henry said, and suddenly his old eyes were steel. 'I did that for you.'

And he had, Allie thought. Henry was an old-fashioned ringmaster, with old-fashioned views on circus animals. It was her distress that had made him retire them.

It was her distress that had put them into this mess?

'They're still okay,' she said carefully, feeling weird.

'We know. We get updates,' Bella said, beaming. She dived into her purse and produced photographs, and Allie found herself staring at pictures of lions and monkeys and two gorgeous, healthy elephants. Maisie and Minnie. She'd adored these animals as a kid. She'd fought for them.

That fight had got them into this mess. What would happen to them now?

'You need to talk to Margot,' Bella urged again, and Allie shook her head.

'I need to talk to Mathew.'

'Same thing,' Bella retorted. 'He's staying with her.'

'How do you know?'

'Of course we know. We were expecting...'

'Enough.' Allie put up her hands in surrender. 'I don't want to know what you were expecting. At least, I do want to know, but I'm not the least sure I can trust you two. I may not want to trust Mathew Bond either, but at least he gives me facts. I'll see him. Meanwhile, you stay well, both of you, and no more conniving. I'll do my best to see what I can save, but you need to leave it in my hands.'

She kissed them both and left. She headed down to the beach and took herself for a really long walk. She thought about elephants and lions and monkeys. She thought about a circus she loved, a team she loved. She thought about a circus sold out for two solid weeks.

And then she went to face Mathew.

CHAPTER THREE

MARGOT'S HOUSE WAS adorable. This whole town was adorable, Allie thought, as she walked past the long row of fishermen's cottages to reach Margot's postcard-perfect cottage.

The rain had stopped. The late afternoon sun was shimmering on the water and the boats swinging at anchor in the bay looked clean and washed. Fort Neptune had once been a major defence port, and the fort itself was still a monolith on the far headland, but the time for defence was long past. The town was now a sleepy fishing village that came alive each summer, filling with kids, mums and dads eager for time out from the rest of the world.

It was Allie's very favourite circus site, and the thought that Henry and Bella had planned their retirement here was a comfort.

Or it had been a comfort, she thought grimly, fighting for courage to bang Margot's lion-shaped brass knocker. It was all lies.

Lies created to save her elephants?

This was her call. Her responsibility. She took a deep breath—and knocked.

Mathew answered, looking incongruously big, stooping a little in the low doorway. Margot's forebears must have been little, Allie thought—or maybe it was just Mathew was large. Or not so much large as powerful. He was wearing a fisherman's guernsey and jeans. Maybe he'd walked on the beach as well—he looked windswept and tousled and…and…

Okay, he looked gorgeous, she conceded, taking a step back, but gorgeous didn't have any place here. He was looking at her as if she was a stranger, as if she had no right to be here, and she felt like running.

If Margot was dying she had no right to intrude.

But what was at stake was her grandparents' future and the future of all the crew. If she didn't front this man she'd have to go back to the show-ground, give orders to dismantle the big top and do…what?

The future stretched before her like a great, empty void.

'I need to talk to you,' she said, but Mathew's face was impassive. She was a loan, she thought. A number on a balance sheet. A red one. It was this guy's job to turn it to black.

The human side of him had emerged this afternoon. Her grandfather's collapse had propelled him into the circus ring and he'd done well, but how could she propel him to do more?

The loan was enormous. She had the collateral of an ageing circus and a bunch of weird animals. Nothing else.

He needed to turn back into a banker and she knew it.

'There's nothing more I can do,' he said, surprisingly gently. 'But how's your grandpa?'

'I…he's okay. They're keeping him in hospital for checks.'

'Maybe it's just as well. It'll keep him off site while the circus is disbanded.'

She felt sick. More, she felt like…like…

No. She had no idea what she felt like. Her world was spinning, and she had no hope of clinging to it.

'Mathew?' She recognised the old lady's voice calling from the living room. Margot. 'Mathew, who is it?'

'It's Allie from the circus,' she called back before Mathew could answer. Margot had always seemed a friend. It would have been wrong not to answer. 'It's Allie, alias The Amazing Mischka.'

There was a faint chuckle in return. 'Mischka. Allie. Come on in, girl.'

Come in...

'How sick is she?' she said urgently, whispering.

'She's decided she's dying,' Mathew said in an under-voice. 'She's only eighty, but her dog died and she's scarcely eaten since. She's spending her time planning her funeral and deciding who inherits her pot plants. Not me, I gather, because I'm not responsible enough. It sounds comic but it's not. She wants to die, and she's making sure it happens.'

'Oh, no.' She looked into his impassive face—and realised it wasn't impassive. He was fond of the old lady, then. Very fond.

'Come in, girl.' Margot's voice was imperative. 'Mathew, don't keep her out there.'

'Don't...' Mathew said and then he shrugged his shoulders. But she knew what he wanted to say. *Don't upset her. This loan is nothing to do with her.*

'Allie!' This time the call was peremptory and Allie had no choice but to brush by Mathew and walk through into the sitting room. She was tinglingly, stupidly aware of Mathew as she brushed past him—but then she saw Margot and Mathew was forgotten.

Margot was sitting hunched over the fire, in a pale pink dressing gown, draped in a cashmere throw.

Allie had met this lady every year, every time the circus came to town. She was tall and dignified, wearing tailored tweeds with effortless grace. For the last few years she'd carried and used a magnificent ebony walking cane and she'd given the impression of timeless beauty.

But now she was shrivelled. Disappearing?

'Oh, Margot.' Her cry of distress was out before she could stop herself. She'd always referred to Margot as Miss Bond. They'd greeted each other with businesslike pleasantries— this woman was a patron of the circus and her grandfather's friend—but here, in her pink robe, her body hunched over the fire, Miss Bond seemed inappropriate and cruel.

She hadn't realised, she thought, how much this lady was part of her history. Even as a little girl, every time the circus was in Fort Neptune she remembered Margot in her tweeds, sitting proudly upright in the front row.

Could she remember Mathew coming with her? No. He'd be older than she was, she thought, and he mustn't have come with his aunt for years.

All these things flickered through her mind as she knelt by Margot and took her hand. 'Oh, Margot…' she said. 'Oh, Grandpa will be so distressed.'

'Your grandfather's ill himself,' Margot said, looking down at their linked hands for a moment and then gently pulling away. 'All my friends are dying.'

It was a shocking statement, one that made Allie sit back and glance at Mathew.

His face was grim.

'You still have family,' he said. 'And friends. What about Duncan? What about me? Just because you lost your dog… Margot, there's no need for you to die as well.'

'Halibut *was* my family,' she said, gently reproving. 'And it's my time. Losing Halibut made me realise it. I'm eighty years old, which is too old to get another dog. I have no intention of lying around until everyone's forgotten me and even my nephew's wrinkled and gnarled as he stands by my grave.'

It was such a ridiculous image that Allie stared at Mathew in astonishment. He looked anything but gnarled.

He was thirty-fivish, she thought, surely not more.

'Wow,' she said to Margot. 'You might have a few more years before that happens. Too old to get another dog? Dogs live for less than fifteen years. Ninety-five isn't such a great age. And Mathew, gnarled? It doesn't seem an immediate danger.' And she chuckled.

Okay, maybe a chuckle was inappropriate. Mathew surely

looked as if it was inappropriate. 'Your business is with me,' he snapped. 'Not with Margot. Come into the study.'

'Not yet,' Margot said, with a touch of the asperity Allie remembered. 'How's Henry? Mathew told me he was taken ill.'

'He'll be okay,' Allie told her, deciding to ignore Mathew's blatant disapproval. 'The doctors say it's just angina after a dose of the flu.' She looked cautiously at Margot, wondering exactly what the matter was. 'If you'd like to risk a few more years to stay friends with him, it might be worthwhile.'

Margot chuckled then, too, but it was a bitter chuckle. 'But Henry's only here in summer,' she said. 'You all go. Two weeks of Sparkles Circus…I can't stick around until next year.'

'And we won't be here next year, anyway,' Allie admitted, and saw Mathew's face darken and thought…uh oh. Hasn't he told Margot what he's doing?

'In the study,' he snapped and it was a command, but Margot's hand closed on Allie's wrist.

'Why not?'

'Because the circus is bankrupt,' Mathew said in a goaded voice. 'Because they've been living on borrowed time and borrowed money for ten years now. Because their time has past.'

'Like mine,' Margot said, and her voice matched his. Goaded and angry.

'You know that's not true.' Mathew closed his eyes, as if searching for something. He sighed and then opened them, meeting Margot's gaze head-on. 'How can you say your time is past? You know you're loved. You know I love you.'

It hurt, Allie thought. She watched his face as he said it and she thought it really hurt to say those words. *You know I love you.* It was as if he hated admitting it, even to himself.

'And I love Sparkles Circus!' Margot retorted, her old eyes suddenly speculative. 'You're declaring them bankrupt?'

'He has the right,' Allie admitted, deciding a girl had to be fair. 'Margot, you've been wonderful. I gather you persuaded Bond's to finance us all those years ago. I'm so grateful.'

'Yet you come here looking for more,' Mathew demanded and there was such anger in his voice that she stared at him in astonishment—and so did Margot. Whoa.

'I'm not here looking for more money,' Allie said through gritted teeth. 'Or...not much. I didn't know about the loan, but I've been through Grandpa's files now and I'm horrified. The circus can't keep going—I know that now—but what I want is permission to continue for the two weeks we're booked to perform in Fort Neptune. We have sold-out audiences. That'll more than pay our way. If we need to refund everyone, it'll eat into your eventual payout and we'll have a town full of disappointed kids. If we can keep going for two weeks then I can give the crew two weeks' notice. The alternative is going back tonight and saying clear out, the circus is over and letting your vultures do their worst.'

'Vultures...'

'Okay, not vultures,' she conceded. 'Debt collectors. Asset sellers. Whatever you want to call them. Regardless, it's a shock and we need time to come to terms with it.'

'You're foreclosing on the loan?' Margot said faintly. 'On my loan?'

'It's not your loan,' Mathew told his aunt. 'You asked Grandpa to make the loan to Henry and he did. The circus can't keep bleeding money. With Henry in hospital, they don't even have a ringmaster. How the...'

'We do have a ringmaster,' Allie said steadily and turned to Margot. She knew what she wanted. Why not lay it on the table? 'This afternoon your nephew put on Henry's suit and top hat and was brilliant as ringmaster. He's here to take care of you. Could you spare him for two performances a day? Just for two weeks and then it's over?'

'Mathew was your ringmaster?'

There was a loaded silence in the hot little room. Margot

had been huddled in an armchair by the fire, looking almost as if she was disappearing into its depths. Suddenly she was sitting bolt upright, staring at Mathew as if she'd never seen him before. '*My Mathew was your ringmaster?*' she repeated, sounding dazed.

'He made an awesome one,' Allie said. 'You should come and see.'

'I did it once,' Mathew snapped. 'In an emergency.'

'And I couldn't come,' Margot moaned. 'I'm dying.'

'You don't look dead to me,' Allie said, and she wasn't sure why she said it, and it was probably wildly inappropriate, cruel even, but she'd said it and it was out there, like it or not. 'If you're not dead then you're alive. You could come.'

To say the silence was explosive would be an understatement. She glanced at Mathew and saw him rigid with shock.

He'd throw her out, she thought. He'd pick her up bodily and throw.

'I'm…I'm sorry,' she said at last because someone had to say something. 'I don't know how sick you are. That was…I mean, if you can't…'

'If you ate some dinner, let me help you dress, let us rug you up and use your wheelchair…' Mathew said in a voice that was really strange.

'I can't eat dinner,' Margot retorted, but it wasn't a feeble wail. It was an acerbic snap.

'You could if you wanted to.' He glared at Allie, and back at Margot, and he looked like a man backed against a wall by two forces.

He loved this woman, Allie thought—and with sudden acuity she thought he loves her against his will. He hates it that he loves her and she's dying.

What was going on?

And he told her.

'It's Margot's decision to die,' he said, sounding goaded to the point of explosion. 'Her dog's died. Her knees don't let her walk like they used to, so she's given up. She's stopped eating and she won't see her friends. She's lost twelve kilos in the last four weeks.'

'You're kidding,' Allie said, awed. 'Twelve kilos? Wow, Margot, what sort of diet are you on? Our Exotic Yan Yan— Jenny to the rest of us—has tried every diet I've ever heard of. She's currently on some sort of grapefruit and porridge diet. Her husband keeps sneaking over to my caravan for bacon and eggs. Maybe I should send Jenny to you.'

There was another silence at that. A long one. She'd trivi-alised something life-threatening, Allie thought. Uh oh.

She glanced at Mathew and saw his face almost rigid with tension. How hard would it be, she thought, to watch someone you loved decide to die? And she'd made light of it. Joked.

But in for a penny, in for a pound. Why not go for it?

'It's Sunday,' she said, to no one in particular. To both of them. 'We don't play tonight, which is just as well as I'm feel-ing shattered, but tomorrow's another day. We're in the middle of the summer holidays and the forecast is for perfect weather. We have performances at two and at seven-thirty. Choose one. Mathew could rug you up and we'd keep the best seat for you like we always do. You could watch Mathew being wonder-ful and afterwards you could talk to Jenny about your diet.'

'You can't want me being wonderful,' Mathew exploded. 'If you think I'm about to make a spectacle of myself again...'

'You enjoyed it,' she said flatly. 'Tell me you didn't. I won't believe you.' She turned back to Margot. 'Mathew took to ringmaster to the manor born,' she said. 'He's seriously awe-some. He could spend the next two weeks playing ringmaster. You could put off dying for a couple of weeks. I could give the team time to figure where we go from here. It's win-win for everyone.'

'You think dying's a whim?' Margot said faintly and Allie took a deep breath and met her gaze head on. She'd been blunt and insensitive—why not just keep on going?

'I guess dying's something we all have to do,' Allie admitted. 'But if you could squeeze in a couple more weeks of living and lend us your nephew while you did, we'd be very grateful. More than grateful. You'd be saving the circus. You'd be giving us—all of us—one last summer.'

'The loan's already called in,' Mathew snapped.

'Then call it out again,' Margot snapped back and suddenly the old lady was pushing herself to her feet, unsteady, clinging to the arms of her chair but standing and looking from Mathew to Allie and back again.

'Mathew is your ringmaster?' she demanded as if she was clarifying details.

'He is,' Allie said.

'I'm not,' Mathew said, revolted.

'If I eat,' Margot said. 'If I manage to eat my dinner and eat my breakfast…if I decide not to die…would you extend the loan for the two weeks Allie's asking? You know I've never touched Bond's money. You know I fought with my family. Apart from that one loan to Sparkles, I've never asked anything of you or your father or your grandfather. I've asked nothing but this, but I'm asking it now.'

'Margot…'

'I know,' she said, and amazingly she grinned and Allie caught the glimpse of the old Margot, the Margot who'd been a friend of the circus forever, who'd sat and cheered and eaten hot dogs and popcorn and looked totally incongruous in her dignified tweeds but who now held the fate of the circus in her elderly, frail hands. 'It's blackmail,' she admitted. 'It's something we women are good at. Something this Allie of yours seems to exemplify.'

'She's not *my* Allie,' Mathew snapped.

'She's your leading lady,' Margot said serenely. 'Mathew, I'm happy to live for another two weeks, just to enjoy the circus.'

'This is business, Margot.'

'It's probably not fair,' Allie ventured. To say she was feeling gobsmacked would be an understatement. She'd come to plead for a two-week extension, not to negotiate a life. 'Margot, you don't have to do this.'

'Don't you want me to live?' Margot demanded, and Allie felt flummoxed and looked at Mathew and he was looking flummoxed, too.

'I came down to spend time with you,' he managed.

'And now you can,' Margot retorted. 'Only instead of immersing yourself in your financial dealings while I die, you can be a ringmaster while I watch. You've been a banker since the day you were born. Why not try something else?'

What had she done? Allie thought faintly. She hadn't just backed this man against the wall; she'd nailed him there. He was looking as if he had no choice at all.

Which was a good thing, surely? It was the fate of the whole circus team she was fighting for here. She had no space to feel sorry for him.

Besides, he was a big boy.

And he was an awesome ringmaster.

'I brought the scripts for the clown jokes for the week,' she ventured, sort of cautiously. The room still felt as if it could explode any minute. 'We swap them around because lots of families come more than once. If you could read them…even memorise them like you did today…'

'He memorised his lines?' Margot demanded.

'He helped with the water cannon joke,' Allie told her. 'He timed it to perfection.'

'My Mathew…a ringmaster…'

'Worth living for?' Allie asked and chuckled and glanced at Mathew and thought chuckling was about as far from this guy's mindset as it was possible to get.

'Yes,' Margot said. 'Yes, it is. Mathew, do you agree?'

It felt as if the world held its breath. Allie had almost

forgotten how to breathe. Breathing was unnecessary, she thought—unless the decision came down on her side.

'Yes,' Mathew said at last, seemingly goaded past endurance, and she couldn't believe she'd heard right.

'Yes?'

'Give me the scripts.'

'You mean it?'

'I don't,' he said through gritted teeth, 'say anything I don't mean. Ever.'

'Oh, my…' Her breath came out in a huge rush. 'Oh, Mathew…'

'You have what you want,' he said. 'Now leave.'

'But I'd like crumpets,' Margot interjected, suddenly thoughtful. 'With butter and honey. Mathew, could you pop across to the store to get me some?'

'Of course.' Mathew sounded totally confused. 'But…'

'And leave Allie with me while you go,' she said. 'If I'm not dying I need company.'

'I'll get them for you,' Allie offered but Margot suddenly reached out and took her hand. Firmly.

'I'd like to talk to you. Without Mathew.'

'Margot…' Mathew said.

'Women's business,' Margot said blandly. 'Fifteen minutes, Mathew, then I'll eat my crumpets and have a nap and you can go back to your work. But I need fifteen minutes' private time with Allie.'

'There's nothing you need to discuss with Allie. Two weeks. That's it, Margot. No more.'

'That's fine,' Margot said serenely. 'But I will talk to Allie first. Go.'

He went. There didn't seem a choice. He needed to buy what Margot required, leaving the women to…women's business?

He had no idea what Margot wanted to talk to Allie about, but he suspected trouble. Margot was a schemer to rival Machiavelli. For the last few months she'd slumped. He'd seen how much weight she'd lost, he'd watched her sink into apathy and he really believed she was dying.

Did he need to fund a circus in perpetuity to keep her alive?

It wouldn't work, though, he thought, even if it made financial sense—which it didn't. For the next two weeks, Sparkles would play in Fort Neptune, Margot would see him as the ringmaster and maybe she'd improve. But even if the circus was fully funded, it'd move on and she'd slump again.

Meanwhile, two weeks with Allie...

Allie.

He gave himself a harsh mental shake, disturbed about where his thoughts were taking him. The last couple of days while he'd been here, watching Margot fade, he'd become... almost emotional.

What was it about a girl in a pink leotard with sparkling stripes that made him more so?

A man needed a beer, he thought, and glanced at his watch. Two minutes down, thirteen minutes to go. Women's business. What were they talking about?

A man might even need two beers.

'You need to excuse my nephew.' With the door safely closed behind Mathew, Margot lost no time getting to the point. 'He doesn't cope with emotion.'

'Um...' Allie was disconcerted. 'I don't think I need to excuse Mathew for anything. He's just saved our circus.'

'For two weeks and he foreclosed in the first place.'

'Grandpa borrowed the money,' she admitted, trying to be fair. 'With seemingly no hope of repaying the capital. Bond's is a bank, not a charity. It's business.'

'And that's all Mathew does,' Margot said vehemently. 'Business. His parents and sister died in a car crash when he was six. His grandfather raised him—sort of—but he raised him on his terms, as a banker. That boy's been a banker since he was six and he knows nothing else. I brought him down here for two weeks every summer and I tried my best to make him a normal little boy, but for the rest of his life... His grandfather worked sixteen-hour days—he did from the moment his son died—and he took care of Mathew by taking him with him to the bank. He taught Mathew to read the stock market almost as soon as he could read anything. Before he was ten he could balance ledgers. His grandfather—my brother—closed up emotionally. The only way Mathew could get any affection was by pleasing him, and the only way to please him was to be clever with figures. And there was nothing I could do about it. Nothing.'

'Oh, Margot...' What business was this of hers, Allie thought, but she couldn't stop her.

'You're the same, I suspect,' Margot said. 'The circus is in your blood; you've been raised to it. I've watched you as a little girl, without a mother, but I always thought having the run of the circus would be much more fun than having the run of the bank.'

'I've never...not been loved,' Allie said.

'You think I can't see that? And I bet you're capable of loving back. But Mathew... He's brought three women to visit me over the years, three women he thought he was serious about, and every one of them was as cool and calculating as he is. Romance? He wouldn't know the first thing about it. It's like...when his family was killed he put on emotional armour and he's never taken it off.'

'Why are you telling me this?' Allie asked, feeling weird. 'It's none of my business.'

'It *is* your business,' Margot said. 'You've thrown him off balance, and what my Mathew needs is to be thrown off balance and kept off balance. Knock him off his feet, girl. If you want to save your circus...'

'Margot...' She'd been sitting on a stool near Margot. Now

she rose and backed away. 'No. I'm not even thinking…I wouldn't…'

'If I thought you would, I wouldn't suggest it.'

'And that makes no sense at all,' she said and managed a chuckle. 'Margot, no. I mean…would a Bond want a kid from the circus?'

'He might *need* a kid from the circus. A woman from the circus.'

Margot was matchmaking, Allie thought, aghast. One moment she'd been dying. The next, she was trying to organise a romance for her nephew.

'I think,' she said a trifle unsteadily, 'that I've won a very good deal by coming tonight. You've helped me keep the circus going for two weeks and that's all I came for. I'd also really like it if you kept on living,' she added for good measure. 'But that's all I'm interested in. You're about to eat crumpets. If you'll excuse me, I think I'll quit while I'm ahead.'

'He needs a good woman,' Margot said as she reached the door.

'Maybe he does,' Allie managed, and tugged the door open. 'But I need a ringmaster and two weeks' finance and nothing more, so you can stop your scheming this minute.'

The pub was closed. Sunday night in Fort Neptune, Matt thought morosely. Yee-ha.

He walked the beach instead.

The moon was rising over the water, the last tinge of sunset was still colouring the sky and the beauty of the little fort was breathtaking—yet he deliberately turned his mind to figures.

Figures were a refuge. Figures were where he was safe.

It had been that way for as long as he remembered.

When he was six years old his family had died. He had a vague memory of life with them, but only vague. He remembered the aftermath, though. The great Bond mausoleum. His grandfather being…stoic. His great-aunt Margot arriving and yelling, '*Someone has to cuddle the child. I know you're breaking your heart, but you're burying yourself in your bank. You have a grandson. If you can't look after him, let me have him.*'

'*The boy stays with me.*'

'*Then look after him. Take him to the bank with you. Teach him your world. Heaven knows, it's not the perfect answer but it's better than leaving him alone. Do it.*'

Thinking back, it had been an extraordinary childhood, and it didn't take brains to understand why he was now really only comfortable ensconced in his world of high finance.

Which was why this was so...bewildering. Walking on the beach in the moonlight, knowing tomorrow he'd be a ringmaster...

Figures. Business.

He needed guarantees, he thought, fighting to keep his mind businesslike. He needed an assurance that in two weeks the handover would be smooth and complete.

He'd draw up a contract. Make it official. That was the way to go.

It was a plan, and Mathew Bond was a man who worked according to plans.

Tonight he'd watch Margot eat crumpets, he'd help her to bed, and then he'd make Allie sign something watertight. He'd make sure it was clear this was a two-week deal. And then...

Okay, for two weeks he'd be ringmaster, and that was that. He hoped that it'd make a difference to Margot but if it didn't there was only so much a man could do.

He'd do it, and then he'd get back to his world.

To banking.

To a world he understood.

CHAPTER FOUR

AFTER LEAVING MARGOT, Allie headed back to the hospital. She reassured herself Henry was okay, she told her grandparents about the two weeks, she brought an exhausted and emotional Bella back to her caravan and settled her and told her the world wasn't about to end, and finally she retreated to the sanctuary of her own little van, her own little world.

Her dogs greeted her with joy. Tinkerbelle and Fairy were her own true loves. The two Jack Russell terriers were packed with loyalty and intelligence and fun.

There'd never been a time when Allie hadn't had dogs. These two were part of her act, the circus crowd went wild with their funny, clever tricks, and she adored them as much as they adored her.

She greeted them in turn. She made herself soup and toast and then she tried to watch something on the television.

It normally worked. Cuddling dogs. Mindless television.

There was no way it was settling her now. There was too much happening in her head. The loan. Grandpa. Margot.

Mathew.

And it was Mathew himself who was unsettling her most.

She had so many complications in her life right now, she did not need another one, she told herself. What was she doing? She did not need to think of Mathew Bond...like she was thinking of Mathew Bond.

'It's Margot,' she told her dogs. 'An old, dying woman playing matchmaker. She's put all sorts of nonsensical ideas into my head, and I need to get rid of them right now.'

But the ideas wouldn't go. Mathew was there, big and beautiful, front and centre.

'Maybe it's hormones,' she said and she thought maybe it was. As a circus performer, hormones didn't have much of a chance to do their stuff.

Hormones… Romance… It wasn't for the likes of Allie. She moved from town to town, never settling and, as Henry and Bella had become older, Allie's duties had become more and more onerous.

It wasn't that she wasn't interested in a love life. It was that she simply couldn't fit it in. She'd had all of three boyfriends in her life and none had lasted more than six months. Trailing after a circus performer was no one's idea of hot romance, and within the circus… Well, no one there exactly cut it in the sexy and available stakes.

'So now I'm thinking about Mathew and it's nothing but fancy, but oh, if I could…' she whispered, and for a moment, for just a fraction of a lonely evening after a hard and frightening day, she gave herself permission to fantasise.

Mathew holding her. Mathew smiling at her with that gentle, laughing smile she'd barely glimpsed but she knew was there.

Mathew taking her into his arms. Mathew…

No! If she went there, she might not be able to pull back. She had to work with the man for the next two weeks.

'This is nonsense,' she told the dogs. 'Crazy stuff. We'll concentrate on the telly like we do every night. Half an hour to settle, then bed, and we'll leave the hormones where they belong—outside with my boots.'

It was sensible advice. It was what a girl had to do—and then someone knocked on the door of the van.

Mathew. She sensed it was him before she opened the door.

He was standing in front of her, looking slightly ruffled.

He was wearing that fabulous coat again.

Mathew.

What was he doing, standing in the grounds of the circus at nine at night, holding a contract in one hand, knocking on the door of a woman in pink sequins with the other?

This was business, he told himself fiercely—and she wouldn't be in pink sequins.

She wasn't. She was still in her jeans. Her windcheater was sky-blue, soft, warm and vaguely fuzzy.

She looked scrubbed clean and fresh, a little bit tousled—and very confused to see him.

The dogs were going nuts at her feet, which was just as well. It gave him an excuse to stoop to greet them and get his face in order, telling himself again—fiercely—that he was here on business.

She stooped to hush the dogs and their noses were suddenly inches apart. She looked…she looked…

Like he couldn't be interested in her looking. He stood up fast and stepped back.

'Good evening,' he said, absurdly formal, and he saw a twinkle appear at the back of her eyes. She could see his discomfort? *She was laughing?*

'Good evening,' she said back, rising and becoming just as formal. 'How can I help you?'

He held up his contract and she looked at it as she might look at a death adder. The twinkle died.

'What is it?'

'It's an agreement by you that these two weeks are not in any way a concession or notice by the bank that we've waived our legal rights. Our control over the circus starts now; you're here for the next two weeks on our terms.'

'I can't sign that,' she whispered. 'Grandpa…'

'You can sign it. You agreed before the show that you

wouldn't interfere with foreclosure. Your grandfather has named you on the loan documents as having power of attorney but, even so, we don't actually need you to have legal rights. We don't need to disturb Henry. As the person nominally in charge right now, all we're saying is that your presence here for the next two weeks doesn't interfere with legal processes already in place.'

She pushed her fingers through her hair, brushing it back from her face. Wearily. 'Isn't that assumed?' she asked. 'That the next two weeks doesn't stop you from turning into a vulture at the end of it?'

He didn't reply, just stood and looked at her. She looked exhausted, he thought. She looked beat.

She looked a slip of a girl, too young to bear the brunt of responsibility her grandfather had placed on her.

'Have you told everyone?' he asked and she nodded.

'I asked Grandpa whether I should tell the crew, and he said yes. He's known this was coming. He should have told us and he's feeling bad. He asked me to give everyone as much notice as possible.'

So she'd had to break the bad news herself.

'I'm sorry.'

'So am I,' she said wearily. 'Do I have to sign this now?'

It could have waited until morning, he thought. Why had it seemed so important to get this on a business footing right now? Was it to make it clear—to himself more than anyone—that he wasn't being tugged into an emotional minefield?

'We might as well,' he said. 'Seeing I'm here.'

'I'll need to read it first. Are we talking a thirty page document?'

'Two.'

'Fine.' She sighed and pushed the door wide so he could enter. The dogs stood at each side of her, looking wary.

How well trained were they?

'They're not lions,' she said, following his look. 'They don't go for the jugular. They're very good at hoops, though.'

They were. He'd seen them at work today and they were amazing. They were two acrobatic canines, who now looked like two wary house pets, here to protect their mistress.

'Basket,' she said and they checked her face, as if to make sure she really meant it, then obligingly jumped into their basket.

It was tucked into a neat slot under the table where feet didn't need to go—about the only space in the van a basket would fit. The van was a mastery of a home in miniature, he thought. Unlike Bella and Henry's, it wasn't cluttered. It looked feminine and workable, and very, very comfortable.

'Nice,' he said approvingly and she gave a sort-of smile.

'It's the way we live. It'll be hard to get used to a house that doesn't move.'

'Will you work for another circus?'

'No!' That was definite. 'Most circuses are nomadic and I can't leave Gran and Grandpa. The only circus that works around here is Carvers and I won't go near them in a pink fit.'

'So what will you do?'

'I'm a trained accountant,' she said and he blinked because of all the unlikely professions…

'I know,' she added bleakly. 'I'm a qualified accountant for a circus that's gone bankrupt. What a joke.'

'But how can you be a qualified accountant?'

'Online university,' she said curtly. 'Doesn't that fit the image? Circus folk. Inbred and weird.'

'I never said that.'

'You never thought that? Why the astonishment, then? Because we're bankrupt? It's not my fault. Professionally, this is a bombshell. I wasn't given the facts.'

'Which wasn't fair.'

'Maybe it was,' she said wearily. 'I wasn't given the facts to protect me. Grandpa could never have afforded to keep our animals into their old age. He took on the debt for me. I loved those elephants, and even now I'll never agree to have them put down, even though I foresee a lifetime of debt in front of me.' She closed her eyes for a brief moment, as if gathering strength for a lifetime of elephant support, then took the document and sat at her table-in-miniature and read.

He stood and watched her read.

Her head was bowed over the paper. Her gorgeous curls were tumbled so he couldn't see her face.

A lifetime of debt…A lifetime of bookkeeping for a girl in pink sequins.

'There might be charities that'll help with the animals,' he ventured at last, and she nodded without looking up.

'I'll sort it. Not your problem. According to this, Bond's owns this circus and all its assets as of today—and nothing we can do in the next two weeks changes it.'

'That's right.'

'And we're in receivership right now. You'll sell us to Carvers?'

'That's up to us,' he said gently and she bit her lip and went back to reading.

'All this document says is that I promise not to try and extend the two weeks, and I don't get rid of any assets in the interim.'

'That's the gist.' She was good, he thought. What she was accepting must be a gut-wrenching shock, but he'd drawn it up in legalese, and she had it in one quick scan.

'So no riding off into the sunset on camels?'

'Um…no.' Unbelievably, she was trying to smile, and something inside him twisted. Hurt.

She read on, then reached for a pen and signed.

'We won't do anything stupid,' she said dully and the smile had gone again. He missed it.

'Thank you.' He took the document, checked the signature—some things were inbred—and tucked it into his pocket.

He should go.

'This is not your fault,' she said suddenly. 'And you have promised to be ringmaster. There's no reason for you to feel bad.'

'I don't.' But he did and she knew it. How? She was watching his face and he had a strange feeling that she could see... much more than he wanted her to see.

'I need to check on Pharaoh,' she said abruptly, standing again, and in the confines of the tiny caravan she was way too close. She'd washed in something lemony, he thought. Citrus. Nice.

He could just reach out and touch those curls.

In his dreams. He was here on business.

'Pharaoh?'

'You met him this morning. Camel. Cough.'

'Right,' he said faintly. 'Don't you have anyone else to do the heavy work?'

'The animals are mine,' she said, suddenly protective. 'I love them. How could I ask anyone else to care for them?'

'*You love camels*?'

'How can I not? Come and make their acquaintance. You've only met them in passing, and they're special.'

He should leave—but the lady of the pink sequins was asking him to go chat to camels.

How could a banker resist an invitation like that?

The ground had dried a little since this morning, but not much. His brogues were suffering. Allie had her boots on again and was sloshing along like a farmer.

She graciously allowed him to carry the feed bucket.

The enclosure was made of cyclone fencing panels, bolted together to form a secure, temporary home. The panels started and ended at a huge truck, opened at the back with the ramp down.

'That's their retreat,' Allie told him, seeing him checking the place out under the temporary lighting. 'The van's their security. The camels hardly use theirs but if they're threatened—for instance we've had hoodlums break in and throw stones, and once we had dogs dig under the fencing—they'll back into the van. The noise they make clattering up the ramp is enough to wake us and we'll be out here in minutes, but we're not worried. We seldom have problems.'

The camels didn't look worried, Mathew thought, as he saw the great beasts greet Allie with what looked almost like affection. Even though he carried the feed bucket, it was Allie they headed for.

She greeted each of them in turn, scratching ears, slapping sides, and as one tried to nuzzle her neck she reached up and hugged him.

'Pharaoh's a softie,' she told him. 'He's the oldest. His cough's getting better. I think we might let him work tomorrow.'

'It won't be too strenuous?' He thought back, remembering the clowns slipping and sliding from the camels' backs.

'They love it,' she said simply. 'These guys are designed to trudge through the desert, going without water for days at a time. I'll take them for a decent workout in the morning, but without the circus work they're bored. If they can't work...' She faltered. 'I'm going to have to find them a desert to roam.'

'On accountancy wages?'

'That's not your problem,' she said again, and grabbed the feed bucket and sloshed it into the trough with something like violence.

'We might be able to find you an accountancy position within the bank.'

He'd said it without thinking. He'd said it because...she

seemed bereft. Alone. She seemed a slip of a girl with the weight of the circus on her shoulders.

He shouldn't have said it, and he knew it the moment the words were out of his mouth.

She didn't look at him, but she straightened and looked beyond the circus grounds, to the foreshore where the moon glimmered over the distant sea.

He saw her shoulders brace, just a little, as if she was preparing herself for what lay ahead.

'Thank you,' she said in a cool, polite voice that had nothing to do with the Allie he was beginning to know. 'But I have Gran and Grandpa, and my two great-uncles—Fizz and Fluffy are really Harold and Frank and they're Gran's brothers. How can I leave them? I can't. Between us we have two dogs, three camels and three ponies. So…an apartment within commuting distance of Bond's Bank… Sydney, isn't it?'

'Yes, but…'

'There you go, then. Impossible.'

'Allie…' He was supposed to be the stand-back, dispassionate banker here. Bankers didn't get involved—had his grandfather taught him nothing? But right now…

He couldn't bear it. He felt so responsible he felt ill.

He put a hand on her shoulder, but the moment he touched her she wheeled to face him. With anger.

'For the third time, it's not your problem,' she snapped, and she was so close…so close…

'I'd like to help.'

'You already are. You're ringmaster. You've extended our time. What else?'

'I could do more.'

'Like what?' His hand was still on her shoulder and she wasn't pulling away. 'Extend the loan? Let us get deeper in debt? Even if you would, we couldn't accept. I know when to call it quits and we're calling it quits now. You've given us two weeks of getting used to the idea, of finding ourselves somewhere to live, of figuring out something. The caravans will be repossessed but they're ancient, anyway. I now know why Grandpa's been so reluctant to replace or even fix them. I'm thinking maybe an old farmhouse somewhere out of town, for a peppercorn rent, some place I can commute to a book-keeping job for a local car yard or something. You don't need to offer any more charity.'

'It's not charity.' She was still so close. His banker bar-riers...his rule about non-involvement...were dissolving be-cause she was so close.

'Giving us that loan in the first place was charity,' she said bleakly. 'No more.'

'Allie...'

'What?' she demanded, and glared up at him and it was too much. It was far too much.

She was too close. The moonlight was on her face. She looked frightened and angry and brave, all three, all at the one time, and quite simply he'd never seen a woman so lovely. She stood there in her ancient jacket and old jeans and her disgusting boots, but the memory of her slim, taut body fly-ing through the air in her pink and silver sequins was with him still.

A bookkeeper for a car yard...

His hand was on her shoulder. He could feel her breathing.

She was glaring up at him, breathing too fast. She should break away. He expected her to, but she didn't.

Why? The night held no answer. It was as if they were locked there, motionless in time and space.

One woman and one man...

Her face was just there. Her mouth was just there.

Don't get involved.

How could he not? Something was happening here that was stronger than him. He didn't understand it, but he had no hope of fighting it.

It'd take a stronger man than he was to resist, and he didn't resist.

She didn't move. She stood and looked up at him in the moonlight, anger and despair mixed, but something else... something else...

He didn't understand that look. It was something he had no hope of understanding and neither, he thought, did she.

Loneliness? Fear? Desperation?

He knew it was none of those things, but maybe it was an emotion born of all three.

It was an emotion he'd never met before, but he couldn't question it, for there was no time here or space for asking questions. There was only this woman, looking up at him.

'Allie, I care,' he said and it was as if someone else was talking.

'How can you care?'

He had no answer. He only knew that he did.

He only knew that it felt as if a part of him was being wrenched out of place. He was a banker, for heaven's sake. He shouldn't feel a client's pain.

But this was Allie's pain. Allie, a woman he'd known for less than a day. A woman he was holding, with comfort, but something more. He looked down at her and she looked straight back up at him and he knew that now, for this moment, he wasn't her banker.

In a fraction of a moment, things had changed, and he knew what he had to do. He knew for now, for this moment in time, what was inevitable, and she did, too.

He cupped her face in his hand, he tilted her chin—and he stooped to kiss her.

One minute she was feeling sick and sorry and bereft. The next she was being kissed by one of the most gorgeous males she'd ever met.

The most gorgeous male she'd ever met. Her banker.

Her ringmaster?

It had been an appalling day. She was emotionally gutted *and he was taking advantage.*

But, right now, she wasn't arguing and he actually wasn't taking advantage. Or if he was, she *wanted* him to take advantage. If taking advantage felt like this...

It did feel like this. It felt like...It felt like...

It felt like she should stop thinking and just feel. For this moment she could stop being lonely and fearful and bereft and block every single thought out with the feel of this man's body.

His mouth was strong, warm, possessive. Persuasive. Seductive? Yes! She was being seduced and that was exactly what she wanted. She wanted to let go. She wanted to forget, and melt into this man's body with a primeval need.

For there was no fear or loneliness or bereavement in this kiss. Instead she could feel a slow burn, starting at her mouth and spreading. There was another burn starting in her toes and spreading upward, and another in her brain, spreading downward.

In her heart and spreading outward?

She'd gone too long between kisses. In a travelling circus, the opportunities for romance were few and far between. How else to explain this reaction?

But did she need to explain? Stop thinking, she told herself frantically. This is here, this is now and there's no harm. For now simply open your lips and savour.

And she had no choice, for her mouth seemed to be opening all by itself, welding to his, feeling the heat and returning fire with fire.

Her arms were wrapping round his gorgeous coat, tugging him closer, closer still. Sense had deserted her. For now all she needed was him. All she wanted was him.

Mathew.

His big hands held her, tight, hard and wonderful. Her breasts were moulding to his chest.

She could feel the faint rasp of stubble. She could smell the sheer masculine scent of him.

She could feel the beating of his heart.

She wanted… She wanted…

She didn't know what she wanted, but what she got was a camel, shoving its nose right between them and braying like an offended…camel?

This was a kiss that needed power to break, but there was something about a camel that made even the most wondrous kiss break off mid-stride.

They broke apart. Allie staggered and Mathew gripped her shoulders and held—but Pharaoh was still between them, his great head looped over their arms, moving in, an impermeable barrier between them.

She heard herself laugh—sort of—or maybe it was more of a sob. At the end of a nightmare day, this had been quite a moment. It was a moment that had lifted her out of dreary and desolate into somewhere she hadn't known existed. It had warmed her from the inside out. It had made her think…

Or not think. Just feel. That was what she'd wanted, she thought almost hysterically. It had been a miracle all by itself. For a moment she hadn't thought at all.

But what now? Pharaoh had broken Mathew's hold on her shoulders. She looked past the big camel and saw Mathew's face and she thought, he's as confused as I am.

Not possible. She was so confused she was practically a knot inside.

Or maybe she wasn't confused. Maybe what she wanted—desperately—was to shove this great lump of a camel aside and will this guy to pick her up and carry her to her caravan. Or not her caravan—that was far too pedestrian for what she was feeling now. What about a five-star hotel, with champagne and strawberries on the side?

Um…not? Sense was sweeping back and she could have

wept. She didn't want sense. She wanted the fantasy. James Bond and the trimmings...

Not James Bond. Mathew Bond, banker.

'Maybe...maybe that was a bit unwise,' the banker said, in a voice that was none too steady. 'I don't make love to clients.'

And with that, any thought of luxury hotels and vast beds and champagne went right out of the window. *Client.*

'And I don't make love to staff,' she managed.

'Staff?'

'With Grandpa in hospital, I'm in charge of the circus and you're ringmaster. Staff,' she snapped and saw a glint of laughter deep in those dark eyes.

Pharaoh nudged forward as if he anticipated the need to intervene again, and Allie leaned against the camel and shoved, so both of them backed a little away from Mathew. To a safer distance.

'But the ringmaster has the whip,' Mathew said softly and, to her amazement, he was grinning.

She gasped, half astonished, half propelled to laughter. But she was grateful, she conceded. He was making light of it. She needed to keep it light.

'There's a new prop edict as of tomorrow,' she managed. 'Whips are off the agenda.'

'I guess they need to be,' he said a trifle ruefully. 'Allie, I'm sorry. I don't know what came over me.'

It needed only that. An apology.

'I don't normally...react,' she said, trying to keep her voice in order.

'To kissing?'

'To anything. You caught me at a weak moment.'

'As I said, I'm sorry.'

They were back to being formal. Absurdly formal.

'You have your contract,' she told him. 'You need to get back to Margot.'

'I do.'

'Goodnight, then,' she said and she clung to her camel. A girl had to hold on to something.

'You don't need more help?'

'I don't need anything.'

'I suspect you do,' he said, his voice gentle. 'You're so alone. But I also suspect you don't need me making love to you. You have enough complications on your plate already.'

'It was a nice kiss,' she managed. 'I quite liked it. But if you think it causes complications you're way out, Banker. One kiss does not complications make. Goodnight.'

He looked at her for a long moment and she looked right back. Firmly. Using every ounce of self-control she possessed to keep that look firm.

She was aware that Pharaoh had swivelled as well, so both of them were staring.

One girl and one camel…the man didn't have a chance.

'Goodnight, then, Allie,' he said gently. 'And to you, too, Pharaoh. Sleep well, and let any complications rest until tomorrow.'

'You're not a complication,' Allie snapped.

'I meant bankruptcy,' he said, even more gently. 'I mean the disbanding of your circus as well as your way of life. I didn't mean me at all.'

And he reached out and touched her, a feather touch, a faint tracing of one strong finger down the length of her cheekbone.

'I need to come early tomorrow to look through your books,' he said softly, as if hauling himself back to reality. Hauling himself away from…complications? 'I'm sorry, but you're right, this is business. We'll make it as easy as possible, though. No whips at all.'

CHAPTER FIVE

HE'D COME TO Fort Neptune to say goodbye to his great-aunt. Instead, he was watching her pack away a comprehensive breakfast and listening to her nudge him in the direction of romance.

'She's lovely. I've thought she was lovely ever since she was a wee girl. Her grandpa used to pop her on the back of the ponies in her pink tulle and she was so cute...'

'I'm not in the market for a woman in pink tulle,' he growled and she grimaced.

'You'd prefer black corporate? Honestly, Mathew, that last woman you brought down here...'

'Angela was caught up in a meeting and didn't have time to change before leaving. She changed as soon as she got here.'

'Into black and white corporate lounge wear. And she refused to go for a walk on the beach. Mathew, just because you lost your parents and sister, it doesn't mean you can't fall in love. Properly, I mean.'

'There's the pot calling the kettle black,' he growled. 'Your Raymond never came back from the war and you dated again how many times? And that guy who calls every morning and you refuse to see him...Duncan. He's a widower, he's your age, he has dogs who look exactly the same as Halibut...'

'They are not the same. They're stupid.'

'They look the same.'

'They come from the same breeder,' she said stiffly. 'Those dogs of Allie's came from him, too. Allie got the smart ones. I got Halibut and he was the best. Duncan got what was left over.'

'You're changing the subject.'

'*You're* changing the subject,' she retorted. 'We were talking about your love life.'

He sighed. 'Okay. We're two of a kind,' he said grimly. 'We both know where love left us, so maybe we should leave it at that. But are you coming to watch today?' But he thought... they'd never had a conversation like this. About love?

When he'd mentioned Duncan, Margot had looked troubled. Why? Had he touched a nerve?

A love life? Margot?

'Tomorrow,' she said. 'My knees are still wobbly.'

'Because you've hardly eaten for months.'

'My decision not to keep on living is sensible,' she said with dignity, and he grimaced.

'It's dumb. There are always surprises round the corner.'

'Like you'd notice them. Corporate...'

'I am,' he said in a goaded voice, 'spending most of my day today with pink sparkles.'

'So you are,' she said, cheering up, and in silent agreement both of them put the moment of uncharacteristic questioning aside. 'For two weeks. I hope I'll be fit to come tomorrow and if I can I'll come every day until the end.'

The end...

The words hung and emotion slammed back into the room again.

The end of the circus?

'You won't go back to dying at the end of the circus, will you?' he demanded.

'You won't go back to corporate?'

'That's not fair.'

'It is fair,' she retorted. 'What's the alternative? Look at you, a banker all your life and nothing else, and will you look at an alternative? Why not get serious about some pink sparkles? It could just change your life.'

'Like you're changing your life?'

'That's not fair, and you know it.' Then she hesitated. 'No,' she said slowly. 'Just because I make mistakes, it doesn't mean you need to join me.'

'Margot…'

'Shoo,' she said. 'Go. I've made my mistakes. You go right ahead and make yours.'

He needed to go to the circus, get into those books and make sure the structure was ready for handover, but the conversation with Margot had unsettled him. Instead, he decided on a morning walk and the walk turned into a run. He had energy to burn.

He had emotion to burn.

Margot was matchmaking. It needed only that. He'd spent half the night awake, trying to figure out how he was feeling, he was no closer now, and Margot's words had driven his questions deeper.

Allie.

Why had he kissed her? There'd been no reason at all for him to take her face between his hands, tilt her lips to his and kiss her—and Mathew Bond didn't do things without a reason.

Nor did he get involved.

Thirty years ago, aged six, Mathew had been a kid in a nice, standard nuclear family. He had a mum and a dad and a big sister, Elizabeth—Lizzy—who bossed him and played with him and made all right with his world. Sure, his father was a busy banker and his mum was corporate as well, but he and Lizzy felt secure and beloved.

That all changed one horrendous night when a truck driver went to sleep at the wheel. Mathew was somehow thrown out into the darkness. The others…Who knew? No one talked of it.

He'd woken in hospital, with his Great-Aunt Margot holding him.

'Mum? Dad? Lizzy?'

He remembered Margot's tweed coat against his cheek and somehow even at six, he hadn't needed her to tell him.

After that, his grandfather had simply taken him over. Mathew was, after all, the heir to Bond's. From the warmth, laughter, the rough and tumble of family life, he'd been propelled into his grandfather's austere existence, and he'd been stranded there for life.

He learned pretty fast to be self-contained. He had two weeks every summer with Margot, but even then he learned to stay detached. He needed to, because when the holidays ended he woke up once again in his great, barren bedroom in his grandfather's mausoleum of a house. He'd learned some pain was unbearable, and he'd learned the way to avoid it was to hold himself in.

His aunt Margot cried at the end of each summer holiday but he didn't. He didn't do emotion.

And now… He'd come down here trying to figure how to keep himself contained while Margot died. Instead, Margot was dithering over whether to die or not, his self-containment was teetering and a girl/woman in pink sequins was messing with his self-containment even more.

So why had he kissed her?

Lunacy.

Margot was right, he conceded, in her criticism of the women he dated. Inevitably they were corporate colleagues who used him as an accessory, the same way he used them. Sometimes it was handy to have a woman on his arm, and sometimes he enjoyed a woman's company, but not to the point of emotional entanglement.

And not with a woman who wore her heart on her pink spangled sleeve.

It was Margot causing this confusion, he decided. His distress for his great-aunt had clouded his otherwise cool judgement. Well, that distress could be put aside. For the time being Margot had decided to live.

Because of Allie?

Because she had renewed interest, he told himself. So... He simply had to find her more interests that weren't related to the circus.

The circus meant Allie.

No. The circus was a group of assets on a balance sheet and those assets were about to be dispersed. Allie was right. Carvers, a huge national circus group with Ron Carver at its head, was circling. The bank had put out feelers already and Carvers could well buy the circus outright.

Keeping Allie on?

This was not his business. Allie was nothing to do with him, he told himself savagely. The way she'd felt in his arms, the way she'd melted into him, had been an aberration, a moment of weakness on both their parts.

He didn't want any woman complicating his life.

He didn't want...Allie?

He jogged on. Soon he needed to head back to Margot's, get himself together and go to the circus.

Actually he was already at the circus. He'd been jogging and thinking and suddenly the circus was just over the grassy verge separating fairground from sea.

And he could see Allie.

Allie was standing by the circus gates, talking vehemently to a policeman.

The policeman had a gun.

Yeah, okay, policemen with guns didn't normally spell trouble, though they usually kept them well holstered. Maybe this was a cop organising tickets for his kids to see a show. Or not.

The gun, the body language and the look on Allie's face had Matt's strides lengthening without him being conscious of it, and by the time he reached them he figured this was trouble.

The cop looked young, almost too young to be operating alone, but then, Fort Neptune wasn't known for trouble. The towns further along the coast would be teeming with holiday-makers. The bigger towns had nightclubs. The police force would be stretched to the limit, so maybe it made sense to leave one junior cop on duty in this backwater.

What was wrong? He was surveying the circus as he jogged towards them.

The big top looked okay but something was different. He took a second to figure what it was, then realised a section of the cyclone fencing forming the camels' enclosure was flattened. The truck's doors were wide open but the truck was empty.

No camels.

He reached them and Allie gripped his arm as if she feared drowning.

'The camels…' she gasped. 'Matt, you need to stop him.' She sounded as if she'd been running. Instinctively his arm went round her and held, drawing her into him.

'Stop what? What's happened to the camels?' he asked, holding her tight.

'They're at large,' the cop snapped. 'Wild animals. You're holding me up, miss. I need to be out looking.'

'The crew's out looking,' she said, distressed. 'And they're not wild.'

'The report I received said three wild animals.'

'Tell me what's happening,' Matt said in the tone he used when meetings were threatening to get out of control. 'Now.'

There was a moment's silence. The cop looked as if he

was barely contained. He was little more than a kid, Matt thought, and a dangerous one at that. Any minute now he'd be off, sirens blazing, on a camel hunt. Wanted, dead or alive...

'Someone broke into the enclosure,' Allie managed. 'They used bolt cutters to drop the cyclone fencing. But I don't understand why they've run, why they didn't just back into the truck. They're tame,' she said again to the cop. 'They're pussy cats. Who told you they're wild?'

'No matter,' the cop said brusquely. 'I'll find them.' He moved towards his car, but suddenly Matt was squarely between cop and car.

'I'm not sure what's going on,' Matt said mildly, but he motioned to the gun. 'But if you plan to shoot anything—*anything*—without a life or death reason—then I'll have your superiors down on you like a ton of bricks.' He'd started soft but his words grew firmer and slower with each syllable. This was Mathew Bond, Chairman of Bond's Bank, oozing authority at each word. 'That's a promise. Allie, is everyone out looking?'

'Yes. I just came back...Constable Taylor said...'

Enough. He didn't want to know what this spotty kid had said. He didn't need to—he could tell by Allie's body language. 'Does everyone have a phone?' he demanded. 'Does the crew have them? Will they phone you, Allie, as soon as the camels are located?'

'Y...yes.'

'And if a member of the public phones, they'll contact you, Constable Taylor?'

'A message will be relayed to me,' the cop said ponderously.

'Excellent,' Matt said and hauled open the passenger door to the front of the patrol car. 'Allie, you ride up front and watch. Constable, you drive, and I'll ride lookout in the back.'

'Lookout?' Allie said faintly and he managed a reassuring grin.

'I'll be riding sidekick to a cop,' he said. 'I've been waiting for a chance to do this all my life. Let's go.'

Riding sidekick? Had he just said that? What did he think this was, the Wild West? But there was no way he was letting this gun-happy cop off on a camel quest with no supervision.

'What gives you the right?' the cop demanded, looking stunned.

'Because I'm the circus master,' he snapped. 'Miss Miski will confirm it. These are my animals and my responsibility, and if you hurt them you'll answer to me.'

The camels had scattered. The cop drove up and down the side streets, with Allie growing more and more anxious, until they received their first call.

Caesar was out on the highway. He'd obviously reacted in panic when he'd first seen the traffic and he was almost two miles out of town. Fizz—Frank—and Fluffy—Harold—had found him. Harold was staying with him, he reported to Allie, while Frank headed back for the trailer to fetch him.

One camel safe.

'One down,' Matt said gently. 'Two more coming up.'

He was sitting in the back seat while they searched, scanning like Allie and the cop were doing, but Allie thought he was doing more than than scanning. He'd calmed things down.

The cop was still looking grim but he was also looking contained, no longer like a boy on a vigilante hunt.

Another call. Jenny and Greg had found Pharoah in a community garden. Pharoah seemed frightened, he had a minor wound on his back, but there was enough enticement in the garden to make a camel think twice about escape. Jenny and Greg took up sentry duty. The trailer would pick him up second, Allie decreed, and turned and found Matthew smiling at her.

'Two safe,' he said. 'One more and we're home free.'

She relaxed a little more, but she was still on edge. The cop's gun was in his holster right by her side. She had an almost irresistible urge to grab it and toss it out of the window.

Mathew's hand touched her shoulder, a feather touch of reassurance.

'Camels are pretty hard to hide,' he said. 'And we're right beside the only gun in town.'

She closed her eyes for a millisecond, infinitely grateful that he was here, that he was right. Australia's rigid gun laws meant no one was going to shoot, and all they had to do was find Cleo.

And finally, blessedly, her phone rang again. It was Bernie—Bernardo the Breathtaking. Allie had the phone on speaker and she sensed his distress the moment she answered.

Cleo was in the yard of the local primary school. Bleeding from a graze on her flank. Edgy. Surrounded by excited kids.

'Isn't the school closed for holidays?' Mathew demanded of the cop as the car did a U-turn and the cop switched on the siren.

'It's used for a school holiday programme,' the cop snapped. 'For kids whose parents work. There'll be twenty kids there, from twelve years old down. A couple of student teachers run it. They're kids themselves. They'll have no hope of keeping the children safe.'

And the threat was back.

Fort Neptune was a sleepy holiday resort where the town's only cop must spend most of his time fighting boredom. Now Mathew could practically see the adrenalin surge. He had his foot down hard, his lights were flashing, his siren blazing, and Mathew thought this was a great way to approach a scared animal. *Not.*

'There's no panic,' Mathew told him. 'It's just a camel.'

'It's wild and wounded,' the cop said with conviction—and relish? 'I need to keep the kids safe at all cost.'

Then they were at the school, pulling up in a screech of

tyres. The cop was out of the car with his gun drawn, but Matt was right there beside him.

It wasn't pretty.

Mathew had watched Cleo yesterday. She'd been a teddy bear of a camel, with ponies and dogs jumping over and under her, but now she did indeed look wild. The school yard was rimmed with high wire fencing. There was one open gate. How unlucky was it that she'd found it? There was no way a frightened Cleo could find it now to get back out.

And she was surrounded. Kids were shouting and pressing close and then running away, daring each other to go closer, closer. A couple of teenage girls were flapping ineffectually amongst them.

Bernie was trying to approach Cleo, trying to shoo the kids back, putting himself between the camel and the kids, but Cleo seemed terrified beyond description.

Any minute now she could rush at the kids to try and find a way to escape. Any minute now they could indeed have a tragedy.

The cop was raising his arm—with gun attached.

'You shoot in a schoolyard, you risk a ricochet that'll kill a kid. Put it down!' Mathew snapped, with all the authority he could muster, and the cop let the gun drop a little and looked doubtful instead of intent.

So far, so good.

But action was required. 'Officer, do something,' one of the older girls yelled. 'If any of these kids get hurt…'

They well could if they kept panicking Cleo, Mathew thought.

Allie was flying across the schoolyard, calling Cleo to her, but Cleo was past responding. She was backing, rearing against the fence, lurching sideways and back again. Everything was a threat.

If the kids would only stop yelling…

Maybe it was time for a man—without a gun—to take a stand.

Once upon a time, as a kid with no home life to speak of, Mathew had joined his school's army cadet programme. He hadn't stayed long—drills and marching weren't for him—but there'd been an ex-sergeant major who'd drilled them. The sergeant major could make raw recruits jump and quiver, and Mathew took a deep breath and conjured him now.

'Attention!'

He yelled with all the force he could muster. Every single kid there seemed to jump and quiver. Even Cleo jumped and quivered. He'd had no choice, but it killed him that he'd frightened her more. She backed hard against the fence and her eyes rolled back in her head.

There was blood on her flank. What sort of wound?

But there was no time for focusing on Cleo. He needed to get these kids in order before anyone could get near her.

'Everyone behind me,' he ordered, still in his sergeant major voice. 'And you...' He pointed to a pudgy boy with a stone in his hand and his arm raised. 'You throw that and I'll hurl you straight into the police car and lock the door. That's a promise. Put it down and get behind me. Every single one of you. Now!'

And, amazingly, they did. Twenty or so kids—plus the two teenage helpers—backed silently, shocked to silence.

Which left Cleo still hard against the fence, with Allie and Bernie to deal with her. But Bernie was obviously not an animal trainer. He was looking at the camel's rolling eyes and he was backing, too.

Maybe he was right, Matt conceded. The camel was huge, lanky, way higher than Allie. Allie looked almost insignificant.

But Allie could deal, Matt thought. She must. Matt's job was to keep his troops under control.

He should order them to return to their classroom, he

thought, and they'd probably go—but there was one complicating factor. He could see from a glance at the teenage attendants what he was dealing with. They looked almost hysterical. Left like this, he knew the story that'd fly around town. He could see the headlines tomorrow—wild animal loose in schoolyard, threatening the safety of our children.

He needed to defuse it, now.

Besides, the cop was still waving his gun. Get rid of the kids and the way would be safe for a single bullet…

He glanced back at Allie. She knew what the stakes were. She knew what was likely to happen, but all her attention was on Cleo. She was whispering to the camel, standing still, blocking everything else out, simply talking to a creature she must know so well…

Okay, Allie on camel duty, Mathew on the rest. Defusing hysterics and rendering one gun harmless.

It was time to turn from sergeant major to schoolteacher.

'Girls and boys, we need your assistance,' Mathew said. 'Can you help? Put up your hand if you will.'

A few hands went up. More kids looked nervously towards Cleo.

'This camel is called Cleopatra,' Mathew continued, ignoring everyone but the kids. 'She's a lovely, gentle girl camel who works in the circus you've all seen down by the beach. Today she's been injured so she's terrified. Look at her side. She's bleeding. We need to get her to the vet. Mischka is trying to calm her down. Have any of you been to the circus yet? Mischka wears pink sequins and rides on Cleo's back. She looks a bit different now, doesn't she? Do you recognise her?'

A few more hands were raised. Wounds, vet, circus—he had their attention.

'Mischka looks worried,' Mathew said, almost conversationally. 'That's because she's been out searching for Cleo for hours. Did you know Cleopatra has a special place in Mischka's heart? Cleo's mother was killed by a road train—

do you know that a road train is? It's a huge truck with three enormous trays on the back. The truck driver wanted to kill Cleo to sell her for dog meat, but the circus crew was travelling the same road, moving from town to town. Mischka saw her and saved her. Now she's a circus camel. Cleo's favourite food is popcorn and her favourite pastime is doing tricks to make kids laugh. But now she's hurt and she's frightened, so we need to keep really still, really silent, while Mischka settles her down.'

'You can't...' the cop snapped, but Mathew had been deliberately lowering his voice, lower and lower, until at the end the kids were straining to hear. The cop's voice was like a staccato blast into the peace.

'Shush!' a pigtailed poppet close to Mathew scolded, and the cop looked from poppet to camel to Mathew—and, amazingly, he shushed.

His gun stayed unholstered, though.

Allie was inching towards Cleo. She was talking to her, softly whispering, growing closer, closer. Bernie was watching the cop, seeing the threat. Matt had a sudden vision of Bernie launching himself through the air at the gun, and he flinched and went right back to talking this down.

'While we wait for Mischka to calm Cleo down, maybe I should tell you about camels,' he told the kids 'Cleo's a dromedary. That means she only has one hump. Her hump's used to store energy and water, meaning she can go for days without drinking. Two-hump camels are called Bactrian camels. They still roam wild in the deserts and mountains of Mongolia. You could ask your teachers...' he smiled at the two young women, imbuing them with more authority than they seemed to have '...to show you Mongolia on the map. Camels were brought to Australia in the olden days to help the early settlers cart goods into the outback. There are lots of stories about the pioneer camels on the Internet.'

And, just like that, he had the two trainee teachers on side.

They stopped being hysterical teenagers and turned into the professionals they'd one day become.

Allie had managed to reach Cleo. She was a slip of a girl holding Cleo's halter and starting to soothe her. The cop's gun was drooping, and Mathew kept right on talking, inexorably turning a Wild Animal into Educational Opportunity.

'Camels were used extensively to open up this country,' he said. 'Cleo's mother was a wild camel, but she's descended from those first camels brought here all that time ago. When people started using trucks and trains, they let the camels loose to do what they wanted. But imagine all that time ago, girls and boys. These camels came from Pakistan. Imagine putting animals like Cleo onto boats not much bigger than the fishing schooners in our bay and bringing them all the way to Australia.'

'They would have been as scared as Cleo,' the poppet said.

'Indeed they would.' The older of the two trainee teachers finally had herself in hand, a professional in training, and, in the face of Matt's calm, she was ready to take over again. 'We'll find pictures of them on the Internet this very day, and we might start a project.' And then she looked at the cop— who still had his hand on the gun.

'Can you please put that away,' she snapped. 'The children have had enough of a fright for one day. Will the camel be okay, Miss…Miss…Mischka?'

'I think she's been shot,' Allie said and they all, without a single exception, turned to stare at the cop.

'Hey, it wasn't me…' he started but Allie shook her head.

'No,' she said soothingly. 'This is from air pellets. Someone's shot her with an air rifle.'

'And they've hurt her?' another of the kids demanded and Allie bit her lip and nodded and turned back to Cleo.

'Well,' the older of the trainees said, 'there's wickedness everywhere, isn't there, boys and girls, and yes, I saw that stone as well, Adam Winkler, and we'll be discussing it as soon as we're all inside. Which is where we're heading now. We'll leave these people to care for Cleo. Please let us know how she gets on, Miss Mischka. Thank you, Officer, for bringing us help so promptly. All right, children, right turn, quick march, back to class single file and we'll leave Cleo in peace. Let's go learn about camels.'

The girl would be a good teacher, Matt thought appreciatively. He would have watched her usher her charges and her fellow trainee back into the school, but he was too busy watching Allie.

The cop decided to guard the gate. He wasn't leaving until the school yard was cleared of camel, but he didn't want any part of persuading same camel into a trailer.

Bernie elected to watch the cop.

This was an act of sabotage and deliberate cruelty, Matt thought, as Allie settled Cleo some more. He had a clear idea now of what must have happened. The camel enclosure had been destroyed and the camels shot with air pellets to drive them crazy with pain. That there hadn't been at least one tragedy was a miracle.

'Have you had vandalism before?' he asked Allie.

'Not like this.' She was picking daisies and feeding them to Cleo. Matt made a mental note to send a gardener in to make reparation before anyone noticed. 'We have kids around the circus all the time, trying to get in to see free shows, checking out the animals, even trying to pinch things from our stalls. But this...' She looked at Cleo's flank and winced. 'Someone's come in during breakfast, which is when we have our performance meeting—it's about the only fifteen minutes in the entire twenty-four when there's no one watching. Everything's securely locked but they used bolt cutters to knock down the enclosure. Then they must have deliberately shot them to make them crazy.'

'But never before? Nothing like this?'

'No.'

She was rubbing behind the big camel's ears but the hand she used was shaking.

She was pale and growing paler.

'It didn't happen,' he said, a little too sharply, enough to make Cleo edge away a little—but Cleo had daisies now, and her own personal person and she wasn't about to tear away in fright. 'Nothing dire happened,' he said more gently. 'Pharaoh and Caesar are safe, no one's hurt and this wound on Cleo's side seems like superficial grazing. Air pellets sting, but unless they hit an eye they don't do lasting damage. I'll call the vet now.'

'The cop would have shot Cleo if you hadn't been here,' she said, just as dully. 'I should say thank you.' Then she seemed to haul herself together. She leaned into Cleo's long, soft neck and sighed. 'I do thank you. I'm so grateful.'

'It's all been a bit much to take in over twenty-four hours,' he said softly. 'I'm sorry.'

'Me, too, for all sorts of reasons.' She closed her eyes for a moment, leaned against the camel and let the warmth of the morning sun rest on her face. It was as if she was gathering strength, he thought, for when she opened her eyes again she looked different.

Moving on.

'How did you know how I found Cleo?' she demanded. 'And how did you know her mother was killed?'

He'd known because Jenny had told him while they were waiting in the wings last night, but he wasn't about to tell her that. He needed to make her smile.

'Spies,' he told her and she glanced sharply at him and saw he was trying to tease. She even managed a lopsided smile in return.

'You have spies? Bugs on the dogs?'

'On Tinkerbelle,' he said promptly. 'The tiny spot under

her left ear isn't a spot at all. If you ever use flea powder we're doomed. It muffles reception no end.'

She grinned. 'Whoa, what a traitor.'

But then her smile died. It was a weird time. They were standing in the schoolyard waiting for the trailer. The sun was warm on their faces, the camel was settling, the cop was on cop duty at the gate, making sure no wild animals got out or came in, and Bernie was making sure the cop's gun stayed exactly where it belonged.

In a moment the trailer would arrive, there'd be the vet to arrange, and the circus was due to start in an hour.

In an hour this woman would be back in pink spangles, in charge of her world, but for now...she seemed bereft and alone, and once again he felt that urge to reach out and touch her.

Protect her from all-comers?

Whoa, that was a primeval urge if ever he'd felt one. This woman didn't want a knight on a white charger even if he wanted to be one.

But...

What if he saved her whole circus?

The thought was suddenly out there, front and centre. He was wealthy by anyone's standards. He could pay off debts, fund those dratted animal retirees, keep Sparkles going into perpetuity.

'Don't even think it,' she said into the stillness.

'Think what?'

'What you're thinking.'

'What am I thinking?'

'The same as I was thinking all night,' she told him. 'I'm looking at you right now and I'm seeing sympathy. I read about you on the web last night. You're not a minion in Bond's Bank—you *are* Bond's Bank. You could fund us a thousand times over. Last night I read about you and I thought this morning I'd head back to Margot's and throw myself on her neck, then get her to bully you into extending the loan.'

'She might do it, too.' He was unsure where to go with this. This wasn't your normal business discussion. This was intensely personal—and he didn't do personal. Or did he?

'I know she might,' Allie agreed. 'So I lay in bed all night and thought about it and decided I have an ageing circus with an ancient ringmaster with a heart condition. I have Bella who'll break her heart when she has to move away from the circus but she already struggles to get up and down the caravan steps and the caravans are ancient themselves. I have geriatric clowns. They're my great-uncles but I can see past that. I can see they need to retire. We have a couple of great acts but most of the circus is failing. Your news is appalling, but how much more appalling if I drag this out longer? If I plead for an extension, then it's on my head, and I can't wear it. I…can't.'

For a moment he thought she might cry, but she didn't. Instead she bit her lip, then tilted her chin and met his gaze straight on.

'The goodwill you get for selling this place, our booking rights, our name, will probably get you enough to cover our debts—apart from the animal refuge debt but I'll worry about that later. I've insisted Grandpa pay into superannuation for everyone—I assume that fund's safe?'

'It is.'

'Well, then,' she said. 'That's that. You've given us two weeks and I don't want more. You're calling in the loan and you have every right. For the next two weeks we might need you as our ringmaster—and our friend—but after that… Thank you, Mr Bond, but that's all.'

CHAPTER SIX

BY THE TIME they had Cleo back at the circus, the vet was waiting. All three camels had pellet wounds. The injuries were superficial but the vet was grim-faced.

'It's a wonder these guys didn't kill themselves with fear. Someone shooting these into their flanks...I'll talk to the police. If we could find out who, we could lay charges, but I'm betting it'll be a bored teenager with a new air gun.'

But what about the fencing? Mathew thought. The bolts between the fencing had been cut with speed and precision. Surely a kid would simply aim an air gun through the wire?

Bolt cutters took strength. Adult strength. And someone must have aimed the gun from the direction of the truck, so the camels couldn't retreat.

He wanted to talk to the cop, but his experience with the town's constable wasn't encouraging.

He glanced at Allie, who was helping wash Cleo's side with disinfectant. He wasn't about to share worries about thugs with bolt cutters with Allie. She had more than enough to worry about.

But assets needed to be protected. That was a rule ingrained into his banker mind since time immemorial. These were the bank's assets, he thought, though as he looked over the wounded camels and watched the geriatric circus crew fuss around them, he thought the word asset hardly applied.

Still, he took himself out of earshot, made a couple of phone calls and felt happier. He'd have security guards here by tonight.

He turned and Allie was approaching him. She looked businesslike, and he wondered how much effort it was costing her to keep herself calm in the face of the future before her. What was she proposing? To spend the rest of her life paying for the keep of geriatric animals?

'There'll be no camel show today,' she said. 'They'll need time to settle but it's fine—I'll put in an extra dog show. We'll leave the camels in view so the kids can see them as they go in and out, and we'll put up a notice saying what's happened. With a bit of luck it might even out our air gunner—there'll be kids who'll know what's happened. Mike's applying lots of bright red antiseptic so their wounds look even more dramatic than they are. Meanwhile I need to amend your cheat sheet.'

'My cheat sheet...' His mind wasn't working like it should be, or maybe he was having trouble switching from banker to outrider to teacher to...ringmaster? Or to the guy who just wanted to watch Allie.

'Your notes for tonight's performance,' she said patiently. 'Tinkerbelle and Fairy can put on an awesome act if needed and they're needed now. Okay, Maestro, time to suit up.'

'Maestro?'

'Maestro, all the way from the vast, impenetrable reaches of Outer Zukstanima,' she said and chuckled. 'It's a circus tradition. That's who we've decreed you are. By the way, when you're not in the ring can I call you Matt?'

'No!'

'I'm not calling you Mathew for two weeks,' she retorted. 'It's a banker's name. It's the same as your grandfather's, according to the website I read. So Mathew is your banking name and Maestro is your circus name. What do I call you when I just want to talk?'

There was a question to take him aback. Or, actually, just to take him back.

'Okay, Matt,' he said, before he could think any more, and it was like a window being levered, opening into the past. Matt was who he really was, in his head, but he admitted it to no one.

His memories of his big sister Lizzy were hazy, but her voice was still with him. *'Matt, come and play with me. Matt, you're messing up my painting. Mattie, hold my hand while we cross the street.'*

And his mother—also a banker...

'Elizabeth, call your brother Mathew. Mathew, call your sister Elizabeth.'

And the two of them grinning at each other and knowing that, regardless of how the world saw them, they were really Matt and Lizzy. He'd stayed Matt in his head, he thought, but only in his head. No one else ever used the diminutive.

'What did I say? What's wrong?' Allie demanded and he hauled himself back to the present with a jerk. 'I'm sorry,' she said, and she was watching his face. 'I've hurt you. The web said your family was killed. Is that what's wrong? Did they call you Matt?'

How intuitive was this woman?

'Nothing's wrong,' he said, more harshly than he intended. 'But Matt is okay.'

And suddenly it was.

For two weeks he was playing ringmaster. Make-believe. Why not extend it? For two weeks he could be Matt in his private life and he didn't have to be a banker at all.

With Allie. With The Amazing Mischka.

He should stay being a banker, he thought. He should insist that at least his name stayed the same, but Allie was moving on, and she was taking him with her. She seized his hand and tugged him forward to her grandparents' caravan, where the circus world in the form of his ringmaster's coat and hat waited.

Memories of Lizzy were suddenly all around him. 'Come on, Matt…'

The pain of knowing she wasn't there…He'd been six years old and the agony was still fresh. Lizzy.

Do not go there. Do not ever let yourself near that kind of emptiness again.

But… 'Excellent,' Allie was saying and the pressure on his hand intensified. Strong and warm—and very, very unsettling. 'Matt is nice and easy to say,' she decreed. 'And it makes you sound far less toffy. We can relax around nice, plain Matt.'

'Nice and plain? Says you who's about to force me into spangly top hat and tails.'

'There is that,' she said and she chuckled. 'Matt and Maestro seem a fearsome combination. For the next two weeks you're our hero. We'll like you in both personas, and we can forget about Mathew the Banker entirely.'

Matt or Maestro? He was thrown off balance by both. He shouldn't answer to either. He felt…he felt…

Okay, he didn't know how he felt. He had an almost overwhelming urge to head back to Margot's, climb into his gorgeous car and go home to Sydney. Taking leave had been a bad idea.

He'd done it to say goodbye to Margot but now Margot had no intention of dying, at least for the next two weeks.

If he left, would she still die?

If he left they'd have no ringmaster. And more. Allie had the weight of this whole organisation on her shoulders. How could he walk away? He couldn't walk away from Allie, he couldn't walk away from Margot, but cool, contained Mathew Bond was feeling way out of his comfort zone.

Allie left him to dress herself. He put on his uniform and

stared at himself in Henry's mirror and thought…what was he doing here?

He knew what he was doing here. He had no choice.

A knock on the van door signalled Allie's return. She'd transformed into Mischka faster than he'd thought possible. How on earth had she applied those eyelashes? They were… extraordinary.

'I'm glad ringmasters don't need fake eyelashes,' he said faintly and she grinned.

'You'd look awesome. I have spares if you'd like.'

'Thank you, but no.'

'No?' She was teasing again, her sparkle returning with her spangles, and he felt like applauding the courage she was showing.

And the way she looked.

And the way she smiled…

'I'm ready,' he said, more roughly than he'd intended, and he stepped down from the van, but she didn't move back like he'd thought she would.

'The vet says you gave him your credit card details and all the veterinary costs of the camels are on you,' she said and she was still far too close.

'I…yes.' He hesitated. 'The circus is in receivership. That's what receivers do.'

'What, throw good money after bad? You realise these camels aren't worth anything? They stand up and get down and kneel, and they don't bite but there's not much else I can teach them. Saving them isn't a financial decision.'

'No,' he said and she looked up at him.

He was still too close.

She was still too close.

'So it's nothing about receivership and I do need to thank you,' she said, and suddenly the desire to reach forward and touch her was almost overwhelming.

Almost. They were in full view of the crowd assembling

for the performance. Any move he made now would be a public move, and he had no intention of making a public move.

Or any move, he told himself harshly. No move at all.

'So let's get this circus moving,' she said a bit breathlessly,
and her breathlessness told him she was as aware of him as he
was of her—which was another reason for him to step back.
And step back he did.

'Let's go show some eyelashes,' he managed.

'One set of eyelashes,' she said and grinned. 'Coward.'

'Story of my life,' he said and turned and headed for the
circus.

Despite the chaos of the morning, the circus ran like well
oiled clockwork. The ponies and dogs did their stuff without the camels. The act was a bit shorter than usual and not
so impressive—but then Mischka moved seamlessly into a
performance with just the dogs and he stopped thinking not
impressive. He started thinking the opposite. Quite simply,
Mischka and her two nondescript dogs left him awed.

One girl in silver sparkles, dancing, turning, tumbling.
Two adoring dogs following every move.

They'd do anything for her, he thought, as he watched them
from his position ringside. She wasn't feeding them, bribing
them or even talking to them. She moved and they moved,
like shadows beside her, in front of her, behind her, depending on her direction. She danced backward, they were up on
their hind legs strutting forward. She danced forward, they
did the same thing backward. She tumbled, they turned somersaults with her. She spun, they spun.

She stood on her head and they jumped across her spread
legs and turned in crazy circles around her head. The crowd
went wild.

She stood and bowed and the dogs bowed with her. A
camera flashed in the front row and he was momentarily distracted—no cameras were allowed and it was in the list of

things he was supposed to watch for as ringmaster—but the guy put the camera away fast as soon as he saw Matt watching him, and Matt thought—why wouldn't you want to take a picture of this girl and these dogs?

'Why doesn't she put this act on all the time?' he asked Fizz as Allie and her dogs disappeared behind the curtains. Fluffy was out in the centre of the ring, setting up the next joke. Fizz and Mathew had a fraction of time to speak.

'It takes too much out of her,' Fizz said. 'That's an amazing acrobatic performance and she still has to do the trapeze act. She's so good we could just about run the circus around her only she'd fall in a heap.' He frowned then and glowered at Matt and Matt knew he wasn't Matt in this guy's eyes. He was the guy who was pulling the rug from under all of them. 'She's falling in a heap anyway. She's not eating. She's not sleeping. Her van light was on all last night, and when we bullied her to eat breakfast this morning she looked like she was going to throw up. But there's nothing we can do about it. Nothing any of us can do.'

He didn't wait for a response—maybe because he knew Matt didn't have an answer to give.

Instead he pinned on his clown grin, he bounced out to join Fluffy and the circus went on.

They took their bows as usual, they started clearing, ready for the evening performance in four hours, and at some stage Allie realised their ringmaster was no longer among them.

Fair enough, she thought as she worked on. He had his own life. He'd agreed to play ringmaster. That didn't mean he had to be hands-on, a true member of the circus troupe.

So why did she feel…empty?

No reason at all, she told herself. She had enough to worry about without Mathew…Matt Bond's continual presence. He sort of…unnerved her.

He'd kissed her.

She'd been kissed before. No big deal.

Yes, but Mathew Bond was a big deal.

'He's Matt,' she told herself and she said it out loud as if the words could somehow make him ordinary.

He wasn't ordinary.

He'd saved her camel.

He was killing her circus.

No. It wasn't him, she told herself fairly. She couldn't hold it against him. Her grandfather had killed the circus the moment he'd taken out that loan, and he'd taken out the loan because of her.

The guilt was killing her.

Everything was killing her. There were so many emotions—and overriding them all was the image of one sexy banker.

But it wasn't just that he was sexy, she thought. Yes, there was an element—or more than an element—of reaction to the fact that he was drop dead gorgeous and he had a killer smile and when he touched her, her body burned—but there was also the way he swept into the ring as if he owned it. There was the way he'd caught the children's interest today and turned kids and trainee teachers from antagonistic to gunning for Cleo all the way. There was the way he'd paid the vet's bills, which would be huge. She knew it was a small amount for him but he hadn't had to do it, and he'd smiled at her and looked worried about Cleo, and he'd stopped the cop shooting her—and then, when she'd asked about his name and he'd said Matt, he'd looked as if she'd pierced something that hurt. A lot.

There were complexities within the man and she was intrigued as well as attracted, but she'd better not be either she told herself, because being attracted to the banker was just plain dumb. Letting him kiss her had been dumb. It was the way to get her life into an even deeper mess than it already was.

'Just do what comes next,' she told herself, so she did. She finished clearing up. She had three hours before the evening performance. She checked her camels again, and then changed into respectable and went to the hospital to see Henry and Bella.

It didn't help. Her grandmother looked worse than her grandpa. It was as if everything was being taken away from her, and the only thing she had to cling to was Henry.

So what was there for Allie to cling to? she thought bleakly as she left them.

Her grey mood was threatening to overwhelm her. She had to get herself together, she told herself harshly. There was another show to put on tonight.

She was so tired all she wanted to do was crawl under a log somewhere and sleep.

She walked out of the main entrance to the hospital—and a gorgeous British Racing Green Rover was sitting in the car park. And Mathew/Matt/Maestro, or whoever this man was, was leaning against the driver's door as if he had all the time in the world to wait, and with one look she knew he was waiting for her.

With her dogs?

Tinkerbelle and Fairy were in the car, their little heads hanging out of the window, their tails wagging almost enough to vibrate the car. What on earth were they doing here? They should be ready for the show. She should be ready for the show.

She glanced at her watch. No, she still had two and a half hours. She was so tired she was losing sense of time.

'Hi,' he said as she walked—very slowly—down the steps towards him. Her legs didn't seem like they wanted to carry her.

'H…hi,' she ventured back.

'Fizz tells me you're not eating,' he said gently as she reached him. 'He said you didn't eat breakfast and you hardly touched lunch. He checked the fridge in your van and he's horrified. I've just bullied Margot into eating dinner and now it's your turn. Hop in the car, Allie. We're going to eat.'

What could a girl do except climb into his gorgeous car and hug her ecstatic dogs and wait for him to tell her what he was about to do with her?

How pathetic was that? But in truth Allie had gone past pathetic. She hadn't slept. She'd spent the morning being terrified for her camels. She'd given a performance which took every ounce of energy she possessed, she'd spent time with an emotional, devastated set of grandparents, and somehow she had to gear up for another performance tonight.

If a tsunami swept inland now, she thought, she didn't have the energy to run.

She didn't want to run. She wanted to sink back into the gorgeous leather seats of Matt's fabulous car and simply stop.

He seemed to sense it. He didn't speak, just quietly climbed into the driver's seat and set the big motor purring towards the sea.

He paused at the strip of shops on the esplanade and disappeared into the fish shop. She could climb out and go home, she thought as she waited, but it'd seem ungrateful. The dogs were on her knees, and they were heavy. She didn't have the energy to push them off and, quite simply, she was past making such a decision.

Passive R Us, she thought mutely, but she didn't even begin to smile.

Mathew returned, booted the dogs into the back seat and handed her the parcel of fish and chips—a big, fat bundle of warmth. He glanced at her sharply and then nosed the car away from the shops, around the headland, away from the town.

He pulled into a reserve on the far side of the headland, by a table and benches overlooking the sea.

'Is it okay to let the dogs loose?' he asked, and she had enough energy to think thank heaven the dogs weren't white and fluffy; they were plain, scruffy brown. They could tear in crazy circles on the sand and still look presentable for the show. So that was what they did while Matt produced a tablecloth from the back of the car—linen?—plates, cutlery, napkins, glassware—and then he fetched the parcel from her knees and placed it reverently in the middle of his beautifully laid table.

'Dinner, my lady,' he intoned in the voice of Very Serious Butler, 'is served.'

The ridiculousness of the whole tableau was enough to shake her lethargy. Haziness receded. She climbed from the car and looked at the table in astonishment. The council picnic table was transformed into an elegant dining setting. Gum trees were hanging overhead, filled with corellas, vivid green and red parrots coming to perch for the night. Behind them were miles of glorious beach, no vestige of wind, the only sound being the soft hush of the surf and the calls of the sandpipers darting back and forth on the wet sand. Down on the beach Fairy and Tinkerbelle were digging their way to China in a setting that was so picturesque it took her breath away.

This was Fish and Chips with Style.

'Margot and I had a discussion,' Matt said, leading her to the table simply by taking her hand and tugging. 'Margot thought I should take you out to dinner, somewhere fancy. I thought you might like to sit on the beach. We've compromised. This is Margot's idea of picnic requirements. She can be quite insistent for someone who's almost dead.'

'She's very much alive,' Allie managed. 'Mathew, I should go back...'

'Did we agree it was Matt?'

'Nobody calls you Matt.'

'No,' he said and she couldn't figure whether there was regret there or not. No matter, he was moving on. 'But you do.
Please.' He unwrapped the paper to expose slivers of golden
crumbed fish fillets and gorgeous crunchy chips. He poured
lemonade into the crystal glasswear.

'I know wine matches the setting,' he said. 'But you have
to hang upside down tonight and I don't want you sleeping
on the job.'

'No, Maestro,' she said and he chuckled.

'Excellent. Maybe I need to be Maestro tonight. The boss.'
He saw her hesitation and he placed his hand on her shoulder
in a fleeting gesture of reassurance. 'Allie, the circus crew
knows where you are—they concur with my plan to give
you a couple of hours off. They're doing everything needed
so you can walk back in the gates at twenty past seven, don
your false eyelashes and go straight to the ring. So you have
two full hours to eat and to sleep.'

'I could go back to the circus and sleep.'

'Would you sleep?' He headed to the back of the car and
hauled out a massive picnic rug and a load of cushions. 'You
might nap,' he conceded, 'but you can nap here. Herewith a
beach bed, my lady, for when you've polished off enough fish
and chips to keep me happy.'

And then he sat beside her and ate fish and chips and
looked out at the sea and he didn't say a word—and she could
eat fish and chips or not—no pressure—but the pressure was
insidious. The late afternoon sun was gorgeous. The dogs
were deliriously happy. She was suddenly…almost happy.

It was the setting, she told herself, feeling totally disori-
ented. The beach was gorgeous. The fish and chips were
gorgeous.

Matt was gorgeous.

Whoa… Concentrate on fish and chips, she told herself
fiercely, and don't think any further.

For gorgeous was scary.

* * *

Once Allie had disposed of enough food to satisfy him—
which was a lot—Matt once again refused her a choice. He
pointed to the rug and the pillows and he gave his orders.

'Lie. Sleep.'

'I can't just lie out here in public…'

'Why not? The sun's great. No one's around. I'm not asking you to sunbathe naked.'

'No,' she said and looked doubtfully at the cushions. They
did look great. The dogs had already settled amongst them
but Matt had ordered them to the edge so there was more than
enough room for her.

She *was* tired.

'So you're standing over me to keep guard,' she said nervously and he shook his head.

'I'm on washing-up duty,' he said and proceeded to toss
the remaining chips to a hundred seagulls who'd magically
appeared and then bundle all the picnic gear into his capa-
cious basket. 'That's that. And then, if you don't mind, I'll
share your very big blanket.'

'You want to share my bed?'

'My nefarious plan's uncovered,' he said and gave an evil
chuckle and she had to smile.

This man was an enigma. Solitary, aloof, ruthless, kind…
Mind-blowingly sexy.

She should argue, but the sun was on her face and she was
full of fish and chips and her dogs were here, which made it
seem…okay…and those cushions… And this man…

She slid down onto the rug and sank into the pillows and
it was like she was letting go.

It wasn't just today that had exhausted her, she thought.
It was…life. Matt was right; this circus was unviable. Even
without the massive debt for the animals, she'd been struggling.

She'd been struggling for years. Her grandparents were

growing increasingly frail. Slowly, imperceptibly, she'd taken over their roles, taking the day-to-day running of the circus onto her shoulders. As more of the performers grew older she'd simply taken on more.

But she couldn't think of that now. She couldn't think past the pillows. All roads led to this place, she thought. All paths led to these pillows, and to this man standing over her simply assuming control.

'It's scary having you hover,' she complained and he grinned and sank down to join her. To sleep with her? Sleep in the real sense, she thought. There was no way she was up for a spot of seduction now.

'I'm only doing this to make you feel better,' he said. 'So you won't feel self-conscious snoozing alone.'

'I don't think I'll snooze.'

'Close your eyes then,' he said. 'Think of anything you like except money and circuses and grandparents and camels.'

'Is this the advice you give to all your clients?'

'Clients?'

'You are my banker,' she said and then caught herself. 'I mean, my grandparents' banker. Mathew who's really Matt.' And then she said sleepily, into her pillows, 'Why did you look upset when you told me you were Matt? Why does no one call you Matt? Is it about your family?'

He'd lain beside her, feeling vaguely self conscious but knowing he needed to do this to make her relax. There was a good foot between them. The dogs were on the end of the rug. This could be totally impersonal.

It wasn't. It was as if there was a cocoon around them, enclosing them in a bubble of space where there could be no secrets.

It was an illusion, Matt thought, but even so, a question which would normally make him freeze was suddenly able to be answered.

'My grandfather was Mathew,' he said. 'My father was

Mathew. My great-grandfather was Mathew. I expect if ever I have a son he'll be Mathew.'

'That doesn't leave much room for the imagination,' she said sleepily. 'But...Matt?'

'My father and my grandfather were...to put it bluntly... strong personalities, and my mother was just as rigid,' he said. 'You've met my great-aunt. Picture her multiplied by a hundred. Even Margot would never consider calling me Matt.'

'But someone did.'

'My sister Lizzy,' he said. 'Elizabeth. As the biography you read told you, she died when I was six, in a car crash with my parents. Matt died with her.'

'I'm so sorry,' she whispered. 'Oh, Matt...'

'It's a long time ago,' he said, more roughly than he intended. 'After the crash my grandfather was even more formal. There was no nonsense about him, no emotion, no stupid diminutives. I didn't want a diminutive anyway.'

'But you think of yourself as Matt.'

He started to say no. He started—and then he stopped.

He did, he conceded. On the surface and all through the exterior layers he was Mathew, but underneath was where the pain lay. To let anyone call him Matt...

'Does me calling you Matt hurt?'

Yes, he thought. It was like biting on a tooth he knew was broken. But he glanced at her, lying sideways on her cushion, drifting towards sleep, and he knew that somehow she was worth the pain.

Something in this girl was inching through the layers of armour he'd built. He knew pain would come, but for now all he felt was a gentle, insidious warmth.

He hadn't felt cold, he thought. He hadn't thought he wanted...

He didn't want. This woman was a bereft client of the bank, and he needed to remember it. He needed to put things back on a business footing, fast.

So talk about her business affairs now?

No. He might be a businessman but he wasn't cruel. He'd brought her here—wise or not—to give her time out and he'd follow through. He'd let her sleep.

But first… She'd exposed part of him he didn't want exposed. Fair was fair.

'How about you?' he asked. 'Who called you Allie?'

'My mother, of course,' she said, but she didn't stir. There didn't seem any pain there.

'But I gather you've been cared for by your grandparents since you were tiny.'

'You have been doing your research.' She snuggled further into the pillows. Tinkerbelle, or maybe it was Fairy, one of the identical dogs with identical tails that whirred like helicopters when they were happy, which would be now, had snuggled onto the pillow beside her and she held her close. 'Gran and Grandpa have been great. I had the best childhood.'

'Without a mum?'

'I know, sometimes I feel guilty for thinking it,' she said. 'Mum took off with the circus fire-eater when I was two. She and Scorcher left for a bigger, better circus where they could make more money, but it didn't last. Scorcher went on to make his fortune in America and we haven't heard from him since. Mum moved on to a series of men, places, adventures. She's currently working as a psychic, reading Tarot cards up on the Gold Coast. She sends me Christmas and birthday cards. Every now and then she whirls in, usually needing money, spins our life into confusion and spins out again. I've figured she does love me, as much as she's able to love anyone, but I'm eternally grateful she and Scorcher left me behind. My family is this circus. Gran and Grandpa, Fizz and Fluffy, the crew, the animals; they've been here all my life. Sparkles is my family.' She sighed then and buried her face in her pillow, so her next words were muffled. 'For two more weeks.'

Matt thought back to the instructions he'd left at head office. Feelers had been put out already. There were circuses—one in particular—hovering, wanting to cherry pick the best of this little outfit. Their bookings. The best of their performers.

The circus was in receivership, like it or not, and instructions were to sell.

'If you wanted you could stay on in the circus,' he said tentatively. 'There are bigger commercially viable outfits that would be very willing to take you on. Your acts are wonderful.'

'But just me,' she said softly and hugged her dog closer. 'By myself. How lonely would that be? As I said, we're family. We'll stay together. I'm not sure about the elephants, though.'

'Let me help,' he said, and he hadn't known he was going to say it until he did. 'Maybe I can take on the retired elephant fund.'

She rolled over then and looked at him—really looked at him. It seemed weirdly intimate. Girl lying on pillows, the sinking sun on her face, her dog snuggled against her. Her banker sitting above her, offering…finance?

'Why would you do that?'

'I like elephants?'

She smiled then, almost a chuckle, but her smile faded.

'No,' she said. 'Um…not. Years ago my grandfather asked a favour of Bond's Bank and it put us into all sorts of bother. I think it's time for the…bonds…to be cut.'

'And the elephants?'

'I've already started contacting welfare groups. I'll find somewhere.'

'Not as good as where they are now.'

'No,' she said softly. 'But that goes for all of us.' She sighed, snuggled even further into the pillows and closed her eyes. 'Nowhere's as good as where I am right this minute,' she said softly. 'Nowhere at all, so if you don't mind, I might just go to sleep and enjoy it.'

She slept.

He watched over her.

It was a curious sensation, sitting on the grassy verge above a deserted beach, watching the sandpipers scuttle to collect the detritus of an outgoing tide—and watching a lady sleep.

He felt absurdly protective. More, he felt…emotional. As if he'd do anything to protect her.

In days of old, when knights were bold…

There was a romantic notion, he told himself, and the thought of himself as knight on white charger almost made him smile.

But not quite, for the notion wouldn't go away. Something in this woman stirred him as he'd never been stirred.

It was because she was needy, he told himself. She needed protection.

But was she needy? She was a feisty, courageous, multi-talented circus performer and accountant, and she'd just knocked back his offer to help.

He was her banker.

He didn't want to be her banker.

Where were his thoughts taking him? Were they turning him into Matt?

Exposing him?

What if…? he thought. What if…?

She looked so vulnerable. She *was* so vulnerable. He could pick her up, he thought, and take her back to Sydney and keep her safe.

Yeah, that was white charger territory again, he thought ruefully. Romantic stuff. He had a very large apartment looking over the harbour. Even so, it'd hardly house Gran and Grandpa and Fizz and Fluffy and Tinkerbelle and Fairy and three ruddy great camels…

He did grin then, thinking of the concierge of his apartment block. Thinking of camels.

Then he glanced down at Allie again and he stopped thinking of concierge or camels.

What he wanted, he decided, more than anything else in the world, was to sink onto the pillows, gather her into his arms and hold her.

But even in sleep he could see her fierce independence. It was engendered by her background, he thought. He knew enough of the back story of this circus now to have a good idea of its dynamics.

Yes, the circus had raised her, but it hadn't been long before Allie had more or less taken over. Everyone his people had talked to when researching the circus had referred to Allie. 'Allie only hires the best. Allie keeps the best animal quarters. Allie's safety standards are second to none.'

This circus…Allie's family… Allie's life.

It wasn't possible to keep it going. He'd looked long and hard at the figures. Even without that appalling pension fund for retired animals, the performers were ageing, the superstructure needed major refurbishment and the whole organisation was winding down.

But she'd fight for what she had left, he thought. He could see her on this farmlet she dreamed of but it wasn't a dream he was seeing. It was a nightmare. One girl working her heart out to provide for the remnants of a finished circus.

That was why he was feeling protective?

That was why he was feeling cracks in his armour?

He needed to get a grip. He was her banker, nothing else. Except for the next two weeks he was her ringmaster.

'Yes, but that's all,' he said aloud and Allie stirred in her sleep and he felt…he felt…

As if he needed to head along the beach and walk, or maybe run. He needed to get rid of this energy, get rid of this weird jumble of heart versus head.

The dogs looked up at him, questioning.

'You guys stay here,' he told them. 'I'm not going far. You're in protection mode.'

They snuggled down again as if they agreed.

He walked but not out of sight. His jumble of thoughts refused to untangle.

He was in protection mode as well, whether Allie wanted it or not.

Whether he wanted it or not.

'Matt,' he said out loud and the sound of the name he hadn't used for years startled him. 'Matt.'

Put the armour back on, he told himself harshly. Turn yourself back into Mathew.

The problem was…what?

He glanced up the beach, to the sleeping woman with her huddle of protective dogs and he thought…

He thought the problem was that he didn't know how to turn back into what he'd been. Mathew seemed to be crumbling.

He'd get himself back together, he told himself, after two weeks as ringmaster. Two weeks as knight on white charger?

She doesn't want me to be knight on white charger, he told himself and hurled a few pebbles into the sea and tried to figure what he wanted.

Sydney. The bank. Normality.

Yeah? He glanced back at the sleeping girl and normality seemed a million miles away.

CHAPTER SEVEN

TWO HOURS LATER he dropped Allie back at the circus. She'd woken subdued. They'd driven back in near silence. She'd hesitated before she left the car but in the end she'd said a simple thank you. Then she'd paused. A guy in a security uniform was standing by the gate.

'You are?' she'd said while Matt waited.

'From Bond's Security,' the man said. 'We have security covered.'

She looked back at Matt, and then she sighed.

'You're taking care of your own?'

'Yes,' he said because there was nothing else to say, and she gave an almost imperceptible nod and disappeared back into a life that was almost over.

He had half an hour to evening performance. He needed to go back to Margot's to put his good trousers and white shirt on so he could don his ringmaster apparel over the top.

He walked in the front door and Margot was bundled up like a snow bunny: two coats, fur boots, mittens, fur hat and rug.

'It's um…summer, Margot,' he said and she snorted.

'Says you who have body fat.' Then she paused and looked at him critically. 'Body mass, I should say. Muscle. You look like you could be Allie's catcher.'

'Rather Valentino than me,' he said, suppressing a shudder. It was the one part of the circus he didn't enjoy—watching Allie fly through the air, totally dependent on a great bull of a man whose grip was like iron but whose intelligence...

'He hasn't dropped her yet,' Margot said gently, watching his face. 'So I can't see why he would tonight. Come on then, get changed. I don't want to miss anything.'

'You're coming?'

'Yes. Hurry up.'

'They can hardly start without the ringmaster,' he said dryly and she cast him a sharp look.

'Neither they can,' she said softly. 'How fortunate.'

Things went well that night. Allie's dog routine was even more spectacular—their time on the beach seemed to have done them good. No one dropped anything or was dropped. The audience roared when they were supposed to roar and they hushed when they were supposed to hush.

Margot had an awesome seat. Tickets had been sold out for days but Allie saw her arrive and someone ran for a chair and she was placed right up the front, supervising all.

Matt was aware of her as he worked.

She was a force to be reckoned with, his Aunt Margot. He knew she disapproved of the way he'd been raised. She'd never criticised his grandfather to him, but he'd overheard a couple of heated conversations with his grandfather. Very heated.

'You're bringing that boy up to be a financial calculator, not a child,' she'd told her brother. *'For heaven's sake, give him some freedom.'*

Margot was a Bond—stern, unyielding, undemonstrative—yet she'd never had anything to do with the bank. She'd lived on her own income. She'd refused family help. She was an independent spirit. So maybe a part of her wasn't a Bond.

A true Bond would choke seeing Mathew Bond in glittery top hat and tails, Matt thought, but Margot cheered and gasped with the rest of them, and at the end of the performance he watched Allie rush around to talk to her and, to his astonishment, he saw his normally undemonstrative aunt give Allie a hug.

As the big top emptied he strolled across to join them. Casually. As if it didn't do anything to his head to see these two women together. Allie was kneeling beside Margot's chair, smiling and holding her hand, her affection obvious, and the old woman, who only days ago had decreed she was dying, was holding her hand back and smiling and chuckling at something Allie was saying.

He'd given the circus a two-week reprieve, he thought, but it had also given Margot two weeks.

And after two weeks?

Worry about that then, he told himself. Maybe he could pick Margot up and forcibly take her back to Sydney...

Yeah. She'd be about as at home in his Sydney apartment as Allie's camels would be.

The women broke apart as he approached, both looking at him critically. Banker in spangles. He could see a twinkle in Margot's eyes and half of him loved seeing mischief again, and the other half thought—uh oh.

'You look splendid,' Margot declared. 'And you make a wonderful ringmaster. I just wish your grandfather was alive to see it.'

'He'll be rolling in his grave right now,' he said, smiling down at her. He loved this old lady and, no matter what, these two weeks were a gift. 'The whole Bond dynasty will be. My father, my grandfather and his grandfather before them. What do you reckon, Margot—should I give up banking and run away with the circus?'

'There's not a lot of money in circusing,' Allie said, smiling but rueful. 'Plus you'll have to look for another circus.'

'I don't know why this one's closing.' Margot suddenly sounded fretful. 'Mathew, you should buy it. You're rich enough to buy it. He is, you know,' she said to Allie, as if

Matt was suddenly not there. 'Rich as Croesus. He's rolling in banking money like his father and his grandfather and great-grandfather before him. Not that it's made any of them happy. Mathew, buy a circus and have some fun.'

Allie's smile remained but it started to look fixed.

'It wouldn't work,' she said softly. 'Thank you for offering,' she told Margot, with only a sideways glance at Matt. 'But, even though this has been an appalling shock and we're not as prepared as I thought we were, this is a circus on its last legs. Look round, Margot. Half our crew is geriatric.'

'They don't look geriatric to me,' Margot snapped.

'You're how old?' Allie said and her smile returned. 'Get real, Margot. Could you manage a trapeze or two? There's a time to move on.'

'Exactly,' Margot said and glared at her nephew. 'That's what I've been telling Mathew.'

'I don't mean dying,' Allie said indignantly. 'Just...not playing with the circus any more. Taking life seriously.'

'Why don't you mean dying then?' Margot said morosely. 'You can't get any more serious than that.'

'Margot...'

'Don't you worry about me, girl,' Margot ordered with a decisive nod. 'Tell me, are you making plans to see these elephants of yours? Mathew tells me you didn't even know where they were.'

'I can't worry about them now. I'll figure...'

'You loved them,' Margot snapped. 'That's why your grandfather asked for my help in the first place. I know he told you he'd sold them to a zoo in Western Australia. I always thought it was stupid, lying to you, but now you know they're local, you could go see them. Mathew could take you.'

And the mischief was back, just like that.

'Where are they?' Allie said cautiously.

'It's an open range sanctuary, part of a farm, only it's not open to the public. You'll need to get more details from Henry but, as far as I can remember, it's on the other side of Wagga.'

'Wagga,' Allie said faintly. 'That's almost three hundred miles.'

'Matt has a nice car.' Margot sounded oblivious to a minor hiccup like three hundred miles. 'The circus doesn't do a matinee on Wednesday. You could be there and back by the evening show.'

'Not even for my elephants,' Allie said, and Matt realised there'd been a faint sheen of hope in her eyes, a lifting of the bleak acceptance he'd seen too much of, but she extinguished the hope fast now and moved on. 'Three hundred miles and back in a day with a show afterwards? That's impossible. When…when we're wound up, there'll be all the time in the world to go look at elephants.'

'But you'd like to,' Matt said slowly, watching her face.

'You have a gorgeous car,' she told him. 'But not that gorgeous. A six hundred mile round trip? Get real. Did you like the show, Margot?'

'I loved it,' Margot said soundly.

'Well, that's all that matters,' Allie decreed. 'Keeping the punters happy. For the next two weeks this circus is going to run like clockwork, and then I'll worry about my elephants. I'll have time then.'

'In between finding houses, settling geriatric circus staff, finding a job…' Matt growled, but she shook her head. She looked fabulous, he thought, in her gorgeous pink and silver body-suit. She looked trim, taut and so sexy she took a man's breath away. She also looked desolate. But, desolate or not, she also looked strong. She was cutting him out of this equation.

'That's not your problem,' she told him. 'Margot, your nephew very kindly gave me time out today—he fed me fish and chips and he gave me time for a snooze. So he's being our ringmaster and he's being kind, but apart from that…I need to cope with this on my own.'

She'd been kneeling beside Margot. Now she rose. Matt held out his hand to help her but she ignored it.

'I do need to do this on my own,' she said, gently but implacably. 'And I will. Thank you for your help, Mathew, and thank you for your friendship, Margot, but I need to go help pack up now. Mathew, you need to take your aunt home.'

Mathew.

My name is Matt, Matt thought, but he didn't say it. Allie was resetting boundaries, and what right did he have to step over them?

'She really wants to see those elephants.'

Settled into his car, Margot was quietly thoughtful. They were halfway home before she finally came out with what was bothering her.

'I know she does,' Matt said. 'But a six hundred mile round trip in a day is ridiculous.'

'Since when did a little matter of six hundred miles ever get in the way of a Bond?' Margot snapped, and he glanced at her and thought she looked exhausted.

How much had tonight taken out of her?

She'd turned away and was looking out of the window, over the bay to the twinkling lights of the boats at swing moorings.

'You know, it doesn't happen all that often,' she said softly into the night, and he had a feeling she was half talking to herself.

'What doesn't happen?'

She was silent for a moment. A long moment. Then…

'I fell in love,' she said at last, into the silence. 'You've seen his photograph on my mantel. Raymond. He was a lovely, laughing fisherman. He was…wonderful. But my parents disapproved—oh, how they disapproved. A Bond, marrying a fisherman. We'd come down here for a family holiday and the thought that I could meet and fall in love with someone who was so out of our world... It was insupportable—and I was insistent but not insistent enough.'

'You told him you'd marry him.'

'Yes,' she said, and her voice was suddenly bleak. She stared down at her gnarled old hand, to the modest diamond ring that had been there for as long as Matt could remember. 'We met just as the war started. I met him on the esplanade. The heel had come off my shoe and he helped me home. We went to two dances and two showings of the same picture. Then Father got wind of it and I was whisked back to Sydney. Soon afterwards, Raymond was called up and sent abroad. We wrote, though. I still have his letters. Lovely, lovely letters. Then, two years later, he came home—for a whole three weeks. He'd been wounded—he was home on leave before being sent abroad again. He came to Sydney to find me and he gave me this ring.'

She stared down at the ring and it was as if she was looking into the very centre of the diamond. Seeing what was inside. Seeing what was in her heart all those years ago.

'He wanted to marry me before he went back,' she whispered. 'And I wanted to. But my father...your great-grandfather...' She shook her head. 'He was so angry. He asked how I could know after such a short time? He said if we really loved each other it'd stand separation. He said...*I forbid it*. And I was stupid enough, dumb enough, weak enough to agree. So I kissed my Raymond goodbye and he died six months later.'

She stared down at the tiny diamond and she shook her head, her grief still raw and obvious after how many years? And then she glared straight at Matt.

'And here you are, looking at someone who's right in front of you,' she snapped. 'Allie's perfect. You know she is. I can see that you're feeling exactly what I was feeling all those awful, wasted years ago and you won't even put the lady in your car and go visit some elephants!'

At the end she was practically booming—and then she burst into tears.

In all the time he'd known her he'd never seen Margot cry.

Bonds didn't do emotion.

He'd seen the engagement ring on her finger. He'd never been brave enough to ask her about it. Once he'd asked his grandfather.

'A war thing,' his grandfather had snapped. *'Stupid, emotional whim. Lots of women lost their partners during the war—Margot was one of the lucky ones. At least she didn't get married and have children.'*

One of the lucky ones...

He hugged Margot now and found her a handkerchief and watched as she sniffed and sniffed again, and then she harrumphed and pulled herself together and told him to drive on—and he thought of those words.

One of the lucky ones...

A six hundred mile round trip.

Allie.

'You can do it if you want to,' Margot muttered as he helped her out of the car, and he helped her inside, he made her cocoa, helped her to bed—and then he went for a very long walk on the beach.

A six hundred mile round trip.

Allie.

Elephants.

One of the lucky ones...

Wednesday morning.

Allie had plans for this morning, but none of them were good. She had a list from the realtors of all the farmlets that were available for rent in the district in her price range. She'd added combined pensions plus what she could feasibly earn as a bookkeeper minus what it'd cost to keep the animals and it wasn't looking pretty. The places looked almost derelict.

She thought of the lovely beachside cottage Henry and Bella had told her they were paying off, and she felt ill.

They'd done this for her.

Henry was being released from hospital tomorrow. They'd kept him in until he was over his virus, but she suspected the kindly staff of the small district hospital were also giving them a break. Tomorrow they'd be back in their caravan and they'd have to face their future.

Maybe one of these properties was better than it looked in the brochure, she thought grimly. Ha.

Deeply unsettled, she fed the animals early, then took the dogs for a long walk on the deserted beach. As she walked back to the circus a helicopter was coming into land on the foreshore.

'Bond's Bank' was emblazoned on the side.

Why?

Maybe this was Matt's…Mathew's staff, she corrected herself. He'd said the circus could operate for two weeks but she was under no illusion. The circus belonged to him, lock, stock and barrel, and if he'd brought in a team to pull it apart…

She felt sick.

She stood back and watched as the chopper came to rest, as the rotor blades stopped spinning.

It was a very small chopper for a team of financiers.

Who was she kidding? she thought ruefully. Sparkles was a very small circus. Why would they need a team?

But this small? Only one guy climbed from the chopper and that was the pilot.

This had nothing to do with her, she told herself grimly.

She walked back to the circus, giving the headland and the chopper a wide berth. She walked into the circus enclosure and Matt…Mathew…was waiting for her. Casually dressed. Smiling at her with a smile that could make a girl's heart do back-flips if a girl's heart was permitted.

Which it wasn't.

She loosened the dogs' leads and the dogs raced to greet him, jumping and yelping as if he was part of the family.

Which he wasn't. He was Mathew.

'Back,' she said to the dogs, but they uncharacteristically ignored her. Maybe because Matt...Mathew...had knelt and was scratching them behind their ears and they were lick-spitting, traitorous hounds and they didn't know this guy was taking away their lifestyle and they didn't know this guy was capable of taking away their mistress's heart...

Only that was a dumb thing to think. She pinned on a smile and moved forward to greet him with what she hoped was dignified courtesy.

'Good morning.'

'Good morning yourself,' he said and straightened and smiled some more and her heart did do that stupid back-flip she'd been telling it not to. 'It's a great day for elephant visiting,' he added.

'Pardon?'

'We have a chopper,' he said. 'An hour there, an hour back, a couple of hours visiting...You'll even have time for a wee nap before evening performance.'

'What...?'

'You might need a sweater,' he said. 'It gets a bit breezy in the chopper. And elephant snacks? What do you take to an elephant you haven't seen for years?'

'I...'

'Just do it,' he said gently. 'You know you want to. Your financial adviser says this is a good idea, so who are you to argue?'

He was serious. The chopper was for elephant visiting. Not only had Matt organised for it to be delivered, it seemed he was flying.

'I've had my licence for years,' he told her cheerfully. 'Joe's spending the day on the beach while I take over his machine. It's economical,' he said as she opened her mouth to protest—if she could think of the words she needed, which she couldn't. 'Two people instead of three. Lots of fuel saved. And don't tell me I don't need to come—Bond's Bank has been financing these elephants for years, and I have a vested interest in inspecting our investment.'

And here was Bella, walking towards her, carrying her jacket. Bella, who spent every waking moment with Henry.

Had Matt lined this up with her Gran? Obviously yes.

'Matt says he'll take Henry and me to see them when Henry's well,' Bella told her, beaming. 'But just knowing you're visiting them today will do your Grandpa good. Give them our love.' And she placed a paper bag into Allie's limp hand. 'Doughnuts,' she said. 'They're very bad but Maisie and Minnie both love them. Sneak them some when no one's looking.'

Maisie and Minnie. Mother and daughter, great, lumbering Asian elephants, third and fourth generation circus bred, docile and wonderful. Allie had loved them with all her teenage heart, and that was what this mess was about. She'd fought for them.

If she climbed into the chopper with Matt, she could see them in an hour.

But what if...and she should...and it wasn't...

She had all sorts of protests and not one would come out.

Bella took the two dogs' leads. 'Come on, guys, your mistress is visiting past loves today,' she said as Matt propelled Allie towards the chopper and Allie let herself be propelled because there didn't seem any alternative. And Matt was large and commanding and he had everything sorted and she thought, just for a moment, wouldn't it be great to put this whole mess in Matt's hands and let him sort it out?

There was a dumb thought. Her mess was nothing to do with him—she'd told him that and she was right.

But right now?

Right now she was going to see some friends she hadn't seen for years.

Where had her grandfather sent them?

Somewhere good, she pleaded silently. Somewhere to make this sacrifice worthwhile.

'Let's go,' Matt said and he helped her into the cockpit.

She sat passive as he adjusted her harness and her headphones and closed her door.

She sat passive as he slid behind the controls, did what he needed to and lifted the chopper from the ground.

She glanced across at Matt and she saw that he was smiling, that faint devil-behind-the-smile glimmer she was starting to know.

It was a smile that made her feel being passive was her only protection.

CHAPTER EIGHT

THE JOB DESCRIPTION for a circus performer didn't come with the label big earner, so a one-time commercial flight from Sydney to Melbourne was the sum total of Allie's air travel. She'd never been in a helicopter.

Now she was in a tiny cockpit beside Matt, the cockpit seemed almost a transparent bubble, and she felt like...

She was flying?

She *was* flying, she told herself, trying hard not to cling to the edge of her seat and whimper. The chopper rose with a speed that took her breath away. She was in a bubble heading for the clouds.

She forgot to breathe.

Fort Neptune grew smaller and smaller. She was in a bubble in the sky with Matt Bond.

The floor beneath her was transparent. She could see miles of coastline falling away beneath her. She could see the Blue Mountains.

'It's safe,' Matt said through her headphones and she tried really hard to catch her breath and act cool and toss him a look of insouciance.

'I'm just...' She saw where he was looking and carefully unfastened her white knuckles from the seat. 'It's just I'm always wary of inexperienced drivers.'

'That would be pilots.'

'Pilots,' she snapped.

'I'm very experienced.'

'You didn't hand me your CV as you got in the driver's seat,' she managed as the Blue Mountains loomed and the chopper started to rise even further. 'I like first-hand knowledge of my…chauffeur.'

'You want to radio for a reference?' he asked. He grinned and she knew, she just knew, that if she took him up on his offer she'd radio and someone would tell her that this man was competent, no, more than competent, an expert, experienced, calm and safe.

Safe.

See, that was half the problem. He didn't make her feel safe. Okay, maybe his piloting skills weren't the issue. Flying above the Blue Mountains in a transparent bubble might make her feel unsafe with anyone, but she was settling, getting used to the machine, starting to be entranced by the landscape beneath—but underlying everything was the way this man made her feel.

Unsafe?

Just unsteady, she told herself and that was reasonable. He'd pulled the rug from under the circus she loved.

No. He hadn't done that. Her grandfather had done it by taking out such a huge loan. Matt had every right to call it in.

And the unsafe bit wasn't about the loan, either, she conceded. She sneaked a quick glance across at him. He was focused again on the country ahead. He looked calm, steady, in control, and she thought—that's what the problem is.

He's more in control of my world than I am.

Concentrate on the view, she told herself. On the scenery.

And on what was waiting to meet her?

'Do…do these people know I'm coming?'

'The park's owners? Jack and Myra. Yes, they do. They're good people.'

'How do you know?'

'We do thorough research before we foreclose,' he said gently. 'We wanted to know where our money was—whether there was any chance of us retrieving it. There's not. Every cent your grandpa paid has been long spent. Jack and Myra are in trouble themselves, but not from mismanagement. It's because they care too much.'

'I'll pay them back,' she said tightly.

'With a bookkeeper's salary?' He sounded amused and she winced. She thought about the amount she was likely to earn and the amount she owed and she could see why he was amused.

And she thought again… He's more in control of my world than I am.

'Don't worry about it today,' Matt said gently. 'Today's not for finance. Today's for seeing your friends again.'

He focused on the machine again, on the myriad of instruments, on the scene ahead, and she thought—he's letting me be. Like the picnic on the beach…he's giving me space.

She felt, suddenly, stupidly, dangerously, close to tears.

This man was in control and she wasn't. She had to be.

The majestic line of the Blue Mountains was receding now, opening to the vast tracts of grassland that grew inland for hundreds of miles, spreading until they gave way to the true Australian outback.

What a place to keep retired circus animals!

'They keep all sorts,' Matt said, and it seemed he was almost following her thoughts. 'It started forty years ago when a grazier called Jack met a circus performer called Myra. Myra was a trapeze artist like you. Jack asked Myra to marry him but Myra wouldn't leave the bear the circus had owned for ten years. So Jack married Myra and Jack's farm has been home to aged circus animals ever since. They've fought to keep it going, but finally they've lost.'

So any thought of asking—begging—them to keep the elephants on for free was out of the question, Allie thought miserably, but, as she thought it, Matt's hand closed over hers. Firm, warm and strong.

'Friends today,' he repeated softly. 'Finance tomorrow.'

Surely only in Australia could such an area be one farm. Jack and Myra's holding was vast. They circled before they landed. Allie saw a vast undulating landscape with scattered bushland, big dams, a creek running through its centre, beef cattle grazing lazily in the sun—and the odd giraffe and elephant.

It was so incongruous she had to blink to believe she was seeing it.

Jack came forward to greet them as the chopper landed, elderly, lean, weathered, taciturn. He gripped Allie's hand. 'Myra's feeling a bit frail. Sorry, it'll be only me doing the tour.'

She owed this man so much money. That Jack and Myra hadn't been paid...

'I'm so sorry,' she started but Jack's hand gripped hers and held.

'You're Allie,' he said. 'We know why your animals came to us. Myra's loved you even though she's never met you. Your animals have had ten years of good living, thanks to you. You tried your best, girl, as did your grandpa, and there's no grudges. Want to meet them?' He motioned towards an ancient mud-spattered truck. 'Let's go.'

'Yes, please.' Friends today, she thought as she glanced at Matt and he smiled and ushered her towards the truck. Problems tomorrow.

And two minutes later, there they were, beside the dusty dam where two elephants soaked up the morning sun.

They were together as they always had been, two elephants lazing by the bank of a vast man-made dam, half a mile from the homestead. Minnie was still smaller than her mother. She declined to rise from reclining on the mud bank, but Maisie started lumbering across to meet them.

Jack climbed out of the truck and called. Maisie reached

Jack, touched him with her great trunk—and then her small eyes moved to see who was accompanying him.

Allie was out of the truck. Maisie and Minnie. Friends.

And Maisie reacted. Her trunk came out and touched Allie—just touched—a feather-touch on the face as though exploring, confirming what she'd suspected.

And it was all Allie could do not to burst into tears.

These guys had been her friends. She'd been the only kid in the circus, home schooled, isolated. Her dogs were with her always, but these two...She'd told them her problems and they'd listened; she thought they'd understood. At fifteen, sixteen, seventeen she hadn't been able to bear the chains around their great stumps of legs. She'd made such a fuss that her grandfather had mortgaged everything.

It didn't matter now. She leant all her weight against Maisie's trunk and Maisie supported her and she thought she'd do it again. Whatever the cost. She'd have no choice.

'The...the lions?' she managed. 'And the monkeys?'

'They're a bit more closely contained,' Jack said ruefully. 'I can't give them a hundred miles to roam, much as we'd like to. They only have a couple of miles we can fence securely.'

A couple of miles. She thought back to the six foot by ten foot cages and she thought...she thought...

She thought she just might finally burst into tears.

He stood his distance and watched.

That these elephants knew this woman had never been in doubt. They seemed to be as pleased to see her as she was to see them—that was if he was reading elephant language right which, he had to admit, was a bit of a long call. But Allie surely knew them. She was between the two elephants, hugging as much as she could of them, looking close to tears.

Maisie, the biggest of the two, lifted her left foreleg and trunk. It was a gesture that even Matt could tell was an invitation that had long been used, for Allie accepted almost before the leg was completely raised. She swung herself up on the great raised leg, she held the trunk and the next minute she was on Maisie's back, leaning forward, hugging as much of Maisie as she could.

'Well, I never,' Jack said placidly, almost to himself. Then the old farmer grinned. 'We have ten of 'em, you know. From the moment they get here we forget they're circus animals—there's no balancing on stools here. They're as wild as we can make 'em. Some we can hardly get near any more—they're the ones that've been mistreated—but these two always like company. We figured they've been treated as right as circus animals ever can be, and their reaction confirms it.'

'We had the best act,' Allie called down to them, still elephant hugging. 'I wonder...you want to see?'

'No stools,' Jack said, and Allie grinned.

'Nope.' She stood up. She was wearing soft, clinging leggings, a baggy jacket and trainers. She tugged off her trainers and tossed them down to Matt, and her jacket followed suit.

She was left in leggings, a close fitting T-shirt and bare feet.

'Let's see if we remember,' she muttered and now she was talking to Maisie—and to Minnie. 'Oi,' she called to Minnie. 'Oi, oi, oi. Top and tail.'

And astonishingly, ponderously, top and tail was just what happened. Minnie had risen to stand by Maisie. Now she shifted to stand close behind her mother, so close they were touching, and she took her mother's tail in her trunk and held on.

As if on cue, Allie slid over Minnie's head, onto Minnie's slightly smaller back. Then she stood, steadied, measured the distance with her eyes—then flipped into a high, tumbling somersault, high over the gap, landing flawlessly, sliding to a sitting position so Maisie didn't get the jarring shock of two feet landing on her.

And as she slid down, Maisie lifted her trunk and trumpeted, as if in triumph, and turned with the girl still on her back and headed straight into the dam.

Matt made an involuntary step forward but Jack gripped his shoulder and held. He was chuckling out loud.

'Let 'em be,' he told her. 'Maisie loves her waterhole like life itself, and she's showing off—and you think your girl wants to get off?'

She didn't. Allie was laughing with incredulous delight as Maisie stomped deep down, neck-deep into the dust-brown waterhole. Minnie lifted her trunk and trumpeted like her mother—and went right in after.

Two elephants, one waterhole, one ecstatic girl. Maisie was lowering her trunk in and out of the water, splashing like a two-year-old in the bath. Allie was under a shower to end all showers.

'I've seen this before,' Jack said in satisfaction. 'There's a bond between elephant and keeper. We've had these two for ten years now but this girl's been an important part of their lives for a long time.'

He couldn't keep his eyes from her. She was drenched, covered in muddy water, happy as…a pig in mud?

An elephant in mud, he thought, changing the analogy to suit the girl and the time and the place.

It was doing things to him. Standing here, in this almost wilderness, on the edge of nowhere, with the sun on his face, the weathered old farmer beside him, more elephants in the distance, these two elephants in the water before him—and Allie, all cares forgotten, happier than he thought he'd ever seen a woman.

More beautiful than he'd ever seen a woman.

Jack was looking at him sort of quizzically and he had a feeling the man was seeing more than he wanted him to see. Or was that just because of the weird, exposed way he was feeling?

'She's beautiful,' the old man said, and Matt thought—
yes, she is.

Allie was standing again, back on Maisie's back. Maisie
was filling her trunk with water and spraying it behind, something they'd obviously done years before and loved. Minnie
was beside them, splashing and spraying as well.

But then…

Suddenly the younger elephant tried the same as her
mother, filled her trunk with water, lifted it high to spray—
but, as she did, she swept her trunk across her mother's back.

Swiping Allie straight down into the water.

No!

She was in the water. She was under the water, and if Matt
couldn't see her, neither could the elephants beside her.

She sank straight under with the impact of the fall. Maisie
shifted around as though searching for her. The water
churned…

And Matt was in there. He was hardly conscious of moving, but one moment he was talking to Jack, the next he was
diving hard and deep, straight through the murk, straight to
the spot where Allie had fallen.

Somehow he reached her. It was instinct, luck, something,
but somehow he had her and hauled her back, away from the
animals moving nervously forward. The water was deep and
murky and the elephants were shifting in alarm but he had
her tight and he wasn't letting go. He hauled her to the surface just as Minnie surged forward.

The elephants could see them now, and they meant no
harm. Maisie lurched as if to block off her daughter, and
somehow Matt hauled Allie sideways and back towards the
bank. Finally he found his feet in the mud and hauled Allie
out of the water and out of danger.

What had just happened? A moment's inattention…

He felt his knees sag as he realised how close…how close…

The elephants were now stock still in the water. Jack had

surged forward almost as fast as Matt—he was knee-deep in the mud—but he, too, stopped.

Then Maisie took one, two ponderous steps forward and lifted her great trunk and touched Allie's face. She checked her out with her trunk as Matt had seen mother elephants check their babies in wildlife documentaries.

Documentaries. Not real life.

In reality, Allie had fallen and if one of these huge creatures had moved sideways before he'd got there...

He was holding Allie hard against him and he felt her shudder. She didn't flinch from Maisie's touch, though. She stood within the circle of Matt's hold and she touched Maisie's trunk in turn.

'I'm sorry,' she whispered. 'I gave you a fright. I forgot to watch Minnie.' *She was talking to Maisie?*

'It's the way accidents happen,' Jack growled in a voice that said he was as shaken, or more, as they were. 'You forget the power of these guys. They know you, girl, and they're friendly but they're elephants, not toys.'

'Which is why they're here and not in the circus,' Allie managed, but she wasn't moving from Matt's hold. 'I should never... That was so dumb. But it was great.'

'Thanks to your man, here,' Jack said.

'He's not my man.' Her knees were giving in on her, Matt thought. He was holding her up and she needed it. It was okay by him; for now, for this moment, he was her man, whether she willed it or not.

She stood still, taking her time to recover, and Matt was happy to hold her for as long as she needed. Jack stood back and waited as well, and the elephants stood and silently watched, as if they, too, were coming to terms with what had happened. But that was crazy. Anthropomorphism, Matt thought—attributing human traits to animals. It was sentimental nonsense.

But as Matt watched Maisie watch Allie, as he felt Allie's

shudders fade, as he stood still while Maisie's trunk explored him in turn, it was impossible not to feel that way.

Maisie's trunk felt like a blessing. *Look after my girl.*

Thanks to your man, here…

That was how he felt right now. Her man.

Because she felt like his woman.

Nonsense. This was emotion, with no basis in reality.

Except the girl he was holding in his arms felt every inch real, felt every inch a woman, felt every inch a part of him.

His woman.

One dangerous moment had shifted his foundations. He needed to get on firm ground—which involved getting out of this dam.

Before Allie could object, he swung her into his arms and strode out of the muddy water, setting her gently on the bank. He held her for a moment, held her shoulders, then reluctantly let her go.

She didn't move far. She still looked white-faced and shocked.

Emotion be damned, he moved back in again. He put his arm around her shoulders and tugged her against him. Just until she'd recovered, he told himself as they both turned to face Jack.

'You're really okay?' Jack demanded and he was white-faced, too, or as white-faced as a weathered farmer could possibly look.

'I…I'm fine,' Allie said. 'Just paying the price for being dumb. I'm sorry I scared you.' She glanced back towards the elephants, who'd obviously decided things were okay, they could go back to water play. 'What…what happens now?'

'With these guys?' Jack's face turned even more grim. He stared at the great elephants and then he turned and looked into the distance. There were beef cattle grazing peacefully close by, but they could see another three elephants behind them. And two giraffes. 'I'm starting to face it,' he said. 'Myra and I run this place on the smell of an oily rag, but we don't make ends meet. The problem is, these guys live for ever. I started this place when I was wealthy, but I'm not any more. People felt sorry for individual animals—circuses and the like. No one wants to be the one to put them down so they've paid to have them sent here. Five years' keep. Ten years' keep if we're lucky. But Myra and I are getting old. We're running out of steam and we've run out of money. That's why I decided I had to pull in what's owing, only people like you are coming back to me saying sorry, there's no more funding. Myra and I need to retire. My son and his wife would take this on in a heartbeat if it was a business proposition but it's not. We have to walk away.'

He looked across at Maisie and Minnie, still cavorting in the water like two kids instead of a forty-year-old and her eighteen-year-old daughter. 'I'm sorry, lass,' he said. 'But I've made so many enquiries. No one wants them. No one has the room or the facilities to keep them right, and I suspect you'll be with me when I say I'd rather put them down than have them go back to the lifestyle we saved them from.'

'All the animals?' Allie whispered and it was as if all the breath had been sucked out of her.

'All,' he said.

'How many?'

'Ten elephants, two giraffes, four lions, three tigers, four panthers, forty-six monkeys, one gorilla, two bears and seven meerkats.' He managed a smile. 'We might manage to keep the meerkats. Building them an enclosure and keeping them happy might keep me happy in my old age, though I'm not sure how they'll go in a retirement village.'

'They'll be awesome in a retirement village,' Allie said stoutly but she was watching Maisie and Minnie, and Matt could see the iron will needed to keep her face under control. He was holding her and her body was rigid. 'Oh, Jack… there's nothing I can do,' she whispered.

'I know,' the farmer said gently. 'You did what you could as a teenager. They've had ten great years because of you. If it finishes now...' He didn't continue. He didn't have to. 'Do you two want towels? Showers?'

We're fine,' Allie said, starting to recover. 'It's hot. We'll dry. Can you show us the lions?'

So Jack walked them across to the lion enclosure and Matt kept holding her because it seemed the right thing to do. She needed him.

After a scare like that, she'd need anyone with steady legs.

That didn't seem important. What was important was that now she needed *him*.

Allie had fallen silent. Had it been a mistake to bring her here? Matt wondered. Would it break her heart? But even if these animals had to be put down, she'd want to have seen them.

Better to have loved and lost than never to have loved at all...

Where had that saying come from? He didn't know, but suddenly instead of Allie and her elephants—or maybe as well as Allie and her elephants—he was thinking of Margot and her soldier fiancé.

Better to have loved and lost...

Why did it feel as if there was armour there and something was attacking it? It was as if armour was being picked off, piece by piece. There was a big part of him that wanted—needed—to retreat, to regroup, to stop holding Allie, to stop looking at Allie. He was thinking...thinking...

He saw Jack glance at him and then at Allie and he wondered how much the old man saw. Jack could read animals. Could he read him?

That'd be hard. He could hardly read himself.

The lions were difficult to see. Their enclosure was magnificently built, double fenced, the fence embedded deep into the ground so nothing could dig through. It must have cost a fortune, Matt thought, as he saw it stretch away beyond their sight. The ground beyond was undulating, with trees and rocky outcrops, natural shelter, another waterhole. It was as close as Jack could make, Matt thought, to the wilds these creatures belonged in.

Jack handed Allie field glasses and pointed to a group far to the left. 'Yours'll be the old man,' he told her. 'Prince is still magnificent and Hilda's loyal to him. Zelda died of natural causes last year. The other three in that pride are all lionesses from a guy's private zoo. He made money in the IT boom, set up a private zoo, but his firm went bust so now...' He shrugged. 'Ah, well. I've done the best I can for as long as I can, but it's over.'

Enough.

All the time he'd been talking, walking, watching, no matter that his emotions were in unaccustomed overdrive, Matt's banker brain had been working. Yeah, he'd been distracted by Allie—who wouldn't be distracted by Allie?—but somehow he now reverted. Focus, he told himself, and he did.

'You say your son would take over here?' he asked Jack. 'If it was a viable business?'

'Yes, but it's not,' Jack said shortly.

'Do you and Myra want to go live in a retirement home—with or without meerkats?'

'There's no choice. The house is falling down. All we have goes into these animals. Myra has arthritis. She needs...'

'Help,' Matt said softly. 'Major help. Would you mind if I looked at your books?'

'There's nothing to see,' Jack said bleakly. 'Outgoings equals incomings multiplied by three.'

'But I can't see a scrap of waste,' Matt said. 'I can't see a hint of mismanagement. You know, Bond's Bank has a vast international reputation. As part of our business model we take on projects that do our corporate image good. Usually they're big and visible and attached to major charities, but this…' He stood and gazed around him, at the vast outback landholding, at the elephants in the distance, at the lions in the foreground. 'There'd be more animals than these needing homes,' he said, and it wasn't a question.

'Every week I get requests,' Jack said heavily. 'I can't take them, and I know they get put down.'

'Allie, your camels could come here. They'd like it here.'

'Camels,' Jack said, and brightened. 'That'd give me stuff to learn about.' But the brightness faded. 'You're talking fairy tales, son,' he said. 'Do you have any idea how much this place is losing?'

'I suspect I do,' Matt said absently. 'And I have a board I'd need to bulldoze. Would you have any objection to the Bond logo going on your website?'

'What website?'

'The website Bonds Public Relations team would build for you.'

'But…'

'We don't do things in halves,' Matt went on, working on his theme. Still not looking at Allie. This was business, he told himself. This was nothing to do with a soaking, bedraggled woman who was looking at him with the beginnings of hope in her eyes. 'If we decide to put our fingers in this pie…' He hesitated. 'It wouldn't be a finger. It'd be a whole fist. Or an arm right up to the chest.'

He glanced across at the decrepit homestead. An elderly lady was standing on the veranda, watching them, shielding her face from the sun. With a flash of intuition, he thought— that's Mrya and she doesn't want to be here because she thinks we're talking about putting these animals down.

'We'd build two houses,' Matt said. 'One for your son and one for you. No, make that three. Let's put in a manager's residence as well so your son can take a break when he needs to. You run beef cattle, to make a living, right? My proposition is that you keep doing that if you wish, but you no longer need

to. We'll take on the entire costs of maintaining the sanctuary, including generous wages for all of you. We'll examine
how much land you have here, thinking about expanding if
we need. If you're knocking animals back…Bond's wouldn't
want them knocked back or put down. You'll need more staff
and we can organise that. Other banks sponsor sports clubs
or car races. I'm thinking Bond's will be in the business of
saving animals instead.'

'But…' Allie said, and she'd lost her bluster. Her voice
was scarcely a whisper. 'But what we owe…What everyone
owes…'

'It'll be retrospective,' Matt said. 'We're taking on these
animals as of now but we'll take on the debts as well. Bond's
has the resources to pull in debts from those who can afford
it but the animals' survival won't depend on repayment. For
those who've paid for years, that'll be deemed enough. If
you wanted to make this place better for your animals, Jack,
where would you start?'

The man looked dazed, as well he might. 'I don't…I don't
know,' he managed. 'My son has all sorts of dreams. Myra
has all sorts of dreams.'

'I'll have my people contact your people then,' Matt said
and grinned and shook his hand. 'This can work for both of
us. As a PR exercise it'll be magnificent. By the way, you
need a name. Does the farm have one?'

'No,' Jack said faintly. 'We've stayed under the radar. Kept
it quiet, like.'

'Then maybe we need to change that. It'll mean more animals come to you; you'll need more resources to handle them,
but we can cope with that. We're talking long-term funding.'

The commercial part of him was kicking in now, seeing
possibilities. He'd hardly touched the structure of the bank
since his grandfather had died. It was a staid institution, in-
sular and secure.

Maybe it was time to break out.

'We need an angle,' he said. 'A name...'

'What about Bond's Unleashed?' Allie said. She'd pulled away from him to use the field glasses but suddenly she was right in front of him, staring up at him with shining eyes. 'Bond's Unleashed, for all of you.'

'Bond's Unleashed...' The words drifted, the possibilities opening. Like the girl before him. Possibilities...

'Letting go,' Jack muttered. He stared around at the animals and he stared back at Matt. 'This'd be me letting go of the responsibility—with your blessed bank taking over.'

'Bonds unleashed all over the place,' Allie said and Matt thought...Matt thought...

Bond's Unleashed. He knew it'd work. He could see it.

But mostly all he could see was Allie.

'You need a great snarly lion on your banking logo,' Allie said and he thought incredulously—this is a businesswoman. She has business smarts.

She's beautiful.

'You could use Prince,' Jack said doubtfully. 'But he's more smug than snarling.'

'If Photoshop can get rid of cellulite it can turn smug to snarly.' Allie's eyes were glimmering with unshed tears and she reached out and took Matt's hands in hers. 'Matt, are you sure?'

'I'm sure.' The way he was feeling, it was all he could do to get his voice to work.

'And your bank can afford it?'

'Yes, it can. A thousandfold if need be.'

'And I can send the camels here?'

'Yes,' he said and he saw a weight slide from her shoulders. Her face lightened and she looked...younger?

The feel of her hands in his...

Bonds unleashed. The way he was feeling...

'We should check on the rest of your animals,' he said

quickly before his thoughts could take him one inch further into territory he was struggling to understand. 'The monkeys.'

She nodded. 'I…yes, please. We should.'

'And you need to meet our meerkats,' Jack said. 'They're not nearly as risky as elephants.' He grinned at Matt, a great, wide grin that made him seem twenty years younger. 'They're playful. You want to play?'

'I'm a banker,' he said. 'I finance this operation; I don't play.'

'You could be unleashed as well,' Allie said softly, and suddenly things seemed right out of control.

'No.'

'No?'

'No,' he repeated and, whether he meant it or not, the words came out explosively. 'Jack, I'll need a rough idea of what you need to keep this place running until we can get long-term organisation in place. Can I talk you through it while Allie greets her monkeys?'

'Sure,' Jack said easily. 'Myra has the books. She might also have a cup of tea.' He grinned. 'Maybe a whisky as well?'

'No whisky,' Allie decreed, casting a mischievous glance at Matt. 'One, he's my helicopter pilot and two, he's my ring-master and he's performing tonight. For now, Matt Bond, that leash stays very firmly on.' Then she tucked her hand in his and chuckled. 'But now I've seen you dive into muddy waters and save me from elephants. Now I know that leash can come off at need.'

Allie checked out her monkeys, who didn't recognise her but they looked gloriously content. Matt checked the books and tried to turn into a banker again.

As he went through the financial figures he understood why Jack was in such financial trouble. He should have folded this place years ago but instead he hadn't compromised one bit. He and Myra were living in poverty but the animals were living in luxury.

Jack and Henry…two old men, following their dreams.

Allie following after.

At least he could save Jack's farm, Matt thought, trying very hard to stay in banker mode as he guided their chopper back to Fort Neptune with a seemingly subdued Allie beside him. The Board might even think it was a good idea—Allie's name was pure brilliance.

But he still couldn't save the circus. No amount of money could make ageing performers young again.

'But it's just us now,' Allie said, almost to herself, but she had headphones and mouthpiece on so he could hear every whisper.

'Just us?'

'With pensions and what I can earn, we can afford a place. It was the thought of paying off that debt that was killing me. And the camels…what was I supposed to do with the camels?' She smiled across at him, a glorious, open smile of sheer gratitude. 'I thought you'd destroyed us, Matt Bond. Instead, you've saved us.'

'We've still foreclosed on the circus.'

'Yes, but that was coming anyway,' she said fairly. 'And it hurts, but it would have hurt whenever it happened.'

'Do you want help finding a place to live?'

'You've done enough for us,' she said gently. 'Matt, back there when I heard you make the offer to Jack, I thought I should refuse. It's charity, but then I realised it's not me you're offering the money to. I talked to Myra while you were going over the books. Do you know how close they were to getting all those animals euthanased? I think you're wonderful, Matt Bond, you and your darling bank.'

'Darling bank…' In all the years he'd worked for Bond's, he'd never once heard his bank described as darling.

'Thank you,' she said, and sniffed and then turned and

looked at the scenery below and he thought—she doesn't know what else to say.

Thank you.

He didn't want this woman feeling grateful to him, he thought.

Why?

'We'll get as much out of this as we put in,' he growled, but she didn't turn back to him. He heard her sniff again.

'I'm sure you will,' she managed. 'I'm sure you're a banker through and through, and this is a very sound business decision. But you're a lovely man, Matt Bond, and you make an awesome ringmaster and I don't even mind if you foreclose on our circus—you are one special person.' And with that she sniffed and subsided.

He focused on the controls for a while.

He was one special person?

He glanced at Allie's averted head and he thought of her cavorting in the muddy waterhole with her elephants and he thought of what she was facing now, her life ahead with a bunch of geriatric circus performers and he thought...he thought...

He thought he wasn't that special person. And he thought more chinks in his carefully built armour were being knocked out every minute.

CHAPTER NINE

HE LANDED ON the foreshore. Joe, the pilot, was there to greet them. 'Successful day?' he asked.

Allie glowed and said, 'Fabulous,' and Matt saw Joe do a double take.

They were both filthy but Allie was the filthiest. She was the one who'd played with elephants, and she'd spent time in the monkey enclosure as well. She'd dried out—the day was so warm her clothes had dried on her—but her hair was tangled, her clothes were smeared with mud and she looked... well, she looked as if she'd just come out of a waterhole filled with elephants. But Matt knew Joe wasn't seeing that. He was seeing the glow, the woman underneath, and suddenly the effort to stay a banker was too much. What was resurfacing was that almost primeval instinct to hold her hard and say, *She's mine.*

Instinct was dumb. Instinct was wrong.

Besides, if she was his, what would he do with her?

Marry her? Take her back to Sydney? Give her the life of his mother and his grandmother? Matriarchs, raising the next generation of Banking Mathews while he banked on?

What was he thinking? Allie was a circus performer, in love with elephants and dogs and aged performers and he... his life was the bank. Margot was getting better by the day. He'd promised her two weeks, but after that he'd return to

Sydney, he'd get his life back and this time in Fort Neptune would fade to the aberration that it was.

Joe was climbing aboard the chopper, waving farewell. 'You're looking good, sir,' he yelled as the rotor blades threatened to drown out speech. 'I'll report back to work that I've now seen you without a tie. And with a girl who doesn't wear a suit. Wonders will never cease. Expect to hit the front page of Business Weekly,' he yelled and then grinned. 'Only kidding.'

And he was gone, leaving Allie and Matt gazing after him.

The roar of the chopper faded to nothing.

They should go.

Where they were standing had been cleared for chopper landing—for emergency evacuation, for urgent transport, not just choppers of itinerant bankers. It was a spit of land reaching out into the bay, with the circus behind them.

The sea was turquoise-blue, calm and still, with the small waves lapping at the shore the only sound breaking the stillness. The fishing boats were all out. There were only the tenders—small rowing boats—swinging at mooring.

It was a perfect day.

A perfect moment.

Where to take it?

It was Allie who made the decision.

She took his face in her hands and she stood on tiptoe.

'Thank you for today, Matt Bond,' she told him. 'Thank you for my elephants.'

And she kissed him.

They'd kissed before. That kiss was still imprinted on his brain, a sweet, tender moment which, for a guy who'd had few such moments in his life, was one he'd remember.

And want repeated? Maybe he did, because he surely didn't step back now.

But, as a banker, Mathew Bond would accept a kiss from

a grateful client—or from a woman who wanted to get closer than he willed—and he'd know what to do with it.

He'd kiss back—lightly. He'd take the woman's shoulders—whoever the woman happened to be—and set her back and smile at her. And he had just the right smile.

It was a smile that said the barricades were up. Very nice kiss, thank you, let's move on.

But this…

This was Allie kissing him, and Mathew Bond the Banker might have every intention in the world of moving on but Mathew Bond the Banker wasn't in charge right now.

This was Matt, the guy underneath all that armour. All day long—or maybe it was since he'd met Allie, something had been chipping away, chipping away. He felt weird, exposed and uncertain.

Or he *had* felt weird, exposed, uncertain. What was surfacing now was something deeper again.

Primeval need.

The need to gather this woman to him and hold.

He'd felt it when Joe had smiled at her and he'd managed to suppress it. He'd been holding back. But now she had his face in her hands, she was right before him, she was on tiptoe, her lips had found his—and she was kissing him.

Hard, fierce, wanting.

This was no kiss of polite thanks. This was not even a kiss of desire for a relationship. It wasn't a kiss of consciousness at all.

It was, quite simply, a kiss of passion.

All day he'd watched her emotions see-sawing. All day he'd seen something he'd never seen before—a woman totally exposed. Her love for those great elephants was deep and real. Her joy in knowing they'd live had unleashed any inhibitions.

But this wasn't a kiss of thanks. It was part of that same raw emotion, and he knew it the moment her lips touched his.

Fire met fire. He took her by the waist and drew her to

him, deepening the kiss, and it felt as if their bodies were fusing to become one.

All day the chinks in his armour had been growing wider. Now it was as if the last of the brittle pieces were falling away, leaving him wide open—and this woman was sliding right in.

She was reaching places he hadn't known existed. The warmth of her, the heat, was wrapping itself around his heart, leaving him crazily vulnerable, but he was loving it. He was holding her and that was what he intended doing. Holding. How could he not hold on to this loveliness? How could he step away from this woman?

Gloriously, she was kissing him still. She'd taken his face between her hands and lifted her face to him. She was opening herself to him and the sensation was indescribable.

What was happening to him? It felt as if all his foundations were crumbling to nothing.

But now wasn't the time for wondering about foundations. Who cared for foundations when he was holding her, crushing her breasts against his chest, feeling her mould to him, feeling her hands twine around his head, her fingers in his hair, feeling her mouth open under his, her tongue search as he wanted to search…

Now was simply for being.

Now was for kissing a woman called Allie.

What was she doing?

She was kissing a man who was twisting her heart as it had never been twisted.

He'd saved her elephants. She'd have kissed him if he was King Kong.

But not like this, she thought, dazed. Never like this.

Why was she kissing him?

It was meant to be a thank you, she thought, but she knew that was just an excuse. She'd been aching to kiss him. Aching to touch him.

Why?

Because he was a banker who'd saved her animals?

Because he was one hot guy?

Because he'd saved her today?

None of those things. She was being honest with herself here. She'd been sitting next to him in the chopper for the last hour and she'd been glancing at his face and she'd been thinking…

He's vulnerable.

Poor little rich boy?

But there was no need to take that to extremes, she'd told herself dryly. There wasn't a lot for her to feel sorry about in Matt Bond's world.

And yet as she kissed him now, as she savoured the feel of him, the strength, the heat, the sheer masculinity of this gorgeous hunk of male, that strange feeling was still with her.

He felt…empty, she thought. Alone.

A loner?

The two things were different.

She'd been brought up in a circus family, surrounded by people who loved her.

Did Matt have anyone who loved him apart from Margot?

Did he want anyone else?

She ought to pull away and think about it, but thoughts weren't operating all that efficiently right now.

Her toes were curling.

Her fingers were in his hair. He had the most gorgeous hair, thick and black and curly. He used some sort of product that tamed the curls when he was in his suit, when he was playing the ringmaster, but today had got rid of any product. He was washed and wind-blasted, there was farm dust in his hair, her fingers were tangling…Ooh.

She might or might not love Matt Bond, she decided at last, but she loved his hair.

And, in turn, his fingers were investigating her tangles,

gently, slowly, as if exploring every fibre—then drifting downward from the crown to her throat.

His fingers...

He was making love to her with his fingers.

She was having an orgasm here. She was standing out on the spit on Fort Neptune's harbour, she was being kissed by a man she'd met only days before, the kiss was public property—anyone shopping on the esplanade could see this kiss—and her insides were melting and this man's hands were driving her wild and he was just touching her hair and her throat, for heaven's sake, and she thought, she thought...

She thought if it was in private she might rip his clothes off right here. Right now.

Um...it wasn't private. She was kissing a banker in full view of the world, and she'd instigated the kiss, and if she didn't stop soon things would get well out of control, and she'd likely be tarred and feathered and run out of town as a scarlet woman.

And she'd deserve it.

Right, then.

Somehow she moved—she must have moved—she must have made some vague motion of pulling away because, appallingly, he responded. He put his fingers to her lips as if it needed touch to break the seal. He pulled back, just a little, and the next moment he was holding her at arm's length and she was looking into those gorgeous dark eyes and watching him smile at her and she was thinking....he's just as confused as I am.

And she was drowning in that smile.

'Good...good kissing,' she managed, and he managed a chuckle in return. She wasn't fooled. He was as shaken as she was.

'It's good that we're practising,' he said in a voice that confirmed it. 'We might get good enough to put it on the circus programme if we keep on like we are.'

'We hardly need to put it on the programme.' She glanced across the road, to the shops, to a small cluster of interested onlookers. 'We're giving a free performance.' She shook herself, hauled back from his grasp, fought for reality. 'Speaking of performance...'

'You have heaps of time.'

'Yes, but I need to go visit Grandpa first. I need to tell him what's happening at the farm.'

'You want me to come with you?'

He said it lightly, but it wasn't light. She knew it wasn't light. It was a suggestion that they might take this further.

Girl kisses boy.

Girl takes boy to visit Grandpa.

Not wise. Not wise at all. She gave herself a quick mental shake, reminded herself who she was, where she was, of all the people who depended on her, of how messy a relationship with this guy could be, and about thirty other very good reasons why she should be wise. Regardless, she almost caved in and said yes, but the reasons were there and she was a grown woman and she had to have some sense. Sense for both of them.

'Thank you, no,' she said, struggling to sound light. 'It's time I got back to normality. Thank you for today, Matt. Thank you for what you've done. Thank you for everything, but now I think it's time to move on.'

'That was some kiss.' He'd barely got in the door before Margot was right in front of him, her eyes twinkling with pleasure. 'I didn't know you had it in you.'

'Margot...'

'In front of the whole town,' she continued. 'In my day that'd constitute engagement.'

'Margot!'

'Well, why not? Oh, Matt, she's lovely.'

'She is,' he said tightly and headed for his room. He needed to shower and change—and he needed time to himself—but he was reckoning without Margot.

She was no respecter of persons, his Great-Aunt Margot, and she was no respecter of privacy. He walked into his bedroom and she walked right in after.

'So now what?' she asked.

'I go and play ringmaster at tonight's performance.'

'That's not what I mean.'

'That's all I'm capable of meaning right now,' he told her. 'She's a great girl but I've known her for less than a week—and I can't see her fitting into my world.'

'Your world of banking?'

'What else do you think I mean?'

'Raymond didn't think I'd fit in at Fort Neptune,' she said stolidly. 'I proved him wrong. It's a pity I lost him before I proved it.'

'This is nothing to do with you and Raymond.'

'No, it's all about courage. You keep your emotions filed under P for private, like the rest of your dratted family.'

'Like you, too,' he said, goaded. 'You lost Raymond sixty years ago and you've buried yourself ever since.'

'Living in Fort Neptune is not burying myself.'

'No,' he said shrewdly. There were things he'd thought about his Aunt Margot, things he'd never said, but if she was goading...and if she'd decided to die anyway... 'But what about Duncan?'

'Duncan?'

'You know very well who I'm talking about,' he said. 'The Duncan who stops by every morning to make sure you're okay. The Duncan who's rung me through the years to tell me things he thinks I ought to know—like when you broke your leg on the cliff and didn't think to tell me. The Duncan who rang me and practically bullied me down here because he's so worried—and he told me he asked you to marry him fifty years ago but you refused because you said you never wanted to forget Raymond.'

'He married Edith,' she said stiffly. 'They had a lovely marriage until she died two years ago.'

'So he fell in love,' Matt said softly. 'But he lost and he had the courage to move on.'

'Well, you don't have the courage to fall in love in the first place,' Margot snapped. 'At least I did it once.'

'And it hurt so much you never did it again.'

'So you don't want that hurt?'

'I did hurt,' he said, his voice lowering to match hers. 'I lost my entire family.'

That caught her. She looked up at him, Bond eyes meeting Bond eyes and he thought—she's almost a reflection of me.

'We're two of a kind,' she whispered, mirroring his thoughts, and he winced.

'Bonds.'

'Cowards?'

'Duncan will be round again tomorrow morning,' he said. 'You jump first.'

'Are you joking? I'm eighty.'

'All the more reason to jump fast.'

'Mathew!'

'I think I'm Matt,' he said softly. 'Some time today I think I left Mathew behind.'

'Oh, my dear,' she said, subsiding, for the anger and aggression had suddenly gone out of her. 'Do you really think that?'

'I don't have a clue. Can you see Allie in my life? Or me in hers? Allie in Sydney or me living in a farmlet with the remnants of Sparkles Circus…?'

'Duncan has ten grandchildren and two Jack Russell terriers,' Margot retorted back at him. 'And I have a cottage I love.'

'So you've decided to die rather than compromise?'

'Compromise is hard,' Margot said. 'As you get older it

gets harder. And you…losing your family and finding the courage to start again…I know how hard it is.'

'And I don't even know if she'd have me,' Matt muttered, and Margot's eyes flew wide.

'So you do feel…'

'Of course I feel,' he said explosively. 'I feel and feel and feel and I have not one idea what to do about it. Yes, I'm like you, Margot, but you've spent sixty years thinking about it. I've barely started.'

There was something wrong. He felt it the moment he returned to the circus. Things were underway for the performance, everyone was busy doing what they needed to do, but there was a stiffness, a silence, a tension that he couldn't place.

Allie was preoccupied and silent. 'Nothing's the matter,' she said stiffly in response to his fast enquiry. 'We just need to make this performance as good as it possibly can be, or better. Your bow tie's crooked. See you in the ring.'

The show went on. It was magic, as usual. Allie did a short but wonderful show with her dogs. The camels were back at their best. The tumblers, the magicians, the clowns were all on top of their game, but still there was something…

Previously at the end of each act, the performers would bounce out of the ring and be greeted with good-natured banter by those in the wings. Now they retreated to silence.

It was as if the volume in the ring was still on normal, but behind the curtain the volume was set to mute.

And the smiles were masks, Matt thought. He did his normal joke routines with Fizz and Fluffy. The clowns hurled themselves into their roles, but underneath the painted clown faces was almost tragedy.

What was going on?

'Are things okay with Henry?' he demanded of Allie in a

fast turnaround of equipment where they both had to work together.

'He's fine.'

'Is he still coming home tomorrow?'

'Yes.'

'And Bella?'

'She's fine, too.'

'Then what's the matter?'

'Nothing that hasn't always been the matter,' she told him. 'We're facing facts, that's all.'

He had no time for more.

Finally it was over. Bows were taken, the crowd dispersed and the clearing up started.

This was normally Matt's cue to leave. He'd figured by now that he just got in the way when he tried to help. This was a well oiled machine, and he simply messed up operations.

He didn't leave tonight, though. He'd been watching Allie's face all evening, watching the tension, watching pain. He was starting to know this woman. He was starting to hurt when she hurt.

Was he throwing his heart in the ring?

She wouldn't know what to do with it, he thought grimly. The heart of a Bond? It'd only complicate her life. He'd do what he had to do on the sidelines and then move away—but he had a feeling that there was stuff to be done on the sidelines now.

He headed over to the camel enclosure. Allie wasn't there but she always came here last thing—he knew that by now. The dogs came to greet him. They had the run of the circus and without their sparkly ruffles they were two nondescript Jack Russells, seemingly empathising now with a worried mate.

'You too?' he asked as he sank down on a bench near the camels and both dogs jumped up beside him and put a head on a knee apiece. 'You're worried, too?'

They didn't move, just sat and waited and so did he, and ten minutes later Allie appeared with a bucket of feed and desolation written all over her.

She stopped when she saw him. He expected the dogs to jump down to greet her but they didn't. He had a weird feeling they were depending on him. *She needs help. Fix it. We're right behind you.*

'You want to tell me?' he said and she stopped short. She stood with the bucket of feed in her hand, as if she didn't know what to do with it. As if she didn't know how to move forward.

She'd shed her sparkles. She was back in her customary jeans and oversized jacket. She'd let her hair out from her performance hairstyle, but residual hairspray was making her curls hang stiffly, at awkward angles.

She'd scrubbed her face free of make-up, but tonight her eyes looked even bigger without the kohl.

Desolate was the only word to describe her.

'Allie…' He rose and lifted the bucket from her hands and set it on the ground. An indignant bray behind him reminded him of priorities. He turned and tipped the bedtime snack into the feed bin, the camels relaxed and he turned back to Allie.

She was still standing where he'd left her. Motionless.

Gutted.

'Allie, tell me,' he said and he couldn't bear it. He moved forward to take her hands, but she did move then. She stepped back in a gesture of pure revulsion.

'It's not your fault,' she whispered but by her expression he could tell she thought it was. 'It had to happen. I…we knew. It was just, I thought we'd have another week before it began. Only of course you have to organise things.'

'Organise what?'

'Carvers rang Grandpa with an offer,' she said dully. 'It's not much. They say we can't even look after our animals. They say they're not paying for our reputation—not when we let wild animals out. Wild—our camels! I'm sure it was Carvers who let them out, using it as a wedge to drive the price down. But Grandpa says what they're offering is all we can expect, so he rang your bank and he accepted. What's worse is that people from Carvers have told every single member of our crew what they thought of them—what their commercial value is. They've offered jobs to five. The rest…well, we all knew it. Anyway, Grandpa got your people here and he signed off on the offer. It's done. We perform for one more week—that's in the offer—but it's finished.'

'Allie…'

'Is that why you took me away today?' she demanded. 'To get me out of the way?'

'No!'

'So your people could come in behind my back?'

Your people…

It would be his people, he thought. The team from Bond's.

Apart from his brief call to organise the chopper, he hadn't been in touch with the bank for days. His foreclosure team back in Sydney would see no need to consult him if Henry received an offer. If Henry was willing to accept, a fast sale to one of the few potential buyers would suit everyone.

It was inevitable, he thought bleakly. It was simply reality hitting home. But now…

Now Matt was the villain of the piece.

Your people.

'Allie, I'm sorry. I didn't know…'

'That you were foreclosing? Of course you did.'

'Yes,' he said. 'I didn't know about today's offer, though. But it does make sense. That's why the team will have moved fast.'

'Your team.'

'Yes,' he admitted. 'I told the team we were giving you two weeks before closing the place down, but we've been putting out feelers for buyers before this.'

'Behind our backs?'

'Henry knew,' he said, firmly and surely. 'It's Henry's circus, Allie. This is not deceit. It's business.'

'Then that's why Carvers will have let the camels out. It's been all over the local papers. Wild beasts from circus roaming town. It's like Carvers wrote the piece. They'll have done it to make sure they get what's left of us for a rock-bottom price. I bet they've been planning it for months. And what they said… They told Fizz and Fluffy they were only fit for geriatric home entertainment—if not inmates. They were triumphant.'

'My people would never have said that.'

'No, but they stood in the background while Carvers said it.'

'I'm so sorry.' He hesitated, but then decided there was no choice but to be honest. 'I've had my phone off, but Allie, if an offer was made, I'd have talked to your grandfather, too, as I'm sure my team has. What they get for the circus goes against your grandfather's debt. It's in all our interests to get a fair price.'

'But to do it so fast… Signing today, and while I was away…'

'Maybe Henry wanted it that way,' he suggested. 'I'm sorry, Allie, but it's your grandfather's decision.'

'I know—' her hands working themselves into fists, clenching and unclenching '—Grandpa has the right. I can't override anything he's done.'

'Would you want it overridden?'

'Done differently. Done…with respect. If I'd known…'

'Allie…'

'Mmm?'

'There is life after this.'

She looked at him, bleak as death. 'Is that what you say to everyone you foreclose on?'

'To be honest, Allie, it seldom happens. We usually do a thorough business appraisal of everyone we lend money to.'

'Unless it's a favour to your Aunt Margot.'

There was a moment's silence. A long moment. More than anything, he wanted to step in to her and take her into his arms. That wouldn't be a usual banker/client gesture of reassurance, he thought, but then Allie wasn't a normal client. With a normal client he could step away.

Her body language said step away anyway.

'They're taking my dogs,' she said, almost conversationally, and he stilled.

The dogs. He glanced behind him and the dogs hadn't moved. They were lying on the bench but there was nothing relaxed about the way they were lying. They were looking straight at him.

Mathew Bond the Villain?

'Grandpa listed all the animals in the asset sheet,' she told him. 'Well, of course he did. They're half the reason people come to see us.' She took a deep breath and stared, not at the dogs, not at Matt, but at the ground. 'People from Carvers have been in the audience for the past few nights. They know what these guys can do. They know they're worth their weight in gold and Grandpa's signed them over. He didn't realise, but it's too late now. All our assets... All our animals. The camels. The ponies. And...and the dogs.'

He stared behind him at the two nondescript Jack Russells. They were circus dogs, but they were also dogs who were loved as pets. He looked at the girl before him and he thought...her heart's breaking.

He moved. Whether she wanted it or not, suddenly he was holding her. He drew her against him, he held her tight, and he felt her body heave with silent sobs. She cried, but not in the sodden sense of the word. It was as if her body had gone into spasm.

A breaking heart? It wasn't an overstatement.

The dogs... The animals... The contract...

How could he solve this one?

Maybe he couldn't. If he knew his team, this sale would be watertight. They'd have brought lawyers. Henry was in hospital so they'd have requested certification of competency before Henry signed. Henry would have signed with as many witnesses as were needed to make things unbreakable.

He thought suddenly of the camera in the audience, and he thought Carvers must have worked on this.

What were you thinking? he demanded of the absent Henry. And then he wondered why he hadn't handled this himself. It wouldn't have happened if he hadn't extended the foreclosure time, if he'd handled the stripping of the circus himself last week.

Or would it? Could he have sensed how much her animals meant to this woman?

And now? All he could do was hold her and wait for the shudders to subside, for her to pull herself together and remember she hated him.

She did pull herself together—sort of—but when she finally pulled away, he didn't see hate. He didn't see anger.

All he saw was defeat.

'I'll talk to them,' he said. 'See if we can organise an exclusion.'

'Are you kidding? They know the dogs are our biggest draw card. Besides, old man Carver hates Grandpa with a vengeance. Two circuses, vying for the same crowds for generations. You have no idea how much Carver will have delighted in today.'

'Dogs shouldn't be for sale. None of the animals should be.'

'They are and they've been sold.' She gathered herself, clicked her fingers and her dogs were instantly by her side. 'The only way we could get out of it is if they won't work. Carvers would never keep them then, but I've trained them to work for anyone. They're wonderful, and now we're paying the price.'

'Allie...'

'Enough. Matt, I need to say thank you. Thank you for your extraordinary generosity towards Jack's waifs and strays. And...and thank you for your very nice kiss. It was...appreciated. Matt, the crew's decided that we'll stick it out for the next week. We won't go out on a whimper, but Grandpa's home tomorrow and if he's home it'll be his last week as ringmaster. We don't need you any more. So thank you, but now it's time for you to go back to being a banker, and for us...for the crew to have our last week being together and then move on.'

He left. She watched him until he was a faint, far off figure in the moonlight.

She slumped onto the bench and her dogs draped themselves over her knees and she thought...

No. She didn't think.

Her world was ending. Her circus was sold. It was the end of life as she knew it.

So why should the hardest part of the night be watching one banker walk along the beach away from her?

CHAPTER TEN

FOR THE NEXT week there wasn't a lot to do, except go back to his original plan when he'd come to Fort Neptune. Make Margot live.

But it seemed Margot had made that decision all by herself, for she didn't have time to die while she was angry.

'I don't understand why you can't buy the circus outright,' she snapped at him. 'You have enough money...'

'I should have bought it,' he conceded. 'But it's too late now.' The sale had gone through so fast he hadn't seen the connotations. Sparkles was no longer a viable business, but for Allie to lose everything...

She hadn't lost everything, he reminded himself. Henry's debts were sorted. Allie and her grandparents could move on, debt-free. Allie would have no further financial commitment.

But she'd have emotional commitment as far as the eye could see. She was still committed to living with her grandparents and great-uncles and she was losing her dogs. The camels and ponies were bad enough, but the dogs?

There was nothing he could do. The contract was watertight. All they could hope for was that somehow the animals proved unsatisfactory and were discarded.

How unlikely was that?

'It's breaking your heart, isn't it?' Margot said and he realised he'd been staring into the dregs of his breakfast coffee for the last five minutes. 'So do something.'

He'd tried to. He'd rung the head of Carvers and offered to buy the animals back, no matter what the price.

Ron Carver had simply laughed.

'I've watched that damned little circus take the best spots, the best crowds, ever since I took over this business. Forty years of watching, and now it's giving me pleasure to rip the guts out of it. Nothing's for sale except what I discard. I'll let you know when I'm in the mood for deciding what's rubbish and what's not.'

Rubbish. The detritus of Sparkles Circus. The detritus of Allie's life.

He was being melodramatic, he thought grimly. Sparkles was a business and businesses closed down all the time. People moved on.

Allie would move on.

So what made his gut clench every time he thought of her?

'I'll take you to the circus this afternoon,' he told Margot.

'Duncan's taking me,' she said, and he nearly fell over. Duncan, town mayor, long-time friend, had been excluded from Margot's life for months. Last night Matt had arrived back at Margot's cottage to find Duncan and his dogs just leaving. Duncan had given him a sheepish grin and he'd thought—whoa...

Stupidly, he'd also had a very adolescent thought. *Margot doesn't need me either.*

He was used to being a loner. What was wrong with him?

Duncan was taking Margot to the circus? How big a statement was that?

'Maybe I shouldn't go, then,' he said slowly. 'It's time I backed away.'

'Oh, for heaven's sake... It might be time Bond's Bank moved away,' she snapped. 'But not us. We have a week left of Sparkles and I'm making the most of it. And you... Your bank has done what it had to do, so now you can close the door on your business dealings and be a friend. Or more. Don't tell me you're not personally involved. You kissed her in front of the entire town. You've fallen hard.'

'I haven't.'

'If you can't admit that to yourself then you're a fool, and one thing I never thought to think was that my nephew was a fool. Help me get ready. We're going to the circus.'

The circus was supposed to be sold out but somehow Margot and Duncan ended up where Margot always sat, in prime position. Matt, however, had no intention of sitting where he could be seen.

Fizz saw his problem, though. 'It might be your bank but this isn't your fault, mate. Allie's told us what you've done for the old animals. Come and stand in the wings. There's a spot where Allie won't be aware of you.'

How did Fizz know he'd rather stay out of Allie's sight? He hardly knew himself, but he stood in the wings that afternoon, that night, the next day…

He watched Henry play his time out as ringmaster. He watched Fizz and Fluff play with their cannon for the final times. He watched Tinkerbelle and Fairy turn themselves inside out for their mistress and quiver their delight.

He watched Valentino catch Miss Mischka, he heard the crowd gasp in wonder and he thought—don't drop her. And then he thought—she's falling anyway. What would her life be away from here?

He cared so much.

He watched on and, the more he watched, the more he knew the armour he'd so carefully built around him was shattered. He'd built the armour to avoid pain but the pain was here with him regardless. It was as if Allie was a part of him, something he hadn't known was missing but now he was achingly aware of its loss.

How could he lose what he'd never had?

How could he move forward from here without his armour? he thought desperately. How could he possibly persuade her to let their two worlds collide?

A banker and a girl in pink spangles.

He had to try.

She knew he was watching her and her heart twisted and twisted. Pain was everywhere.

She wanted him to go away.

No. She didn't. The last thing she wanted was for him to leave, but it had to happen.

Her life was the remnants of this circus and she was committed for as far as the eye could see and further. He was heading back to Sydney. She was headed to a ramshackle farm and poverty and caring.

She wouldn't have it any other way, she told herself fiercely as the week wore on. This was her choice—she chose family.

Matt was a man who walked alone. For a glorious short time she'd let herself fantasise about walking by his side, but that was all it had ever been.

Fantasy.

Friday night. The final performance was the next day. The air of impenetrable gloom was settled hard. Even those who'd been offered new jobs, who were continuing with Carvers, seemed grey. Their performance had been impeccable, but Matt saw the professionalism that masked the sadness.

During the week Duncan had been great, the elderly mayor now Margot's permanent escort, but tonight was his granddaughter's ballet performance. So Matt took Margot home after the circus, settled her with hot cocoa, watched her being sad as well—and then left.

'You're going back to talk to her?' Margot demanded.

'Yes.'

'Make sure you get it right.'

'I don't know if there is a right,' he said heavily. 'But I need to try.'

'Like I'm trying with Duncan,' she said approvingly. 'Good boy.'

The camels' last meal was more a midnight snack. Camels were supposed to be able to go for a week between meals, Allie thought as she fed them, but no one had ever told these guys.

Would Carvers want them? The contract said that Carvers had first rights to all the animals, but if they didn't perform to expectation they'd be returned. Win-win for Carvers, she thought grimly. There'd be no long-term care expenses for animals past their prime for Carvers.

'I'll offer to take you back when you're ready for retirement,' she told them sadly. She thought the ponies would come back—they were getting old and slow. She'd organised space for them in her life plans.

And if the camels were returned? Jack would love caring for them.

Matt would pay.

She'd been aware of him in the wings every performance for the last week. She knew he'd been talking to all the guys except her. Because he'd been ringmaster, albeit briefly, the crew treated him as one of them.

But he wasn't. He was a banker, in the wings, waiting for the curtain to close. She avoided talking to him and he didn't push it.

What was it about Matt that made her feel desolate? More desolate even than losing the circus.

As desolate as losing her dogs? At the end of tomorrow's performance, Carvers would move in and they'd be gone.

They were lying on their customary bench now, watching

her scratch Pharaoh's ears, just watching. They knew something was wrong.

She couldn't bear it.

'Allie?'

She didn't jump. It was almost as if she'd expected it—Matt's voice coming from out of the dark.

'I've almost finished,' she said inconsequentially, and stopped scratching Pharaoh and turned to face him.

He was a shadow in the night, dark and lean. He was wearing his gorgeous coat. Even though she could hardly see his eyes, she knew what his expression would be. She knew his eyes would be filled with concern.

All week she'd felt his concern. He was concerned for all the crew, but for her... She felt as if he was ready to scoop her up, lift her from this world, take care of her as he'd taken care of her animals.

'Allie, you can't do this on your own,' he said, and his words confirmed it.

'Do...do what?'

'Margot's friend, Duncan, is the local mayor and his son's the town's realtor. He says the place you've found to live in is basic. Really basic.'

'It's fine.' She'd looked at all the places they could afford to rent, and had found a big old weatherboard house, a mile out of town, with four bedrooms and enough land so if Carvers discarded the ponies...*when* Carvers discarded the ponies...

The dogs.

Don't go there. Think of the house, she decided, not the animals.

Basic pretty much described it, but it'd fit Allie, her grandparents and Fizz and Fluffy. They could afford it—just.

'What will you do out there?' he asked.

'I've already talked to the local accountant. He's offered me bookkeeping work.'

'And the others?'

'They'll figure it out,' she said, a little bit desperately. 'Everyone has to face retirement.'

'It'd be better if you had a place in town.'

'You know we can't afford it.'

'Let me help.'

She stilled. Closed her eyes. Knew what she had to say.

'Long-term care for ageing circus performers as well as circus animals? I don't think so.'

'I can afford…'

'I know you can,' she said. 'But allow us some pride. We need to move forward, Matt, without Bond's Bank.'

'I'm not talking about Bond's Bank,' he said. 'I'm talking about me. And you.'

She didn't answer. She couldn't. She couldn't think of a thing to say.

'Allie, I think,' he said softly into the night, 'that I've fallen in love with you.'

There was an even longer silence at that.

Love.

Matt.

This wasn't how it was supposed to happen, Allie thought at last, when her mind was capable of rebooting. Girl meets rich, kind and sexy hero. Really sexy. Hero rides to girl's rescue. Hero tells girl he loves her.

Girl loves hero back?

And it hit her, standing in the moonlight with her camels at her back and her dogs watching her, that it wasn't all fantasy. It was possible she did love this man. Or it was more than possible.

For how could she not? He was the kind of hero that fairy tales were made of. He was rich and kind and sexy and he'd ridden to her rescue and he was pretty much all-round fabulous.

But it was more than that. She'd known him for almost

two weeks. Was that long enough to see behind the façade, to see the vulnerability, the need, the boy behind the man?

Was it long enough to sense that in this man she'd found someone she could spend the rest of her life with?

Maybe in fairy tales, she told herself, for that was where happy ever after occurred. In fantasy land. In the world where pink sparkles reigned supreme, where there were no feed buckets and mud-spattered boots, where there was no retired circus family, shattered already, and if she walked away...

She couldn't. She knew she couldn't, and so did Matt. She could tell in the stiffness of his body language, by the way he held himself back when she knew—*she knew*—that every inch of him wanted to walk forward and take her into his arms.

She knew it because that was what she wanted. With all her heart.

The fairy tale. The fantasy that was the dream.

'I can wait,' he said even more gently, and something inside was coming apart. Tearing, ripping, the pain was almost unbelievable.

'Don't,' she said. 'You've done enough.'

'This isn't doing anything for you,' he said, and she heard it then, a pain that matched hers. 'This is doing something... asking something for me. Allie, I need you.'

He did move then, but she hardly noticed him moving. One moment she was standing, numb and still and alone, the next she was folded in to him, wrapped in cashmere, feeling his strength, his warmth, his heart.

'We can do this,' he said roughly, harshly. 'If you feel as I do... Do you?'

'I...maybe. Maybe I do.'

'Allie!'

'But there's no use feeling...like I do.' Her voice was scarcely a whisper. 'There's no way we can be together.'

'If you love me...'

'How can I love you? What use is that?'

'We can work things out. Let me help.'

'Do you honestly think Grandpa would let me take any more of your money?'

'If I married you he would.'

And her world stilled again.

Marriage. The ultimate happy ever after.

Maybe. She'd always been dubious of fairy tales and here it was, the ultimate test.

She could let herself stay folded in cashmere—or she could face the truth? Come on, Allie, she told herself harshly. This was time to be a grown-up.

She was still folded against him. She should pull away but there was only so much a girl could do in the face of…what she was facing…and pulling away from this gorgeous coat was not within her capabilities. Pulling away from this man…

She had to. In a moment. Soon. Even Cinders had her moment of feeling all was right in her world.

Before reality hit—but reality was now.

'You know, I've always been dubious about Cinderella,' she managed and thought—how can I find the words to explain? She must. 'Matt, I don't have anything to offer.'

'You don't need to offer…'

'How would it work? My family needs me. You know they do. There's no way they—we—could live in the city. Would you come here every Saturday, share a ramshackle bedroom and return to your bank on Sunday? It'd wear thin very fast.'

'It might be fun,' he said. 'And you could come to Sydney. We could share.'

'Sharing's being part of each other's lives.' She took a deep breath, trying to work it out for herself.

'Matt, maybe this sounds dumb, but fairy tales don't work. I'm thinking that in that vast, extravagant palace, with her prince out on princely business six days a week—and Margot's told me how hard you work, Matt Bond, so don't even think of denying it—Cinders must have been pretty lonely after her prince swept her off her feet. And me? Yes, I could get a job in Sydney but every moment I'd be worried about everyone down here. And down here…what would you do? I can't see it.'

She pulled back from him then, meeting his gaze in the darkness, willing him to understand—and knowing that he already did. The bleakness in his face told her he did.

'No,' she said softly. 'Matt, you'll always be our friend…'

'I don't want to be your friend.' It was an explosion in the stillness of the night, and Tinkerbelle—or was it Fairy?—stood up and barked. Not like she meant it, though. Maybe she was as confused as her owner.

'That's it, then,' she said, and somehow she made her voice sound sensible. 'It's time for us to move on. You've been wonderful.'

'I don't want to be wonderful!'

'You can't help yourself,' she said and she even managed to smile. 'You just are. Matt Bond, superhero. Prince to the rescue. Off you go on your white charger and find yourself some other maiden.'

'Allie…'

'Matt, no.'

And there it was. She'd said it.

He stood and looked at her for a long, long moment. 'I'll figure this out,' he said at last and she smiled again, but her smile was bleak.

'I know the truth about magicians,' she said. 'Magic's not real.'

'I'll figure it.'

'Matt…'

'There will be an answer,' he said, and he took her hands again, holding her hard, his grip warm and strong and sure.

'And pigs will fly,' she whispered. 'Matt, don't.'

'Anything's possible in a circus. I *will* find an answer.' He tugged her close and she shouldn't let him, she shouldn't, but how could a girl not? She let him. She even tilted her face. She even stood on tiptoe in her disgusting boots so she could meet him face to face.

So his mouth could claim hers.

And she even surrendered. She let herself melt into his kiss. Her arms came round and held him. He held her close, closer, closer. She kissed and she kissed and she kissed and for one last, glorious moment—or maybe longer than a moment—maybe much longer—she let herself believe in the fairy tale.

She kissed her prince and he kissed her back. She loved him with all her heart, with everything she possessed, and then, when the kiss had to end, as even the most wonderful, magical kisses must end, she made herself stand back, look at him one last time and step away.

The fairy tale was ended.

He walked home along the beach. The night was almost moonless. The only sound was the faint lapping of the waves. There was nothing to intrude on his thoughts.

His thoughts should be bleak as death. They weren't.

Would Allie's superhero disappear into the ether without a trace?

He would if he thought there wasn't any hope, but things had changed.

One little word. *Maybe*. Maybe she loved him, and the way she'd said it…

She did, he knew she did, so it only needed…

A miracle?

'Superhero stuff,' he said into the silence. 'Where would a superhero start?'

Find the nearest telephone booth to change into Lycra? Lift her up and carry her bodily back to his lair?

Did Superman have a lair?

How about James Bond?

Forget the superhero, he told himself, and forget the fairy tale. Allie had rightly rejected it out of hand.

His thoughts took off on a different tangent.

He didn't mind the superhero analogy but he agreed it was a one-sided equation. Allie had rejected the notion of hero on white charger and he got it. Equality. Superhero needs superheroine.

He couldn't take her with him. She needed her own lair.

A lair to share?

This was ridiculous, but his thoughts were in free flight.

Go back to basics, he told himself. Go back to what he knew. When faced with a dilemma, he encouraged his employees to brainstorm. Now he was doing it all by himself.

What were the problems? Face this logically. Lay everything on the table and look at every last piece of the equation to see what unbending factor would be bent.

One geriatric circus crew who Allie regarded as family. The odd geriatric animal as Carvers rejected them.

One dilapidated circus.

One Allie who'd learned to be a bookkeeper but looked magnificent in sparkles.

One banker who was solidly based in Sydney, with occasional forays overseas. Who only knew life as a banker.

Margot. He threw her into the mix for good measure.

Camels, ponies, dogs.

Dogs…

That was Priority One of the puzzle, he thought grimly. He needed to find some way to get her dogs back.

But Carver was enjoying this power. It was a triumph, taking the Sparkles' showstopper as well as Sparkles.

An alternative?

Buy Allie a puppy? After all, one Jack Russell was very like another.

Yeah, right. There spoke a man who'd never owned a dog. As if Allie would think that.

Yeah, right... And there went the tangent again.

He'd stopped and was staring out to sea.

One dog was very like another.

One showground was very like another.

One town was very like another.

Unless you knew them. Unless…

He was thinking further. He was looking at every single thing on the table. A girl who lived and dreamed circus. A banker.

A jumble that surely must fit into some sort of order.

It was as if a jigsaw was being thrown up and landing in another frame.

Another picture.

Dogs. Dogs first.

He turned and started striding up the beach, then striding wouldn't do it. He had a contract to pull apart.

He had a girl to win.

He had a magician's hat to pull on.

Striding wouldn't do it. He started to run.

CHAPTER ELEVEN

ONE MONTH LATER, and her life was transformed.

She'd done it. She had all her ducks in a row.

They had the farmhouse almost liveable. For the first couple of weeks Fizz and Fluffy and Bella and Henry had looked grey. The caravans had gone, bought as part of the Carver package, and their belongings had simply been dumped in the sheds here.

It had taken Allie weeks of bossing, of being determinedly cheerful, of threatening and cajoling, but finally they'd all stirred and sighed and decided they might as well get on with it. The house was coming together.

Bella even thought she might start a garden—which was excellent, Allie thought, as once the house was sorted she didn't actually know what everyone was going to do.

Except her. She was going to work and coming home. Her new job was eight until five, Monday to Friday, coping with the basic accounting of five Fort Neptune businesses—the supermarket, two filling stations, the butcher and the funeral home.

It was so boring that after four weeks she was starting to look longingly at the funeral home.

Today was Friday. Five-thirty. She was heading home for the weekend.

Home. The new normal. Grey. No matter how much

bounce she put on for the rest of the household, all she saw was grey.

She could stop in and say hi to Margot, she thought, but Margot was doing okay. Every time she went past Margot's cottage she saw Duncan's car outside or Duncan and his dogs going in and out. His dogs were Jack Russells. She couldn't look at them.

And, worse, Margot looked a little like Matt, and every time she thought about Matt she felt sickeningly sad.

Her dogs.

Her circus.

Matt.

There was a great hole where her heart should be.

Get over it, she told herself. Move on. It's not as if it's a real tragedy. Just pin that dratted smile back on and…

And stop.

She did. Her foot eased off the accelerator.

She'd turned into the farmhouse gate and there was a line-up on the veranda.

Fizz and Fluffy.

Bella and Henry.

Margot and…Duncan?

And Matt.

Matt.

And Duncan's dogs. Jack Russells. Two…

No, three.

Four?

She pulled up and everyone was beaming. Even the dogs.

Matt was beaming.

He had two dogs under his arms.

Duncan had two dogs under his arms.

Matt set his dogs down. The dogs Duncan held wouldn't be set. They were trying to lick Duncan to death.

The two Matt had been holding quivered, stared down at her as if they couldn't be sure—and then they were racing across to her, two balls of canine joy, flipping somersaults, delirious with happiness, and she was down on the ground ruining her prim bookkeeping uniform, trying to hold every inch of them.

And look at Matt at the same time.

He didn't have his coat on. He was wearing jeans and faded pullover. He looked...He looked...

He looked like Matt. She hugged her dogs and she thought she could never love anything as much in the whole world as she loved these two. But Matt was smiling at her and she knew she was wrong.

'We have our dogs back,' Henry boomed unnecessarily from the veranda, and she tried to surface from the dogs enough to ask questions. 'Plus our ponies. Plus our camels.'

'H... How?

'Carver brought them, of course,' Henry said. 'Or his henchmen did. Drove up and practically threw them out of the trailers. Said they were useless, and if the contract hadn't stipulated they be returned to us rather than be put down, that's where they'd be.'

'I've been having them watched,' Matt said mildly. 'We always expected the ponies and camels to be returned; Carvers didn't need them, but the dogs were a different matter. It worked out as we hoped, but I've had undercover security watching over them all the same. Until Carver cracked and tossed them back at us.'

'But... But...' She didn't have the questions to ask.

'Well you may "But",' Duncan said ponderously. 'Too right you had them watched, young man. Of all the risks... If Margot hadn't said she'd consider marrying me if I did it, I'd never have agreed. It wasn't your dogs at risk, miss.'

'They were Duncan's,' Margot said and beamed and somehow, between the dogs, she tucked her arm into Duncan's. 'Wasn't that brave of him? And noble.'

'Very noble,' Allie said faintly and then as the dogs jumped around her feet, she stooped again to hug them. 'No. How can it be noble when I don't understand?'

'Sleight of hand,' her grandfather said and chuckled. 'A feat to be proud of. Your young man is quite a magician. Even I suspected nothing. Fizz did, but apparently Matt thought if he told us all we might give it away.'

'Give…give what away?'

'That last night.' It was Fizz, the old clown, beaming wider even than the painted face he'd worn for so long. 'When the dogs finished in the ring it was me who took them back to your van. That night Carver's men were waiting, collecting everything, but somehow, in the shadows of the wings, two dogs turned into two different dogs.'

'You remember when you got them?' Margot said. 'You bought these two in Fort Neptune. Duncan's two girls are their half sisters. Only they're stupid.'

'Hey!' said Duncan.

'Nice but…placid,' Margot said and smiled. 'And identical to yours. So Duncan took your two girls home, and no one suspected anything. Matt put a discreet watch on all the animals— if there'd been any bad treatment Matt's watchers would have been there in an instant—and when Carver's handlers couldn't do anything with them except make them beg for food, finally he sent them back. It's taken a month. We're sorry it's taken so long, dear.'

'It has, though,' Matt said softly, smiling down at her, 'given me time to put a few more variations to the contract in place.'

'You know,' Margot said thoughtfully, 'if I were you, Matt Bond, and I'm not, so I can't give you advice, but it seems you've been giving me lots of advice lately so maybe you could take a little…If I were you and a girl was looking at me like Allie's looking at you…maybe you could take her somewhere else and tell her the rest. Somewhere six people and four dogs aren't listening.'

But Allie had something to do first. She was up on the veranda and she was hugging Duncan—or she was hugging as much of him and his dogs as she could.

By the time Duncan emerged from her embrace he was laughing, flustered, and Matt was right beside her, ready to take over the hugging, ready to take Margot's advice.

'I have this really comfy car,' he told her. 'There's room for two dogs on the back seat.'

'But…' She was having trouble breathing. 'What are you going to tell me?'

'I'm not going to tell you anything,' he said. 'I'm going to ask you. Isn't that how it's done?'

'It was in my day,' Duncan said and the elderly town mayor looked at Margot and chortled. 'And my day's still right here.'

He drove her back to town. She was silent for the ten-minute drive. She should ask…but she wasn't brave enough.

She'd sent this guy away. She'd said what was between them was impossible.

It still was impossible, but for now, with her two dogs draped over her knee—yes, they should be in the back seat but discipline had been a bit slack at Duncan's and they approved of being lapdogs—it seemed anything was possible.

For this moment she could pretend that anything was possible.

She hugged her dogs and stared straight ahead and waited for them to reach the beach, but, instead of going to the car park that led to the sand, Matt turned off just before, to the spit of land on the foreshore, to the site of Sparkles Circus.

To the ex-site of Sparkles Circus. Now there was nothing but bare headland. The circus was over.

She climbed from the car and looked at the empty site, at the grass already starting to regrow, at her favourite circus site in the world.

Next year Carvers Circus would play here.

'Next year Carvers Circus can't play here,' Matt said as he came around the car to stand beside her. 'There's been a hiccup.'

'A hiccup.' She was past being astonished.

No, she wasn't. She was pretty much totally astonished.

'Health and Safety issues,' Matt said mournfully. 'Have you noticed how narrow the neck of the spit is? Twenty yards at high tide, and once the circus is out here, there's no other evacuation route, other than by boat. And Carvers Circus is twice the size of Sparkles. Duncan's the mayor. I can't believe he hasn't seen the dangers before this. It only took a nudge, however, and he moved. A man of action, is our Duncan.' He grinned. 'Especially after our watchdog officer showed him a picture of *his* dogs in cages. Next year the circus site will be on the football ground.'

'But the football ground's on the other side of town,' Allie managed, trying to get her head around this. 'You won't get the crowds there.'

'Ah. We knew you were a businesswoman,' Matt said smoothly. 'That's what Duncan's counting on. Fort Neptune has a reputation for keeping its holidaymakers happy. No Sparkles, no happy tourists. So, as any good mayor would, Duncan approached our bank for a business plan to take the town forward. And now we have one.'

'Which would be what?' She'd finally got her breath back. She was still astonished but she was able to look at this guy with suspicion. His eyes were dancing. He looked... Machiavellian.

He looked like Matt, but she was ordering her hormones—desperately—to get over that.

'We propose to turn the spit into a permanent amusement site,' Matt told her, as if he didn't even sense her inner turmoil. 'Funded by the Council, sponsored by Bond's. It'll spread out onto the esplanade, so safety's not an issue. It'll consist of a permanent nautical market, heritage-based, things bought and sold as they would have been bought and sold a hundred years ago. We've asked Margot if she'll take over the organisation and she's already in Bossy R Us mode. Everyone we've talked to is enthusiastic but we need a centrepiece. A showpiece at its heart. Something like an old-fashioned circus.'

'Matt…'

'We see it as a permanent attraction,' he said, and the twinkle had gone now. He sounded deadly serious—banker spelling out business proposition. 'It'd be small, cosy, family-oriented, and it wouldn't have to be spectacular. We see it—Henry, Bella, Duncan and I…'

'Grandpa knows about this?'

'We have talked,' he admitted. 'We had to do something while you did all the town's taxes. Can I go on?'

'I…yes.' Her voice came out a squeak and he grinned.

'Right. Business modelling. Three shows a week maybe, but with added extras. We've talked to the local schools. They'll bring the kids and use it as part of the curriculum. They hope you might be able to teach kids basic circus tricks, so they can treat this as a permanent, loved part of the town. And more. Duncan's talked to the mums' groups, the nursing home, the kindergarten. Everyone wants to be involved. Everyone wants to learn. Allie, Carvers will still come to Fort Neptune, as they have the right to come, and they'll probably still get their audience—people have cars—but they only have the right to be here for two weeks of the year and you're here for ever.'

'Me?' she said blankly.

'That's if you'd like to be a ringmaster,' he said softly. 'Instead of a bookkeeper. For Henry's not going to be able to do it for ever. Though with the show I'm envisaging, age old doesn't matter. We'll just lower the trapeze.'

'I don't…I don't…'

'The bank would finance new equipment,' he said, hurriedly now as if he was afraid she'd think of objections before he could get it all out. 'We'd provide a new big top, new equipment, everything you need. And you have a team. Our dog-watcher reports that even those who were offered jobs with Carvers are already unhappy. You can choose who you want.' Then he hesitated, seeing her confusion. 'But we're not forcing you, Allie. This is something the town needs. Duncan and Margot and I are setting it up, and if Sparkles doesn't want to take up our offer we'll put it out to tender. Carver might even be interested.'

And that hauled her out of open-mouthed, goldfish-goggle mode like nothing else could.

A tiny circus. A permanent site. A job for the crew as long as they wanted it.

A home.

She saw it. Take away the high risk acts, she thought. Increase the acts that everyone loved, that everyone waited to see, year after year.

Tell Fizz and Fluffy to increase their jokes.

Shine up the cannon.

'Don't you dare offer it to Carver,' she managed. 'If it's okay with you, I think we might negotiate a deal.'

'Consider it negotiated.' He hesitated. 'Only there is a stipulation.'

'Which…which is?' They were standing on the wide grassy site of circuses past. Behind them was the tiny fort town. Before them was the sea. The breeze was warm and full of salt. The town's fishing fleet was swinging on moorings in the bay as the setting sun played over them.

A plover and his mate were calling to each other somewhere in the grass behind them. Apart from that, there was nothing, nothing and nothing, but a man and a woman with their whole lives stretched out before them.

'I'm the financier of this project,' Matt said, his voice becoming gentle, unsure, as if this last part of the plan was the most likely to be rejected. 'As as financier, I need a hands-on role. You'd have to hand the bookkeeping to me.'

'I'm a bookkeeper.'

'Yes, but the circus you book-kept went bust,' he said, sounding stern. 'How could Bond's possibly finance a venture with such a record unless they took a personal interest? A very personal interest.'

'Which…which would be?' He was so big, she thought inconsequentially. He was so…male. He was Matt.

Mathew Bond of Bond's Bank.

No. Just Matt. A guy with a proposition to take her breath away, with a body to take her breath away, but, at the core, still that hint of uncertainty, as if he, too, was being asked to take a step into the unknown.

'I'd need to live in Fort Neptune,' he said and her breath was taken away all over again.

'Wh…why?'

He hesitated. Thought about it a little. Fought to get it right.

'You know,' he said slowly, as if he was talking through an idea he was only now coming to terms with, 'ever since I can remember, from the day I was born, it was always assumed I'd be the Chairman of Bond's Bank. With my family holding, I'm the major shareholder. I've been trained since birth to sit in the director's chair, to take control of the day to day running of the bank, to *be* Bond's Bank. It was only when I met you that I thought…why? Do I need to be the Chairman of Bond's Bank? Four weeks ago I stood on the beach and did some brainstorming and put everything on the table. Or on the sand. Just like I've taught my employees to do. I put Chairman of the bank on the sand as well, and suddenly I thought—I don't need to pick it up again.'

'But…Matt, it's what you are.'

'Is it? Why?'

'I…' She couldn't think of an answer. She struggled. 'Because you get to wear gorgeous coats,' she said at last and he grinned, and finally, finally he reached out and took her hands and tugged her to him.

'I have three coats,' he said. 'That's enough for one man for a lifetime, especially as I propose moving aside, keeping a seat on the Board but not staying as operational Head. That means I won't spend half my life in Europe's winter, where cashmere coats are needed to keep me warm. I have a helicopter. I can travel. Jack needs a good financial adviser at the farm and I'd like to be hands-on at Bond's Unleashed. I'd like to revamp Bond's public image, but a lot of that can be done online. So I was sort of hoping...no, make that really hoping, that if I bought a house here, commuting at need but basing myself here in perpetuity, I might have something else...*someone else*...to keep me warm.'

'Matt,' she said again, but this time it was different. It was a breath when she was struggling to breathe. It was almost a prayer.

Matt.

'I love you,' he said and her world stood still.

'Love...'

'I've told you before, Allie. You knocked me back because you didn't fancy playing beggar maid to my King Cophetua. This way it'd be different. We'd share a house, we'd share a life, but it would be sharing. You'd be taking Sparkles over from Henry and your life would be based here. Duncan and I think Sparkles could run at a profit almost immediately. You'd be independent.'

'And you...you'd be independent, too?'

'You're pretty good with marketing,' he told her, caressing her with his eyes. 'I suspect there'll be times, lying in bed late at night or early in the morning, when I say, "Love, what do you think about this?" And I was acting ringmaster for a whole week so I pretty much know about circuses. I'm hoping you might do the same.'

'Bed,' she said faintly, because of all the images his words conjured up, that was the biggie. Lying in bed beside this man. Waking up beside him, over and over, for the rest of her life.

Living here. Running the circus here. Watching Henry and Bella enjoy their retirement. Watching Fizz and Fluffy with their pride restored. Watching Margot decide to live.

And at night, home to bed, home to Matt, home to her love.

'Allie...' And she heard his tension. He was holding her, he was smiling at her, he was promising her the world, a future, love, a home and hearth and him.

And he didn't know. He wasn't sure.

'There'd....there'd be stipulations,' she managed.

'Stipulations?'

'Yes,' she said, and her voice cracked a little but she made herself go on. 'You would need to do banking business. There'd be times you would need to go away.'

'There would be,' he agreed, the tension building.

'Then we'd have to always have an alternative.'

'An alternative?'

'An alternative ringmaster,' she said and she smiled and smiled, her eyes misting with tears, her heart swelling so she thought something down there might burst but she didn't care. 'So that if you need to travel, I get to come with you.'

'Allie!'

'I won't stay in my Cinders kitchen,' she said. 'Or the wings of my circus either, for that matter. And I'd really like a bit of hands on involvement in your life, in your bank if we can swing that and in Jack's sanctuary as well.'

'Yes,' he said, just like that, and she looked at him, she really looked at him, and everything sort of dissolved. Melted. It was as if her past was falling away and there was only this man, this moment, this love.

'I love you,' she whispered, finally, at last. 'Matt, I don't... I don't really care about stipulations.'

'It's important to get it right,' he said gravely. 'This is a very important contract you're entering into and, as a banker,

I have to warn you to check the fine details. Allie, will you marry me?'

'Yes.'

His eyes darkened and gleamed and he tugged her tighter. 'Didn't I just warn you?'

'You can warn me all you like,' she said and this time it was Allie doing the tugging. 'But you've offered and I've accepted. I have two dogs who witnessed every word. Contract made, Mathew Bond, and there's no way you're getting out of it now.'

'Matt,' he said, because suddenly it seemed important.

'Matt,' she whispered, lovingly, surely, and she held him and held him, and when he tilted her chin to claim her mouth, as she melted into his arms, as her night dissolved into a mist of love and truth and happiness she thought:

Matt.

Superhero.

Ringmaster.

Love.

It was a strange place to have a wedding reception.

Matt and Allie married in the church at Fort Neptune, the church Margot had decreed would be used for her funeral before she'd decided that this wedding would come first. It was even possible now that baptisms would happen before funerals as well, Margot thought happily, as she watched Matt and Allie take their vows. And there might even be another wedding. Duncan was dining at her cottage every night now and the locals were starting to gossip. She'd promised him she'd consider marrying him and maybe she should. A Bond had to be careful of her reputation if she was to stay living in such a small town, and right now living looked good.

But they weren't in Fort Neptune now. They were at Jack's animal sanctuary. *Bond's Unleashed.*

Duncan was holding her hand as Jack made a speech. Matt

and Allie stood side by side in their bridal splendour, smiling and smiling, while Jack spoke about the future, about what Matt and Allie had achieved and what they had before them.

For, after this morning's ceremony, the guests had all been transported to the sanctuary. They'd set up a canopy by the dam. There was a small chance that the elephants might be interested enough to move in on the ceremony, in which case the guests were instructed to grab the trays of food and re-treat, but the elephants seemed to know. They stood back, Maisie and Minnie and three more of their now permanent herd, and watched as these strange human creatures did what strange human creatures did.

The formal opening of the fresh and newly funded Bond's Unleashed animal sanctuary had been last week. This place was safe in perpetuity. Allie and Jack, newly elected members of the newly formed board, would see to it.

'It's our life's work,' Matt had said. 'And our children's and our children's children. I was bequeathed a bank and a destiny as a banker. Our children—and not one called Mathew, by the way—can do what they like, but we'll raise them to care.'

'How could they not?' Allie had said, and Margot, watching the two newlyweds, could only agree.

These two were right. These two were fine. The future stretched before them magically, wonderfully, and on impulse she turned to Duncan.

'I will marry you,' she said. 'As long as I can share your dogs.' And Duncan whooped like a teenager and whirled her right off the ground so Margot felt like a girl again and not like an aged spinster who should watch her dignity.

And from the dance floor, where Jack had spread planks over the grass and dust, where Allie and Matt had been per-suaded to dance a bridal waltz, Allie whispered to Matt, 'Look at Margot. Look at Duncan.'

Matt looked and smiled—and then he looked down at his

bride and his smile grew wider, more tender, enveloping her in a warmth that would stay with her for the rest of their lives.

'Maybe they've found what we've found,' he said, and he took the first steps of the bridal waltz, holding her close, finding the steps worked automatically because Allie's body in her beautiful white bridal gown simply melted into his, and it was as if one body was dancing. One heart.

'Maybe it's catching,' Allie whispered, holding him tight. 'Matt, I love you so much.'

'I love you so much I'm willing to share,' he said grandly, sweeping her round the makeshift floor while their audience, half of Fort Neptune, all of the circus, so many from Bond's Bank, erupted into applause. 'If you knew how hard it was to get all these people all the way here…'

'Just so they can share,' Allie said, and looked around at the audience, at their friends, at the elephants far in the background, and she held Matt and she thought…sharing.

She'd always shared, she thought, but she'd been isolated in her sharing.

Matt had simply been isolated.

But two islands had suddenly become the mainland, the centre, the base on which the future would grow.

'How many kids?' she asked as Matt reached a corner of the dance floor. He was concentrating on a tricky turn, steering his bride so he didn't take her off the boards, so he didn't lose her to the dust.

Her question, though, almost made him mis-step.

'Kids?' he said. He'd thought about them in the abstract, but…real?

'Kids,' she said happily. 'Kids and dogs and ponies and camels and gran and grandpa and uncles and all of Fort Neptune. You'll never be alone again, my Matt.'

'I'll never want to be,' Matt said and then stooped and whispered into her ear. 'Will you wear sparkles on our wedding night?'

'I surely will,' she said and smiled and smiled. 'As long as you wear your top hat.'

'Just wave your magic wand and decree,' he said grandly. 'Who said circuses are all about illusion? Magic does happen. It's happening here.'

* * * * *